The EAGLE and the CROSS

The
EAGLE
and the
CROSS

R. J. PINEIRO

A TOM DOHERTY ASSOCIATES BOOK
NEW YORK

This is a work of fiction. All of the characters, organizations, and events portrayed in this novel are either products of the author's imagination or are used fictitiously

THE EAGLE AND THE CROSS

Copyright © 2008 by R. J. Pineiro

All rights reserved.

A Forge Book
Published by Tom Doherty Associates, LLC
175 Fifth Avenue
New York, NY 10010

www.tor-forge.com

Forge® is a registered trademark of Tom Doherty Associates, LLC.

ISBN-13: 978-0-7653-5375-7
ISBN-10: 0-7653-5375-X

First Edition: September 2008

Printed in the United States of America

0 9 8 7 6 5 4 3 2 1

For Cameron

Enjoy Wake Forest

And

For St. Jude, saint of the impossible, for
continuing to make it possible

Author's Note and Acknowledgments

I began *The Eagle and the Cross* in 1991, soon after my first novel, *Siege of Lightning,* was acquired by Berkley, and almost two years before the start of a very long and wonderful relationship with Tom Doherty and Robert Gleason from Tom Doherty Associates, who published my next twelve novels over the course of seventeen incredible years.

At the time I was exploring genres, trying to find my own voice, my own direction in the literary world. This novel began as a writing experiment fueled by a childhood obsession about World War II, but it soon evolved into something very special—so much that I chose to put it aside while I developed my writing style through a series of computer and military thrillers over the following decade.

I picked up *Eagle* again soon after the turn of the millennium, investing a year developing it further, bringing to life a multinational cast of characters thrown into the bloodiest war of the twentieth century, WWII's Eastern Front. But again, I decided to give it another rest while devoting several years to explore the world of artificial intelligence and nanotechnology through works like *Cyberterror, Havoc,* and *Spyware.*

In late 2007, I embarked on *Eagle*'s last revision, finishing a story written from the heart over the course of almost two decades.

Along the way, many individuals provided support, including:

My wife, Lory, for twenty-five wonderful years of marriage. I'm looking forward to the next twenty-five.

My son, Cameron, now almost nineteen years old and in college. When *Siege* was first published way back when, he was barely five years old. My God, where did the time go?

My family, spread all over the place, from Texas and Louisiana to El Salvador and Venezuela.

My veteran agent, Matthew Bialer, for twenty years of support and guidance.

My friends at Tom Doherty Associates, including Tom Doherty, Bob Gleason, and Eric Raab, for so many years of good books and good times.

Linda Wiltz, for spending time proofreading the manuscript.

Finally, a special thanks to all my colleagues at Advanced Micro Devices, where I am celebrating twenty-five amazing years of excellence in semiconductors.

PART ONE

Summer of 1941

"Russia must be disposed of. The quicker we smash Russia the better."
—Adolf Hitler

1

Lebensraum for Aryans

Hrubieszów, Poland
June 22, 1941

Dawn stained the crystalline moonless sky over eastern Poland with vivid hues of orange and yellow, giving Luftwaffe Oberleutnant Erich Steinhoff a false sense of tranquility. The distant siren from a Soviet coal train chugging across the Bug River while puffing its way into the German side of the Russo-German frontier mixed with the doleful howling of the base's patrol dogs.

Erich eyed his Messerschmitt Me 109F "Franz" single-engine fighter on the foggy clearing that led to the two-thousand-foot-long grass runway. His ground crew was already working on the Franz, which appeared unusually small parked next to several Me 110s—the pitifully slow and awkward dual-propeller heavy fighter that had cost the lives of many of Erich's friends during the initial stages of the Battle of Britain.

Erich wore a fly-fronted, single-breasted flight blouse with no cuffs or external buttons on that cool and humid morning. Aside from the lapel ranks consisting of two stacked wings supported by two oak leaves, the only other insignia on Erich's dark gray blouse was the Luftwaffe national emblem on his right breast—an eagle with unfolded wings clutching the swastika. His baggy trousers, also dark gray, were tucked into knee-high black leather boots. A thick brown belt, from which a holstered sidearm hung, kept the blouse in place over the trousers.

Erich yawned, rubbed his eyes, and stretched his arms. His body had still not gotten used to the short nights of the Russian summer, when the sun barely set, something the Russians called "white nights."

"What a peaceful morning. Isn't it, Oberleutnant Steinhoff?"

Erich turned his head and looked into the light blue eyes of his gruppenkommandeur, Major Hans Barkhorn—the tall and bony native from Nuremberg, Bavaria, who was in charge of Jagdgeschwader, or fighter wing, fifty-two (JG52), Gruppe 1. The JG52 consisted of four gruppes spread along the border from the city of Hrubieszów down to Przemyśl, with orders to provide air support for Army Group South. Adolf Hitler had divided the attack on Russia along three army groups. Army Group North would head toward Leningrad. Army Group Center would march to Moscow. Army Group South would conquer Kiev and the Caucasus.

Barkhorn's flight uniform was identical to Erich's with the exception of the lapel ranks, which consisted of three stacked wings surrounded by a wreath of the same embroidery of Erich's oak leaves, and of the Knight's Cross hanging down from his neck. Barkhorn had earned the coveted decoration after fifty aerial victories.

"It won't be for long, sir," replied Erich with a tone melancholic enough to raise Barkhorn's right eyebrow. He instantly regretted the response. In addition to his duties with the Luftwaffe, Barkhorn was also an honorary member of the Schutzstaffel, Adolf Hitler's SS.

"This is one of the Reich's proudest moments, Oberleutnant. The racially lower and mentally weak Slavs are about to become a part of the German empire. Their agricultural lands will bring prosperity to our people. They are about to pay the price for their inferior intelligence from interbreeding with Mongolian stock."

Erich nodded. "Of course, Major."

"You mustn't underestimate the power of the Reich, Oberleutnant. You are one of our finest. Today we shall make history. Remember the führer's words, 'Just kick in the Russian door and the whole rotten structure will collapse.' Today we kick in the Russian door. We shall tour Moscow in ten weeks. We shall replace the red flag in the Kremlin with the swastika!"

Before Erich could reply, Barkhorn turned and headed for the communications tent.

Erich exhaled. *Spoken like a true Aryan.*

Nazi obsessive hunger for *lebensraum,* or living space, continued to spread the Luftwaffe too thin. But as he had learned months ago, when his government had ordered the slow Me 110s into Britain and Erich had reacted negatively, the Nazi Party did not expect Erich to understand its war directives, but it *did* expect him to obey them. And to think that for a short time he had actually believed in the party.

Erich shook his head. His mother had been right in assessing the Nazis as nothing more than power-hungry fanatics, but he had no choice. He loved his Deutschland as much as he loved flying. His mother, an enthusiastic pilot and instructor of a boys' glider club, had taught Erich to fly a glider by the time he was fourteen. A year later, Erich too had become a licensed instructor for the Glider Group of the Hitler Youth. After Erich graduated from secondary school in 1939, he decided to put off his father's plans for him to become a doctor and enlisted in the Luftwaffe. A year later he earned his fighter pilot wings, and at the age of twenty, Erich was sent to the Western Front, where he soon discovered that the Luftwaffe was indeed as glorious as he had hoped it would be.

Unfortunately, working under the Nazi umbrella, he found himself following orders issued by civilians during military situations—orders that often led to disaster. Erich saw the frustration of Luftwaffe officers when trying to argue Berlin's demented orders and were told to follow them blindly. And there were always the ever-present SS officers, who were nothing more than Hitler's spies, keeping a watchful eye on the pilots.

Erich frowned.

He detested the SS officers, but they were Hitler's right hand. In order to continue flying, Erich had to coexist with them.

"Ready, Erich?"

Erich smiled when Leutnant Werner Haufman, the short and stocky street fighter from Augsburg who always seemed to be looking for a way to stir up a fistfight for money, slowly walked up next to him and tilted a pack of cigarettes toward Erich.

"No, thanks, Werner. I'm trying to quit, remember?"

Haufman rolled up his eyes and grunted. He pulled out a cigarette with his lips, struck a match against the sole of his right boot, lighted up, and took a long draw. "Suit yourself." He slowly exhaled and closed his eyes.

Erich checked his watch and shifted his gaze back to his plane.

"You're too tense, Erich. Barkhorn pissed you off again?"

Erich nodded. "Him and the rest of the power-hungry Nazis. They want too much too soon."

"Easy, buddy. The SS has many ears."

Erich glanced at his friend from elementary school. Haufman was also a pilot, but unlike Erich, the dark-haired junior officer belonged to the dive-bomber wing of the Luftwaffe. Haufman flew the single-engine Ju 87 Stuka, a machine that had already proven itself as a powerful and accurate bomber over France and Poland. Erich didn't mind showing his concerns in front of Haufman. The volatile lieutenant had already gotten in trouble once by punching an SS junior officer at a party in Augsburg two years before. Only Haufman's academic record and promise as a top aviator saved him from prison—the place where everyone who disgraced a member of Hitler's glorified special armed forces usually ended up.

"Screw them," Erich said. "They are spreading us too thin while cutting back on resources."

Werner exhaled through the side of his mouth and

winked. "I'm usually the one bitching about life in the German milita—"

Suddenly, the lights in the compound flickered off and on while loudspeakers shouted a single word over and over.

"Dortmünd! Dortmünd! Dortmünd!"

Erich closed his eyes. The code word was the final signal from Hitler that Operation Barbarossa—the invasion of the Soviet Union—was to proceed. Dozens of pilots left their tents and headed for their airplanes.

"It's time," Werner said. "I'll see you tonight."

"Careful, old friend. You take too many chances in those dives," said Erich, well aware of Haufman's reputation for pulling up at the last possible minute to achieve maximum accuracy on his runs.

"Relax. *You* take care, you hear? And watch your tail." Haufman sprinted toward for the other side of the airfield.

Erich inhaled deeply and decided he was ready. He had been ready since the night before, when the final details of the operation were revealed to the pilots.

He approached his Franz fighter, whose long main landing gear and tiny tail wheel made it sit at a very steep angle. Its nose pointed skyward.

"Morning, Erich," said a black ground-crew member.

"Hello, Mathias," Erich responded to his servant. Mathias was a native of Algeria, in northern Africa. In traditional Nazi Germany military fashion, an officer above the rank of leutnant was entitled to a servant. Erich found his during a brief station in Africa while on transit to the eastern front. Unlike other officers who maintained a master-slave relationship with their servants, Erich developed a friendship with the African to the point that he had Mathias trained in the Luftwaffe and got him the rank of hauptgefreiter, or corporal. Mathias knew the Me 109Fs better than any German technician.

Erich walked around to the left side of the plane, climbed onto the wing root from the trailing edge, and gently walked up. He grasped the windshield handles, swung his right leg into the cockpit, followed by his left, and slowly lowered his 180-pound body over the seat while ducking under the canopy. He slid into the seat and instantly felt right at home. The Franz's cockpit, though not that spacious, was comfortably efficient, allowing Erich to easily find and reach all instruments.

He extended his legs until the soles of his boots came in contact with the rudder pedals and slid the insteps into the straps.

"Good hunting, sir!" said Mathias as he climbed onto the wing and closed and locked the heavy canopy.

Erich raised his right hand and extended his thumb toward the sky. All three members of his ground crew walked away to a safe distance except for Mathias, who sat on the wing to guide Erich to the runway. The Franz's nose-up attitude greatly impaired Erich's forward vision while on the ground.

Erich threw the master switch and powered on the avionics, radios, and magnetos. He set the propeller pitch at full increase and reached with his left hand to set the engine fuel-air mixture to full rich. He signaled Mathias sitting on the leading edge of the right wing. The African nodded.

Erich pushed the starter button. The Daimler-Benz engine fired after a couple of jerks. A few puffs of black smoke spat from the stubby exhaust stacks, and the propeller spun into a clear disk.

He set the throttle to idle and looked through the armored-glass canopy at the other eight Me 109Fs that made up his *staffel,* or flight squadron. All eight planes already had their propellers spinning. A ground-crew member sat on the right wing of each craft. Erich dialed a prearranged frequency into his communications radio and spoke into the microphone attached to his headset.

"Black Clove Five Oh Five to Cloves. Taxi into position and hold."

"Yes, Staffelkapitan!" was the unanimous response.

Erich managed a thin smile as he slowly pulled back the throttle to increase RPM. Unlike American, British, or Soviet airplanes, the Messerschmitt throttle was pulled back to accelerate and pushed forward to slow down.

Erich released the brakes and followed Mathias' signals to the end of the runway. The stiff landing gear made him feel every bump on the ground.

The moment he reached the runway, Erich turned his craft into the wind. Mathias quickly jumped off the wing and ran toward the edge of the seventy-foot-wide runway.

Erich checked his watch. It was just past three o'clock in the morning. He pressed both feet on the rudder pedals to apply the brakes and slowly pulled back the throttle handle to achieve twenty-three hundred RPM for a few seconds. Black smoke puffed out of the exhausts. He brought the engine back to idle and repeated the procedure three more times until no smoke came out during rev-up.

Satisfied that he had cleared any carbon deposits on the engine's plugs, Erich turned the plane back to face the runway, added twenty degrees of flaps, made the sign of the cross—a habit he had picked up from his mother—and slowly opened the throttle.

Mathias jumped and waved his arms. Erich felt the powerful acceleration pressing him back against his seat as the engine began unleashing thousands of pounds of thrust in an ear-splitting crescendo.

He inched the throttle slowly; otherwise the brutal torque induced on the fuselage by the engine could cause the Franz to roll over. Power had to be added gradually while increasing right rudder and aileron to compensate for the torque and also to keep the Messerschmitt lined up with the runway's center line.

Indicated airspeed quickly increased. Erich added a dash of forward pressure on the control stick. The tail rose and the nose dropped to the horizon. At last Erich could see directly ahead of him. He shifted his gaze back to the airspeed indicator.

Eighty knots . . . ninety . . . one hundred knots.

Erich maintained enough forward pressure to keep the

plane on the ground until the airspeed indicator needle scurried past 115 knots.

He released the forward pressure, and without having to apply any rear pressure to pull up the nose, the well-balanced plane left the ground at a shallow angle of climb.

He slapped the gear lever with his left hand, wound up the flaps, and watched his airspeed dash past 160 knots while climbing at nearly three thousand feet per minute.

Erich indulged himself in one brief backward glance.

The second fighter from his staffel was already making its takeoff run. A third had taxied into position and was holding.

He checked his watch once more. They were right on schedule.

2

Nonaggression Pact

Lvov, Ukraine
June 22, 1941

The distinct sound of heavy artillery echoing in the distance, Colonel Aleksandrovich Nikolai Krasilov bolted out of bed, put on his pants and boots, and raced outside the one-story brick building across from the dusty airfield.

He blinked several times to clear his sight as he made his way to the communications building on the other side of the short runway. To his surprise he was the first one outside. Other pilots ran out of the building just as he pulled on the front door and stepped inside.

The base's primitive communications room consisted of two ten-year-old two-way radios and three operators, who were pacing nervously. The trio turned to him.

"What is happening? The artillery rounds are coming from the west!" he asked, even though he feared he already knew the answer.

"Ye—yes, Comrade Colonel!" responded the youngest of the operators. "We're under attack by the Germans!"

Krasilov, a twenty-year veteran of the Red Air Force, knew better than to jump to conclusions based on his gut feeling plus a comment from a young enlisted man, but the fact still remained that someone had ordered the artillery to fire. The sound was too far away for Krasilov to tell which side the guns belonged to, but the thundering blasts were definitely coming from the border.

"How do you know this information?"

"The radio, sir. Our bases by the border . . . the screams, sir . . . the planes at Novovolynsk are being strafed on the ground . . . their radio just went dead."

Krasilov felt a headache in his temples.

"But how can that be?" asked another operator. "We have a nonaggression pact with the—"

"This is Colonel Vasili Petrosky, anyone come in, come in!"

Krasilov raced for the microphone on the table. Colonel Petrosky was in charge of the defense for the border town of Rava-Russkaja, fifty miles northwest of Lvov.

"This is Aleksandr, Vasili. What is your situation?"

"Flames, Aleksandr! There are flames everywhere. Our fighters are burning! Our tanks are burning! We need help immediately or we'll be forced to retreat. The German panzers are just a few hills away! Their planes fill the sky!"

"Hold in place, Vasili. We'll contact Kiev!"

"I'm not certain how long we can—"

A blast of static invaded the room.

Krasilov gripped the microphone. "Vasili? Vasili?"

No response.

Krasilov pounded a fist on the table. Petrosky's cry for help was all the convincing Krasilov needed. "Get me Kiev Military District headquarters immediately!"

"Yes, sir!"

The young radio operator jumped on a chair and dialed a new frequency while Krasilov went back outside. His pilots' gaze was on him. They looked as confused as he was.

He saw fear in some of their eyes. None of them said a word, though. They waited for Krasilov to speak.

After months of warnings, the inevitable—at least in Krasilov's mind—had happened. The undeniable signs that something significant was about to happen were everywhere: German planes flying reconnaissance missions over Russia for months; German ships pulling out of Soviet ports in a hurry; German embassy officials in Leningrad, Stalingrad, and Moscow burning documents and getting ready to depart. Yes, the signs had been there, but what had been more incredible than the reports themselves was Stalin's refusal to publicly acknowledge them.

Krasilov faced his men. No one could close his eyes to the German threat any longer.

"All I know is that we're under attack. Get to your planes and wait for my order. Move!"

The pilots looked at one another. Krasilov understood their hesitancy. Communiqués from TASS—the official Soviet news agency—over the previous two weeks had indicated that the two nations were at peace and that war was not a possibility. In fact, many Red Air Force pilots of the Baltic, Minsk, and Kiev Military Districts had been allowed to go on leave by Moscow Military District headquarters after a recently completed night training exercise that left them not only short on fuel, but also short of sleep.

The pilots continued staring at Krasilov.

"Are you deaf? Move it! To the planes! Now!"

The pilots ran off.

"Sir?"

Krasilov turned. The young operator stood by the doorway.

"Yes?"

"The rifle division at Mostiska briefly came in. They were also pleading for help, sir. Then communications ceased."

"Damn! Where is Kiev?"

"I've just got them on the line, sir."

Krasilov stormed past him and reached for the microphone. "Kiev Military District, this is Colonel Aleksandrovich Krasilov of the Red Air Force in Lvov. We're under attack by German forces . . ."

"You must be insane, Colonel Krasilov! Why is your message not in code?"

Krasilov narrowed his eyes at the odd response. "Did you hear me? I said we're under attack! German forces are wiping out our border defenses this minute! Where is General Kirponos?"

Another voice came through on the radio. "Colonel Krasilov, this is Colonel Timoshenko. General Kirponos received orders yesterday to move his headquarters to Tarponol. They are en route. His orders were that no action must be taken against the Germans without Moscow's consent. Comrade Stalin has forbidden our artillery to open fire and our planes to fly."

With the sound of his own planes revving up, Krasilov's grip tightened around the microphone. The response was unsound. Was Stalin that far out of touch with reality? And why were his generals so afraid to act on their own out here in light of such blatant violation of the nonaggression pact? The answer lay in the fact that over the past two decades, the paranoid Stalin had done a masterful job of purging the armed forces of all of its finest generals, replacing them with his own clowns. The result was this havoc, this inability to make real-time decisions in time of crisis—this total dependence on Moscow to tell them exactly what to do.

Krasilov pressed further. "We must fight back! Our troops are being killed. Towns are in flames!"

"The order stands, Colonel! No attack must take place against the people of—" The line went dead just as a powerful explosion shook the base.

Krasilov dropped the microphone and ran outside. He took a quick breath when spotting hundreds of enemy planes across the sky, like a swarm of angered wasps. He turned and saw the cause of the explosion. Three planes were burning at the edge of the runway from the strafing run of a German Messerschmitt fighter, which rolled its wings before disappearing behind the trees that bordered the airfield.

Enraged, Krasilov raced for his old Polikarpov I-16. His ground crew stood by the short, stubby plane as he climbed into the open-canopy cockpit, quickly went through the preflight check, set the air-fuel mixture to full rich, and threw the engine starter. The propeller turned a few times before the engine engaged with a cloud of smoke that quickly blew away in the slipstream.

Another explosion.

As he added throttle, Krasilov spotted a German plane pulling up. Four I-16s were in flames less than a hundred yards away as two other Messerschmitts entered a dive. Krasilov could see their muzzle flashes and the resulting lines of dust streaking toward three parked airplanes on the other side of the base. The planes exploded a few seconds later. A gigantic sheet of fire reached up to the sky followed by billowing smoke. One of the German planes flew through it before lurching skyward.

Krasilov reached one end of the airfield. A plane in flames halfway down the runway blocked his planned take-off path.

Frowning, realizing that he would have to get off the ground quicker to clear that burning obstacle, Krasilov pressed the top of the rudder pedals, applied full power, and lowered flaps. The forty-five-hundred-pound plane trembled under the conflicting commands. RPM increased to twenty-seven hundred. The tail rose and the nose dropped to the horizon under the powerful pull. Krasilov eased back the stick, used the elevators to control the nose's attitude, and waited. Three thousand RPM. He could hear the rivets squeaking as the stress on the monocoque structure reached the outer edges of the design. Krasilov held out for a few more seconds while firmly clutching the control stick. The craft began to slide over the ground.

He lifted his feet off the pedals and the I-16 snapped forward. His eyes shifted back and forth between the pulsating flames straight ahead and the airspeed indicator.

Speed, speed.

Eighty knots . . . ninety.

The flames rapidly accelerated toward him.

One hundred knots.

He spotted a German fighter breaking through the heavy smoke billowing over the burning I-16. Its wing-mounted guns came alive with muzzle flashes. Tracers flashed to his left and right, peppering the sides of the runway.

Krasilov pulled back on the stick and squeezed the trigger. The slow I-16 left the ground. Krasilov pointed the nose directly toward the incoming German craft flying at fifty feet aboveground heading directly toward him.

3

Dogfight

Skies East of Lvov, Ukraine
June 22, 1941

Erich Steinhoff expected the Russian plane to break its takeoff run, but the pilot had pulled up and was now firing while flying directly toward him, as if the Russian pilot's intentions were to either shoot him down or ram him. Erich swung the stick right and up, setting his Messerschmitt into a steep climb and turn.

Krasilov stopped firing the moment the German plane, which he now recognized as an Me 109F Franz, broke its run and cut high and to the right.

He cleared the burning wreck, broke through the dark smoke, and also pulled up, but could not even attempt to catch up with the departing Me 109F. The German plane outperformed him by over a hundred knots.

It didn't matter. He was airborne with full tanks and a full load of ammunition. Besides, the Franz was not his primary target. Krasilov fixed his eyes on the large bombers that the German fighters were trying to protect.

Pushing full power, the Russian colonel set his single-engine plane in a fast climb.

Erich made a wide sweeping turn and came back around looking for the stubborn Russian plane. He scanned the skies and spotted him at ten o'clock headed for a formation of Junkers Ju 88 bombers en route to Kiev.

Without a second thought, Erich prioritized the lone I-16 over multiple ground targets and swung the Messerschmitt in its direction, quickly closing the gap.

He pulled back throttle to avoid approaching it too fast and risking overshooting. In his opinion anyone could shoot down a plane if given enough ammunition, but it took an expert to do it on the initial run and with a minimum number of bullets. To accomplish that he had to get close to the Russian craft.

Real close.

Erich inched the throttle to gain some airspeed while executing a steep right turn to stay with the Soviet.

The bombers almost within reach, Krasilov cut right to fly past them, turned again, and faced them head-on to avoid the deadly guns on top and aft of the craft.

As he made his turn he noticed something behind him.

An Me 109F.

Erich noticed that the enemy pilot had finally realized he was on his tail. The Soviet executed a steep dive and turn. Erich easily followed while cutting power to avoid ramming it.

The I-16's tail less than fifty feet away, Erich squeezed the trigger.

The two 7.9mm cowl-mounted machine guns began to vomit rounds at the rate of one hundred per minute. They had a total capacity of 150 rounds per gun, providing Erich with just under ninety seconds of firing time. To avoid using up his ammo too fast, he limited himself to short controlled bursts while fine-tuning his aim.

Krasilov watched his airspeed alarmingly increase past three hundred knots, almost fifteen knots above the maximum rated speed of the I-16, and he felt it in the powerful windblast that the short windshield barely deflected. Its high-pitched screeching mixed with the roaring engine and the creaking and snapping of the trembling wings.

He had to slow down or face midair disintegration. But slowing down meant giving the Messerschmitt glued to his tail an even better chance of nailing him.

Several bullets ripping through the wooden skin of the right wing told him that the German was going to get him regardless of his speed. At least at slower speeds he had some maneuverability in his favor. Krasilov abruptly cut the throttle and pulled up the nose. A few more rounds blasted through the left wing.

Erich had to break hard left to avoid a midair collision. The Russian had decided to slow down, and in doing so, he had forced Erich to pull away, but only momentarily. Erich skillfully executed a tight three-sixty and in less than twenty seconds was once more in pursuit. This time his throttle was almost on idle as he set his plane in a forty-five-degree dive and opened fire for one second. Smoke began to come out of the Russian craft's nose.

4

Smoke and Sunflowers

Skies East of Lvov, Ukraine
June 22, 1941

The dense smoke spewing out of the grumbling engine blinded him. Krasilov wasn't sure what section of the machine the German had hit, but it had at least left him with enough power to remain airborne.

He pushed full throttle and the engine responded but at the price of puffing out more smoke. He looked behind him. The German remained with him, but the pilot had stopped firing. Suddenly, the German broke left and got next to him. Their wingtips couldn't have been more than ten feet apart. Krasilov noticed the large black clove painted right behind the propeller hub. Next to it he read the letters SONJA.

He shifted his gaze to the cockpit and saw the pilot behind the thick metal frame supporting the glass-paneled canopy. The German brought his right hand up and touched the middle finger against the side of his helmet.

Krasilov frowned. He had heard about the chivalry displayed by German pilots, but only now did he realize that it was not just another Nazi propaganda tool. The German had wounded his craft and was simply making sure Krasilov was going down. He obviously had no wish to make Krasilov's plane explode in midair by pumping more rounds into the I-16's aging body.

The German continued to salute for a few more seconds, apparently waiting for Krasilov to salute back, but Krasilov refused. The Germans were the enemy of his people. He would not salute a Nazi.

Krasilov eyed the altimeter as it dropped below five thousand feet. The German waved, broke left, and flew away at great speed after flying a circle around him. Even if Krasilov had wanted to take him, the fast Messerschmitt had already come and gone past his line of fire. The fighter headed back to their original target: Krasilov's base.

The Russian's eyes filled. The Germans were picking their targets at will and blowing them up. There was no defense. He was the only fighter who had gotten airborne. Five planes burned on the runway and dozens were in flames on the side of the field. The communications building was also burning. From this high up he could see the Junkers dropping load after load of bombs on Lvov!

Flames quickly spread across the city.

"Not on the city you bastards!" he screamed into the wind, his voice drowned by the deafening noise. Krasilov's wife and two daughters lived on the outskirts of Lvov.

Through tears of rage, Krasilov spotted a pair of Messerschmitt Me 110s. The heavy twin-engine fighters flew in formation a thousand feet below him as they made their run over the city.

Krasilov pointed his plane in their direction and idled the engine to reduce smoke and improve visibility. It worked. In a dive, his I-16 gained airspeed but without engine power. The Me 110s were five hundred feet below and closing awfully fast. He lined up the right-most bomber in his sights and squeezed the trigger.

Nothing.

Startled, he squeezed it again.

Nothing.

Damn!

The Franz must had damaged something vital to the I-16's weapons system—or else the dated machine-gun system was malfunctioning as it sometimes did.

The Me 110s were two hundred feet away now.

As Krasilov stared at the large white-on-black cross painted over each wing another possibility for attacking the bombers occurred to him.

Perspiration beads rolling down his creased forehead,

Colonel Krasilov aimed for the right wingtip. He had to get the entire aileron or the bomber might survive the attack.

One of the Me 110's cannons began to swing in his direction. Someone on the plane had spotted him.

Airspeed rushed above three hundred knots. The I-16 trembled from the windblast on all leading edges. The attitude indicator told him he had achieved an eighty-degree angle of dive, beyond the Polikarpov's specifications.

Muzzle flashes broke out of the single cannon now pointed at him. Sparks flew out in all directions as the Me 110's rounds struck the massive radial engine, but it was to no consequence. Krasilov maintained his dive.

The wing got closer.

Airspeed now was 320 knots.

Clutching the control stick with both hands, Krasilov saw the white-on-black cross grow larger until it filled his entire windshield. He lowered his head at the very last moment.

The soul-numbing impact shook him violently as a blurred vision of fire engulfed him.

Krasilov let go of the stick and put both hands over his face as the heat intensified. The back of his seat caught on fire, but the heavy Russian fighter held together.

He pressed his back against the flight seat to put out the flames while staring at the propeller bent over the fuselage. Flames covered the entire tail as the plane glided toward the ground.

He had to land fast to avoid an explosion. Smoke spewed out of the engine. Krasilov turned it off to prevent more fuel from reaching the front, and pulled on the fuel-dump lever on the side of the seat to minimize the chance of an explosion during his emergency landing.

The smoke subsided and enabled him to pick a spot to land, but before he could do that, Krasilov lifted his head and searched the skies for his victim.

He grinned when spotting the Me 110 with a missing wing gyrating in a fatal spin several hundred feet away.

The wind intensifying the flames behind him made

Krasilov focus on his own problem. He still had to find a place to set this plane down.

He slowly eased back on the stick and held his breath. The nose rose a few degrees. Airspeed decreased below three hundred knots. He tried to lower the flaps, but they didn't work. He tested the rudder and ailerons, and they responded.

Krasilov pulled up the nose several more degrees, bleeding more airspeed.

Altitude two hundred feet. Speed two hundred knots.

A field of sunflowers extended toward Lvov. Krasilov glided toward it.

One hundred feet. One hundred fifty knots.

Still too fast for a controlled landing, but he didn't have a choice. He was approaching Lvov at great speed. He had to slow down, but without flaps he was forced to set the plane down at that speed or risk running out of room or stalling.

The burning buildings rapidly grew in size.

Krasilov breathed deeply, held it, and lowered the nose just as the ground came up to meet him.

The landing gear hit hard, rattling the plane. Krasilov didn't mind the vibrations as long as he could keep the plane in—

He ran into an irrigation ditch. In a flash, the nose dove into the shallow ravine and the tail went up in the air. The I-16 flipped once before landing on its side.

Krasilov smashed his head against the windshield, bounced, and crashed his back against the flight seat.

Disoriented from the blow, half his body outside the cockpit, the Russian colonel opened his eyes and through blood he saw smoke and sunflowers.

The airplane lay on its side. The left wing was gone. The right one stuck straight up in the air. He kicked his legs and pushed himself away from the wreckage.

His back burned and so did his forehead. He felt the torn flesh above his eyebrows. It was in shreds, but he had survived.

Slowly, Krasilov managed to put enough distance between the wreck and him, and simply lay there. His body hurt too much to move. He tore a sleeve off his shirt and bandaged his forehead as best he could to stop the bleeding. He closed his eyes and breathed deeply. The sounds of German fighters mixed with explosions and cries.

The smell of gunpowder and smoke filling his nostrils, Krasilov got up and stumbled toward the outskirts of the city. His family was there . . . somewhere.

5

Fighting Back

Skies East of Lvov, Ukraine
June 22, 1941

His fuel supply nearly depleted, Erich turned the Franz back to base. In the initial hour of fighting, he had shot down one fighter and damaged a dozen more on the ground. In a way he should feel proud of this accomplishment, but he didn't. Concern wormed in his stomach about this new enemy. Today he had seen what was supposed to have been a weak Slav fighter pilot—according to Nazi propaganda—fight back with fierce intensity to the point of committing suicide as long as he could take a few Germans along with him. That was an entirely different kind of Russian warrior from what his superiors had described as a soldier lacking the will to fight.

As Erich cruised over the Bug River, he spotted a flight of Stukas going back into Russia for another bombing raid.

He reached for the radio.

"Jericho leader, Black Clove Five Oh Five."

"Black Clove, Jericho. Enemy fighter situation?" Erich heard Haufman's voice crackling through his headset.

"The airways are clear of enemy fighters, Jericho leader. Low on fuel. Good hunting."

"Thanks."

Erich saw the Stukas going for a steep climb before reaching Lvov. He rocked his wings.

6

Dive-Bomber

Skies over Lvov, Ukraine
June 22, 1941

Cruising at seven thousand feet, Werner Haufman eased the stick in both directions to return Erich's salute while maintaining the lead of his "finger-four" formation flying at a comfortable 130 knots. The name of the formation was derived from its similarity to spreading the fingers of a hand with the thumb tucked in. Haufman flew the middle finger.

His current target was the same one of his previous run: the destruction of three- and four-story buildings on the outskirts of the city of Lvov, where German intelligence believed Soviet snipers could hide and become a nuisance to the advancing army.

In his previous run, Werner and his *schwarm*—a four-craft squadron within the gruppe—had destroyed three of the required seven buildings in their sector of interest.

"Enemy fighters?" he asked his gunner to double-check Erich's information.

Sitting directly behind him and facing the rear of the plane, the gunner, who manned the single MG15 7.92mm machine gun on flexible mounting in the rear cockpit, was responsible for defending the Stuka from enemy fighters. He replied, "None, sir. Skies are clear!"

"Jericho leader here," Haufman said to his schwarm. "Prepare for single-line dive ahead."

"Yes, Schwarmführer!" was the unanimous response.

Haufman advanced the throttle, and the twelve-cylinder, liquid-cooled Junkers Jumo 211J-1 engine belched dark smoke off the side exhausts before accelerating the fourteen-thousand-pound dive-bomber to 150 knots.

He glanced backward and saw his Stukas lining up behind him with two hundred feet in between. The lack of enemy fighters made his job easier by allowing his schwarm to dive over the target one at a time. That not only gave them a better chance of hitting the target, since one plane's miss could be covered by the next, it also reduced the risk of collision because they avoided diving in formation—something his schwarm would had been forced to do if enemy fighters were present.

The Stuka was a slow plane. Diving single file meant that after completing a dive run, the craft had to circle overhead and wait for the others before regrouping and returning to base. That was when they were the most vulnerable to enemy fighters.

Werner rolled the Stuka over on its back, pulled the nose down, and trimmed for 220 knots.

"Air brakes everyone!" he said after satisfying himself that there was no antiaircraft fire visible.

Werner had mixed feelings about the newly installed air brakes, which were supposed to buy him a few extra seconds of diving time, thus increasing bombing accuracy, and also cut back on the Gs when leveling out. The price for that, however, was that his Stuka would be exposed for a longer period of time to the enemy's guns, but the lack of Soviet defenses eliminated the risk today.

A few scattered clouds dotted the scene. Werner slammed the air brake handle, and a ten-inch-wide surface on the trailing edge of both wings lowered by sixty degrees from the wing roots all the way to the ailerons.

Barely feeling the vibrations on his control stick, Haufman concentrated directly ahead, aligning the horizon with the lines painted at various angles on the cabin's side panels, achieving an eighty-degree angle of dive.

Six thousand feet.

Werner heard the "Jericho Trumpets" winding up as airspeed increased. The roar of a Stuka going for a dive was intimidating enough by itself. However, someone in the Luftwaffe dreamed up the idea of adding two small wooden propellers, which mounted on the undercarriage spats, spun by the slipstream. Their pitch and intensity increased dramatically the moment Werner broke two hundred knots, and grew as the Stuka gathered more speed.

Five thousand feet at 205 knots.

Werner entered a small cloud. Everything turned white for a second before the target reappeared again.

Four thousand feet at 210 knots.

The noise from the trumpets blasted against his eardrums in spite of his helmet and airtight canopy. Rivulets of sweat rolled down his forehead and into his eyes, stinging them. He controlled the urge to rub them. Both his hands were busy—one on the stick and the other on the throttle.

Three thousand feet. Two hundred twenty knots.

Werner finally got a building centered in his sights, but he had to wait before releasing his load. Accuracy was paramount when carrying only one large bomb.

As the earth blasted toward him at astonishing speed, Haufman felt elation taking over his senses. This was what he did best. Nothing else gave him the same sense of uninhibited euphoria as the last few seconds before he pressed the stick-mounted release lever while looking straight down at the growing target.

He saw people running in all directions as the altimeter scurried below one thousand feet.

The sirens reached an ear-piercing shriek.

Now!

He pressed the lever.

The five-hundred-kilogram bomb, mounted on swing links on the craft's underside directly below the cockpit, lowered and swung forward on release so that it could clear the propeller arc.

Haufman hauled back on the stick and cut power, and four Gs drove him into his seat. His vision tunneled for a few seconds until he leveled off at three hundred feet. He glanced back and noticed with satisfaction that his bomb had hit dead center.

The building collapsed under the powerful explosion and caught fire. The next Stuka was already making its run on an adjacent building. Haufman set his craft into a gentle turn and climb as he wiped the perspiration off his face.

He reached two thousand feet a few seconds later and waited for his Stukas to complete their run. In all, two buildings had been completely destroyed, and a third partially damaged. The craft regrouped and headed back across the border to reload.

7

Train to Hell

West of Lvov, Ukraine
June 22, 1941

The sudden jerk awoke her.

Dazed, confused, Dr. Zoya Irina Krasilov rubbed her burning cheek, where the Hitlerite had struck her with the stock of his rifle when she had fought back to keep from getting raped, like the other women ahead of her in line at the train station.

As she lay on the hay-littered floor with dozens of other female comrades in a noisy train car that smelled like cattle, feces, and urine, Zoya realized that despite her best efforts, the animals had ravaged her while she had been unconscious.

Fighting back the tears filling her dark eyes, Zoya—also a captain in the Red Army—felt the wetness between her bruised thighs. She performed a quick check and verified that the Germans had not inflicted any permanent or life-threatening injuries.

But they had certainly raped her.

Bastards.

Swallowing hard, she looked about her again, discerning the soft cries of nearby women mixed with the rattling car and the distant rumble of artillery rounds.

A woman in her late teens hugged herself while laying next to Zoya with her eyes closed. She remembered her from a month ago, when the girl had applied for a marriage permit at the commissary. They sent her to see Zoya at the military hospital to get a clean bill of health before they would grant her a marriage license. Her shredded clothes revealed purple blotches on her pale thighs.

Beyond the young woman were others just like her, beaten, raped, scourged. Their cries seemed louder now, amplified by the stark reality of their situation, by the shifting shadows as sunlight forked through the few windows and many slats of the cattle car.

An older woman leaned over and vomited, the stench filling the car. Another one, in her early forties, like Zoya, braced herself, lips trembling, urine and blood dripping down her thighs.

A beam of light momentarily flashed over a girl of around fifteen. She was on her knees, hand clasped in front of her face, her young eyes locked on the ceiling, her lips moving as she prayed. She was half naked from the waist down, raped like the others.

Zoya's only consolation was that she could not have any more children after giving birth to her twin daughters nine years ago. She would not end up pregnant with a half-German baby like some of the women wheezing or crying around her.

But the Nazi animals had done more than just rape her. Although she wasn't hemorrhaging, her vagina burned, as if they had forced acid up her.

Acid. Urine.

The Germans had raped her and then pissed inside her.

Unless she found a way to rinse herself, a vaginal infection would likely set in.

Mustering strength, the military doctor managed to stand and peek through one of the slats of the rumbling cattle car. She saw the steppes projecting beyond the train station and the vast meadows surrounding Lvov, now crammed with German tanks and soldiers beneath a sky peppered with their planes.

Insanity!

Clutching the bars of the window, the wind swirling her dark hair, Zoya watched the Germans advance east without any apparent resistance.

Where are our troops? Our Planes? Our soldiers?

Where are you, Aleksandr?

Swallowing spit, perplexed at the lack of Soviet troops defending the Rodina, the motherland, Zoya felt anger worming in her gut, displacing surprise. She couldn't understand why the Soviets weren't fighting back. There were many Red Air Force and Red Army bases in the Ukraine, yet she saw no attempt to stop the enemy, to prevent it from destroying her land.

From destroying our way of life.

Her heartbeat rocketing, fully awake now, Zoya thought of her daughters, alone in their apartment while she had been working at the hospital, located just two blocks away from her home. The Germans had beaten most of the men with clubs and rifle stocks, in some cases killing them, before shooting the rest in the abdomen, leaving them thrashing in pain while taking the women away in a truck.

Then the bombs had torched Lvov.

Zoya looked away from the thick smoke coiling skyward from her hometown, her eyes finding the girl praying on her knees. Zoya remembered her Catholic upbringing, remembered her religious mother, remembered the God she had forgotten after joining the Socialist Party, which she had to do in order to enlist in the Red Army and then attend the university in Kiev to get her medical degree.

Captain Zoya Krasilov quietly began to pray, began to implore to a God she now sought as her world burned around her, as it became evident that the Socialist Party—that her own Red Army—would not be able to care for her, to guarantee her safety and that of her family. Zoya prayed with sudden fervor that her daughters were all right, that they had managed to leave Lvov before the Nazis turned it into the smoking rubble backdropping the sea of swarming panzers.

Lvov.

Her city.

The home of her family.

Life as she knew it vanished in the distance as the train gathered speed, as it churned, toward Poland.

Poland.

She shivered, aware of the rumors of prisoner camps built by the Germans to control the population of conquered nations. For months the Lvov commissary had received reports pieced together from the personal accounts of Polish refugees, from tales of inhumane living conditions, of tortures, of terrifying medical experiments, of . . .

You must be strong.

Filling her lungs with resolve, Zoya Krasilov decided at that moment that she would find a way to survive—would find a way to return to her home, to her husband, to her daughters. She had to believe that they were alive, that they had survived the initial onslaught and were now heading east. She had to believe that to keep from going insane, to keep from collapsing into total despair.

Despair.

She could see it in the eyes of the women stuffed inside the cattle car. She could taste it in the back of her throat as she swallowed, as she filled her lungs with putrid air, as her vagina burned from a certain infection she wasn't sure how she would treat without medical supplies.

Zoya rallied the courage becoming of the officer she was, of the warrior that she had become before being a doctor, of the trained fighter who had been taught to face adversity directly and fight it with all of her heart.

Panzer columns marched across sunflower fields, crushing everything in their path, followed by troop carriers and trucks towing artillery units—and soldiers, thousands and thousands of them, extending as far as the eye could see.

Clutching her aching lower abdomen, Zoya watched them in silence.

8

Lonely Graves

Lvov, Ukraine
June 22, 1941

The dive-bombers had temporarily stopped, although Krasilov didn't think they could destroy much more. There wasn't a single building intact. Most had collapsed over the streets or were about to from the intense fire.

He reached his street, where he spotted two girls in the middle of it . . . *two kids*!

Krasilov's heart jumped, and he ran, desperately hoping they were his daughters—

"Colonel! Please help us, Colonel. Please!" The girls, one around eleven years of age, the other a few years older, wore white nightgowns and kept on screaming as they ran up to him and clung to his pants.

He recognized them. They attended the same school as his daughters.

"My wife and daughters, girls," Krasilov asked as he pointed to a three-story building that had collapsed into itself. "Have you seen them?"

"The Germans, sir . . . they raided the hospital and took our mother and also Doctor Krasilov."

Krasilov's stomach knotted at the mention of his wife, Zoya, who was one of the resident doctors at the military hospital and would had been on duty at the time of the attack.

"They took her? Where?"

"To the railroad station, sir," said the younger of the two girls, her face darkened by the same smoke that stained her soiled garment. "They all got on a train and headed for Poland."

Krasilov felt a lump forming in his throat. The rumors from Poland about concentration camps made him want to scream in anger, in frustration that his beloved wife, his beautiful Zoya, could be headed to those death camps.

But his military training took over his emotions, forcing control. Instead, he asked, "What about Marissa and Larissa? Have you seen them?"

The younger girl lowered her gaze while the older pointed at the rubble that had been Krasilov's building.

"Please, Colonel!" said the younger girl suddenly, tears welling in her eyes. "We're hungry! Please, help us! Help us!"

His hands trembling, Krasilov pulled out two small dark chocolate bars from his pocket. "Here," he said with haste. "Take this and run out of the city! Lvov isn't safe anymore. The Germans will be here very soon. Tell everyone you see to head east. You got that? Head east!"

The girls snagged the chocolate and ran away.

Krasilov faced the ruined structure. His family lived on the third floor. The choices facing him seemed just as grim. Either the Germans abducted his daughters or they had perished in the rubble. They could have also managed to escape, but something told him the chances of that happening were negligible given what he had just learned from the two girls.

Steeling himself, Krasilov began to climb the mound of rubble, searching through the debris while praying that he would not find them, then praying that he would. Perhaps they escaped the Germans. Perhaps they survived the explosions and managed to flee the city in time.

Time.

Beads of sweat rolled down the sides of his face as he moved rock, brick, and wood aside. His muscles burned and his head throbbed, but it did not matter. He had to know. He needed to know.

An overwhelming sense of despair gripped him the moment he shifted several planks of wood aside and exposed the bodies of his twin daughters. They wore their nightgowns.

The two girls in the street had been right.

Finding the strength he desperately needed to remain calm, Krasilov inspected their bodies, which were faced down and appeared unharmed.

He turned the first one over . . . her face and chest were gone.

Trembling, Krasilov let go of her shoulders and leaned to the side, controlling the first convulsion, but a second reached his mouth. He couldn't even tell which of his daughters that was!

His body tensed as he vomited, as he let it all out.

Slowly, Krasilov straightened up, breathed deeply, and stepped over to his second daughter, turning her over.

Larissa.

Although not maimed, her dead eyes stared back at Krasilov.

Stretching his arms to the hazy sky, the Russian officer bellowed a loud scream of anger, frustration, and pain, before he burst into tears.

Later that morning, as German planes flew overhead and panzer divisions rumbled across the Ukrainian plains, Krasilov headed east. Hordes of Russians civilians ran past him as they fled the advancing German army.

But he didn't run.

He wasn't afraid of the Germans. There was nothing else they could take away from him besides his life.

And that would be a blessing.

There were dozens of airstrips between Lvov and Kiev. Krasilov headed toward them. War had come to his home. To his country. War had taken away his loved ones.

As his Rodina burned under Germany's crushing attack,

under Hitler's boots, Aleksandrovich Nikolai Krasilov decisively concluded there was nothing left for him to do but fight back with uncompromising resolve.

He had sworn that over two lonely graves in a sunflower field outside Lvov.

9

Make a Difference

Outside of Rzeszow, Poland
75 Kilometers from the Ukrainian Border
June 24, 1941

Zoya Krasilov felt as if she had just swallowed molten lead. Fear gripped her intestines at the sight of the German soldiers forming two long lines, creating a narrow corridor from the train platform to the barbed wire entrance to the prisoner's camp, backdropped by jagged mountains.

They were armed with whips and clubs.

Women jumped out of train cars and were forced at gunpoint into the corridor. The Germans insulted them, spat on them, urinated on them, and also showered them with blows as the women ran crying down to the camp's entrance.

Those refusing to go through the reception line were dragged by their hair kicking and screaming to a freshly dug pit to the right of the main gate, where they were shot in the stomach and left howling in pain as they slowly bled to death.

Dear God, she thought, staring at the commotion beyond the train tracks, at the bloody prisoners staggering out of the other end, some barely standing. Those who fell and lacked the strength to get back up were kicked to death on the spot and then dragged to the mass grave. The groans and cries from the women nearly drowned out the shouting of the Germans and the cracking of whips.

Please, Lord, get me through this.

Making the sign of the cross, Zoya jumped off the train car along with the next wave of disembarking prisoners. Her shoes had barely touched the gravel flanking the tracks when a soldier jammed the muzzle of his rifle into her torso, directing her toward the line formed in front of the mouth of the corridor.

Her ribs burning, the pain magnified by the infection that had developed in her vagina, Zoya joined the group of women of all ages. Many trembled while urinating from fear or from similar vaginal infections as they waited their turn in line, when they would shield their faces and plunge into the madness.

An old lady fell to her knees after a soldier whacked her on the head with a metal pipe. Three soldiers kicked her in the head repeatedly when she failed to get back up, cracking her skull, splattering her brains on the ground. The same soldiers dragged her away.

A girl in her teens made it halfway before landing head-first after a soldier tripped her. She never survived the onslaught of kicks that followed. The woman running behind her also fell, but managed to stand, only to fall again when a soldier lashed her across the face with a whip. Clutching her bleeding face, she staggered to her feet and made it out of the other end.

And so it went, woman after woman, some making it through the ordeal and some dying brutal deaths in the process. Several times she watched women running too fast down the line, dodging most blows, only to be dragged to the side, where soldiers stripped them naked and then forced them through the line again, breasts flapping in the air as they cried while using their arms to protect their heads.

Go too slow and risk death from an excessive number of blows. Go too fast and you are forced to go again naked.

Forcing logic into her mind, she watched the ones who made it through to the camp's entrance, paying close attention to how fast they ran, to how they shielded themselves

using not their hands but their forearms turned to the outside, thus preventing damage to any arteries.

Her knees quivered, but not just from fear. She felt very
weak from the infection and from traveling for two days
without any food or water and without a bathroom, forcing
her to relieve herself on the floor of the train car—which
her infection made it feel as if she were urinating broken
glass. Of course, most women riding with her were in a
similar condition, making the stench unbearable. Zoya had
momentarily welcomed the fresh air, until the realization
of what lay ahead had almost made her vomit—only she
had nothing to vomit.

Clenching her jaw, anger displacing her fear, Zoya felt
nothing but hatred against these animals, these beasts who
dared call themselves soldiers when they were nothing but
cowards striking down harmless women.

Anger.

Rage.

Zoya felt it bottling up inside of her, injecting her system with renewed strength, with the desire to emerge from
that line on her two feet, to make it through this first day,
and then through the next, and the one after.

Survive one day at a time.

Inhaling deeply as the woman in front of her raced into
the chaos, disappearing amid a shower of sticks and clubs,
Zoya began to pray again for strength, for—

"Move, Russian whores!" screamed one of the soldiers
guarding them.

Zoya plunged herself into the havoc, cringing when the
first blow struck her on the shoulder, followed by another
one on her left forearm, which shielded her face. A German with a whip slashed her on her back, the blow feeling
more like a burn, stinging her.

Keep the pace, she told herself, cringing in pain but
maintaining her momentum, forcing her legs to keep moving, but not too fast, giving the Germans ample time to
whip her, to bathe her with their swinging sticks, most of

which landed on her arms and back. Someone struck her buttocks and another her knees, trying to make her fall.

Do not fall! her mind screamed, remembering vividly the fate of those before her who had tumbled to the ground.

Mustering strength, she remained standing and staggered forward, blood trickling from her forearms, her mind screaming in agony, in the despair that her lips refused to acknowledge. The blows continued, scourging her, burning her, making her lose control of her bladder muscles, but she took the punishment in resigned silence, refusing to fall or to let the soldiers hear her cry—even as urine dripped down her legs. She did not ask for mercy, nor did she scream in terror like the others. Zoya even slowed down at the end, defiantly fast-walking past the last two soldiers in line, one of whom kicked her in the butt, propelling her onto the gravel, where she crashed headfirst.

Bastards!

In a blur, her right cheek burning, she watched the same two soldiers approach her.

Her instincts commanded her to get up as fast as she could, which she did, running away before they reached her, scrambling toward the entrance behind the last prisoner.

The soldiers returned to their position in line to deal with the next prisoner.

Bleeding, her arms and back on fire, her face burning from the fall, Zoya reached the gate, flanked by stolid guards, and lost herself among the crowd of roughly one hundred moaning and sobbing women huddled by the large clearing at the front of the camp, which extended to the foot of the mountains.

Some were naked, purple blotches and cuts spotting their pale bodies. Others, like Zoya, were still clothed but their garments were in shambles.

Soldiers walked around the group carrying bread baskets, throwing chunks at the crowd. The subdued prisoners around her exploded in a frenzy, clawing at one another for the chance to grab a bite to eat. She got pushed into two women fighting over a piece of bread and got kicked in the stomach.

Before she knew it she was on the ground gasping for air. Realizing that she risked getting trampled by the maddened mob, she staggered back up, trying to steer clear of the crazed women, whose shouts mixed with the laughter from the soldiers.

Then the feeding stopped and the crowd settled back down. Dizzy from the blows, Zoya performed a quick damage check, flexing her arms, her hands, each finger, verifying that nothing was broken. The cuts and bruises would heal, as long as she could find a place to wash off the dirt. Her main problem remained her vaginal infection, which continued to sap what little energy she had left. She already felt feverish as her immune system tried to fight off the infection.

Her breathing steadying, she inspected the unfamiliar surroundings from behind her shield of women. Large wooden buildings lined the left side of the compound, each marked by a large sign in both German and Russian. There was a commandant's building, dormitories for the guards, as well as a kitchen and dining facility, which also appeared to be for the guards. She saw an infirmary as well as many smaller and plainer structures to her right, which she guessed were the prisoners' quarters.

Thick posts, spaced ten or so meters apart, ran down the center of the camp. Three meters tall, each had ropes hanging around head level.

While imagining the dreadful reason for the posts, she heard a voice in heavily accented Russian flowing from overhead loudspeakers, which instructed them to line up in rows.

Soldiers began to push and shove the prisoners around to force them into rows—along with a muzzle jab or a blow with the stocks of their weapons.

Zoya received another prod even though she had already managed to get herself into a line.

As she trembled from this most recent strike to her

bruised abdomen, she saw the first resident prisoners. About a dozen of them emerged from one of the larger buildings, marked SUPPLIES, hauling black-and-white-striped prison uniforms like the ones they wore. The women prisoners followed two officers dressed in black tunics.

She stared at their shaved heads, at their gaunt faces and pale complexions, at their sunken eyes encased in purple sockets. Zoya stared at death itself, at the walking skeletons blindly following their captors, silently going through the motions, walking down each row and dropping a uniform in front of each new prisoner, but without looking into their eyes.

The same voice on the loudspeaker instructed them to remove all clothing and put it in a pile behind them, but not to put on the uniforms yet. They were to remain naked for inspection.

The women looked at one another, then at their male captors sneering at them in the muddy clearing.

Zoya began to undress right away, removing her soiled dress, her brassiere, and her underwear, letting it all fall to the ground while keeping a hand covering her pubic hair and an arm over her breasts.

Taking a deep breath, her military training forcing savage control, she made a neat pile behind her and just stood there, her gaze on the uniform by her feet.

Most women complied, just like her. Two teenagers, however, hesitated, removing their dresses but not their undergarments.

The soldiers were all too happy not just to rip them off of them but to drag them by their hair to the front of the group, where they gang-raped them.

Their cries echoed across the camp as the Germans took their turns, grounding them into the mud. But no one—not even Zoya—dared to protest. Everyone just gazed at them with the resigned look that was quickly becoming the norm among prisoners.

On their backs, their slim legs forced apart, their ankles held high in the air, the girls took soldier after soldier in a surreal display of evil power that seemed to drag on forever.

When they were finished, the soldiers tied the girls' hands over their heads to the posts Zoya had seen earlier. They left them there crying, violated, scourged, blood and semen dripping down their bruised and dirty thighs, their young eyes wet with tears.

Zoya swallowed the lump in her throat. The sight contrasted sharply with the picturesque backdrop of green mountains beneath a clear and sunny June sky.

A man wearing a white lab coat marched out of the infirmary building, a stethoscope hanging from his neck. A half-dozen prisoners hauling what appeared to be medical supplies followed him.

The German doctor, a short and stocky man with a full head of silver hair, a wide chin, full lips, and icy-blue eyes, worked his way through the group, inspecting each woman, looking into their mouths, listening to their hearts, giving them an cursory check before asking them something she could not hear. Then the doctor would either keep them in line or motion for the guards to remove them from the group.

Zoya stopped breathing when the guards dragged away the first woman who had apparently failed to pass this rudimentary fitness exam. They took her back outside the camp.

The lone gunshot silenced her screams, chilling Zoya, making her heart pound in her chest with sobering power. The inspection continued, resulting in more women also being dragged out, disappearing from sight, their bellowing screams ended by the cracking shots. But the majority passed the inspection. Zoya figured that if they had been strong enough to get through the welcoming committee, they ought to be strong enough to also get a passing grade from this doctor, who now stepped in front of Zoya accompanied by his prisoner assistants. Unlike the walking skeletons who had brought them their uniforms, these ones appeared better fed, healthier.

The doctor regarded her with indifference, placing his

hands on her face, opening her mouth, inspecting her teeth. He then checked her heartbeat with the stethoscope and nodded before asking in fluent—though heavily accented— Russian, "How do you feel?"

"I have a vaginal infection," she replied, regretting saying that a moment later.

The doctor gave her a puzzled look before nodding at the guards, who came and grabbed her by the arms.

"Wait," she pleaded. "I am a doctor! I can be of assistance to you here!"

A woman in the row in front of Zoya's, who had already passed inspection, turned around.

"Take me instead!" she said. "Don't take the doctor! Take me!"

The German doctor shifted his gaze between Zoya and the stranger, before asking, "Do you know each other?"

Both women shook their heads in unison.

"Then why are you willing to volunteer to die for her?" he asked the stranger.

"I'm a Catholic nun. Take me instead of her, please. She is a doctor and can help you here."

The German doctor turned to Zoya, still flanked by the guards. "Do you have formal medical training?"

"Yes," Zoya replied, her heartbeat throbbing in her temples. Things were happening too fast. Why was the nun volunteering to take her place?

"Which school?" the doctor asked skeptically.

"The University in Kiev," Zoya replied. "I . . . I also trained for two years at the University of Moscow."

"Your name?"

"Doctor Krasilov . . . Zoya Irina Krasilov."

The doctor rubbed his chin, his blue eyes shifting between the two women before saying, "Very well. I could use some help in the infirmary. Report to it after this inspection." He scribbled something on the back of her hand while whispering, "If you are lying, *Russian whore,* we will execute ten of your fellow prisoners."

Before Zoya could reply, the doctor pointed at the nun and said, "Now get this Catholic trash out of my sight!"

Zoya's eyes filled as she stared at the nun, who smiled at Zoya before they led her away. "Make a difference, my blessed child," she said. "Make a difference, Zoya Irina Krasilov."

Zoya stood there frozen, finally closing her eyes when a single shot cracked across the compound.

One of the two assistants trailing the doctor risked a brief look at Zoya, winking and smiling ever so slightly.

Zoya breathed deeply, her mind in turmoil. That woman—that Catholic nun—had just sacrificed her life for her. In a flash, Zoya's Catholic upbringing flashed in front of her eyes. She remembered her mother, a devoted Catholic—remembered the old priest at the church down the street. She also recalled walking away from it all to join the party, to better herself, to become a soldier and a doctor, to serve the Rodina, the homeland.

And it had not been the Red Army, or the Socialist Party, or her colleagues in the medical profession who had come to her rescue in her time of need.

It had been a nun.

As she stood there naked, her eyes on the distant mountains, Zoya felt a surge of confidence sweeping through her. Perhaps she might make it through this after all. That nun had just given her a once-in-a-lifetime chance. She had just bought Zoya a second chance, an opportunity to fight back, to make a difference.

Zoya Irina Krasilov swore at that moment to find a way to use both her medical and her military skills not just to remain alive . . . but to help her fellow prisoners, to resist the Germans, to fight back.

And make a difference.

10

German American

Dniester River
North of Lvov, Ukraine
June 24, 1941

"Remain behind the panzers!" Oberleutnant Christoff Halden shouted to his men as they moved toward one of the last pockets of resistance this side of the Dniester River. A few dozen Russian soldiers had entrenched themselves around the entrance to a bridge, setting up machine-gun emplacements and a pair of mortar launchers in a feeble attempt to prevent the Germans from crossing it.

Overhead, a pair of Stukas dropped over the Russians like black eagles, strafing their positions in an earth-trembling display of power, ripping through their sand-bagged defenses, tearing out a large gap across their line.

Sheets of fire erupted across the Russian trenches. Three men climbed out of a ravine just south of the bridge head, their backs in flames, but they still clutched their rifles while firing at the departing planes.

The panzers moved in, firing salvo after salvo against enemy positions, trying to root them out, but the Russians refused to retreat, refused to give up their bridge. One round went off in between the trio of Russians still blasting away at the Stukas.

The clearing smoke moments later revealed one almost unrecognizable body. The second Russian had been cut in half. His upright torso sat next to his legs. Oddly enough, the man was alive, his arms and head jerking in the inky haze. The third Russian had lost an arm, but still managed to reach for his sidearm and continue fighting until another round vaporized him and his severed comrade. The remaining Russians in the trenches and machine-gun emplacements held their positions even as Germans rounds dismembered their comrades.

Clutching his MP43 assault rifle, which Christoff had set in full automatic fire, the young lieutenant shook his head at the carnage, at the Russians' suicidal defiance.

Why don't they surrender?

Not only did the Germans vastly outnumber them, the Russians defending the bridge lacked artillery guns or other heavy weapons capable of stopping a panzer column.

The lead panzer steered directly toward the closest enemy machine-gun nest, Russian bullets sparking off its thick armor. The deep-rooted enemy didn't let up, firing right up to the moment when the tracks crushed their position.

Instead of advancing, the panzer momentarily rotated in place, grinding down the trench, squashing the trapped Russians into a pulp amid agonized shrieks, kicking up dirt mixed with minced body parts and blood.

Another panzer ran over a Russian trench, but unlike the lead panzer, the driver made the mistake of continuing toward the bridge.

A Russian soldier surged from the ground behind the panzer and clamped a tubular object to the rear of the German tank.

Christoff and one of his subordinates, Sergeant Johan Wiltz, fired their machine guns, cutting down the Russian just as a loud explosion turned the panzer into a mobile ball of yellow flames. The blazing figures of the panzer crew jumped out of their damaged tank, rolling on the ground to put out the fire.

Russians emerged from another trench and fired on the burning Germans, before vanishing again.

To his immediate left, following a pair of panzers, marched Christoff's commanding officer, Hauptmann Meinhard Schmidt, leading the main charge against the bridge. Christoff covered his captain's right flank while a third group of soldiers covered Schmidt's left flank.

It happened quite abruptly, just as he had experienced during the early days of the invasion of Poland, when enemy troops had fought back fiercely, inflicting casualties among the German ranks. In a suicidal move, two Russians cut across the panzer lines while firing their machine guns and throwing grenades at the soldiers behind the tanks. Clouds of sizzling shrapnel enshrouded Hauptmann Schmidt and a handful of his soldiers, tearing them apart, their maimed bodies sprawled on the ground when the smoke cleared a moment later.

"Go, go, go!" shouted Christoff at his men, who had been momentarily distracted by the gory sight. Taking command of the strike, he led Johan and the rest of the infantry around the tanks, killing the two Russians, shooting at anything that moved, running over the enemy positions, overwhelming them with a mix of machine-gun fire, hand grenades, mortars, and forks of orange fire from the flamethrowers.

Russian artillery suddenly started raining on them. Christoff saw it coming from the opposite bank of the river. They had been hiding, waiting for the Germans to get in range.

A round cracked the panzer in front of him like an egg, splattering burning metal in all directions.

Instincts overrode his surprise, forcing him down face first. Losing his machine gun, Christoff rolled away from the burning tank, hands shielding his face from the inferno.

The shells continued to fall, continued to shake the ground around him.

He stopped rolling when no longer sensing the heat. Opening his eyes, he saw havoc among the front of the German attack on the bridge. Soldiers ran in every direction to seek shelter from the Russian rounds, which pounded the terrain like giant hammers, kicking up columns of dirt and molten debris, swallowing entire platoons in seconds.

In between two artillery shell explosions, Christoff spotted his platoon's radioman huddling behind a wrecked Russian tank thirty meters away.

Raising to a deep crouch, Christoff charged in his direction, ignoring the explosions around him. He needed the radio, needed his own artillery and the Luftwaffe to put pressure on the Russians across the river.

He dove the last three meters, landing next to the trembling soldier, whose eyes were fixated on the ground while rocking back and forth.

Christoff slapped the top of the radioman's helmet to get his attention.

The radioman, still in his teens, burst into hysteria, screaming that they were all going to die.

Christoff punched him hard in the face.

The kid quickly came around, staring at the lieutenant in disbelief.

"The coordinates!" Christoff screamed while pointing at the distant figures across the river. "Call them out to headquarters! Request artillery and air support!"

The radioman tried to reach into his backpack to pull out a map, but his trembling hands prevented him from grabbing it.

Christoff snagged the map and opened it in front of them as more shells descended around them.

The smell of cordite and burned flesh assaulting his nostrils, Christoff ran a finger across the map, finding the exact location, then conveying the coordinates to the radioman, who turned on his equipment and began to relay the information to the German units two kilometers behind them.

"Good!" Christoff told the boy, a hand on his helmet. "You did good! Hang in there! Help is on the way!"

Christoff Halden left him there to go find any able soldier to launch a new attack the moment the Russian artillery went silent. He had taken less than ten steps away when an invisible force punched him in the back, sending him tumbling out of control.

Dazed, disoriented, Christoff sat up, holding his right shoulder, which he had just skinned against the dirt. When he turned to see the site of the blast, he saw the radioman's limbless torso next to the torn radio a few meters away.

Invoking strength, he crawled away from him, peering

through the haze at two of his men in a foxhole waving him over.

Where is our damned artillery? Where are those Stukas? he thought while dragging himself along the ground like a snake. *We're being slaughtered!*

Christoff moved toward his men as more shells devoured the world around him, bathing him in dirt and rocks.

"Come, Lieutenant!" one of the entrenched men shouted. "This way, sir!"

Christoff narrowed his eyes, struggled to see the two soldiers through the boiling dirt and smoke, but failed to make out their faces protruding above the foxhole. He also couldn't recognize their voices because of the incessant artillery thumping and the intense ringing in his ears.

But the shells exploding all around him forced Christoff forward, toward the hole, where he might be able to weather the Russian attack until his—

A thunderous artillery round hit the middle of the foxhole just as Christoff was about to reach it.

Dirt and body parts engulfed him as he watched in disbelief the brutal and explosively fast carnage.

The German lieutenant froze, uncertain what to do, where to go, his eyes fixated on the headless torso that had landed just a meter from him, blood and smoke sizzling out of the neck.

The roaring blasts of German artillery units brought focus back to his mind, informing him that his request had made it through to the crew manning the large guns. Seconds later the opposite bank of the river became engulfed in a cloud of flames just as a swarm of Stukas began to make their rounds.

Getting to his feet and grabbing the nearest machine gun, which he quickly checked to make sure it was loaded, Oberleutnant Christoff Halden raced past the destroyed foxhole, jumping over maimed bodies, splashing across pools of fresh blood and sizzling entrails, his eyes zeroing in on the two Russian soldiers running on the bridge toward the stack of dynamite that the pilot from a Stuka had spotted an hour ago.

Johan Wiltz, the rugged Bavarian who had joined Christoff's company during the initial days of the Polish campaign, caught up with Christoff just before reaching the bridgehead, as the German attack gained momentum once again. Johan's eyes first blinked in relief that Christoff had survived the Russian attack, then shifted to understanding what his superior officer was attempting to do.

Panzers continued their advance now free from the danger of Russian artillery units, which had vanished behind columns of fire and smoke. The remaining Russians in the trenches and foxholes perished under the Germans' tank tracks.

As the slow-flowing waters of the Dniester reflected the late-afternoon sun, Christoff Halden thumbed the fire selector of his MP43 to single-shot mode as he took careful aim, firing twice into the back of the closest Russian on that bridge. The brown-uniformed soldier fell over the wooden surface of the bridge just as Johan fired twice more, his excellent marksmanship skills scoring two hits just beneath the soldier's neck, nearly severing the head.

Lowering his rifle, Christoff exchanged a glance with his subordinate. Preventing the Russians from blowing up the bridge had been his primary objective. They had succeeded, but at the price of losing his captain and dozens of men.

Breathing heavily from the short but intensive charge, Christoff patted his subordinate on the back.

"Good shooting, Johan. Go check the bodies and also remove the fuses from the dynamite."

"Yes, sir," said Johan, almost three years his junior.

Christoff turned around, momentarily taken aback by the line of panzers and men advancing toward the captured bridge. Even though they were on his side, the sight was still frightful, and once again the young lieutenant frowned at the suicidal stupidity displayed by the Russians.

Or was it courage?

In the end it didn't matter. He knew Germany would win. It was just a matter of how many stubborn Russians they killed in the process before achieving Hitler's objective—and how many of his comrades in arms died in the process.

As he walked back to rejoin his men, Christoff spotted four dead Russians in a trench, all missing body parts. But the gruesome sight wasn't what caught Christoff's attention. The German officer had seen far worse during the Polish campaign. What gripped him were the ropes tied to the ankles of the Russians, securing them to wooden stakes, preventing them from retreating, forcing them to fight to the death.

It was at that moment of apparent victory, as his troops shouted in joy and praised Hitler, that Oberleutnant Christoff Halden suddenly wondered if Germany had made a paramount mistake by attacking these people, who were showing a level of unyielding determination that exceeded even the brave Polish cavalry, which had tried in vain to stop German panzers with horse-mounted troops. To this day, Christoff could still remember the killing fields in Poland, littered with mutilated humans and horses. What a huge miscalculation on the part of the Polish government, which should have just surrendered to avoid such useless bloodshed.

So why didn't Christoff have the same feeling of superiority here, even after having crushed the initial wave of Russian defenses?

Perhaps it was the historical resilience of this nation to survive the worst attacks, like that of Napoleon more than a century before. Or perhaps it was its vast natural resources and huge population. Or maybe what concerned him most was the thought of opening a second front on this war.

Whatever the reason, in the end this felt like a mistake.

A mistake.

The word repeated itself in his mind—it made him think of an even larger mistake: coming to Germany.

As his men searched the area for survivors, as panzer units crossed the bridge and continued their advance, as the Luftwaffe dominated the Ukrainian sky, Christoff Halden knelt by the maimed body of his captain and broke off the military tag hanging at the end of a chain around his neck.

Holding the bloody piece of engraved metal in his hands, he remembered the day he'd answered Germany's patriotic call in early 1937. The son of German immigrants who had settled in central Texas in the 1920s, Michael Christoff Halden had grown up listening to his parents' stories of their Deutschland, had learned to speak German before English, and had been thoroughly blinded by the prospects of helping rebuild Germany from the ashes of World War I. So the nineteen-year-old had exchanged his American first name for his German middle name and headed to prosperous Berlin, further ahead in technology and standard of living than an America still recovering from the Great Depression.

And at first his dream of a better life had come true. In Berlin, Christoff found prosperity, new friends, new opportunities, especially those provided by the military. Following the footsteps of his father, who had fought for Germany during the First World War, Christoff didn't waste any time before enlisting and enrolling in the Wermacht's officer's course, earning the rank of leutnant months later.

But then came the invasion of Poland, and with it the realization that Germany wasn't building such strong military just to ensure national security. Its goal was to expand, to conquer, to stomp on its weaker neighbors before exploiting them, and in many cases enslaving them, as he had seen firsthand in the concentration camps now dotting the Polish countryside.

But through it all, Christoff—a soldier at heart, not a murderer—had managed to maintain his honor by volunteering for the most dangerous assignments. This kept him honing his warring skills as well as busy fighting against *soldiers,* sparing himself and his men from being forced to participate in the massive executions of civilians, women and children labeled as spies.

Christoff shook his head.

Spies my ass.

Ironically, it was this same display of courage under fire that not only kept him from becoming a criminal but earned him a field promotion to the rank of oberleutnant.

A criminal.

Christoff had tried very hard to avoid becoming one. Yet, as he stared at the maimed bodies of Russians and Germans alike, he couldn't help but wonder if what had taken place here would qualify as criminal.

11

Stubborn Silence

Northwest of Lvov, Ukraine
June 24, 1941

That evening, as German forces continued their drive inside Ukrainian territory, Oberleutnant Christoff Halden's troops were given the opportunity to rest for the evening. Hitler had been pleased with the initial victories and had proclaimed that Moscow would fall in less than two months.

"Is it possible that we will conquer the Soviet Union that soon, sir?"

Drawing on a cigarette, Christoff regarded Sergeant Johan Wiltz, sitting amid several of his men. They were either smoking, like Johan, or sleeping, despite the distant rumbling of German and Russian artillery, whose flashes ignited the horizon like a lightning storm.

Christoff wanted to accept the führer's words but had stopped believing in the Third Reich after the atrocities his country had committed in Poland. However, as a German officer he had to promote a sense of patriotism among his men.

"The Soviet Union is a big country," he said, measuring his words very carefully, lest he wished to end up imprisoned—or even shot—for daring to speak up against Hitler. He had learned long ago that the führer's SS was everywhere. "But our forces are quite formidable. Could we do it in two months? It will be difficult . . . but not impossible."

"But . . . what do you really think, sir?" insisted Johan. Christoff had developed a close bond with these men while fighting as a unit in Poland, to the point that they always wanted his unofficial ratification before they believed anything that came out of Berlin.

Grinning, he said, "Well, Johan, I for one plan to spend this autumn back in Berlin after another glorious victory."

The soldiers who were still awake exchanged glances while nodding and smiling, obviously liking his answer.

They were good men, loyal to Germany, like him. But *unlike* him, most of them were also faithful to Adolf Hitler, and some were even members of the Nazi Party.

Christoff had not been able to bring himself to join them, especially after the slaughter he'd witnessed in Warsaw. And if he'd had his way, he would have resigned his commission and headed back to America. But by the time he had realized his mistake, it had been too late to go back, too late to undo the damage. He didn't even have the proper papers to travel, having turned in his American passport in order to enlist in the Wermacht. But at the time his juvenile ideology had driven his decisions—an ideology crushed by the madness he had seen in Poland.

You can't go back.

But even if you could, would you?

Much had happened both in Germany and in America since he'd left in the spring of 1937. Not only was traveling from Germany to America restricted, but he wasn't sure if he could return to the life he had left behind after having been a part of the German war machine for so long. How would his family react? How would his friends treat him? Would his community of New Braunfels, Texas, made up of Nazi-hating German immigrants, accept him? Or would he have to return incognito, perhaps settling in another region of the country, always living with the fear of one day being recognized for who he had been during the early years of this war?

You are stuck here, pal, he thought as he left his men behind and continued to stroll around the camp smoking a cigarette and contemplating his grim options.

He reached the barbed-wire fence where the Russian prisoners rotted away under the watchful eyes of several German soldiers.

The sight unsettled him.

Christoff had seen prisoners in France and Poland, but these Russians were different. For one thing, they didn't complain about their appalling situation. They simply stared into the distance with the stubborn silence that came from having nothing to lose, with the same utter defiance that had made those soldiers earlier today anchor themselves in the trenches, willing to fight to the death, even when facing terrifying odds.

He watched them carefully, sitting or laying on the muddy ground with their untreated wounds, their exposed entrails, their burned faces and missing limbs. Flies buzzed around them, feeding off the festering injuries whose stench made his stomach knot. One soldier had lost his lower jaw, his upper teeth exposed in a macabre leer that turned toward the German oberleutnant.

Christoff locked eyes with the man, who was also missing most of his left arm. Large horseflies crawled over his maimed face. He would likely be dead by morning, along with some of his comrades. The rest probably wouldn't last a few days. But even on the eve of their death he sensed an air of strength oozing from their wounds, from their stolid stares, from their refusal to let their captors hear them moan, cry, or protest about the terrible pain they were in, about the lack of medical treatment or the brutal conditions of their captivity. The Polish wounded had cried and the French had squealed, begging their captors for morphine, for anything to alleviate their suffering. Some had even pleaded for a bullet in the head.

But not these Russians. Not these—

"Oberleutnant Halden!"

Christoff turned around. One of the senior officers of his army division, Oberst Günter Dörnitz approached him. The gray-haired colonel was followed by two of his aides. Behind them marched a man of short stature wearing the black tunic and pants of the Schutzstaffel, the SS. His right lapel sported double white lightning bolts, and like a good Nazi, he wore his red armband displaying a black swastika inside a white circle.

Christoff's throat went suddenly dry.

The SS, headed by Heinrich Himmler, was assigned by Hitler himself to control the general population of conquered territories. The SS was feared not just by the enemy but by all of the branches of the armed forces, from the Wermacht and the Luftwaffe to the Kriegsmarine, as Hitler had empowered it to do pretty much as it pleased. The SS had been responsible for the fall of many good officers who had made the mistake of complaining about the often insane directives originating from Berlin.

Christoff snapped to attention while bringing the tip of his right palm to his right temple.

"At ease," said Oberst Dörnitz.

He complied, gazing into the narrowed light-blue eyes of the tall colonel, whose lips were compressed as he inspected his young subordinate before shifting his stare toward the captured Russians beyond the rolls of barbed wire. "I see some managed to survive."

"I'm afraid not for long, Herr Colonel," replied Christoff in a tone more melancholic than he had intended. "They are in need of medical attention."

Dörnitz frowned.

"Our supplies are strictly limited for our own wounded, Oberleutnant!" shouted the stocky SS officer, his chiseled face beneath a full head of ash-blond hair tight with tension.

"Halden, this is Standartenführer Hans Kurtz," said Dörnitz. "He is in charge of population control in this region of the Ukraine."

"Yes, sir," Christoff replied. Kurtz held the equivalent rank in the SS of a full colonel, or oberst, which made him Dörnitz's equal, though as an SS officer Kurtz probably could intimidate even a general.

"These Russians shall rot before we spend a single deutsche mark curing them. They are not even worth the kerosene we will have to use to burn their carcasses to prevent the spread of disease."

"Yes, sir," repeated Christoff, used to dealing with SS officers. In his mind the bastards were little more than sadists wearing a military uniform. They seldom engaged in battle but were quick to show up the moment a territory had been secured to terrorize harmless civilians.

"We have plans to solve the problem of their overpopulation," added Kurtz with pride. "We are making certain that their inferior ethnic group does not prevail another generation!"

Waffen SS or not, this guy was really beginning to annoy Christoff, but he chose to play it cool, simply nodding while staring straight ahead.

After an awkward moment of silence, Dörnitz motioned one of his aides to bring a small leather box, which the general then presented to a puzzled Christoff, who just held it in his hands, not certain what to do with it.

"Field Marshal Gerd von Rundstedt, commander of Army Group South, was very pleased that you prevented the Russians from blowing up that bridge this morning."

Christoff shrugged. "Just doing my job, sir."

Dörnitz pulled out a piece of paper from his tunic and read, "For bravery and leadership displayed in the battlefield, even after your commanding officer, Hauptmann Meinhard Schmidt, was killed in action by the Russians, the führer has awarded you the iron cross. Congratulations." Dörnitz took the coveted medal and tied it around Christoff's neck so that the cross hung just over his Adam's apple.

"Thank you, Herr Oberst!"

"You have also been officially promoted to the rank of captain," added Dörnitz, shaking Christoff's hand while handing him his new rank insignias. "You may wear them in the morning to lead your new company into battle."

Christoff was momentarily at a loss for words. "Yes, sir. Thank you, sir."

Standartenführer Kurtz leaned forward and also shook Christoff's hand before saying, "Congratulations, Hauptmann Halden, and remember that there is no place for mercy for one's enemy in the Third Reich. No place. The Bolsheviks must be treated like the subhuman species that they are. Keep up the good work."

"Thank you, Herr Standartenführer."

They left him there with the soldiers guarding the prisoners. Christoff watched them walk away until they faded in the fog rapidly engulfing the camp.

At twenty-two he was probably one of the youngest captains in the Wermacht. His men would be happy for him, proud of his well-deserved promotion and award, yet Christoff didn't feel like celebrating.

It's the Russians' eerie silence, he decided. It had somehow drowned his spirits far more than Hitler's empty promises—the lies that had drawn him to this corner of the world, to this hell on Earth.

There was no going back, not today, not tomorrow, not ever.

You'll have to play this through to the end.

Whatever that end might be.

12

Firing Squad

Babi Yar Forest, North of Kiev, Ukraine
July 26, 1941

Blisters covered most of his hands as he worked along with thousands of other prisoners while the Germans looked on.

Colonel Aleksandrovich Nikolai Krasilov ignored his blistered palms as he clutched the shovel and continued to dig the irrigation ditch. Yet he knew that the long ravine he had been excavating for the past two days—since being captured by a German patrol—would not be used as a waterway.

Krasilov maintained a steady pace, breathing slowly as he thrust the shovel into the soil, pressed the sole of his flight boot into the back of the shovel to drive it in deep before pulling it back and up, throwing the loosened dirt over his right shoulder and up to the top of the ditch. A large group of women and children waited along both sides of the trench under the watchful eye of dozens of German soldiers.

Krasilov worked without pause, lest he end up shot in the stomach as had so many men when they had collapsed from exhaustion. He had to stay alive, had to keep making himself valuable to his captors—even if doing so meant digging his own grave. He had to bide his time until an opportunity to escape presented itself to him.

The staccato machine-gun fire reverberated across the dense forest, rattling not just Krasilov but all of the men in the ditch. An instant later, amid screams, bodies began to fall on him.

First a woman, then two children, their chests and abdomens ripped open, their blood and viscera splattering around him.

As the deafening reports from the machine guns nearly drowned the shrieks, Krasilov tried to look up as more bodies rained on the men. He watched the helmeted silhouettes of German soldiers at the top of the ravine backlit by the sunlight forking through the thick canopy overhead. The flashes from their muzzles created a stroboscopic effect as the ground around him burst with multiple explosions, and filled with the inert bodies of men, women, and children, their limbs and heads turned at unnatural angles.

The man next to him trembled, letting go of his shovel as a round struck him in the middle of the face, blowing out the back of his head, splashing the trench wall as he collapsed.

Krasilov knelt by a woman shivering by his feet, blood and foam oozing from her mouth and nose as she breathed.

He embraced her, tried to console her in the middle of this madness, as the ear-piercing blasts of the machine guns echoed down this mass grave they had dug for themselves, as he whispered in her ear that this should all end soon, that they would all soon find peace from these monsters, from these—

A white-hot pain in his head blinded him. Colors exploded in his mind before all went dark.

13

Doctors of Death

Outside of Rzeszow, Poland
75 Kilometers from the Ukrainian Border
July 27, 1941

Dr. Zoya Krasilov leaned over the Polish girl and pressed her stethoscope against her chest, praying that her heart had stopped beating—even if it went against her medical oath and her renewed Catholic faith.

She closed her eyes in disappointment when listening to the rhythmic pulses in her instrument and somehow managed to hold back her tears. She'd rather get raped again than tend the wounds of the patients of this so-called infirmary. But she had not only taken the oath a long time ago, she had made a silent promise to the Catholic nun who had sacrificed herself for Zoya. She had sworn to make a difference in every way she could. And she could do so as a doctor by helping her patients heal, even if the healing process would lead them to more suffering at the hands of the German doctor.

At least that's what he calls himself, Zoya thought, inspecting the burns covering the girl's entire body—burns the ten-year-old had suffered when the Nazis immersed her in boiling water for thirty seconds to study the reactions of humans to burns. The camp's head doctor, an SS colonel known only as Dr. Helmut, had explained that the results from this revolutionary medical experiment would help German scientists determine how many burns an average soldier could endure before medical attention was required.

Animals!, she thought, staring at the grotesquely blistered skin covering the girl's chest and arms. Only her head and neck had been spared.

The girl was unconscious thanks to the injection of morphine Zoya had administered after ten hours of nonstop crying, when Zoya had begged Helmut for a dose of the precious painkiller.

The SS colonel—the same doctor whom Zoya had pleaded with the day of her arrival—had reluctantly agreed when Zoya had explained that in order to make the experiment as realistic as possible the patients would have to be treated just as the wounded soldiers would. Otherwise the data collected could lead to the wrong conclusions.

With a final sad glance at the scalded skin, Zoya moved on to her next patient, a woman with both arms broken as part of an experiment to determine how many times arms could be broken before they would not heal anymore. Zoya had hidden her dismay when learning that the count for this particular patient was ten over a period of one year.

The bastards have broken her arms over and over the moment they healed.

Only the discipline she had learned from years in the Red Army and then as a military doctor kept her from breaking down in front of this gaunt Polish woman of around forty, who regarded Zoya with an indifferent stare from sunken brown eyes.

They've broken her spirit.

The woefully thin arms were in slings to allow Dr. Helmut to inspect the condition of the bones, which Zoya now did, but carefully, as humanely as she could, slowly feeling the bones beneath the skin, a task made easier by the appalling lack of muscle tissue. Like so many other long-term prisoners, she looked like a living skeleton, and also like most prisoners, she lacked the will to refuse cooperation, accepting her fate without mustering a word of complaint.

Zoya knew that the inspection she was currently performing should be painful, yet this Polish woman didn't utter a word, her silence speaking volumes about the brutal suffering she had undergone for so long.

Just as she had been instructed by Dr. Helmut, Zoya made an entry in the log, indicating that the bones on her arms seemed to be healing just fine—an update that would mean another round of breaks in a wooden contraption Helmut had left next to her bed as a morbid reminder of what was to come.

I have to get out of here, she thought. *I have to join the resistance—find a way to fight back.*

She continued her rounds, checking the broken arms of another victim of the same morbid experiment, only this one was just seventeen years old. Dr. Helmut wanted to evaluate the effect that age had on the healing process.

"How are you feeling, Tasha?" she asked. Tasha Burojev was one of the two girls who had been publicly gang-raped on the first day at the camp. They were subsequently sent to the infirmary to become human guinea pigs.

"They hurt, though not as much as much as they did yesterday," she replied.

Zoya admired the girl's courage. Tasha had not uttered a single moan when Helmut had ordered her arms broken four weeks ago, and again just yesterday, when her young bones were nearly healed. She had taken the pain on both occasions with silent defiance.

"Rest, my dear," Zoya said, gently stroking her hair before checking her pulse and administering a strong painkiller.

Tasha drifted into deep sleep moments later, as the injected chemical took effect.

In a way, Tasha was lucky. Zoya's next patient, the other gang-raped teenager, was participating in an experiment to determine how certain brain functions were affected by measured blows to specific parts of the head. This girl had first lost her ability to speak, then her ability to write, then her sight, followed by her hearing in her right ear. Her shaved head had been sectioned with a red pencil to indicate the injured areas and the effect they had.

Zoya controlled the urge to vomit. The Germans had run this experiment dozens of times, to the point that they could nearly predict the exact consequence of each blow to specific sections of the head. This teenager was just another data point in a morbid experiment that ended when the patient became a complete vegetable.

And on she went, patient after patient, blocking her feelings, keeping them from surfacing as the terrifying sights tore at her sanity, at her values.

But she continued, tending their wounds, trying to provide hope in a place that had no hope.

Trying to make a difference.

14

Mass Grave

Babi Yar Forest, North of Lvov, Ukraine
July 27, 1941

The pain in his head awoke him. It felt like a splinter wedged deep in his brain.

Colonel Aleksandrovich Nikolai Krasilov opened his eyes despite the throbbing pain. He blinked rapidly to clear his sight.

Slowly, a face materialized in front of him.

He saw . . . eyes—the eyes of the woman he had tried to console right before . . .

The slaughter.

The cries.

The horror.

He breathed in slowly while bringing a hand to his head, cringing when his fingers came in contact not with his skull but with something soft just above his right temple.

Dear God!

His brain was exposed. The pain he had felt right before passing out had been a German bullet cracking his skull.

But why am I still alive?

The only explanation that made sense was that the round must have bounced off. He didn't relish the thought of the bullet still being inside his head. But if the bullet had indeed pierced his head, he doubted he'd be alive.

With great care, he found the edges of the wound, his fingertips brushing against the jagged bone. It felt roughly a centimeter wide and twice as long.

Slowly, with great effort, he shifted the pale body of the woman enough to see beyond her, above the trench, his eyes searching for the German soldiers.

He saw none, just moonlight glowing through branches swaying in the warm summer breeze, amid buzzing flies.

How long have I been out?

The Germans had taken his pilot's watch the morning they captured him, as well as his wedding band and his papers. The foul smell told him that he must have been out for many hours.

His head throbbing as if he had a blaring migraine, Krasilov remained still for several minutes just listening, trying to discern any sounds beyond the whistling breeze and the rustling of leaves.

Nothing.

Quietly, he slid from beneath the woman, worming his way to the top of the layer of humans littering the bottom of the ditch, the terrible odor assaulting his nostrils, making his stomach convulse.

Forcing control, he once again looked around him, searching for any movement, any sound, convincing himself that he was indeed alone—alone with thousands of rotting bodies and a million flies. Now in the open he felt several flies settling on his head wound. He swatted them out of the way, careful not to hurt his gash.

In his twenty-some years with the Red Air Force, Krasilov had seen his share of death and destruction, but the slaughtered bodies extending beyond him propelled him to an unsurpassed level of horror. He sat in a sea of twisted bodies oozing gasses, decomposing in the summer heat.

Get away from here.

The Germans could return at any moment with more prisoners or simply to fill the hole with dirt and cover this massacre.

As he reached the nearest wall he felt warm drops trickling down the right side of his head. Krasilov removed the shirt from the same man who had been shot in the head just before he was, and wrapped it around his head like a bandanna to protect his wound, which was still bleeding. It was then, his eyes adjusted to the darkness, that he noticed everyone around had been shot in the head.

That made sense, he decided. After machine gunning the crowd, the Germans must had jumped into the ravine and walked around shooting everyone in the head to eliminate the possibility of someone escaping. His head wound must have been enough to keep the executioners from shooting him again.

Lucky bastard.

Crawling out of what would have been his grave, Krasilov didn't feel so lucky. Not only had the Germans taken his wife, killed his children, and were exterminating civilians, they had crushed all border defenses and were now driving deep into Ukraine. Soon they would enter Russia, and, if not stopped, Moscow.

Moscow.

He tightened his fists.

Over my dead body, he thought, clawing his way up, slithering over the mounds of excavated dirt, staggering to his feet in the leaf-littered forest.

Light-headed, thirsty, nauseated, he gave the grave behind him one final glance before heading west.

15

The Procedure

Outside of Rzeszow, Poland
75 Kilometers from the Ukrainian Border
August 30, 1941

The routine was always the same. She would finish her rounds at midnight and step inside the small nurse dormitory wedged in between the infirmary and the German doctors' quarters.

As the only prisoner-doctor in the compound—and also because of her outstanding medical skills—Zoya had been given the special privilege of having her own private room.

A privilege and also a curse, she decided as she headed for her room at the end of the row of bunk beds, where a dozen prisoner-nurses slept.

Totally exhausted from a twelve-hour shift that always left her not just physically and mentally drained but taxed her emotions beyond what she thought she could handle, Zoya settled herself in her small bed and tried to go to sleep. But she knew it would be useless.

As expected, the door to her room inched open a few minutes later, and a short, stout figure walked inside.

Dr. Helmut.

Zoya Krasilov had learned awhile back how to behave during the procedure—and in her mind that's *all* this was: a procedure, nothing else. Silence was vital to appease the doctor's desires.

She remained still, arms by her sides, eyes on the wooden ceiling as he sat on the bed and pulled down the covers. He began to undress her, slowly, prolonging the procedure, exposing her breasts, her mound of pubic hair, which she had shaved in the shape of a heart at his request.

Then came the hand, massaging her stomach, her breasts, the inside of her thighs.

Controlling her breathing, silently cursing not just the German but this body and face of hers that awoke the most primitive of instincts in her captors, Zoya's mind slowly traveled beyond this room, past the barbed wire encircling the camp, across the border into Ukraine, and beyond. She wondered what had become of Aleksandr, her husband, friend, and lover. She tried to imagine a reunion with him and with Marissa and Larissa; tried to picture what it would be like to hold them again, to kiss them again.

Aleksandr. Marissa. Larissa. Lvov. Sunflowers. Blue skies.

The images filled her mind, carrying her away from the hands spreading her legs, from the figure crawling over her, from his stinking breath as he kissed her, as he pressed his hairy chest against her.

"Russian whore," Helmut whispered in his broken Russian

while nibbling her left ear before entering her hard. "Take this, Russian whore."

Zoya cringed as he insulted her, as he mumbled in the dark how Germany was raping the Soviet Union just as he was now raping her at will.

"You are enjoying this, my Russian whore," he whispered, smiling as she trembled, as a heat flash rushed through her system.

Zoya closed her eyes, trying to regain control, not wishing to see the German's dominant stare, the one that told her she had been conquered.

Aleksandr. Marissa. Larissa. Lvov. Sunflowers. Blue skies.

She went back to the images, to the reunion, to that precious moment when they would all be together again, when her Red Army would drive Germany back, when the red star would replace the swastika.

The end came suddenly for the German doctor as he abruptly stopped his thrusts, shivered, and released inside of her, remaining still for a moment, his perspiration dripping on her face.

He withdrew slowly, finally getting off, dressing in a hurry before leaving the room.

Zoya just lay there, hands on her heaving chest, her legs crossed, her heart pummeling her chest. The bastard had won again, had managed to force her body to respond.

Do what you have to do to stay alive, to survive.

She remembered the promise she had made to herself the day she'd arrived over two months ago, when that Catholic nun had sacrificed herself for her: survive one day at a time and make a difference. The work at the infirmary was both taxing and heartbreaking, but at least she had an opportunity to provide moral support to the victims of the German's experiments, and she used their suffering as a way to put these midnight rapes in perspective.

In the scheme of things, what the German doctor had done to her paled in comparison to the experiments conducted next door. She could not get pregnant, and she trusted that being a German doctor, he would not be transmitting any diseases to her. But if he did, she had access to plenty of medication to combat an infection, just as she had cured her own vaginal infection two months ago.

Survive one day at a time.

Make a difference.

As her body slowly settled down, her mind grew tired. Slowly, she fell asleep.

16

Opportunity

Outside of Rzeszow, Poland
75 Kilometers from the Ukrainian Border
August 31, 1941

The gunfire echoing from the front of the camp pulled her away from her patients.

Dr. Zoya Krasilov stood, exchanged a glance with Tasha, whose nearly healed arms were scheduled to be broken tomorrow, and rushed to the front of the infirmary.

Several guards lay dead on the mud while others ran toward the rear of the compound as a wave of men in civilian clothes fired at them from the other side of the barbed-wire entrance. Several men climbed over the top and landed inside the compound.

Partisans!

Fire broke out from the compound's observation tower, where the Germans had installed a machine gun. In an instant two of the partisans inside the compound fell to the German rounds. Others raced for cover, unable to open the main gates for their compatriots. Those outside did not have a good angle to fire on the tower, which meant they could not provide covering fire to those making it over the top to unlock the gates.

Zoya dropped her stethoscope, her military training abruptly superceding her medical profession as she rushed toward the fallen German soldiers and picked up a machine gun. It was a model with a long magazine for sustained firing.

She had never used this weapon, but gun mechanisms weren't all that different. She found the action bolt, pulled it toward her, verified that there was a round chambered, and leveled it at the observation tower, firing several bursts. The rounds cracked across the compound, drawing the attention of the German machine-gun emplacement toward her and away from the partisans.

The ground to her right exploded.

Zoya rolled to her left, away from the bullets, rose to a crouching position behind a water barrel, and started shooting again, providing the much-needed covering fire for the partisans, who finally got the door open and burst into the prison camp in large numbers, driving back the Germans.

She sensed movement to her immediate left and watched Dr. Helmut emerging from the officers' quarters adjacent to the infirmary. He was followed by two Waffen-SS colonels and a major—the heads of the camp. They were reaching for their sidearms.

Zoya swung the weapon in their direction and swept it at waist level while releasing a long burst, cutting them down. She returned her attention to the pillbox atop the tower just as two partisans reached her position, releasing another burst.

"Who are you?" one of them asked in Polish as he crouched next to her by the water barrel.

"Captain Zoya Krasilov . . . of the Red Army," she replied, trying to concentrate to speak Polish while keeping the pressure on the Germans.

A half-dozen partisans reached a vantage point on the clearing and joined in the fight, peppering the tower with machine-gun fire, silencing it.

Keeping her weapon pointed in the direction of the tower,

Zoya turned to see the face of her liberator, a fair-skinned man in his thirties, with eyes as dark as his thick hair.

"What are you doing here, Captain Krasilov?" he asked.

"The Germans destroyed Lvov . . . my hometown," she replied, breathing deeply, the events unfolding too fast. More than fifty partisans now crowded the front of the prison, some disappearing into buildings in teams of five or more to clear the place of Germans, who were shot on the spot. The partisans didn't take prisoners, and that suited the female inmates just fine.

Some of the women prisoners attacked a pair of wounded soldiers with their bare hands, clawing at their faces as the Germans screamed for mercy. The partisans looked on as the women stripped the soldiers naked and castrated them with a pair of the same shears they had used to shave their heads.

Zoya closed her eyes, finding it hard to believe that this was actually happening, that they were being liberated.

"It is a pleasure making your acquaintance, Captain Krasilov," the partisan said, smiling. "I'm Aris Broz, leader of the resistance movement in this region." He placed a hand on her shoulder and patted it while adding, "We had better get going. The survival of our movement hinges on hit-and-run strikes. This place will be swarming with enemy troops within the hour."

She lowered her rifle, exhaling heavily.

"Is there anything we can do for you in return for your help today?" Aris asked.

Zoya stared at the opened gates and the train tracks beyond it—at freedom, and the opportunity to fight back, to avenge what the Germans had done to her country, to her family, to her.

Her gaze momentarily landed on the horde of women prisoners running toward the entrance with the assistance of the partisans. Zoya glanced at the dead Germans in front of the officers' quarters.

As Aris Broz looked on, she walked toward them, stepping in front of Helmut, the SS colonel, the doctor, the monster. She had shot him once in the abdomen, leaving him alive.

Their eyes locked as she stepped up to him.

Zoya gathered her phlegm and spat on him before hissing, "This is one Russian you shall never rape again." She fired once at his groin and watched him roll in pain.

As Dr. Helmut screamed in agony, Zoya turned to a perplexed Aris Broz and said, "You asked me what you could do in return?"

The partisan leader gave her a puzzled smile and a tentative nod.

"Then get me back to my country. Just get me back to my people."

PART TWO

Winter of 1942

"For the enemy and his accomplices unbearable conditions must be created in the occupied territories. They must be pursued at every step and destroyed and their measures must be frustrated."
—Joseph Stalin

17

Yanks

Bahrain
November 1, 1942

Zipping up his black leather aviator jacket, U.S. Air Force Captain Jack Towers took a long drag from his cigarette while staring at the large merchant ships quietly steaming north toward the port of Abadan, Iran. He slowly exhaled through his nostrils as he stepped away from the edge of the hill and walked back toward the dusty, makeshift runway where he had landed the night before. His back still ached from sleeping on the floor, but as Jack saw it, at least he'd had a relatively quiet place where he could get a few uninterrupted hours of sleep without being disturbed by gunfire. That alone was a luxury these days.

On the way to the small mess tent, Jack walked next to his plane, a Bell P-39D Aircobra he had baptized *The Impatient Virgin*. It was named after one of his wilder girlfriends during his short but busy stay at Cochran Field, Georgia, where Jack had trained side by side with Royal Air Force pilots on advanced dogfighting techniques with the Aircobras. From there Jack had been transferred to Dale Mabry in Florida for additional dogfighting training. Eight months later, Jack, along with two dozen other pilots who had logged over one thousand hours, spent a week in Camp Kilmer, New Jersey, where they boarded a ship loaded with four hundred P-39Ds destined for the Red Air Force as part of President Roosevelt's Soviet-American lend-lease program.

In the year and a half that Jack spent training with the air force, he never suspected that his first official overseas post would be training Soviet pilots to use their new equipment. But the aircraft that he had learned to master turned out to be one that neither the U.S. Air Force nor the RAF picked after the development of the faster and much more agile Curtiss P-40 Kittyhawk. The surplus of P-39Ds were shipped to the Soviet Union, where their fighter aircraft technology lagged the West by a few years.

But the real motive behind this not-so-glorious duty had to do with the fact that Jack was born under the name Jackovich Filipp Towers. His mother was a Russian nurse with whom his father had fallen in love during World War I. He had married her after the war and settled in Indiana.

Raised mostly by his mother, Jack spoke perfect Russian by the time he was three years old, and his mother saw to it that Jack didn't forget it by refusing to speak to him in English—something she did to this day.

Jack smiled as he rubbed his hand over his jacket and felt the letter—written in Russian—he'd received a few days before from his mother.

He always got letters from his mother but never from his father. Jack's father was always too busy running his used-car lot. He had always expected Jack to take over the business, but Jack had other plans for his life. Although his father never criticized his decision, Jack felt certain that was the reason he never got any letters from the old man.

That's just as well, reflected Jack. All his father wanted to talk about was cars anyway. He couldn't care less about Jack's aviation career.

There had been a time, Jack remembered as he walked around two parked Jeeps in front of the mess tent, when his father had a chance to pull him closer. It was during Jack's seventeenth birthday. Jack had wanted a car more than life itself, and in his mind he'd hoped his father would get him one. So much did Jack expect the car that he had told his friends he was getting one. That proved to be a grave mistake, because to Jack's surprise, the old man failed to show up for the party. *I had a last-minute customer,* Jack recalled him saying when arriving empty-handed three hours late.

The car-less son of the car salesman.

His friends gave him a hard time about that for weeks.

Jack shrugged and exhaled as he reached the front of the tent. Maybe that experience was the reason Jack felt as if he was always treated unfairly and his current assignment seemed to reinforce that belief.

He pushed the canvas flap and stepped inside the mess tent. The cafeteria line dominated one side of the place—that's if one could call two Arab cooks with a pot filled with eggs and another with a white soggy substance that aspired to be grits a cafeteria line. On the opposite side were two midsize tables with six chairs each. Jack grabbed a metal plate, got some eggs and grits, and walked to one of the tables, where a pilot ate his chow.

"This is a warm meal, Jack. Might as well enjoy it while it lasts," said Colonel Kenneth Chapman, Jack's commanding officer. Chapman was also fluent in Russian. "Heard up north the Ruskies are undergoing food rations."

"That's just great, sir. I can't wait." Jack sat down and filled up his mouth with two spoonfuls of eggs.

Chapman pushed his plate to the side and downed a glass of water. "The latest news from the eastern front is that shit's just about to hit the fan in good ol' Stalingrad, Jack. Better enjoy the runny eggs while you can. Most Russians are on a bread-and-butter diet, but heck, at least that's better than the Germans. Last I heard, those Nazi bastards are eating their own dogs and horses. Guess that's good for them assholes."

Jack saw Chapman's wide grin. His commanding officer had gold caps on his two front teeth. Jack couldn't hide a frown.

War wasn't going exactly as he had planned it.

He had visualized himself fighting Messerschmitts over the English Channel and across the French and German countryside, not in freeze-my-ass-off eastern Russia, but orders were orders. He had to go where the air force sent him. He did get to participate briefly in the battle of North Africa. Flying his *Impatient Virgin,* Jack had distinguished himself by shooting down three Italian Macchi MC.202 single-engine fighters over Libya in the week he'd spent there.

Chapman checked his watch. "We're leaving in an hour, Jack. Our red buddies got a couple of hundred planes just sitting around waiting for us to show them how to use them. No sense in making them wait, right?"

"I guess so, sir."

"Good. Don't forget to pick up a set of long johns from the supply tent. It's gonna be one motherfucker of a winter." Chapman got up and left.

Jack slowly shook his head.

His mother had told him stories of people freezing in minutes at forty below zero, and because in her days as a nurse she had seen more than her share of amputations due to frostbite. Jack got lecture after lecture on how to dress not just warm, but warm for a Russian winter. *There is a difference, my dear Jackovich Filipp,* she'd told him several times. *The Russian winter will rob you of your heat, freeze you to the bone, and then cover you with so many inches of snow that your stiff body won't surface until the following spring.*

The grits tasted terrible and stuck to the roof of his mouth. Jack ate them anyway, then went back to the line for seconds.

18

Airlift

Stalingrad Front
December 13, 1942

Colonel Aleksandrovich Nikolai Krasilov allowed his Lavochkin La-3 fighter to reach ten thousand feet before easing the control column forward. He checked his flanks and nodded approvingly when spotting his seven-plane squadron adopting an arrowhead formation.

A soldier from the Soviet Fifth Armored Division had spotted a formation of German bombers possibly carrying supplies for the trapped German Sixth Army of General Paulus in the Stalingrad pocket. Krasilov's mission was simple: destroy all enemy planes in the region with priority to bombers.

Disappointed at his government's poor intelligence reports, Krasilov scanned the skies and saw nothing but blue. Today was a rare day in the Soviet winter, but Krasilov didn't mind. He hoped temperatures would warm up to ten below so his men could get some relief from what had been a bitter winter. On the other hand, the cold winter affected the Germans far more than the Soviets. Krasilov had grown up in these regions and was used to the long, cold months—and was also well dressed for them. The Germans, on the other hand, were still wearing their summer uniforms. Paulus' army had taken Stalingrad in early September just to find that all that remained from the once picturesque city were the charred facades of the few buildings that still stood. The Soviet people, by order of the Soviet High Command in Moscow, set fire to all buildings, equipment, and anything else that could be of any use to the Germans that couldn't be hauled east in time. The Russian winter caught General Paulus and his glorious but exhausted

Sixth Army thousands of miles from home in a ghost city with fresh Soviet troops attacking from all flanks. Hitler had ordered the Sixth Army to adopt a hedgehog, or all-round, defensive position and to wait for relief. That created the Stalingrad pocket, where the Germans now slowly starved to death by an ever-decreasing channel of supplies.

I hope they all rot, Krasilov thought. After all the atrocities that the invading troops had committed in his motherland, he had not one ounce of pity for them. The Soviet colonel firmly believed that the Hitlerites should be not only repelled from Russia but followed all the way to the heart of Berlin.

"Germans! Three o'clock high!" came the voice from Krasilov's right wingman, Lieutenant Andrei Nikolajev.

Krasilov snapped his head to the left and spotted the formation.

"Scramble, comrades! Scramble! The Hitlerites shall not get their supplies today!"

The craft broke formation in pairs. Krasilov pushed full power. The Shvetsov fourteen-cylinder radial engine puffed two clouds of black smoke before pulling the craft with monumental force. Even at a twenty-degree angle of climb Krasilov watched the airspeed indicator rush past 350 knots and climb as fast as the altimeter.

He closed the gap in under a minute. Andrei remained glued to his side.

The bombers, which Krasilov now recognized as the large Heinkel He 177s, opened fire from all angles, but after a few encounters with the bombers, Krasilov had learned that the Heinkels were most vulnerable underneath, where there was only one machine-gun pod. The other five guns were scattered on the top, front, and rear, but were ineffective from underneath.

To protect themselves from such attack, the German bombers had opted to fly in a combat-box formation, which resembled a slanted flying wedge with the lead squadron in the middle and the rest stacked three hundred feet from the lead squadron's flanks. This arrangement enabled the bombers a clear field of fire for the front gunners and also allowed for coordinated cross fire against the attacking fighters. Each bomber covered the other one's bottom.

That formation, however, had one flaw. The planes on each end of the formation were the most exposed, though usually protected by escort fighters. Krasilov saw no escorts in sight as he approached the left-most Heinkel.

Although the La-3 was a remarkable improvement from the old I-16s he had flown on that terrible day in June of last year, the plane was still not as fast and maneuverable as the Messerschmitt Me 109F or the even faster Me 109G.

The Heinkel's underside dual machine-gun pod, located between the wings in the forward fuselage, swung in his direction and opened fire.

Krasilov broke left, away from the formation. The gun followed him, leaving the bomber exposed to his wingman.

"All yours, Andrei!"

Krasilov saw a few rounds exploding through his Lavochkin's wooden skin.

The craft shuddered but remained airborne. A backward glance, and Krasilov watched Andrei unload a long burst on the Heinkel's belly.

The gun-pod emplacement exploded.

Andrei broke its run while Krasilov made a three-sixty and came back around for his pass. This time there was nothing defending the bomber.

Krasilov made the turn wide enough to allow him ample time to fire. He completed the turn, aligned the Heinkel center fuselage using rudders and ailerons, and squeezed the trigger.

The dual cowl-mounted 20mm cannons came to life, firing at the rate of two hundred rounds per minute in synchronized fashion through the propeller. One in every ten rounds had a phosphorus head that burned bright yellow the moment it left the muzzle. Krasilov used the tracers to guide his fire as it tore open the belly of the large plane.

Pieces began to come off the wounded bomber. Krasilov pulled back the throttle to allow himself an extra second or two of firing time before he had to pull—

A bright explosion and the tail separated from the front of the plane, catching Krasilov entirely by surprise. The tail section flew down while the front fuselage shot up and to the left, blocking Krasilov's planned tight left turn. Breaking right was out of the question. Dozens of Heinkel guns would be waiting for him in a deadly cross fire.

Krasilov continued to fire and kept his run.

Another explosion.

The left engine went up in flames, tearing the Heinkel's wing along with it.

Krasilov rolled the wings ninety degrees and flew through the debris and flames between the torn wing and the fuselage. Fire engulfed him for a second, before turning to thick smoke followed by blue skies. He had flown through the fallen wreckage undamaged.

Krasilov watched in satisfaction as the wounded bomber's right engine continued to run, pulling the remnants of the Heinkel against an adjacent bomber. The two went up in a huge fireball that engulfed a third.

The remaining bombers, which Krasilov had estimated at thirty, continued their trajectory toward the pocket.

"Messerschmitts! Five and ten o'clock!"

"Got them! Break left, Andrei! I'll handle the right!"

Krasilov cut right and saw an Me 109G Gustav coming straight ahead. He leveled off and approached it head-on.

The German opened fire.

Krasilov's index finger reached the trigger and pressed it, but the game didn't last long. With a combined speed of over eight hundred knots, the two planes closed in incredibly fast.

A bullet crashed against Krasilov's propeller hub and bounced away. There was no smoke.

Krasilov waited until the very last second before breaking left. The German broke right and tried to execute a tight three-sixty. Krasilov was about to do a left three-sixty but instead he swung the stick back to the right, instantly pulling a few negative Gs.

The restraining harness kept him from crashing against

the canopy as he completed the maneuver while the German pilot was still halfway through the turn. The Hitlerite had apparently failed to consider Krasilov's change of strategy, and was caught with his entire side exposed. The Gustav's pilot had made a basic but fatal aerial combat mistake. Krasilov was surprised—German pilots were much more disciplined than that.

Krasilov smiled as his finger squeezed the trigger. At such close range the Messerschmitt broke apart after a three-second burst from the 20mm cannons.

As debris slowly fell from the sky, Krasilov cut left and raced after the bombers, most of which already had their payload doors fully open. The Stalingrad pocket was less than a minute away. The Heinkels went for a dive to increase the gap between them and the pursuing La-3s.

Krasilov cursed, wishing someone had informed them earlier about the incoming bombers. Maybe they could have intercepted sooner and taken out more bombers, but just like dozens of times before, all his squadron had was a ten-minute warning from field spotters.

Krasilov watched in utter disappointment as packages dropped from the bomb bays. Bright white parachutes opened a few seconds later.

Krasilov pressed on. There was still a chance to prevent some of the droppings.

He approached a Heinkel from the rear at full speed and with the cannons blasting. He adjusted fire to take out the rear gun emplacement of the closest bomber. The guns swung in his direction, but before a single round left them, the tail section blew into three large pieces just as the packages began to drop. Krasilov did not let up. He maintained his run while keeping the pressure on the trigger.

C'mon, blow, dammit. Blow!

Like a heavenly chastisement, the sixty-six-hundred-pound craft went up into a fiery ball that also engulfed Krasilov's plane for several seconds, enough for the waterproof lacquer protecting the La-3's wooden skin to catch fire.

He left the burning debris behind and immediately cut back power and pushed the stick forward. He had to reach land before the craft exploded, but at an altitude of three thousand feet, he doubted he'd make it. Most of the wings and rear fuselage were already covered by flames. It was just a matter of time before the heat caused the gas tank to blow.

Krasilov leveled off the plane, turned it upside down, and pushed the nose just a dash below the horizon to get the tail out of the way.

He slid the canopy open and pulled on the release mechanism of his restraining harness.

The windblast punched him in the chest as he free-fell through the open canopy, clearing the vertical fin by a couple of feet. The shock kept him from breathing for a few seconds as the earth, the burning craft, and the blue skies changed positions over and over, a peaceful feeling of isolation suddenly overtaking him.

Although it felt as if he was just standing still in midair, Krasilov knew he was plummeting to earth at over 150 miles per hour.

He reached for the rip cord and pulled it hard.

The pilot chute came up and dragged the main canopy, which deployed in a bright red color while giving Krasilov the tug of a lifetime. Fortunately for him, he had managed to fly far away enough from the German pocket before bailing out. Krasilov didn't think the starving Hitlerites in Stalingrad would treat well a downed Soviet pilot who had just been shooting down supply craft—not that the Germans treated Soviet prisoners of war with any decency.

He watched most bombers in the distance drop their payloads before turning back while the remaining Messerschmitts kept the rest of his squadron busy. Krasilov shook his head in disappointment. They needed more time to intercept, and better planes.

He silently glided over the River Volga.

19

Doberman Pinscher Stew

Pitomnik Airfield, Stalingrad Pocket
December 13, 1942

Major Christoff Halden, recently promoted like so many others due to sheer attrition, peered through the broken windows of his new post. The fierce air battle was slowly ending and the surviving Luftwaffe bombers were making their runs, some dropping supplies and others landing at the few airfields still operational in the pocket. White parachutes descended over the city.

If this place can be still called a city, he thought, gloved hands behind his back as he stared at the distant mounds of rubble that had been a beautiful city just a couple of months ago, before the bombings started—though by then the Russians had already done their share of destruction before retreating.

Dozens of smokestacks remained standing where modern factories had once spread across the many square miles of this former industrial city by the River Volga. It had always struck Christoff as ironic that the tall chimneys had survived the nonstop onslaught. But as it turned out, they were not only sturdily built, with many layers of bricks, but their slim profiles made them very difficult targets, often remaining erect as buildings collapsed around them.

Sighing, Christoff regarded his new quarters with despise, an old hangar just off the single runway, where some of the Luftwaffe planes that broke through the shield of Russian interceptors were landing and beginning to offload supplies before hauling the wounded out of the pocket. The rest of the planes simply dropped their cargos over the city.

The supplies, however, were far short of what was required not just to keep the Sixth Army holding the city, but to keep its two hundred thousand soldiers from starving to death. The Sixth Army required 650 tons of supplies a day to survive. On a good day the Luftwaffe would deliver about half that, and on days like today, the tonnage might not reach the one-hundred-ton mark.

Silently cursing Reichmarshall Hermann Wilhelm Göring, the head of the Luftwaffe, for promising to deliver all of the required supplies and then failing to meet that promise, Christoff stared at the empty bowl on the desk next to him. He had just consumed his morning ration of Doberman pinscher stew, which, he had to admit, tasted better than the horse meat the day before.

But at least he was *eating* something of substance—and warm—unlike many of the troops battling it out with the Russians in the city, who would go days without food, forced to eat anything they could lay their hands on, including rats. If they didn't perish from Russian bullets, they would starve to death, and those who managed to survive long enough often lost one or more limbs, noses, or ears to frostbite.

This morning the temperature had dropped to thirty below zero, which made it nearly to impossible to prepare food unless there was a way to make a fire; otherwise everything turned to stone, from bread and eggs to horse meat.

Christoff had been ordered to this remote frozen hell on the outskirts of the city by General Günter Dörnitz, one of von Paulus's generals, to provide security to one of the primary supply channels to the pocket.

"Why me?" he had asked Dörnitz, not relishing the thought of becoming just a guard. Christoff was a soldier—and a damned good one at that. If he had to be a part of this struggle, he'd rather be in the front lines fighting the enemy than maintaining the peace at this airfield.

"Because the last four men we assigned to the post fled south in the planes," the general had replied, adding that all four had been court-martialed and shot for abandoning their posts. Dörnitz trusted that Christoff would learn from their examples and display the same degree of courage that had gotten him this far in the Wermacht.

Followed by his two bodyguards—something Christoff did not as a display of power but for his own protection—the young major ventured onto the controlled havoc dominating the snow-covered airfield.

Men cried out in anger, fear, agony, or frustration. The military police, formed by his most trusted men—including recently promoted Oberleutnant Johan Wiltz—screamed back at the crowd, usually firing over their heads to maintain control, on occasion shooting those who refused to hold their place behind the barricades delineating the waiting area.

No man could board the plane until *after* all of its supplies had been transferred into the armed personnel carriers that would haul them to the various distribution centers scattered in the pocket. After the plane had been offloaded, Christoff himself would verify discharge papers to ensure their authenticity. There were not going to be any deserters on his watch. If he had to stay back and fight the Russians, so would every able man in this army.

Frustration stinging his gut, his officer's hat firmly planted on his head to prevent it from blowing off in the chilling wind sweeping across the barren steppe, Christoff approached Johan, guarding the only entrance to the oversized Heinkel He 177.

"All under control, Johan?"

"Yes, Herr Major," he said, his cheeks red and chapped from the blistering cold. Like most everyone standing in the open this frosty morning, Johan constantly shifted his weight from one leg to the other in order to keep warm. He used the muzzle of his machine gun to point at the two lines of wounded, one for those who could walk either on their own or with the help of crutches, and another one for those on stretchers. All supposedly held the medical passes that would give them the right to board a flight out of this hellhole.

The disturbing thunder of Russian artillery rumbled in

the background, shaking the frozen ground. Christoff didn't think he would be able to hold the field for long. Every day Russian tanks tightened the noose, squeezing the decimated, starving, and poorly armed German troops, who for the most part had lost the will to fight.

Christoff could see the determination to win vanished from the eyes of everyone around him. The only thing preventing a general panic was the dim hope that General von Hoth's 4th Panzer Army would break through the iron shield the Russians had deployed around the pocket and create an evacuation channel—or at least get close enough to Stalingrad for von Paulus to make an attempt to break out and meet them halfway. Von Hoth's panzers was part of the Army Group Don's expeditionary force led by Field Marshal Eric von Mainstein, who had launched a relief expedition to Stalingrad the day before and had already put a dent into the rear of the Russian 57th Army, which controlled the southwest section of the ring surrounding Paulus' Sixth Army, also part of Army Group Don. But in order for the plan to work, Paulus also had to make a run southwest to try and join up with von Hoth's panzers to create a channel.

But Christoff knew better. He had accompanied his superior, General Dörnitz, in a tour of the front three days ago. What he had seen appalled him more than the wounded littering his airfield. The soldiers of the once-glorious Sixth Army—one of the finest fighting units of the eastern front—had been reduced to a mob of emaciated men lacking the will to fight; of pale, robotlike humans with sunken and vacant eyes in gaunt faces. The experience had made him question Paulus' ability to break out of the pocket.

Staring at the desolation around him, Christoff clapped his gloved hands to promote the flow of blood to his rapidly numbing fingers. Defeat, not victory, festered the chilled air he breathed. He could smell a tragic loss with every wounded soldier that he signed off to board the plane, with every breath of frigid air he took, with every communiqué that arrived from Berlin praising the heroes at Stalingrad for holding strong, for refusing to surrender, for living up to the high standards of the Third Reich.

My men are starving to death and instead of supplies Hitler gives us speeches and commendations.

Christoff suppressed such thoughts, for they would only get him shot—though at the moment that would probably be a blessing. Like everyone else in the trapped Sixth Army, he didn't relish the thought of becoming a prisoner of the Russians. He had seen firsthand the atrocities committed by the German army in the past year and a half. The Russians would not be merciful. They will strike back, and when they did, Hitler's main dilemma would not be the loss of Stalingrad or the oil-rich fields in the Caucasus, but the loss of Germany itself as the Red Army obliterated German forces in Europe and Poland, marching straight into Deutschland.

The wind whipped his face raw and for a moment he longed for those hot Texas summer days, for warm lakes and meandering rivers under blue skies, for times long gone, replaced by the nightmare around him.

The inspection of the medical permits began with little incident. Christoff compared each physical wound to the information scribbled on the medical tag and then nodded at Johan and his soldiers to let them through. First those on stretchers were allowed to board, stacking them against the walls of the airplane. Then would come those who could walk.

Two soldiers carried a man on a stretcher up to Christoff. He lacked a medical permit but was bleeding from a wound to his upper thigh.

"I have been wounded, Herr Major!" claimed the soldier, in his twenties, his bearded face blackened by smoke and dirt. "I have witnesses . . . I need medical help!"

Johan removed the field bandages, revealing the telltale powder burns of a self-inflicted wound.

"Get this traitor out of my sight!" exploded Christoff, who had little sympathy for soldiers shooting themselves to escape the pocket. He hated them as much as he despised being here, forced to fight his own people instead of the enemy.

The military police hauled the wounded man away as he pleaded for mercy and dumped him in the pile of frozen bodies to the right of the runway. Paulus' standing orders for such offense was death, but Christoff could not bring himself to order fellow Germans shot because of the pigheaded strategic mistakes of men who were warm and well fed back in Germany.

But just the same he couldn't let them go without some show of punishment; otherwise word of his insubordinate benevolence would reach Paulus' headquarters and Christoff would be replaced by someone who could be trusted. And while the idea of getting relieved of this shit duty was appealing, the thought of failing at his assigned task was not.

So he had come up with a better idea. Rather than shooting the traitors—under the pretext of saving bullets—Christoff had ordered his men to just leave them on the field for their friends to tend to. Some of the wounded froze to death within the hour, but many were hauled back to one of the German-controlled sections of the city by compassionate comrades in arms.

And so it went, wounded after wounded, some making it through, others being turned back to either fight or die of exposure or from their wounds. Then the doors closed and the Heinkel revved up its engines and began taxiing into the wind.

The runway, lost beneath a layer of ice and snow, was marked by the frozen legs of horses—easier to find than wooden posts—hammered into the terrain, compounding the surrealism. A dozen men suddenly emerged from behind the snowbanks flanking the runway and raced toward the moving plane, jumping onto the wings.

The first time Christoff had seen that happen he had mistakenly ordered his men to open fire on them, nearly causing the plane to crash on takeoff. He'd realized then that doing nothing was the best and safest option for the plane, crew, and human cargo.

About half of the men managed to anchor themselves down as the plane gathered speed. The rest rolled off in the slipstream, crashing on the hardened surface and tumbling out of the way. The He 177's engines increased pitch as the pilot pushed full throttle.

A few more men fell off the moment the plane took off and began climbing toward the low layer of cumulus clouds at great speed in order to escape the Russian antiaircraft batteries, which started peppering the sky with dark puffs of smoke. Then the pilot rocked its wings just before it disappeared in the dark clouds, shaking off the remaining men, who dropped to their death over the Russian positions.

As one plane left, a second, already empty, taxied into position to pick up the next load of wounded.

Christoff stared at the runway, and beyond it at the disappearing taillights of a plane that would take those aboard to safety. Forcing his mind back to the task at hand, but nonetheless wondering what it would take for him to be allowed one day to board one of those planes, he resumed his work.

20

Black Clove

Thirty Miles North of the Stalingrad Pocket
December 13, 1942

A layer of cumulus clouds floating above him, recently promoted Major Erich Steinhoff pushed the control stick and tried to line up one of three Russian fighters that somehow had managed to stumble across his gruppe's path.

Erich was escorting Werner Haufman's Stukas for a strafing run of a column of southbound Soviet tanks, and he had already lost a rookie pilot and his Gustav to a crazy Russian, whose plane had just gone down in flames after having come too close to an exploding Heinkel.

The Russian fighters scrambled the moment they noticed the Germans closing in. Erich picked one and closed the gap. Vapor condensation poured off the wingtips as the Gs blasted on the enemy plane struggling to pull out of the dive. Erich also felt the pressure one second later while he instinctively swung the stick back and slammed full throttle.

Now the clouds were directly overhead as he adopted a vertical chase profile. The altimeter needle went crazy while his Me 109G Gustav pushed for altitude. The Soviet disappeared in the clouds. Erich reached the low cumulus and broke through the layer five seconds later, his airspeed rapidly bleeding.

He let the nose drop to the horizon and circled underneath while dipping his left wingtip in the sea of white. He narrowed his eyes when he noticed the Soviet maintaining the climb instead of diving to avoid a stall.

Have the Soviets developed a more powerful engine?

The answer came a few seconds later, when Erich saw the Soviet stall and fall into a reverse spin.

As the Soviet pilot tried to recover, Erich completed his right turn, climbed three hundred feet, and lined it up in his sights.

It can't be that easy, he told himself. Was that pilot so inexperienced as to underestimate the power of his machine and stall?

Almost feeling sorry for the unlucky pilot inside that plane, Erich floated his Gustav right behind the spinning Soviet and let go a three-second burst. Smoke came out of the enemy plane as it spun out of control, disappearing in the clouds.

Erich followed it, diving through the cumulus, breaking through, and verifying that the enemy plane was indeed going down.

He watched it fall over a remote section of forest, a burst of orange flames followed by smoke marking the crash site.

Erich rejoined his gruppe.

"Black Clove Five Oh Five here, where are the other Soviets?"

"Shot down, gruppenkommandeur!" responded his wingman as he brought his Gustav behind Erich.

"Jericho, Jericho. You are clear. Repeat. You are clear."

"Thank you, Black Clove," responded Haufman.

"We're flying on vapor, Jericho. Heading back to base."

"Thank you again, Black Clove."

21

G-Forces

Five Miles North of the Stalingrad Pocket
December 13, 1942

As the top of his canopy grazed the clouds, Werner Haufman inverted and dove toward the advancing Soviet column putting pressure on the trapped Germans. His altimeter read ten thousand feet and his indicated airspeed shot above two hundred knots. He dropped toward the single-file formation as ground fire ignited. Haufman frowned as he spotted dozens of small black clouds three thousand feet below.

He eyed the diving reference marks on the side panel and eased back the stick when he achieved an eighty-five-degree dive. No air brakes this time—too much ground fire. Besides, he was not dropping a bomb in this dive. Unlike the previous versions of the Stuka, the stick-mounted trigger on Haufman's Ju 87G-1 controlled two wing-mounted 37mm Flak 18 cannons, or "tank busters" as his air group usually called them. The addition of the heavy guns, made mostly to cope with the Soviet's increasing number of tanks, had come at the expense of removing all underside bomb mounts. The "eastern front" Stuka was not capable of dropping bombs on the enemy, but was more than adequately equipped to blast through the armor of any Russian tank.

Nine thousand feet at 230 knots.

The slipstream-driven Jericho trumpets screeched as the Stuka approached maximum operating speed. The vibrations on the stick became so intense that Haufman had to set the friction on the throttle control to bring a second hand around the convulsing stick. The angle had to be maintained.

Seven thousand feet.

His wings bit into the small black clouds left over from the antiaircraft fire. The clouds themselves did not present any danger. They simply marked the location where a few seconds before flak blew in every direction with metal-ripping force. If the impact ever came, Haufman would see no cloud. Just a loud explosion before an inferno swallowed him.

Six thousand feet.

The narrow road below widened. Airspeed dashed beyond 260 knots; the Stuka's wings began to wobble. Haufman had exceeded maximum speed, but he was unable to adjust throttle.

Move a hand off the stick, Werner, and you'll never control it, he told himself as his index finger caressed the trigger, but did not press it yet. He was still too far up. Due to the large-size projectile, the cannons came with a limited number of rounds. He had to use them wisely.

In spite of the extreme cold temperature, Haufman felt warm from the adrenaline rush, the euphoria of the moment gripping him as ground fire intensified.

Four thousand feet.

His craft trembled with every near-miss, but he was untouchable. His Stuka had not been hit once in more than a hundred sorties. He had the speed and the determination. His senses were absorbed in the excitement of the moment.

Three thousand feet at 270 knots!

Haufman clenched his teeth. At such speed the Gs would

crush him during pull-up, but he didn't have a choice. He had to keep the dive-bomber right over the Soviet column.

Two thousand feet.

The tanks, dozens of them, filled the winding road below. He inched the stick back and felt a light pressure.

Fifteen hundred feet.

He squeezed the trigger and the vibrations from the savage recoil of the powerful guns rocked the plane with every blast. Two every second, pounding his mind—his soul.

One thousand feet.

The earth accelerated toward him at a staggering rate. Haufman swung the stick back while reaching for the throttle and pulling it back to idle.

The Gs smashed his shoulders, squeezed his head. He felt light-headed.

His vision tunneling, Haufman remained focused on the road, pressing the trigger for another second before easing the stick forward at five hundred knots to maintain a shallow dive. The entire road exploded with antiaircraft fire. The Gs subsided. Haufman breathed deeply.

He released the trigger, broke hard left, and pushed full throttle while descending even farther down.

Two hundred feet.

He had to get out of the range of the guns.

One hundred feet at 230 knots.

The road disappeared behind the trees. Nothing but white countryside expanded below. Haufman exhaled and turned the plane ninety degrees to get a glimpse of his attacking squadron.

"Confirmed kills?" Haufman asked his gunner, who faced the rear of the plane and had a much better view of the damage inflicted on the Soviet column.

"Three burning tanks, Staffelkapitan!"

Haufman nodded and saw another Stuka completing the run, and a third halfway through the—

"Jericho Five, Staffelkapitan! It's on fire!" screamed his gunner.

Haufman cursed the moment the diving Stuka, hit by

flak, went out of control and disintegrated in midair. The burning wreckage crashed several hundred feet on the opposite side of the road.

That was one of the risks of dive-bombing. If hit during a dive, nine out of ten times the plane would spin out of control, and at that speed, it typically came apart in midair, not giving the pilot and gunner the opportunity to bail out.

A few minutes later, Haufman and his surviving Stukas climbed above the clouds and headed back to their base.

22

Angel of Death

Stalingrad Pocket
December 13, 1942

The German Stukas vanished in the distance after another attack against the ironclad Russian forces encircling the devastated city, which stretched along the west bank of the Volga for a few miles. At the upper end of the city, amid freshly fallen snow, stood the Barrikady Gun Factory and the Red October Factory, both former sources of weapons for the Red Army. The constant attacks, however, had long turned them, and the adjacent workers' settlements, into empty structures surrounded by mounds of icy debris. South of the Red October stood what was left of the Lazur Factory, a former tractor-manufacturing facility. West of the Red October and Lazur plants rose Mamayev Hill, a strategic post whose control had flip-flopped between the Russians and the Germans in past months and was currently under German control. The hill overlooked the factories to the north and downtown Stalingrad to the south, including the primary railroad station and the main ferry landing. Farther down the Volga stood the Dar Gova Railroad Station, adjacent to the grain silos.

The German private followed his sergeant as they stepped over the collapsed front porch of a warehouse somewhere in the downtown area a block north of Red Square, in the vicinity of the Nail Factory—though it was hard to tell anymore. The nonstop shelling and bombing had transformed this section of town into heaps of rubble, which the winter then covered with several inches of snow. At least the chimneys had survived the onslaught, and his platoon used them as landmarks to determine which building they were currently searching.

Although the front porch and part of the roof had collapsed, there were still several floors standing, but with gaping holes marking the location of detonating shells. These were the places now used by Russians snipers as vantage points.

Russian snipers.

The young private sighed. Germany's Wermacht lacked proper training for urban warfare. The hundreds of vacated buildings still standing in this former industrial city provided a third dimension to the fight—a dimension foreign to Germany's open-field warfare tactics, forcing them to learn the hard way after losing countless lives to the better trained Red Army. Those initial brute-force methods used by the Wermacht during the early days of the battle for Stalingrad had resulted in thousands upon thousands of casualties at the hands of well-positioned Russian teams.

The smell of gunpowder mixed with that of excrement assaulted his nostrils—a telltale sign of nearby enemy positions. While freezing, fresh human refuse would expand and degas, releasing the foul odor that his sergeant, a veteran of the eighteen-month-old Russian campaign, followed to pinpoint the hideouts before calling in a mortar attack.

Just a month ago, the platoon would use trained dogs to assist in pinpointing enemy locations, but most dogs had already been slaughtered to feed the starving troops.

His search-and-destroy team, formed by the surviving members of decimated divisions who had tried to engage the Russians muzzle to muzzle in close combat, relied instead on mortars to do the bulk of the work before following by foot to sweep up any enemy survivors.

The team advanced single-file over a sea of blocks of concrete, iron beams, pipes, and garbage—all protruding through the layer of snow and flanked by the listing walls supporting the front of the building, which threatened to collapse on them at any moment. Sunshine forked through the holes in the floors above the large entrance, casting a dim glow in the otherwise murky interior.

The sergeant raised his right hand in a fist, ordering the platoon to stop by the entryway, obviously pondering his next move. The veteran soldiers immediately began to sweep the area around them, on the lookout for the Russians, who often seemed to materialize out of nowhere, fire their guns, and then vanish just as quickly, before the Germans could mount a proper counterattack.

Slowly now, with caution, the sergeant stepped inside, his hands clutching a black machine gun, his helmeted head shifting in every direction, searching for—

He jerked back, as if he had stepped on a nest of scorpions, pivoting before racing toward his team.

"A trap! It's a—"

Multiple reports cracked the morning air, echoing off the towering structures. The sergeant's head bobbed back when a bullet tore apart his face in an explosion of blood.

The private swung around.

The shots had not been fired from *inside* the building but from behind them.

There, across the wide avenue, roughly a hundred feet from them, merging with the snowscape, stood a dozen figures dressed in white coats and pants, the muzzles of their weapons alive with gunfire.

With the German soldiers flanking him already clutching their bleeding chests while collapsing, the young private dove behind a snowbank partially covering a large block of concrete, nearly impaling himself on a rebar hidden beneath the layer of snow.

Cringing in pain, nearly losing control of his bladder muscles, the private braced himself as two grenades went off to his immediate right, followed by three others to his left.

He checked his flanks when the breeze sweeping the clearing blew away the smoke. Terror stabbed his gut when he realized that most of his platoon had been annihilated in seconds. Their maimed bodies were sprawled over the frozen debris, their warm blood and entrails splattered around them, hissing in the glacial temperature. One of the German soldiers was still alive, jerking while crying out in pain. The shrapnel had shredded part of his face. An eyeball swung from his socket and he had lost most of his left arm.

Just as quickly as it had started, the gunfire ceased, followed by hastening footsteps mixed with the agonizing cries from the crippled soldier, a new kid from Bavaria, like the young private.

Reaching for his weapon, he brought it up and around, searching for a target, finding none.

Where are you bastards? he thought, raising to a deep crouch as the wounded soldier stopped moving, his one good eye fixated on the young private.

His heartbeat pounding his chest, the German soldier began to sweep his weapon across his field of view, trying to find the—

A single round ricocheted off his rifle's handle, screeching past his left ear.

The sound of the near-miss still ringing in his ears, and realizing that this time the shot had come from the building itself and not from the position of the Russians who had ambushed them, the young private turned around, his eyes blinking surprise when staring at the face of a woman, also dressed in a white winter uniform.

Large brown eyes on an angelic Slavic face burned him with hatred. Her red lips and the rose color on her cheeks contrasted sharply with her otherwise pale skin.

Momentarily taken aback by this glimmer of natural beauty in the middle of hell, the German, realizing he didn't have a chance, dropped his rifle and raised his hands.

The Russian woman fired twice.

His groin and abdomen burning, the soldier remained standing while dropping his gaze, staring in horror and disbelief at the mangled mess the first bullet had made of his genitals. The second round had pierced his midabdomen, where blood gushed out.

Screaming while locking his terrified stare with that of his executioner, feeling as if a hot claw was raking his intestines, the young private fell to his knees in the snow, trembling but still glaring into those beautiful eyes, into the passive face of the Russian woman standing tall in front of him holding the huge rifle draped in white towels, merging it with her winter uniform and the surrounding snow.

He tried to talk, tried to beg for mercy, but instead he vomited blood, which froze almost instantly after splashing the snow.

Feeling light-headed, dizzy, he fell back, breathing through his mouth, his stomach churning from the blood, sensing the end nearing, until slowly, very slowly everything faded away.

23

The Hunter

Stalingrad Pocket
December 13, 1942

Red Army Major Zoya Irina Krasilov regarded the young German soldier as he died, and she felt no pity for him in spite of his age and willingness to surrender. She had lost all compassion for Germans after what they had done to her in that prison camp what now seemed like a lifetime ago.

They can all rot in hell for all I care, she thought, dropping her spent magazine and inserting a fresh one before chambering a round, getting her weapon ready to kill more Hitlerites.

Standing on the frozen clutter littering the exterior of the warehouse, adjacent to a hive of former shops and small factories that had become slaughterhouses just last week, Zoya inhaled the cold and humid air while regarding her search-and-destroy team checking the area for any survivors.

Zoya was attached to the 62nd Army, commanded by General Vasili Chuikov, the man who had recently promoted her after a series of daring attacks to flush entrenched Germans in the Beer Factory, which overlooked the Volga in downtown Stalingrad.

She directed her young team inside the warehouse, its gutted interior cavernous, murky, and humid.

Letting her eyes adjust to the darkness, she grimaced at the stench emanating from a bucket filled with feces warmed by blazing coals. She had set up the bait three hours ago and had been surprised that it had taken the Germans this long to find it.

A chilling breeze whistled through the sunlit holes on the opposite side of the structure, created by the months of ceaseless skirmishing. The ensuing creaking as the powerful wind swept the unstable building made Zoya wonder how long it would be before this warehouse joined so many others that had crumbled into heaps of brick, concrete, and twisted iron. Several panels of corrugated metal ceiling flapped in the wind, their sporadic drumming echoing inside the rickety place.

The cold stung her as she stepped away from sunlight and ventured in the shadows dominating the guts of this building, but she still silently thanked her superiors in the Red Army for the wool socks and the pair of *valenki*—felt boots—preventing frostbite to her toes as she led her patrol through their fifth straight day hunting Germans.

The glow forking through the gaps cast a twilight around her, enough for her to see the remnants of the fierce battle that had taken place here a month ago between factory militia and German units. Russian and German bodies, hundreds of them, frozen in place where they had fallen, had been turned to stone by the violent winter. If she looked close enough at the layer of human debris, Zoya could find at least one pair of dead, frozen eyes staring at her.

She walked over twisted and mangled corpses, past severed body parts and headless torsos, forcing indifference in her mind, struggling to avoid staring down at this vision of Dante's Inferno while scanning her surroundings with her machine gun. As major and leader of a hit-and-run patrol operating deep in German-controlled sections of Stalingrad, she had to set an example for her younger and relatively inexperienced subordinates—some of them sixteen- and seventeen-year-old girls who had forged their birth certificates in order to be allowed to fight. Zoya also had to remain on full alert, lest she join the sea of corpses projecting in every direction.

The seasoned officer peered at the blocks of rubble from fallen walls amid this sea of human refuse—perfect hiding places for enemy snipers. Just as many Germans had fallen victim to Russian snipers, so had Russians also perished from the marksmanship skills of the Germans.

She dropped to a deep crouch, relieved that the arctic weather had temporarily sealed what would otherwise have been an unbearable stench, an explosion in the rat population feeding on decaying bodies, and the associated spread of disease.

Her team, trained to read her moves as they followed her, split two ways behind her, not only creating a wider front of fire but dispersing to make it much more difficult for an enemy sniper to shoot more than one or two of them before they could counterattack.

Empty, she thought, walking around a three-meter-high stack of crushed bodies beneath a fallen section of the floor above. A Russian soldier who had lost both legs when the many tons of concrete had collapsed over him had managed to drag the remainder of his body for a few meters before bleeding to death. The cold had not just preserved the position of his arms as he tried to pull himself toward the cover of a large machine, but also the twisted mask of agonizing pain and raw horror lining an otherwise handsome Slavic face. His glistening light blue eyes stared at Zoya, who blinked and looked away.

Slowly, with caution, she proceeded toward the rear of the warehouse, which faced Red Square and what was left of the theater and the Univermag Department Store. The latter had once been the pride of Stalingrad, a well-stocked shopping store for the working-class population of this 350-year-old city.

Now nothing but freestanding walls and a few exposed upper floors that had not yet collapsed projected beyond the square, backdropped by the frozen Volga.

In the past week the ice on the river had become thick enough for General Chuikov to dispatch some tanks and *katyushas*—multiple rocket launchers carried on the back of trucks—from his 62nd Army to cross over into Stalingrad from the east bank and assist street fighters in the struggle to battle the trapped Germans into submission.

Meanwhile, Chuikov's boss, Marshal Georgi Zhukov, chief of staff of the Russian armies and architect of the plan to defeat the Germans at Stalingrad, had ordered the majority of his heavy weaponry and multiple infantry divisions south to stop General Hoth's panzers' attempt to break through the Russian ring and create an escape path for the trapped German Sixth Army.

Zoya's hit-and-run team, originally designed to flush out Germans troops, now served a far more strategic purpose: demoralize the enemy by not letting it rest even in its own territories. The partisan Aris Broz had taught her long ago the value of this guerrilla-style warfare—one that the Germans with their 1930s textbook approach to war found difficult to cope with, choosing instead to keep throwing more soldiers, tanks, planes, and bombs at the problem.

Zoya remembered the Yugoslav-born partisan with affection. Aris had not only rescued her from the nightmare of that women's prison camp. He also escorted her across most of Ukraine and into Russia, reaching a partisan-controlled pocket west of Smolensk in early December 1941, when the Red Army launched its first major counteroffensive against the invading Germans, pushing them away from the outskirts of Moscow. From there Zoya and the partisans had continued on horseback to a second partisan pocket south of Vyazma, and less than ten miles from the Russian front lines. Then had come what Zoya feared would have been the most difficult part of the journey: getting past the German lines and through the no-man's-land in between the warring armies, and finally into Russian-controlled territory.

Lucky for her, the Germans had been in a panic and in full retreat to the safety of the west, many half frozen and without rations. Tired and demoralized from the six-month-long offense, just to be stopped short of Moscow by a combination of a powerful Russian counteroffensive and the bitter winter, the Germans had not spotted the small partisan group as it crossed their lines and reached the Russian trenches.

Zoya nodded.

The winter had certainly caught the enemy unprepared. She still remembered the frozen bodies of tens of thousands of Germans still wearing their summer uniforms.

And that serves the bastards just fine, she thought, her mind shifting from Aris to her family, whom she missed dearly and didn't know if they were dead or alive—or worse, imprisoned.

In the year since she had joined General Chuikov's 62nd Army, she had tried multiple times to find out if her husband and their daughters had survived the Nazi juggernaut. Her inquiries had been met with silence by Moscow, the only place with some semblance of order in an otherwise chaotic nation. Although disappointed, Zoya wasn't too surprised at the lack of response. If her family had moved around as much as she had, the chance was slim that she would find them until after the war, when locating missing relatives would become a priority. Until then, her country, which had already lost around two million people, had far more important issues at hand than finding the estranged family of an army major currently fighting in a city where two out of three Russians died each day.

Zoya reached a two-story-high hole in the rear of the warehouse, shaped by the twisted rebar projecting from the jagged edges of the demolished concrete. Icicles from a broken pipe overhead draped over a section of the opening, creating a translucent curtain that broke up the shimmering sunlight into an explosion of colors. Some of the ice had expanded over exposed sections of twisted rebar, which acted as the metal skeletons of mind-boggling and often grotesque ice monsters overlooking the ocean of still bodies, like Satan's guards patrolling a section of hell.

She peeked through a foot-wide opening between the concrete wall and one such amorphous shape, which eerily resembled the limbless and headless body of a four-meter-tall creature.

Zoya looked beyond the disturbing sight at a dozen soldiers setting up three machine-gun emplacements behind mounds of rubble in the back of Red Square, in front of what was left of the Univermag Department Store.

Her stomach knotted as she could think of only one reason why a team would be coming toward her so quickly: the first group of Germans she'd killed on the other side of the building had been the bait while another team waited nearby to cut them down as soon as they showed themselves.

Are the Germans getting desperate enough to sacrifice some of their soldiers just to find me?

If true, then that alone told Zoya that her partisan tactics were working. She was inflicting enough terror on the enemy for it to go to such extremes. But that also meant that she too had to be more careful and cunning than ever in order to continue to prevail.

Zoya motioned her team to take up sniper positions along the back of the building and wait for her command. But as her team raced to take up their posts, the shrilling sound of incoming mortar shells resonated inside their enclosure.

Instincts overcame surprise, forcing her to dive into the space created by a fallen section of wall and a cast-iron stove, landing hard on her side, exhaling on impact, her right shoulder burning.

Closing her eyes, praying that her team would react just as she had trained them and seek cover without giving out their positions to the soldiers in the pillboxes by warning each other out loud, she braced herself for the unavoidable.

The first shell rattled the ground behind her with deafening force, peppering the old stove with shrapnel. Ice shattered, crashing down over her hideout, followed by debris raining from the ceiling.

Three more rounds followed in rapid succession, striking all around her in clouds of smoke, kicking up debris and body parts, cracking more ice, which created secondary explosions as it struck the frozen rubble.

Then silence, followed by sharply spoken German. Rolling out from her hideout, Zoya ignored her throbbing shoulder and rose to a deep crouch while once more gazing out of the nearest opening, watching several soldiers zigzagging over the uneven terrain in her direction, backed by the steel-helmeted men laying behind their machine-gun emplacements.

The craters from the mortar attack oozing smoke, the smell of cordite filling her nostrils, she raced away from her position, clambering up a half-collapsed wall, reaching the floor above, and moving all the way to the left side of the building just as staccato gunfire broke out of several places almost at once on the clearing, providing covering fire for the approaching German soldiers.

She reached a vantage point overlooking Red Square, her eyes searching for the easiest target, which she found a moment later: two soldiers running along the edge of the park while firing their rifles toward the first floor of the building. The lack of explosions around them told her that her team was not returning the fire. Beyond them weapons from the three pillboxes rattled away at the building, their muzzles flashing like stroboscopic lights. Her team was either dead from the mortar attack or pinned down by the machine guns.

Although the emplacements would make better targets than the two Germans running—particularly because she had a better line of sight than her team pinned down on the first floor—she still could not get a good enough angle from the second floor.

Her options narrowed, Zoya chose to take the closest threat first, taking careful aim at a spot just in front of the lead soldier running toward the warehouse, waiting until he reached it a couple of seconds later, then firing once, watching his chest explode before switching targets and firing a second time.

Following her partisan training, she went immediately into a roll, which proved to be lifesaving. Her sniper post was peppered with machine-gun fire moments after she had taken down the second German.

You need a new vantage point.

Zoya found it by crawling toward a metal pipe running in between floors and climbing it to the third floor, then racing to the rear windows and positioning herself behind a waist-high opening roughly a meter wide by half as high, large enough to get a clear line of sight on the right-most machine-gun emplacement, manned by two Germans, one clutching the handles of the weapon and the second feeding the ammunition belt into its side.

Once more she blocked everything but her new target, ignoring the possibility of being spotted by either the other two emplacements or the rest of the German soldiers scattered around the square waiting for the opportunity to run toward the warehouse.

No longer feeling cold, the adrenaline rush heightening her senses, Zoya Krasilov fired four times in rapid succession, striking a direct hit not just to each head but twice against the machine gun itself, watching in satisfaction as metal pieces blew from its top.

Then came the roll, to her left, but unlike the previous time, the Germans on the ground didn't respond. The reply came instead via more mortars, screeching as they arced over the building.

The warehouse shook as the rounds blasted through the five-story-high ceiling and detonated to her far left with concrete-ripping force, the powerful reports pounding her eardrums.

Taking up a new position, Zoya searched for the second machine-gun nest, spotting it just as it sprayed the floors below with covering fire for a second excursion of Germans—four of them.

She took aim against the pair manning the machine gun, but before firing she also located the third one, making certain that it too was busy protecting the running infantry and not hunting for her.

Her eyes switching from one emplacement to the other, she made her decision and fired at the center one, killing both Germans and shifting her aim to the last one without firing at the machine gun itself, as she had done the first time. She did this to conserve time, centering the crosshairs of her weapon on the two soldiers sprawled behind the blazing weapon, firing twice more, watching blood burst from their shattered skulls before searching for the running Germans.

Two of them fell to their knees before she could reposition herself, victims of the bullets from members of her team, now free to fire after the German supporting fire had been eliminated.

Zoya took a moment to fire at the machine guns themselves, permanently disabling them, preventing others from replacing the soldiers she had killed.

Satisfied that her team would be able to handle the foot soldiers, she slid down the tube to the second floor and climbed down the wall to the first. By the time she reached it, the gunfight had ended.

One by one her team emerged from the twilight of the warehouse.

Zoya just stood there a moment, watching her warriors, all females, their faces marred with ashes and smoke, their eyes bright, alert. Pride swelled her chest. They had reacted just as she had taught them—just as Aris Broz had once taught her—hiding from the incoming shells before resuming the fight, avoiding suicidal moves, letting the Germans make the mistakes by relying too heavily on their firepower, on their mortars and machine guns.

This last skirmish marked the tenth successful encounter with the enemy in a row. Deciding not to push her new troops anymore until they had gotten a chance to rest, she said, "Come. Let's cross the Volga and rest awhile."

24

Augsburg

JG52 Gruppe 1, Fifty Miles North Of Rostov
December 13, 1942

Standing next to a barrel filled with the burning wood from a downed Russian plane, Erich Steinhoff read the preliminary mission report Mathias had just handed to him. Four Soviet fighters were destroyed at the price of losing four bombers and a single Messerschmitt. The report went on to explain exactly how each plane had been destroyed. The remaining bombers had managed to drop their loads over the pocket.

Erich breathed in a lungful of frigid air, deciding it was the least his group could do: provide as much escort support as he could to the bombers to keep the Sixth Army from starving to death until General Hoth and his column of panzers finally broke through the Soviet stronghold to create a life-support corridor and give the two hundred thousand men trapped in Stalingrad the supplies they needed to counterattack, or at least to hold their ground through the winter.

Erich looked into Mathias' weathered eyes. The African had lost a considerable amount of weight in the past few months, and so had most of his men. The Russian winter had taken a toll not only on their bodies but on their equipment. The brand-new Gustavs didn't respond well in thirty below. Problems from frozen canopy hinges to faulty fuel pumps continued to ground part of his fighter force, but at least he was in direct command of the men and planes on this base.

He had earned this promotion not just because his number of kills had passed the two hundred mark, but also because Barkhorn had been transferred to head of Gruppe 3 after their commander was shot down.

As gruppenkommandeur, Erich now faced the challenge of escorting the supply planes as well as providing air support for Hoth's rescuing army. To achieve this he had at his disposal a meager sixty Gustavs and two dozen Stukas.

And half of them grounded because of the damned weather or lack of spare parts.

Erich briefly closed his eyes at the insanity of what lay ahead, his mind longing for the early days of the war, when Luftwaffe groups were the epitome of efficiency, with their well-oiled machines and trained pilots.

Look at us now, my dear Sonja, he thought. *How are we supposed to win this war?*

Disgusted, he crumpled the piece of paper and tossed it into the fire.

"Things will get better, Erich," said Mathias with the heavy Algerian accent that struck other pilots as entertaining.

Erich slowly shook his head. "We got mostly good pilots and good machines, Mathi. The problem is that we're being asked to spread our forces too thin. We're outnumbered by the Soviets."

"Yes, they have the numbers, but we have the experience."

"Sometimes," Erich said, thinking of the inexperienced Soviet pilot he had killed that day because of a foolish maneuver. But he also thought of his own rookie who was shot down at the hand of that suicidal Russian pilot, whom Erich watched bail out of his burning plane after surviving the cloud of fire from the exploding German bomber. "Unfortunately, the enemy is learning, and they fight with passion. I think it is just a matter of time before . . ." He let his words trail off.

"What about the planes without propellers Berlin has been promising us for some time?"

Erich smiled. "My intuition tells me that the jets, as our engineers call them, might not come into play until later on. In the meantime I'm afraid we'll have to continue fighting in the same way, Mathi. There is no other choice."

The African lowered his gaze.

"Tell me when the new war directive comes through."

"Yes, Erich. I will let you—" Mathias stopped, then pointed at the horizon. "The Stukas, Erich. They're returning!"

Erich closed his eyes and heard the distinctive high-pitched whirl of Junkers engines in the distance. Mathias had a fine ear. He shifted his gaze toward the tree line by the end of the runway, and a few seconds later the first black-painted Stuka loomed over the forest, idled the engine, and softly touched down.

"That's one, Mathi."

Over the next five minutes, seven more Stukas landed, including, to Erich's relief, Haufman's craft—the only Stuka of the bombing wing that had an all-yellow empennage instead of just a band like the other planes.

Seven out of nine.

Sighing, Erich walked up to Haufman's plane as his friend's servant climbed up the side, slid the canopy back, and helped Haufman, who had just been promoted to the rank of oberstleutnant.

"What's the count?" Erich asked as Haufman, wearing a brown, fleece-lined flying suit, removed his parachute, crawled out of the cramped cockpit, walked down the wing root steps, and jumped onto the frozen ground. Like Haufman, Erich also wore a winter flight suit, with the difference that his was dark gray.

"Seven confirmed kills, nothing of any significance. That column must have had a hundred tanks. We need more planes and more pilots! It is insane to continue fighting like this, Erich. I'm sending my report straight to Berlin!" Haufman's eyes were burning.

"Now, now, don't go do anything stupid," Erich noted in a tone as casual as he could make it. Haufman was known for writing very emotional, and oftentimes colorful, reports of his sorties—reports that had cost him a six-month delay in his promotion to oberstleutnant. "Why don't you tell me what happened and I'll write it for you. I promise to be objective."

"How can you talk like that, Erich? How many planes did you lose today?"

"Just one. A young pilot . . . too inexperienced. He should have stayed in flying school for another month or two."

"See what I mean? Those idiots in Berlin are not training them long enough! They send them to us to complete their schooling in battle! It's insane!"

"Keep it down, please," Erich said, leaning closer to his friend. "See that pilot sitting by the fire over there?"

Haufman briefly turned his head and nodded. "Yeah. What about him?"

"The dead pilot was his younger brother. I've already spent thirty minutes trying to calm him down. The poor bastard was ready to grab a Gustav and go searching for a Soviet airfield . . . you know, like in the First World War days? Challenge the best pilot around for a one-on-one air duel?"

Haufman shook his head. "I'm telling you, man, this is not good. Morale is going to shit very quickly around here. Berlin has no idea what they're doing by forcing us to—"

Erich exhaled, deciding it was time to put on his gruppenkommandeur hat, saying in a firm tone: "Listen,

Werner, I recommend you go and rest for a couple of hours. We'll talk again after you get some sleep and write your report."

Haufman turned around and stomped toward his tent.

Shivering, Erich walked to his own tent and lighted the small kerosene lantern standing over the table. He placed both gloved hands over the glass and closed his eyes as the warmth reached his palms and slowly spread up his forearms.

His thoughts drifted first to Sonja, his fiancée and childhood sweetheart. He had not seen her in nearly six months. After his one hundredth kill, Erich had been allowed a week's leave in Augsburg, his hometown. At first Erich had been thrilled. A week with Sonja was more than he could have asked for, but soon their superiors revealed the main reason for the unusually long leave from the front in such critical times. The central Messerschmitt assembly and research factory was also located in Augsburg. As it turned out, Erich spent just two days with Sonja—two days that he would never forget—and the rest of the time locked inside the Messerschmitt factory testing the turbojet engines and powerful gun system of a revolutionary single-seat fighter called the Me 262. The project was so top secret that all test flights were conducted at night, and when he'd completed his work, Erich was directly transferred back to the front.

So you are right, old Mathi, Erich thought as the lantern's heat became so intense he had to lift his gloves off the glass cover and keep them a short distance over it. That first prototype had both impressed and scared him. The speed had been enormous. Although he'd had a hard time judging speed due to the night, he did recall seeing the indicated airspeed go as high as 520 knots.

Erich breathed deeply at the thought of that type of plane in volume production at this very moment. It could mean the difference between victory and total defeat. He could only hope his superiors shared his vision.

But there was a huge difference between designing a prototype and full-blown production. Messerschmitt engineers had spent more than three years perfecting the M109 fighter, and it had been in the prototype stage for two years before that. If the Me 262 followed the same track, then Erich guessed it would be at least two years before volume production.

And by then it will be too late.

His chest felt cold in spite of the warmth in his hands and arms. Erich pulled out his only photo of Sonja and also reached for the half-empty bottle of vodka from a case his men had found in Rostov. Erich was not a habitual drinker, but in such freezing weather, where one's breath crystallized upon exhaling, there were very few things that could warm a man. Since Erich could not have his first choice, he opted for his second while staring at the first and remembering those glorious two summer days in Augsburg.

25

Enigma

Sixth Panzer Division, Aksai River
December 13, 1942

On the battlefield, generals have two particular areas of concern: the area of influence and the area of interest. For Generalleutnant von Hoth, his area of influence lay straight ahead—the direct drive to Stalingrad, the operational area in which his advancing army was capable of fighting the Soviets using manpower and equipment assigned to him by Berlin. Von Hoth's area of interest extended beyond the area of influence to include any enemy forces capable of affecting his current operations within the area of influence. Since the Soviets were closing in on both flanks of his advancing column, General von Hoth considered his flanks his area of interest.

Sitting in the back of the wireless communications

truck, von Hoth finished dictating his directive to the Luft-waffe's JG52 headquarters in Rostov: send all available fighters and Stukas to support Operation Winter Gale—the drive by von Hoth's tanks in support of Field Marshal Mainstein's drive to liberate General Paulus' Sixth Army—while keeping a prudent number of fighter aircraft escort-ing the constant wave of bombers loaded with badly needed supplies for the Stalingrad Pocket.

"Code it and send it," he said to one of two operators sit-ting in front of a wooden box.

"Yes, General!" replied the youngest of the two before opening the box's lid and exposing an Enigma coding ma-chine.

Enigma looked much like a typewriter with the standard three-row keyboard but without numerals, punctuation marks, and other extras. Above the keyboard the entire al-phabet was repeated in the same order, but the letters were not on keys but in small round glass holes that could be lighted up one at a time. Above and to the left of this last set of letters were three slots that covered three wheels or drums. The wheels were half embedded in the machine such that the German operator could only see the top of each through the slots.

The operator pulled up the small lid covering the wheels and exposed them. Each was about three inches in diameter and contained all twenty-six letters of the alphabet engraved on its perimeter around the wheel. Each wheel had on either side twenty-six contact points of entry and exit. The contacts from one wheel came in direct contact with those of the ad-jacent wheel, creating a path that varied depending on the setting of each wheel relative to the next. The wheels were labeled I, II, and III, and could be removed and their respec-tive positions swapped. He opened the Enigma master-code handbook and flipped to the correct date. The manual told him the correct order of the wheels and also which letter on which wheel should face up for that day's particular setting.

Skillfully, he arranged the wheels in the prescribed or-der, closed the wheel cover, and flipped each wheel such that the precise letter appeared through the slot. Next he reached above the wheels for the plugs, which looked like those on a switchboard, except that there was one plughole for every letter of the alphabet. Once again, the manual told the operator which pairs of plugs were to connect which letters that day.

The operator powered up the battery-operated Enigma and slowly began to type the message one letter at a time. The moment he struck the first key, an electric pulse was released. This pulse went through the plug system, through each of the three wheels from right to left, entering and exiting each wheel from one of twenty-six different contact points, bouncing off the left-most wheel and going back through the wheels in the opposite direction through a different set of contact points, back through the plug system again by a different route, and finally on to illuminate one of the letters above the keyboard. The letter was never the same one the operator had initially struck, and furthermore, the next time he struck that same letter, a different letter than the first time would be lighted, because the right-most wheel rotated one notch for every key stroke. After twenty-six rotations, the middle wheel would move one notch and so on.

The soldier next to the operator took note of the coded letter and transmitted it via Morse code on an adjacent telegraph machine to the airfield of JG52 Gruppe 1 near Rostov, where another Enigma operator, armed with an identical machine and handbook, already had his machine preset in the prescribed manner for that day to decode the message one letter at a time.

By the time the telegraph operator had finished transmitting the first letter, the Enigma operator had the next letter waiting.

Satisfied that his message was being transmitted, General von Hoth stepped away from the vehicle and stared at his advancing army. A column of panzers extended as far as he could see, marching across the frozen steppe toward an objective that many of his fellow German senior officers felt was unreachable. Not only was the extreme cold slowing progress, but the constant Russian attacks continued to erode the warring capability of his army.

Von Hoth grimaced, realizing his Sixth Panzer Division walked a very fine line. If he advanced too slowly, the Russian troops massing in between him and Stalingrad would make it impossible to break through, even if Paulus somehow managed to launch a drive south to meet him halfway. If he advanced too fast, he risked stretching his column too soon and further exposing his flanks—and even his rear—to the Russian attacks from the east and the west.

I could get stuck in a pocket, just like Paulus, he thought, the thought chilling him far more that the wind sweeping across the valley.

Von Hoth watched his panzers in silence.

26

Interceptor

HMS Liverpool, Aegean Sea
December 13, 1942

The radio operator quickly jotted down the back-to-back Morse-code transmissions while a second operator used the direction finder to get a bearing on the sources. He was well aware that the letters he was writing down would make absolutely no sense to him, but understanding a German coded message was not his responsibility. His official title was that of interceptor, and that was what he did best, scanning through frequencies looking for anything that remotely resembled German wireless traffic.

The messages were relatively short. That much he could tell, because although the messages were coded, he knew enough about the German Enigma machine to realize that it translated letter for letter. The Enigma did not add or delete letters from a transmission. It simply converted each letter into any one of the other twenty-five possibilities.

The interceptor glanced over to the direction finder operator.

"Got a heading, mate?"

"I got mine, but I need Baghdad's."

The intercept operator nodded while his colleague tried to get a second bearing from a different location. The trick of the D/F was to get two bearings from the origin. The transmission would then be located at the intersection of the two bearings, give or take ten kilometers.

"I'm trying, but the bloody weather in Baghdad isn't helping. There, I've got one. Looks like it's coming from the vicinity of Augsburg."

"Augsburg? That's the first time we've gotten anything from those bloody bastards in that region. How about the second?"

"Hard to tell, mate. Somewhere near the Aksai River would be my best guess. That's all the chaps at BP are going to get from this intercept."

The radio operator began to transmit the message using a secret frequency to a relay station in Athens, where it was relayed to another British ship in the Mediterranean, which passed it on to an intercept station in Madrid. The Spanish station sent it on to England.

27

Visitors

For Colonel Aleksandrovich Nikolai Krasilov the nightmare had returned. His wounded I-16 plummeted to earth
in flames. He had no control of the air surfaces or engine.
Through the flames pulsating from the exhausts he could
see the bent propeller. His face began to burn from the intense heat.

He looked behind him and saw the Messerschmitt's silhouette through the inky haze trailing his wounded fighter.
The one with the black clove painted across the nose.

The pilot waved at him while his cannons took out the
I-16's tail. Pieces of wood blew in all directions, some
striking Krasilov in the back as the craft went into a reverse
spin with the nose pointed at the heavens. Krasilov saw the
blue sky while desperately reaching for the release the handle of his restraining harness, but he could not find it.

Sweating, the rumbling noise of the cannons abruptly
stopping, the Russian colonel looked to his left and
watched the German pilot salute him and laugh. The bastard was laughing as Krasilov hopelessly struggled with his
harness.

The Messerschmitt remained there, as if hovering next
to him. The pilot continued to smile. Krasilov could not release his harness. The heat intensified. The heat . . .

"Colonel Krasilov? Colonel Krasilov! Wake up, sir.
Wake up."

Krasilov opened his eyes and saw Andrei Nikolajev's
round face.

He took a deep breath, sat up, and rubbed his eyes with
the palms of his hands, slowly remembering.

Krasilov had finally arrived at the base two hours ago totally exhausted and nearly frozen from his five-mile trek in thirty below until a T-34 tank from the Second Mechanized Division picked him up and brought him to the air base, where it took him an hour to thaw and less than a minute to fall asleep.

Krasilov ran his tongue inside his mouth, which felt dry and pasty. He reached for the bottle of vodka next to the bed and took a swig, inhaling as his throat and chest warmed up.

He stared at Andrei's clean-shaven face once more. Excitement glimmered in his subordinate's soft eyes.

Andrei, a recently graduated pilot from the Red Air Force, had joined Krasilov's fighter wing six months ago, and had since worked his way to the top, taking second to no one but Krasilov. In fact, Andrei had already shot down more than sixty enemy fighters with a loss of only three planes, a record that only Krasilov, with more than a hundred air victories, could surpass. Krasilov liked the young pilot from the Ukraine who enjoyed women and dancing as much as he loved flying.

"What is it?" Krasilov asked, taking another sip, letting the alcohol do its magical work.

"We've got company, sir. Americans."

Krasilov bolted to his feet. *"What?"*

"Americans, sir. Actually only *one* American but thirty-six American fighters. *Thirty-six*, sir!"

"Calm down. So soon? They weren't supposed to be here until—"

"They're here, sir, and the fighters are being unloaded from the cargo planes as we speak."

Krasilov put on his skin boots and heavy coat and followed Andrei outside, where five huge American cargo planes were parked on the far left side of the snow-covered runway. He must have been really sleeping to not have heard them landing.

Although he was relieved that his men would have more weapons to fight the Hitlerites, as a true Bolshevik,

Krasilov didn't care for the Americans and their flying machines. He wanted more Lavochkin La-3s and perhaps a squadron of the newer but still scarce La-5s. But given the large need for fighters to support the Russian defense and new winter counteroffensive, Stalin had agreed to the American lend-lease program. This was one of the first shipments.

He spotted a dark-haired man wearing a black leather jacket and matching boots and gloves, and dark sunglasses. *So it is true then,* Krasilov reflected as he walked away from his bunker. *American pilots do wear sunglasses, even on an overcast day.*

Krasilov approached him, flanked by Andrei and two other pilots. The American smiled and extended his hand. Krasilov didn't take it. The smile on the American's face vanished. He removed his sunglasses and stared back at Krasilov with indifference.

"You were not supposed to have been here for another week. What gives you the right to barge into my airfield with little warning?" Krasilov asked in Russian, not expecting a response from the American.

"Is that how you welcome your allies, Colonel?" responded the American in flawless Russian. "I'd hate to see what you do to the Germans."

Krasilov was impressed, although he didn't show it. The young man knew the language well.

"I shall consider you my ally when my men have been trained and your planes prove themselves in my eyes. What is your name?"

"Captain Towers. Jack Towers." He put the sunglasses back on.

Krasilov didn't respond right away. He simply stared at his own reflection on the American's glasses and pointed toward a single tent on the other side of the runway. "You will sleep and eat there, when there is food. When there is none, you will starve with the rest of us. There will be no special privileges for you. You will answer to me while training my men, and the moment the training is complete you shall leave my base at once. Is that understood, Captain?"

"I will only answer to my superior officer, Colonel Kenneth Chapman, sir."

"Is that so, Captain? And where is this Colonel Chapman right now?"

"He's training another fighter wing a hundred miles north of here."

"Like I said, Captain. You will report directly to me while on my base!" Krasilov turned and headed back for his tent. "Andrei, show him what he needs to know!"

"Yes, Comrade Colonel!"

28

Volunteer

Kalach Airfield, Twenty Miles West of Stalingrad Pocket
December 13, 1942

Jack frowned as he watched the burly Russian stomp away.

What's eating him?

This wasn't exactly the type of reception he'd had in mind, but then again, nothing had gone his way since he'd joined the air force. Why should this be any different? The Russian colonel with the scarred forehead and the strange patch of exposed scalp just above his left ear looked like he could eat his young.

Perhaps that's the kind of personality required to run a base like this one, he thought. Then again, maybe Krasilov simply was one of those proud, American-hating Russians who hated to come to terms with the sad fact that in order to defeat the Germans they had to accept American help.

"Charming fellow," he finally said to Andrei. "Your colonel's a piece of work."

Andrei smiled and extended his hand. Jack shook it.

"I'm Lieutenant Andrei Nikolajev. Please forgive him, Captain Towers—"

"Jack."

"Jackovich?"

Jack laughed. "Sure. That's fine too."

Andrei smiled, nodded, then frowned. "Colonel Krasilov lost his family last year to the Germans during the early days of the invasion. So don't take him too seriously, especially today. He got shot down early this morning and spent the last seven hours getting back to the base through the snow. He's not in the best of moods."

Jack tilted his head, deciding he would also be in a terrible mood given all of that. "Can't say I blame him," he finally said, deciding to let it go.

"How long before the planes are ready?"

Jack shifted his gaze to the transports and the army of Russians dressed in white camouflage jackets unloading the P-39Ds wingless fuselages down the rear ramps. "I'll say another day at the most. Maybe less. How many pilots are available?"

"Plenty. We just need a more competitive machine than the La-3. We lose too many of them in every battle."

Jack exhaled. The P-39D Aircobras were relatively faster than the La-3s, but not as fast and maneuverable as the Messerschmitts. "How good are they?"

"Excuse me?"

"Your pilots. How good are they?"

"We have the will to learn and the will to fight, Comrade Jackovich. We are all prepared to die for the Rodina."

"Well, let's hope it doesn't come to that, Andrei. The best pilot, in my opinion, is a live pilot."

The Russian gave him a puzzled look that didn't surprise Jack one bit. Chapman had warned him about the courageous—and at times suicidal—Soviet pilots. Jack wondered if perhaps that kind of spirit was paramount to winning a war. Maybe his cool American attitude was not what got things done, but the bold, take-no-prisoners approach that the Russians were so famous for.

A worming feeling in his gut told him he was about to find out.

"This is a war, Comrade Jackovich. Our lives are expandable. We all must fight to defend the Rodina."

Sure, Andrei, Jack thought as he stared into the Soviet's ice-blue eyes crowning the remnants of what appeared to have been once a boyish face. The lines on Andrei's forehead and around his eyes told Jack that the young Russian pilot must have already seen more than his share of battle—probably more than Jack would ever get to experience.

"Would you die for your country, Jackovich?"

Jack considered that for a moment before replying, "That's why we're here, right? Why do you ask?"

"Our perception of the American pilot is one of more self-glory than commitment for his country. That's what we get told anyway. I think that's part of the reason the colonel reacted the way he—"

Andrei's words were cut short by the high-pitched sound of an engine in full throttle very close to ground.

"I hope that's one of yours," Jack said as he scanned the skies.

Andrei turned to the source of the noise while pressing the edge of his palm against the top of his forehead to cut down the glare. Squinting, he stared at the eastern horizon. Then he said, "I'm not that sure which kind of plane that could—it's a Gustav!"

They ran for the shelter on the far right side of the concrete runway. Jack crouched next to Andrei as the Messerschmitt zoomed over the runway.

"Damn! The Aircobras!" Jack shouted glancing at the wingless fuselages wrapped in thick green canvas stacked next to the cargo planes.

Without firing a single round, the Messerschmitt pulled up and rolled its wing while maintaining a vertical climb. The German executed the corkscrew until nearly reaching a low layer of cumulus clouds some five thousand feet high.

"What's he doing?" asked Jack.

"Challenging."

"What?"

"He's challenging the best of our pilots for a one-on-one duel."

"Are you shitting me?"

Before Jack got an answer, Andrei leaped forward and raced toward Krasilov and the other pilots already gathered next to the La-3s.

"Please. Let me handle it, Colonel," Andrei said as Jack finally reached the group.

Krasilov looked around as the Messerschmitt continued to circle overhead. "Any other volunteers?"

The rest of the pilots raised their hands. Krasilov fixed his gaze on Jack, who remained a few feet behind the group. "How about you, Captain Towers? Would you like to show us the real capability of your airplane? Up there is a good opportunity to do so." Krasilov pointed at the German plane and then at the Aircobra he had flown while escorting the cargo planes.

All eyes landed on him. Jack scanned the curious Soviet faces before replying, "I wish I could, Colonel, but my orders are very strict. I'm only supposed to train—"

Krasilov raised his right palm and waved him off. "Andrei! The Hitlerite bastard is all yours!"

Andrei raced for his craft followed by the other pilots. Krasilov stepped up to Jack and stared at him long and hard. Jack thought he saw a condescending smile flicker across the Russian's scarred and hardened face.

"There is an old saying in my hometown of Lvov, Captain Towers," Krasilov finally said in a low voice. "Knowing and not doing is the same as not knowing at all. This is a war. Up there is the enemy. You are a pilot and that is your airplane. It is all very simple out here. There are no politics getting in the way of our task. You see the enemy and you kill the enemy before the enemy kills you."

Jack didn't reply.

"But then again," Krasilov added. "You didn't lose your family to the Germans, right? You didn't lose your hometown

to the Germans, right? Your country isn't the one getting
raped and pillaged by the fucking Nazis, right? So why
should you volunteer to fight someone else's war?"

"America *is* at war with Germany, Colonel."

"Then? Why won't you fight?" Krasilov turned and
walked to the other pilots already gathered by the side of
Andrei's craft to wish him good luck.

Jack closed his eyes and frowned.

29

Heart of a Warrior

Kalach Airfield, Twenty Miles West of Stalingrad Pocket
December 13, 1942

Andrei Nikolajev pushed the Lavochkin's throttle handle
forward and taxied the aircraft onto the wide runway. He
thought about taxiing to one end, but decided he had more
than enough runway on either side of him for a short takeoff.

Turning into the wind, he pressed the brakes, lowered the
flaps, and applied full throttle. The liquid-cooled Klimov
bellowed dark smoke for a few seconds before beginning
to drag the seven-thousand-pound plane over the icy surface.

Andrei let go of the brakes and the La-3 shot forward.
He pulled the stick when the indicated airspeed read 120
knots, and the fighter left the ground.

Andrei raised the flaps and gear, trimmed the elevators,
and turned off the auxiliary fuel pump. The La-3 cleared
the trees and sprinted upward. The moment he reached the
Messerschmitt, the German plane flew next to his right
wing. Both pilots looked at one another for a few seconds
before breaking in opposite directions.

Andrei went for another climb and reached a cumulus
cloud ten seconds later.

The German vanished from sight as the cloud engulfed the Russian lieutenant. Andrei leveled off inside his shield of white, pulled back the throttle, lowered flaps, and began a slow and tight three-sixty turn.

Next to the runway, Jack squinted as he lost Andrei in the clouds. He anxiously waited for him to reappear at the other end, but the Lavochkin remained hidden. He spotted the German craft circling the area looking for the Soviet.

Andrei inverted his craft and continued his turn while slowly descending. He did six more revolutions before the canopy broke through the clouds. His head felt about to burst from the blood pressure of being upside down. He remained like that for a few more seconds as he looked up toward the ground, his eyes searching for . . . *there*!

He smiled when the German fighter came into plain view a thousand feet below him.

The Soviet pulled the stick back and the machine adopted an inverted dive profile. Airspeed quickly began to gather. Flaps up. Full throttle. The German kept the shallow turn. Three hundred knots. The German was no more than five hundred feet away, and still had not seen Andrei.

The Gustav's pilot finally spotted him and abruptly inverted and started a dive, but Andrei already had more than enough speed to close the gap in another five seconds.

The Gustav's tail filling his windshield, Andrei squeezed the trigger. The single, nose-mounted 20mm cannon began to fire. Dozens of rounds ripped through the Messerschmitt's rear fuselage. Three more seconds and Andrei pulled up to avoid ramming the German, whose plane shuddered under the punishment before the tail broke off from the rest of the structure.

"Left, left!" Andrei screamed at himself as he changed his evasive tactic at the very last second, opting for a hard left instead of a climb to avoid flying into the tail, which floated upwards as the rest of the Gustav dropped toward the ground.

A mild two Gs pressed him against his seat as he continued the turn at the same altitude while looking backward and down at the falling craft.

Without a tail section, the Messerschmitt, whose engine was still running, spun out of control along all axes for another minute before crashing next to a stream a mile east of the runway. Andrei saw no parachute.

Jack watched the La-3 rock its wings and make two full-speed low passes over the airfield as the pilots broke into a loud cheer.

The Lavochkin came back around, dropped its landing gear, softly touched down, and taxied back to the side of the runway. The pilots gathered around the craft. Jack saw Krasilov staring at him as Andrei jumped out of the plane and climbed down the wing root. The Soviet colonel shook his head, smiled, and turned around.

Jack silently cursed the air force for sending him here.

30

Telegrams

JG52 Gruppe 1, Fifty Miles North of Rostov
December 13, 1942

Inside his tent, Erich Steinhoff bolted out of bed after Haufman told him of the single Gustav that had taken off a half hour ago.

He looked into Haufman's eyes. The Stuka pilot had a cigarette hanging off the corner of his mouth.

"Who was it?"

Haufman told him. It was the brother of the rookie pilot who was killed that same morning. "I thought that you had cleared him."

"Hell no! Everyone in my gruppe knows better than to

leave without a wingman! Dammit! What did he think he was going to accomplish? Kill himself? He probably did just that."

"And took a Gustav along with him," said Haufman.

Erich exhaled and shook his head. "I can't even fall asleep for a few hours without—"

"Erich?"

Erich turned his head toward the entrance of his tent. It was Mathias.

"What is it?"

"Two reports, Erich. They arrived while you were sleeping." Mathias held two pieces of paper in his hands. He handed them to Erich, who briefly glanced at them, and then back at Mathias.

"These are two hours old! Dammit! You know you're supposed to wake me up when we get any coded messages!"

Mathias lowered his gaze.

"Hey, hey. Calm down, pal," Haufman interjected. "I *ordered* him to let you sleep. This was the first undisturbed rest you've gotten in forty-eight hours. Besides, with the insane orders we always get from our superiors, perhaps we're better off not—"

"Don't say it. I don't want to hear it. We're Luftwaffe pilots and we follow orders from our superiors without dispute."

Haufman raised both hands, palms open. "Whatever you say, man. You're in charge."

"All right, Mathi. That will be all. I'll call you if I need you."

"Yes, Erich."

Mathias left and Erich sat on a wooden chair next to the table in the center of his tent. He began to read two decoded reports while Haufman looked on. The first was from General von Hoth's panzer division. It was a request for air support. The time and place were specified. That directive did not surprise him at all. Erich was well aware of von Hoth's needs to support Field Marshal Mainstein's Operation Winter Gale.

Erich took a sip from his bottle of vodka, and closed his eyes as the clear warmed him. He set the bottle back on the table and read the second report. It came from Augsburg. A moment later he stormed outside.

"Where are you going?" Haufman asked as he raced after him.

"Get my plane ready, Mathi! I must leave right away! Perhaps there is still a chance to win this war!"

"What are you talking about?" Haufman began to ask while Mathias ran toward Erich's Gustav.

"I can't discuss it until I get back. I'm leaving you in charge, Werner. By the way, there's a message from General von Hoth requesting air support. I need you to coordinate it!"

"Me? Where are *you* going? What is going on?"

Erich eyed his old friend. "Augsburg. I must reach Augsburg immediately."

"*Augsburg*? Home? What in the—"

"Trust me, Werner. You're in charge till I get back!"

31

The Cryptographers of Bletchley Park

Bletchley Park, Buckinghamshire, England
December 13, 1942

The early evening air was cold and invigorating.

Royal Air Force Captain Peter Myers stepped outside Hut Three and took a short stroll around the grounds of the estate fifty miles northwest of London, which his government had purchased before the war to house its Codes and Ciphers School.

He walked past the handful of nineteenth-century-style buildings that first struck Myers as ridiculous even by the most generous standpoint of the day. The excessive use of heavy wooden paneling suffocated him—the reason Myers made it a habit to walk outside every couple of hours because, unlike the buildings, the surrounding grounds were pleasant to the eye, including a small garden and a pond in front of the modest stable block.

Very few people visited BP, as it was commonly called. The general rule around the place was once in, never out . . . with few exceptions, of course. The only transients, as they were called by the local staff, consisted mostly of officers who came to BP to learn the necessary ciphering skills to handle material at faraway intelligence posts. Other than that, not even the queen herself was allowed inside without a valid reason.

Myers checked his watch and headed toward Hut Seven, the building where most of the information from field locations came through and got properly typed on a piece of paper the size of a post office telegram. From here the message headed to Hut Six, where a large part of the deciphering took place. The deciphered information—sometimes limited to a point of origin and time of day—went on to Hut Three for translation into English and for interpretation by an air adviser from either the RAF or the USAF. They decided if the information merited the attention of that command's superior headquarters in London.

Myers walked up the wooden steps and pushed the door. Hut Seven, like its sister buildings, Hut Three and Hut Six, was a long and narrow single-story structure divided into rooms of various sizes on either side of a narrow corridor.

He closed the door behind him and walked halfway down the hall, opening the door to his left. Two women worked inside wearing headphones and mouthpieces. They shared a long wooden table and busily typed intercepted messages real-time, as they arrived. Both were from London, and both were also the fastest and most accurate typists Myers had ever seen.

Actually, Hut Seven was filled with such fast typists, two per room. Each room received messages from a specific European area. That way messages could be sorted out

according to their geographical point of origin from the
start. That precaution also saved message-interpretation
time. Messages from a specific field location would be
translated and interpreted by BP personnel very familiar
with the goings-on of that particular area.

Myers' responsibility included the support of all messages intercepted to and from the southern section of the
eastern front—a geographical area that originally lacked
the glamour of France, Spain, or Switzerland. Lately it had
grown in importance as both England and the United
States realized the real significance of Hitler's war with the
Soviet Union. Although the media advertised England and
America's aid to the Soviets as a result of the atrocities
committed by Hitler's army, Myers knew the real reason
for the aid. It was not because Churchill and Roosevelt
sympathized with Stalin, but because of simple mathemat-
ics: if those three million German soldiers and their war
equipment weren't busy invading Russia, Hitler would
most likely have that vast firepower facing west—something
the Allies were not prepared to handle just yet.

"I'll take it these are the latest intercepts?" Myers said,
grabbing five sheets of papers next to one of the typewrit-
ers. One of the women lifted her gaze from her typing
enough to nod, and went back to work.

He picked them up, returned to Hut Six, and went into
the first door to his left.

"What took you so long, sir? I was getting ready to go
look for you."

"Don't worry about it, Charlie. Here we have five more
transmissions. Let's see you figure out . . . these two. They
both came from an intercept ship in the Aegean Sea."

Charles Rosset, a young cryptographer trainee, breathed
deeply and took the pieces of paper that Myers handed to
him. Myers read over Rosset's shoulder.

"Well, according to the D/F, the first message originated
somewhere near the Aksai River . . . that's roughly eighty
miles south of Stalingrad, right, sir?"

"Correct. What does that tell you?"

"I'm not sure, sir. Someone's trying to contact General Paulus' Sixth Army, maybe?"

Captain Myers tilted his head. "Possibly. If you recall this morning's eastern front report, General von Hoth is heading north with the Sixth Panzer Division and they are roughly in the vicinity of the Aksai. For the time being, why don't we make the assumption that von Hoth sent it?"

"All right."

"So, what's next, Charlie?"

"Ah . . . we look for cribs, sir?"

"Splendid," said Myers when Rosset referred to one of the classic ways of cracking Enigma code. A crib was anything that suggested that the message contained one or more known phrases. "Get the menu for General von Hoth. We shall try to reconstruct today's settings of the Enigma machine."

Rosset left the room and came back a minute later with a brown file containing all transmissions that to the best of BP's knowledge were originated by General von Hoth's Enigma operator.

Myers opened the file and examined previously used cribs. For one thing, the Enigma operator always finished the message with the words "signed: General von Hoth." That alone gave a lot of information. An address was also something that helped tremendously.

"What's the origin of the second intercept?"

"Augsburg, sir."

"Good, that might give us a second crib for today's settings."

It was common knowledge among the BP community that the entire Nazi coding system worked off the same encoding handbook. The settings for the Enigma machines were the same for a particular day. Multiple messages, each with its own crib, provided a bonanza of information and a way to cross-check results.

Myers put the enciphered German text from von Hoth below the crib. From his experience with cracking German codes, which included extensive work with two Enigma machines BP had received from the Poles, Myers had discovered that in the German coding machine no letter of the alphabet could ever be enciphered as itself, thus an X would be turned into any other letter but an X. That was a weakness of the Enigma design, and it was the first key to breaking Enigma—and also the basis behind the theory of using cribs.

The crib—the phrase the cryptographer believed lurked in the enciphered message—would be compared to a section of the message where the cryptographer felt the telltale phrase could exist. A letter-to-letter comparison would be made between the suspect phrase and the coded message. If any letter was the same in both the crib and the coded message, then the wrong section of the message had been selected because none of the letters could match.

Myers placed the German words "Generalleutnant von Hoth" over the end of the coded message.

"See any repeats, Charlie?"

"No, sir."

"That's a step in the right direction. Let's feed this crib to the bombe."

"Right away, sir."

The bombe was a machine that employed fifteen hundred radio tubes and an array of photoelectric cells to read the crib—in this case von Hoth's name and title—and its enciphered version, and permutated the letters against one another at the rate of five thousand characters per second until it found the correct setting and order of the wheels and plugs of a German three-wheel Enigma machine that would create that type of enciphering. The trick to get a solution from the bombe was to have a perfect alignment of the crib with the enciphered code. A misalignment of just one letter meant many hours of wasted bombe computing time. Knowing the name of the originator of the message was good, as long as one avoided a pitfall: sometimes the Germans, aware of this flaw in their coding system, would append characters at random at the end of the message.

With this in mind, Myers looked at the code once more and moved the crib over one space to the left. None of the letters matched. He did it once more and found three matching letters.

"Why, Charlie, looks like a worst case of one appended character."

Rosset nodded.

"Let's get a runner back in here for another pass, shall we?"

Rosset picked up the phone. A minute later a young private walked in. He looked about eighteen.

"Yes, sir?"

"To the bombe. Hurry now."

The soldier took the two pieces of paper and the brief instructions Rosset had jotted down and ran outside the building.

Myers turned to Rosset. "Now, Charlie, let's assume that the first message didn't exist. How shall we go about deciphering the message from Augsburg?"

Rosset took the piece of paper in his hands while Myers poured himself a cup of tea.

"Care for some, Charlie?"

"Ah, no, sir. Thanks."

Myers smiled to himself. Rosset had been assigned to him only three weeks ago and he was already breaking German code.

32

New Orders

Pitomnik Airfield, Stalingrad Pocket
December 14, 1942

Major Christoff Halden snapped to attention when General Dörnitz stepped in the tent followed by Standartenführer Hans Kurtz, the same SS officer who had scolded him during the early days of Operation Barbarossa for having shown compassion toward the Russian prisoners. Today, Christoff suspected that the reprimand would come because of his public display of benevolence toward German soldiers who had wounded themselves to try to get airlifted out of the pocket.

Christoff remained calm, relaxed, with the self-confidence that came from not only having defied and defeated death, but having nothing to lose. He was already in hell. Death by firing squad at the moment felt like an upgrade from the frozen misery of his life.

"We seem to have a problem, Major Halden," started Dörnitz while clapping his gloved hands to promote the flow of blood. His breath condensed as it left his trembling lips, and his shoulders seemed to sag. Black circles encased his sunken and bloodshot eyes. Stalingrad was certainly taking its toll on the once proud and powerful Dörnitz—just it also sucked the life out of everyone else.

"A problem of the utmost urgency," added Kurtz while leaning close to Christoff. He looked just as ragged as Dörnitz, and he also reeked of vodka, which was in high demand these days to fight the cold.

Christoff crinkled his nose just enough to let Kurtz know that he could smell it. Although he despised the sight of an SS officer, Christoff was glad some got trapped in the pocket so they could share in the misery.

The SS colonel took a step back and looked over at Dörnitz, who added, "There seems to be a group of Russians, mostly women, who are attacking our troops with partisan-style warfare, and they are doing it in sections of the city that are supposed to be under our control."

Christoff, albeit relieved that these two weren't here to punish him, sensed that he was about to get signed up for a new duty.

Dörnitz continued. "Yesterday alone we lost thirty men to the female fighters. Half of those killed were from a special squad that General Paulus himself sent to eliminate them."

Kurtz added, "Paulus is outraged and demands that we fix the problem immediately because it is demoralizing the troops."

Christoff did his best not to chuckle at that. The Sixth Army was trapped in Stalingrad. Thousands were dying each day from war wounds, starvation, or frostbite—plus a recent breakout of typhus—and Paulus was upset because some group of Russian women were killing a few dozen men?

If Paulus wants to motivate his men, then get them proper food, ammunition, and medical supplies!

He shifted his gaze between the two officers. The intensity and borderline desperation in their stares told him not to voice his thoughts.

Dörnitz said, "General Paulus will start allowing a fixed number of officers with special skills to board the planes along with the wounded."

Kurtz nodded while adding, "Paulus will also allow our heroes to leave the pocket, so that the Russians don't lay their dirty hands on our top talent."

Christoff narrowed his eyes. These two had suddenly caught his undivided attention.

"On the outside chance that Stalingrad falls before General von Hoth can create a channel, our cautious führer wishes to preserve our best leaders and fighting men for the spring counteroffensive."

After a moment of silence, Christoff said, "Permission to speak, General."

Dörnitz nodded.

"Is the general offering me the chance to leave the pocket if I find and kill this elusive group of Russian female fighters?"

Dörnitz nodded again, followed by Kurtz.

"Do I get to choose my own men and weapons?"

"Of course, plus full freedom of action within the pocket," replied Dörnitz.

"Then it will be my privilege to hunt and kill this Russian menace and please our führer," said Christoff, choosing his words carefully.

"In that case, Major Halden, you are relieved of your post at Pitomnik."

33

The Führer

Messerschmitt Assembly Plant, Augsburg, Germany
December 14, 1942

Still dressed in his heavyweight fleece-lined flying suit and black leather boots, Erich Steinhoff crawled out of the motorcycle dispatch's seat that had taken him from the local airport, and began to walk up the steps leading to the front entrance of the giant factory and fenced-in test field.

Someone waited for him at the door—someone he had only seen before in pictures.

Erich stopped, his eyes blinking once to make sure they weren't playing tricks on him.

He stared at the World War I ace himself, now a bit overweight, but still standing with the same pride and elegance that Erich had seen on many portraits. The head of the Luftwaffe, Reichsmarshall Hermann Wilhelm Göring, waited for

Erich by the entrance dressed in his trademark dove-gray full-length coat, black leather boots, and peaked cap.

Erich steadied his breathing and walked calmly up the steps. He had mixed feelings about Göring. Although Erich considered him a good pilot and strategist, Göring had not fought hard enough to provide the Luftwaffe with the amount of equipment needed to sustain the Reich's increasing demands on the German air force. On the other hand, the reichmarshall had sent Erich a personal letter congratulating him for his two hundredth victory, and had been instrumental in getting Erich his promotion and the one-week pass several months back.

"Did you have a good flight, Major?" Göring asked while pointing at him with the marshal's baton he held in his right hand.

Erich noticed the elaborate work on Goering's cap—gold laurel leaves embroidered into the material along the entire cap band. His collar patches featured an eagle on the right, and crossed batons on the left, both surrounded with gold laurels to match the cap. He decided there was enough money and effort in Göring's uniform to build a couple of Gustavs.

"I did, sir. Thank you. I must say that it is an honor to finally—"

"Yes, yes, I know. Follow me, Major. There is someone else who wants to meet you." The reichmarshall turned and walked inside.

Puzzled, Erich followed him across the spacious lobby and down a long hall. Göring turned around.

"Wait here, Major."

"Yes, sir."

Göring went inside. Erich stood there uncomfortably still for a few moments, wondering what in the hell this was all about. *What is Göring doing there? And why am I here? Did I do something wrong?* Just last week he had achieved his 235th kill. His Gruppe 1, ever since Barkhorn left for Gruppe 3, had nearly doubled its number of kills per week while reducing the amount of ammunition needed by two-thirds. This was mostly thanks to Erich's indoctrination in the art of opening fire on the enemy only when it was so close that the Soviet's craft filled the entire windshield. The technique of blasting away the enemy and then flying through the smoking debris had become standard practice among Gruppe 1 pilots.

The door opened. "Come in, Major Steinhoff. Show yourself."

Intrigued, Erich stepped inside. A single lightbulb at the end of a black cord hanging from the high ceiling in the center of the murky room swung gently the moment Göring shut the door behind them. The dim bulb cast a pendulum of light over the reichmarshall's face as he stood by a round table next to Hans Barkhorn.

Well, I'll be damned, if it isn't the good old Aryan himself.

"Major Barkhorn," said Erich with a slight bow.

"Hello, Major Steinhoff. It's been some time."

"Yes, it has."

"I've heard about all the changes you've made since I left Gruppe 1. You didn't agree with the way I conducted the gruppe, Major?"

Erich shrugged. Barkhorn was an ass a year ago, and he was still one. "I'll let my gruppe's record speak for itself."

"That's enough, gentlemen," Göring said. "Put your differences aside. You're both among the Luftwaffe's finest and both happen to be assigned to a very critical front at the moment . . . which brings me to the reason you have been summoned here today."

With that, the reichmarshall took a few steps back. Erich noticed movement in the back of the room but couldn't tell who or what it was. Then the shadow became more visible.

A man was walking very slowly. A man of medium stature and medium build, a bit on the overweight side, but not by much.

Then Erich saw the face, the eyes. The rhythmic strokes of light and shade etched the lines of strain spidering around the weathered eyes. The sight threw chills up and down his body. He felt his knees about to buckle and struggled to remain erect. Barkhorn and Göring snapped to attention a second before Erich realized what he had to do, and he too clicked his boots. The trio raised their right arms at a forty-five-degree angle in front of their bodies with the palms open and facing down.

"Heil Hitler!"

Adolf Hitler barely raised his right hand to return the salute. He remained quiet and continued to walk. He eyed Göring and gave him a tired nod. The reichmarshall nodded vigorously in response.

Hitler then approached Barkhorn. The major stood still, like a rock. Hitler extended his right hand. Barkhorn shook it firmly.

Erich breathed in deeply, held it, and let it out slowly through his nostrils. He did it twice more as Hitler walked toward him.

The führer stopped and faced Erich. In front of him stood the man responsible for the war, and all Erich could do was merely control his body enough to lift his right hand and shake Hitler's. The handshake wasn't as firm as Erich had thought it would be. It felt more like the handshake of a woman than that of the supreme commander of the German armed forces, but it was definitely him.

Erich stared into a pair of dark eyes that conveyed nothing. He saw no emotion, no life, not even anger.

After a minute in the room, Hitler had still not said a word to Erich or Barkhorn, and he never did. The Nazi leader simply walked by Göring, murmured something in his ear, and then left the room.

The moment the door closed, both men turned their heads toward the reichmarshall.

"You now have an idea of how important your mission is to Germany's future, gentlemen. Please step outside. A technician is already waiting for each of you to go over all the details you need to know before your departure."

Barkhorn and Erich exchanged a glance. Neither said a word.

"Good luck, gentlemen," Göring said as he opened the door and motioned them to go outside.

Barkhorn left first. Erich waited a few seconds before he slowly started walking toward the door. His eyes leveled with Göring's.

"We're leaving right away, sir?" Erich asked with a trace of concern in his voice.

The reichmarshall smiled thinly. "Relax, Major Steinhoff. I wouldn't want one of my best experts to go on such mission with something else on his mind besides the mission. I have arranged for a one-hour visit inside the factory after the technical meeting and the briefing. After that you're heading back to your gruppe."

34

Crazy Bastards

Kalach Airfield, Twenty Miles West of Stalingrad Pocket
December 14, 1942

Jack Towers had an audience of seven pilots, including Andrei and Krasilov. The grumpy and scarred Soviet colonel had already told Jack that he had no interest in participating in the class, but since his new La-3 would not arrive for another two weeks, he had no other choice in order to remain airborne.

Temperatures had risen to ten degrees below, creating what most Russians considered a warm winter day. The sky, however, remained heavily overcast and a light breeze swept over the clearing.

Andrei and Jack had dragged the heavy P-39D simulator outside so he could go over cockpit basics before they test-flew their new planes, courtesy of a government interested in the Russians killing as many Nazis as possible.

There had been an instant chemistry between Jack and

Andrei. The young Soviet pilot's openness and friendliness had made up for Krasilov's querulous behavior. From Andrei, Jack had learned that he was the younger of two brothers. His older brother, Boris Ivanovich, had been reported missing during the battle of Moscow a year ago. Jack saw pain in the Slav's green eyes as he related the incident to him. Andrei's only hope was that his brother had been taken prisoner, but that hope was also a curse. Death was often preferable to a German prison camp for what the Nazis considered a lower race.

Jack stared at his audience, all professional fighter pilots, most of whom had probably seen more aerial combat than Jack ever saw during his post in North Africa, and probably more than he would ever see during the entire war.

He shifted his gaze from the pilots to the runway, where the P-39Ds, already assembled and their engines tested by Krasilov's expert mechanics, were parked inside shelters made of earthwork and wood, and spaced roughly 150 feet apart. The precautions were designed to protect the aircraft from enemy fragmentation bombs, and also to minimize the chance of one plane's explosion igniting others.

"All right, listen up," he began as all eyes focused on him. "As most of you probably realize by now, the Aircobra is a bit different from Russian fighters. Although it does have a pair of landing wheels beneath the wings like most conventional fighters, it lacks a rear landing wheel. Instead, it has a nose wheel, making it a tricycle-style landing gear. This will make your landing a bit different because right before touchdown you will have to pull the nose up and let the main gear touch down first. After that, don't force the nose gear down, simply cut back power and let it fall by itself. Everyone with me?"

Jack noticed a few of the pilots barely nodding. "All right. Next thing that's not conventional is the engine location. As most of you have probably heard from your mechanics, the Aircobra's engine is located directly *behind* the pilot. That has both advantages and disadvantages. On the positive side, in addition to providing better overall balance because of its proximity to the plane's center of gravity, if the engine catches fire, the flames and smoke will be directed away from you. That's good. Also, for the most part, unless you make a basic dogfighting mistake and get broadsided, the enemy will try to shoot you down from the rear . . . well, with the Aircobra you don't have to worry about getting your head blown off. There is a ton of aluminum and steel behind you to absorb the bullets. That is also good.

"Now, on the negative side, since the engine is in back, most of the ammo is carried in the nose. That has the effect of changing the weight ratio of the plane as the ammunition is consumed. The more you fire, the lighter the nose will get, and the more you will have to trim the elevators. It will be awkward at first, but with time it'll become second nature.

"Something that will feel strange in the beginning is the use of the 37mm nose-mounted cannon. From what Andrei has told me, the highest caliber that you have in your La-3s is 20mm. Well, 37mm is an entirely different beast. It will take some time to get used to its recoil, so go easy on it at first. The Aircobra also has two 50-caliber machine guns in the nose and one more in each wing. Any questions so far?"

He got no response. Jack took it as a yes and continued for another thirty minutes covering everything from the locations of the instruments, weapon systems, radios, and throttle controls, to critical airspeeds, maximum speed, and Gs.

When he finished, he stepped away from the simulator and looked at the Soviets. "Any questions?"

All of the pilots glanced at Krasilov, who simply nodded and headed for his Aircobra. The other pilots did the same.

"Wait, Andrei. What in the hell is going on?"

"No man will dare ask a question unless the colonel asks it first."

"Are you kidding me? You mean to tell me that those pilots will rather risk their lives and try out something they're not sure about rather than just ask?"

Andrei raised his eyebrows.

"We are all professional pilots, Jackovich. To us a plane is just a plane. We get far less training than this when Moscow sends us new models." The Soviet pilot walked away and joined the others.

"Crazy bastards," he murmured in disbelief as he headed for the nearest burning barrel in the base. Thirty minutes outside in ten below had stiffened Jack's muscles.

As he reached the barrel, Jack pulled out his gloved hands from inside his leather coat's side pockets and extended them in front of the fire. The P-39Ds came alive one after the next.

Jack turned his head and watched the pilots play with the throttle controls, elevators, rudder, and ailerons, before taxiing away single file behind Krasilov.

"Crazy bastards," he hissed again as the pilots reached the runway and positioned themselves in pairs.

A ground crew member fired a green rocket, and the first pair rolled down the runway, roughly two thousand yards long by about one hundred yards wide and running east-west to go along the region's prevailing winds. The surface was made up of octagonal concrete paving slabs about two yards across. As Andrei had explained to him earlier that morning while they dragged the simulator, hundreds of civilians had laid this surface in a vast interlocking honey-comb pattern soon after the ground had been leveled by Red Army engineers. Jack saw the advantage of such a runway when it came time to repair it by simply replacing individual slabs.

In all, the base was built with safety and practicality in mind. All ammunition and fuel was stored in underground dugouts, and all the buildings and hangars had camou-flaged roofs.

"Aren't you going to join the crazy bastards, Captain Towers?" said a low and deep female voice behind him.

Startled, Jack spun round and stared at a tall woman dressed in an old-fashioned aviator suit—the type he'd seen in World War I pictures, with the high sheepskin boots, heavy leather helmet, scarf, and thick jacket. A pistol leaned into her slender waist as she bent to pick up another log and throw it into the barrel.

"Fire's dying out," the woman said while she pulled off her leather cap. She wore an elegant silk helmet underneath, which she carefully removed, folded, and tucked away in a coat pocket. She let her long blond hair fall down to her shoulders, tousled it up, and then regarded Jack with a mix of curiosity and amusement.

"Anything wrong, Captain?"

Jack was shocked to see such an attractive woman in such harsh place.

Her inquisitive hazel eyes remained fixated on him, expecting an answer.

"Ah, . . . no. I'm not allowed to go along with the pilots. I'm just here to train them, Miss . . . ?"

"I'm pilot Natalya Makarova, Captain," she responded with an air of confidence that Jack was not used to seeing in a woman. Much less a woman pilot.

"You're a pilot?"

Natalya tilted her head. "Does that surprise you, Captain?" she asked with humor. The hazel eyes crinkled slightly as she grinned.

"I just never thought that—"

"A woman could fly a fighter plane? Welcome to the twentieth century, Captain Towers. There are several female pilots in this field alone."

Jack couldn't help but smile.

"You think it's funny I'm a pilot, yes?" This time her tone of voice became a bit more serious.

"Oh, no, no. It's nothing like that. You'll have to forgive me, Natalya, but this is the first time that—"

"It's all right. I've seen that reaction before."

Jack flashed his best smile and extended his right hand, "It's a pleasure to meet you, Natalya Makarova."

She pumped his hand firmly. "The pleasure is mine, Captain Towers."

"Call me Jack, please," he replied, deciding that his stay

at this base might not be as bad as he had first imagined. He wondered if all of the other lady pilots were this beautiful.

"All right."

"So, what kind of planes do you fly, Natalya?"

She frowned. "What plane I would like to fly? Or what plane Colonel Krasilov makes me and the other women pilots fly?"

Before he could say a word, Natalya added, "Although I'm qualified to fly the fighters, I mostly fly something you would never dare touch." She gave him a final smile and started to walk away from him.

"You never told me how you knew my name."

She looked over her shoulder without stopping her stride. "News travel fast."

"Natalya, wait."

She turned around, still smiling, arms crossed.

"I . . . is there a place on this base where a man can buy a beautiful woman a drink?"

The smile vanished as her eyes became as cold as the Russian winter. "This is war, Jack. There isn't time for anything else. I'm having a hard time proving myself to these pilots as it is. I don't need . . . *complications,* especially with an American. But it was interesting meeting you."

Jack exhaled in disappointment, watching her walk away and disappear behind some tents on the other side of the airstrip.

Resigned to the fact that his stay here would be as bad as it had first appeared, he turned to the fire and extended his gloved hands over it once more. These Russians were certainly different from the jovial crowd he knew in his mother's family.

He raised his gaze and saw the formation of P-39Ds in the distance.

Crazy bastards.

35

Revelations

Bletchley Park, Buckinghamshire, England
December 14, 1942

Charles Rosset raced into Captain Peter Myers' small office with a paper in his hand.

"Charlie? What is going—"

"We got it, sir! We bloody got it!"

Myers saw the excitement in the young man's eyes, stood up, and put on his black, thick-rimmed glasses. "All right, Charlie. Relax and tell me what's happening."

Rosset vented his lungs in and out a few times to catch his breath as he handed Myers the single sheet of paper.

Myers read both messages already converted into English. He had been right. The first message was indeed from General von Hoth, but it was not directed to General Paulus, as they originally had thought. It was a request for air support to start in—he checked his watch—exactly eight hours from now fifty miles south of Stalingrad. The report also indicated that General Paulus was planning to coordinate an attempt to break through the ring and meet up with von Hoth just south of the city. Between the two armies, they hoped to establish a new ground corridor to either boost the supplies into Stalingrad or provide a quick escape route should the situation become unbearable and the German Army be forced to retreat until the spring.

"This is bloody incredible," he muttered as he stared into Rosset's eyes. "They're actually are going to try to create a corridor."

"Sir, you mean—"

"Hold on," Myers interrupted as he read the second message. That one didn't say much except that a pilot was being summoned to Augsburg for something of the highest importance. Myers shrugged. That one was for the USAF adviser to figure out. Something interesting, however, was the fact that both messages had been sent to the same address and recipient. Luftwaffe Major Erich Steinhoff. Jagdgeschwader 52 Gruppe 1 in Rostov.

"Get both messages to the USAF adviser, Charlie. We might still be in time to intercept the air strike, and if we're lucky, the Russians might also do something about keeping Paulus busy so he doesn't have the time or resources to coordinate a breakthrough."

Rosset ran out the door.

36

New Orders

62nd Army Base, Across the Volga River from Stalingrad
December 14, 1942

Sitting alone in a tent, Zoya Krasilov disassembled her weapon slowly, with practiced ease, carefully inspecting the firing mechanism.

Though it was thirty below this evening, the tent's weathered canvas and the glowing coals inside a spent artillery casing provided enough warmth to allow her to work on the weapon without the burden of gloves. Smoke coiled through a ventilation pipe.

Satisfied that the firing pin remained operational in spite of the heavy usage in recent weeks, she used a solvent and a small brush to strip off the accumulated gunpowder before using fine engine oil to lubricate it.

She paused to reach for a mug of steaming coffee, holding it with both hands while bringing it to her lips, taking a sip, closing her eyes as the hot drink warmed her core.

Setting it down, she resumed her work, taking great care

while cleaning and reassembling her weapon, her most valuable asset while operating behind enemy lines.

Zoya completed the assembly and dry-fired the rifle while pressing her left ear to hear the mechanism.

Confident that she held a fully operational weapon, Zoya inserted a new magazine, chambered a round, and thumbed the safety lever, leaving it safe but ready to kill more Germans.

Kill more Germans.

Zoya sighed, uncertain if her insatiable desire to kill enemy soldiers was driven more by her experience in the prison camp than by the patriotic movement to hold the invading army at Stalingrad.

Take this, Russian whore.

Aleksandr. Marissa. Larissa. Lvov. Sunflowers. Blue skies.

Zoya braced herself while holding back the tears. The horror of what she had done to survive mixed with the uncertainty of the whereabouts of her family, tearing at her sanity. She hated herself for having become a whore for the Germans as much as she hated her government for turning down her requests for information, replying that all of the Rodina's resources were consumed with fighting the enemy. There were to be no exceptions, not even with her growing fame.

I risk my life every day for my country, killing more Germans than any other Russian, and they still refuse my request for information.

Controlling an anger she knew would only lessen her focus and probably get her killed, she turned her attention to her upcoming mission. She reviewed the hand drawings and notes made by the most recent scouts, who ran round-the-clock reconnaissance missions of various sectors of the city and sent their coded observations across the frozen Volga using runners.

The Germans were setting up several machine-gun emplacements and mortar stations on Mamayev Hill, southwest of the Red October plant to bolster the defenses in anticipation of a Russian attempt to take the coveted hill. Zoya's mission was simple: establish a series of vantage points along the upper floors of the Red October plant overlooking the German positions across the stretch of land between the hill and the factory, which was known as no-man's-land. After setting up her team, she was to hold any sniper attacks until the tanks and infantry of the 62nd Army—which would be coming from the north—reached the foot of Mamayev Hill.

The orders came straight from General Vasili Chuikov himself, along with a commendation from the great leader for her heroic efforts to destroy German morale and accelerate the fall of the trapped Sixth Army, which had a far larger strategic significance than the capture of two hundred thousand starving Germans.

Chuikov's letter stated that every day that the Germans held out in Stalingrad was another day that the Red Army had to keep a half million soldiers tied up forming a ring around the city. Those soldiers, Chuikov explained, could instead be reinforcing the Russian troops batting Germany's Army Group South in the Caucasus and possibly create a second pocket that could encompass General von Hoth's panzers driving north to free the Sixth Army. Capturing the strategic hill would not only deliver an emotional blow to the already demoralized German Sixth Army, but it also had a strategic importance. According to Russian intelligence sources, this was the hill General Paulus planned to use to oversee his army's attempt to break through the Russian ring and meet with von Hoth.

And it all hinges on our ability to put enough pressure on them to force an early surrender while also making it difficult to establish a corridor, she thought while staring at the handwritten orders bearing Chuikov's signature.

"Comrade Major?"

Zoya turned to the entrance of her tent, feeling a rush of bitterly cold air invading her refuge through the opening in the canvas as one of her subordinates peeked inside. She recognized the pale and slim face of Tasha Burojev framed by a white hood. She held a white-draped sniper rifle in her gloved hands.

"Come in, Tasha. Come, come," Zoya said, waving her to the center of the tent.

The young soldier complied, setting her weapon down and sitting next to Zoya by the radiant coals. Tasha, a native of Kiev, had lost her parents and older sister to a German mortar before being captured and sent to the same concentration camp as Zoya. Tasha had been gang-raped on their first day at the camp, before being sent to the infirmary, where Dr. Helmut had broken her arms numerous times before the partisans liberated them.

Like Zoya, Tasha had profound personal reasons to hate the Germans—an unspoken trait that Zoya looked for in her recruits. Given the highly dangerous nature of her assignments, Zoya preferred soldiers with a deep-rooted hatred for the Nazis and also who had nothing to lose.

Tasha removed her gloves and hood, revealing a short haircut, like Zoya's; easy to care for.

Turning open palms toward the coals, Tasha asked, "Do we have a new mission?"

Zoya nodded. "We leave in the morning." She went on to explain the details of the mission. When she finished, Tasha closed her eyes in obvious apprehension.

Zoya put a hand on her subordinate's shoulder and squeezed gently, aware of Tasha's concern. The survivability of her team depended on mobility, on hit-and-run tactics, on surprising the enemy with a sudden strike and then leaving the area before German reinforcements arrived. This mission required that they remained stationary, providing cover for General Chuikov's tanks and infantry.

Closing her eyes, Zoya prayed to the same God who had sent the partisans to the prison camp to liberate them from the nightmare, asking for another miracle. Stopping the trapped Germans' ability to leave the pocket meant sealing their fate, which Chuikov believed also meant turning the tide on this war.

37

Silence

Major Christoff Halden worked in the machine shop assisted by Johan as they unpacked the long cylindrical tubes and attached them to their brand-new rifles just as specified in the manual he had received from Berlin today along with the sophisticated hardware.

"General Dörnitz apparently meant what he said, sir," commented the lanky sergeant, Christoff's most trusted man in this most desolated land.

Christoff nodded. He had made one request via telegraph to Berlin, and the advanced equipment and instructions had arrived in the next available Luftwaffe plane twenty hours later.

"Will accuracy be reduced, sir?" Johan asked.

Christoff shrugged, trying to remember his hunting days with his father back in central Texas. The elder Halden, a hunter at heart, had figured a way not to scare off deer if he missed a shot. The device consisted of a cylindrical tube roughly six inches in length lined with cork and filled with metal washers in its center, leaving a hole large enough for the bullet to exit, while absorbing most of the gun's report. It was a crude silencer by today's standards, but it had done the trick—though at the expense of some loss in accuracy. Plus, it was limited to about a dozen shots before it lost its ability to absorb the sound.

"Accuracy won't matter much, Johan. The idea is that these sound suppressors will allow us to get close enough to the enemy to fire our shots and continue undetected. But we shall test it first to make sure that Berlin's design is not only reliable but also durable while minimizing loss of accuracy."

Johan watched with interest as Christoff screwed in the eight-inch-long bulky silencer to the muzzle of the new sniper rifle, already draped in a gray foam material—like the rest of the weapon—not only to match the gray winter uniforms and boots that had also arrived from Berlin hours ago but to insulate the firing mechanism from the severe cold.

"The methods of warfare that you have described, sir . . . they are different from our training."

Christoff smiled inwardly. That was one thing he had learned while growing up in America that Germany lacked: the ability to quickly adapt to new situations. Americans were exceptionally good at learning from their mistakes and rapidly adjusting their tactics.

"Have you ever hunted, Johan?" he asked while inspecting the entire assembly. At least it all seemed to fit together. Next step would be to fire at targets with and without the sound suppressor to quantify the loss in accuracy and also to test the reliability and durability of the attachment.

"Yes, sir, as a boy. My father would take me to the Black Forest. A lot of game there . . . still to this day."

"What is the most important thing about hunting?" Christoff asked, opening the box of a second silencer and attaching it to a second rifle.

"Silence, sir. It's all based on the hunter's ability to sneak right up to the prey unnoticed."

"Precisely. Silence is paramount in a successful hunt, and that is what we all must become. Hunters. Only the prey isn't game."

Johan slowly bobbed his head once, his tired eyes blinking understanding. "The platoon of Russian women."

"Correct. They have also adopted the same tactics."

Johan looked troubled, grimacing before looking away.

"What is it?" Christoff asked.

"What chance do we really have, sir? After all, it is no secret that the Russians and the partisans have already been using such tactics on us."

"That's exactly why it is going to work, Johan. Because our beloved Wermacht has been unable to adapt, choosing instead to fight back with artillery, panzers, and sheer brute force. They will not be expecting a group like ours. But the key is silence, my dear friend," Christoff said, patting the second silencer after having screwed it into the muzzle of the rifle. "Silence at all cost."

38

Wonder Machine

Messerschmitt Assembly Plant, Augsburg, Germany
December 14, 1942

For Erich Steinhoff, the revelation came very suddenly the moment the Messerschmitt scientists led him and Barkhorn into a hangar and turned on the lights.

There they stood, just as he last remembered seeing them six months ago, the two Me 262 prototypes; the propellerless aircraft that Mathias had talked about, but that Erich had been forbidden to discuss with anyone.

The planes, painted in a light-purple camouflage pattern on top and light gray underneath, still had the traditional landing gear fitted with tail wheel instead of the promised tricycle-style landing gear, but Erich saw that as a minor thing. His eyes were fixed on the turbines. One under each wing.

Erich approached one of the jets and ran a hand over the smooth curved contour of the nose. Since the engines were out of the way, the designers had packed four 30mm cannons in the nose, giving the plane unprecedented firepower . . . at an unprecedented speed.

The alloy surface felt cool to the touch. Erich could not find a single straight angle on the fuselage or the wings. It all curved one way or another and fit together with a high degree of precision, much better than the fittings on the latest Gustavs.

The rivets were flush with the body, giving it a smooth feeling, but it was also done for another reason: aerodynamics. At the high speeds that the Me 262 flew, the smallest disruption of airflow over a surface could cause devastating effects.

He reached the side with the built-in steps and froze when he saw a black clove painted on the nose, and his name airbrushed above the wing. He spun around and looked at the group of technicians and engineers.

"You understand the importance of your mission, Major Steinhoff?" Göring asked as he walked past the silent group of scientists and reached the jet's wingtip.

The head of the Luftwaffe took off his hat and set it on the wing. "These are the initial prototypes, Major. Only two. Our engineers are building two more, but it will take them almost six more months to complete them. These two, however, are ready. You have tested one. Major Barkhorn tested the other a month earlier."

"Sir," Erich said, walking closer to Göring. Barkhorn approached them. "I still don't understand. What are we supposed to do with them? Just *fly* them?"

"These are your new fighters, gentlemen. You are not allowed to use any other but these. You shall use them during each of your sorties. I'll make sure that each of you has enough spares to keep them airborne as much as the Gustavs. Given your records, I trust you will not get shot down and destroy them."

"Sir?" Erich asked.

"Yes?"

"Permission to speak freely?"

"Go ahead, Major."

"Well, if we had a hundred or more of these fighters, we could really deliver a devastating blow to the Soviets and the British, but what are we expected to accomplish with only two fighters?"

Goering smiled thinly. "What do you think, Major Barkhorn?"

Barkhorn smiled. "These are propaganda planes. Morale boosters for our men."

Göring's smile grew. "Thank you, Major Barkhorn. You mustn't underestimate the power of morale among the troops, Major Steinhoff. It could make the difference between winning and losing a battle . . . or even the entire damned war. High morale is what drives our men to push hard in difficult times. To come through during tough situations, like driving through Russian positions around Stalingrad and liberating the Sixth Army, which our strategists believe is imperative to maintain the momentum on the eastern front. You take away morale, and all you are left with is scrap metal and fearful men. Do you understand now, Major Steinhoff? Do you now see why we picked you and Major Barkhorn? You are our finest. We must minimize the possibility of anything happening to those planes. The future of the Luftwaffe is riding on you two. We need the men in Stalingrad as well as General von Hoth's army watching you blast Russians out of the sky. That in turn will instill in them the belief that we can still win, that we can still accomplish what no other army in history has been able to do: defeat the Russians in their own land. Now go. Make us proud."

39

One Last Time

Messerschmitt Assembly Plant, Augsburg, Germany
December 14, 1942

Ten minutes later, a soldier led Erich to a room in an adjacent building.

"One hour, Major," the soldier said before closing and locking the door.

"Erich?" a voice said behind him, mixing with the fading footsteps of the soldier.

His heartbeat rocketing, Erich turned around, anticipation filling him an instant before he stared into Sonja's eyes across the large room. She stood next to a pair of open windows. White curtains swirled in the midafternoon breeze along with her long black hair, which was much longer than the last time . . .

Thoughts washed away as she ran into his arms. Erich closed his eyes, buried his face in her hair, filled his lungs with her perfume. Minutes went by. Her lips met his and time stood still, his arms embracing her petite frame.

Erich felt her breasts firmly pressed against his chest and wanted to take her right then and there, but he knew Sonja wouldn't have it that way. She had always wanted to wait until after they were married. Erich had respected her wish then, and he respected it now.

"Oh, Erich. It's been so long," she murmured in his ear.

"Only six months, two weeks, five days, and a few hours."

They both smiled. Save for the longer hair, she hadn't changed one bit.

She crinkled her nose and rubbed a hand over his three-day stubble. "You look better clean-shaven, Erich Steinhoff."

"You're welcome to come by every day and do the honors," he replied.

They laughed again, then stopped, the futility of their situation washing away the joy of the moment. Erich was due back to duty in fifty minutes, and this time around he had the feeling he would be gone for much longer than six months. The Russian campaign had turned against the Germans. The dreams of an easy victory and return home had been replaced with the grim reality of a long and painful war—and even the possibility of losing that war, as Göring had suggested.

Erich could see the pain in her eyes now. He could see the fear and the anger of having to live like this. Sonja slowly pushed herself away from him and turned around.

"Come, Erich. There's something I want to give to you."

Sonja walked toward a door in the rear of the room. Puzzled, Erich followed her. She opened the door and stepped inside.

The curtains were drawn most of the way, but they left enough light through to cast a dim shadow over the bed Sonja now sat on.

"Are you—"

"It's all right, Erich. Please come."

Slowly, Erich approached her and sat next to her, not really knowing how to act. He had been with women before, but this time it was his Sonja, his childhood sweetheart, the future mother of his children.

Slowly, she took his hand and placed it under her blouse as she inched over and kissed him on the neck. A bit slow and soft at first, then with the growing intensity that clearly defined her intentions. Erich tried to control his feelings, but soon found himself fumbling in the twilight of the room as they undressed each other, as they crawled in bed, as their passion took them away from this place, from the madness of this war, from the horrors awaiting him in the eastern front. Sonja took it all away, absorbing his frustration, his anger, his fears as they moved in unison, as their passion became the only reality in the room.

They loved for the little time they had, creating memories that Erich hoped would carry him through the long and cold Siberian nights, through the insanity of his orders, through the agony of combat.

When they finished, they lay side by side, exhausted, their bodies filmed with sweat, their stares locked, as if in a trance neither of them dared break.

"This doesn't change a thing, Erich," Sonja suddenly said. "I still expect you to come home and marry me."

Erich smiled and cupped her face in his hands. "I promise you I'll be back."

40

Hidden Warrior

Lazur Plant, Stalingrad Pocket
December 14, 1942

Major Christoff Halden jumped swiftly and silently over the waist-high remains of a crumbled brick wall, rolling once as he landed to spread the impact across his body, surging to his feet and immediately seeking the shadowy shelter of a towering machine that resembled a giant wheel connected to a control booth housing many levers and dials.

The map obtained from a recently killed Russian platoon showed the route it had taken when crossing the Volga, infiltrating into the German-controlled section of the city through the narrow corridor between what remained of the State Bank and the Beer Factory.

Christoff swept his silent rifle in front of him before checking the edge of the exposed floors above him, failing to spot anything amid the twisted rebar projecting beyond the jagged concrete edges delineating sections of collapsed floor.

Satisfied that the immediate area was clear, Christoff ventured away from the odd-looking machine to signal his team, huddling among the frozen rubble on the other side of the wall.

Unlike other patrol commanders, who assigned the dangerous lead post to a subordinate, Christoff had assumed the role from the start, certain that the survivability of a patrol hinged on the patrol lead's ability to detect danger. He was the eyes and ears of his team, probing the terrain and verifying its safety before exposing any of his men.

Johan emerged from the shadows beyond the collapsed wall and crossed over it, before taking a defensive position next to Christoff, who waited until the last of his ten men had joined him before advancing once again through the desolation of the Lazur Plant, adjacent to the larger Red October.

According to the map, Russian patrols proceeded to this remote location to hide and rest after spreading havoc among the German ranks. The wrinkled and stained piece of paper, however, failed to mark the actual Russian hideouts in the vast complex, which Luftwaffe planes had bombed extensively during the autumn offensive.

Christoff's current objective was to locate the main Russian hideout as part of his plan to find the elusive platoon of female warriors.

As he moved beyond the impressive machinery and other surrounding hardware, some partly buried by the debris from the floors above, Christoff stared at a pile of maimed bodies to his left, factory workers who had perished in the bombings. The cold had preserved them just as they had died, faces contorted in pain when the sizzling shrapnel tore at them, dismembering some, disemboweling others, before the winter created this Russian version of a horror wax museum.

Christoff ignored their dead stares, their long-silenced screams, the frozen layer of blood and viscera beneath his fleece-lined boots, his mind pressing him to go on despite the inhumane temperatures and the sheer insanity of his situation,

Fighting a losing battle while surrounded by a million Russians far away from home.

Home.

Christoff sighed while peering beyond the jagged edges of a broken window at a large square packed with broken machinery and huge bomb craters—all beneath a thin layer of snow. His mind, however, went farther, beyond this frigid nation and the conquered territories, past the fatherland and Britain, across the Atlantic.

Home.

Christoff contrasted the bone-chilling desolation surrounding him with warm, sunny, and peaceful New

Braunffels, central Texas. He thought of cool swimming holes and blue skies, of making love in the back of his father's Ford truck under a starry night. Christoff could recall such moments with vivid clarity—as vivid as the shocked faces of his family and friends when he had decided to join Hitler's Germany.

When he had become the enemy.

Christoff blinked the past away, his predatory eyes once again focusing on his own enemy, the one Germany had created by raping, looting, and massacring its way across this vast land while hoping for another easy victory, like France and Poland.

But the Soviets stopped us, he thought. The Russians had drawn a line in the frozen tundra and anchored down, opting to fight to the death, just as those soldiers had done on the first days of Operation Barbarossa, tying themselves to their trenches, choosing death over surrender while taking as many enemy soldiers with them as possible. It was that kind of unyielding determination that had halted the German offensive in 1941 within sight of Moscow, and now a year later in this forsaken city.

A gust of wind, like a belch from hell, shot through the window, forcing him to look away.

Christoff led his team around the square and deeper into this seemingly endless factory, determined to find these female Russian warriors.

His ticket out of this nightmare.

41

Jet Power

Messerschmitt Assembly Plant, Augsburg, Germany
December 14, 1942

Erich reached the Me 262 parked on the ramp. A ground-crew member standing next to the left wing saluted him. Erich saluted back.

The Me 262's three-piece canopy, made of bulletproof glass, was hinged on the right side. Erich climbed on the left wingroot, reached the cockpit, and eased himself into the seat, which felt considerably roomier than the Gustav's. The instrument cluster, however, was arranged in nearly the same way as his Me 109G.

He carefully went through the pretakeoff checklist before powering the avionics and starting the turbines, smiling the moment the high-pitched whir from the dual engines broke the silence of the test field. He glanced over to his left and saw Barkhorn climbing atop the second prototype.

A small push on the dual throttle handles, and the fourteen-thousand-pound Messerschmitt moved forward under the powerful thrust of the Junkers Jumo 004 engines.

Erich taxied the jet toward the end of the runway as the sun stained the late afternoon sky orange and yellow.

Lowering the sun visor, the oxygen mask hanging off the side of his helmet, he aligned the jet's nose with the runway's centerline, added a mild ten degrees of flaps, and slowly advanced the throttle handles to the fully forward position.

Both turbojets responded by unleashing a combined thrust of four thousand pounds, kicking Erich in the back as the Messerschmitt dashed forward at great speed.

The acceleration was both exhilarating and terrifying.

The power-to-weight ratio of the plane was such that in less than ten seconds after applying full throttle, the airspeed indicator needle blasted past 150 knots.

He waited until it read 170 before easing the control stick back. The Me 262 gently left the ground. He lowered the nose when he reached ten feet above the tarmac, slapped the flaps handles, and raised the gear.

Speed quickly soared to four hundred knots.

In a show of force and skill, Erich swung the stick back and the jet went vertical while several Gs jammed him against the back of the seat.

It was hard to believe that an engineering marvel like the revolutionary and perfected jet he flew could come from the same government that had started a war against the Soviet Union, thus opening a second front.

How can Berlin have the brilliant vision to develop such a technologically advanced fighter, and then turn around and make such poor decisions in the battlefield?

That puzzled Erich tremendously, but as he had already been reminded more than once, the Nazi Party didn't expect him to agree with all of its war directives. It did, however, expect him to follow them without hesitation. And Erich did. Not for the Nazi Party or for the Luftwaffe, and certainly not to assist Hitler's glorified dreams of an Aryan world. Erich did what he did best for the benefit of his Deutschland. Erich flew for Germany.

He reached a layer of cumulus clouds at twenty thousand feet, and leveled off at thirty thousand, where he eased back on the throttles to conserve fuel and slowly circled over the city waiting for Barkhorn to make his takeoff roll. They had a long flight ahead of them.

42

Free Hunters

Kalach Airfield, Twenty Miles West of Stalingrad Pocket
December 15, 1942

REF: CX/MSS/T347/67   HP3434

ZZZZZ

(HP 3434 & 3434 CR ONA GT QX YKE GU 7 & 7)

Orders at one two zero zero hours twelfth for thirteenth. Firstly, Major Erich Steinhoff, Jagdgeschwader 52, Gruppe 1 to attack ten miles north of Aksai River in support of German tank attack in the Kotelnikovo area. Second alternative target crossing the Myshova. Generalleutnant von Hothzzzzz

AM
CR   150700/12/42

Holding the piece of paper that a Soviet radio operator had just passed to him, Captain Jack Towers jotted down the Russian equivalent at the bottom, and a minute later, he entered the briefing bunker, where Colonel Krasilov and his pilots had gathered to go over the day's next mission.

Krasilov's mood seemed to have improved from the day before. The Soviet colonel was laughing loudly as he and Andrei slammed two empty vodka glasses on the table.

Krasilov's face was streaked with oil from a heavy leak in one of the last La-3s in the base. Krasilov, as Andrei had told him earlier that chilly morning, had gone on a two-plane hunting trip looking for Germans, but instead of taking one of the new Aircobras, the stubborn colonel had opted for a weathered La-3. As it turned out, the engine began to leak oil shortly after takeoff, and Krasilov had to make an emergency landing.

As Jack got closer to the table, he could see the imprints of Krasilov's oily fingers on the empty glass. His flying helmet, also stained with oil, lay on the table next to a thick belt with a holstered pistol. The Russian colonel lifted his head.

"Ah, comrades, look. It's the impatient virgin!"

Three pilots roared with laughter, fell to the floor, and slapped the top of their legs with mirth. Andrei slowly shook his head.

Jack frowned before sitting across from a smiling Krasilov. The smile froze on the Russian's face as Jack slid the piece of paper across the table.

The Russian's scarred face wrinkled.

"This just came in for me, Colonel."

Krasilov read on for a minute and then his face turned red. He abruptly got up, tipping his chair and stomping his large fists on the table.

"It's too late to intercept! What took this message so long to get here?"

"It went through a lot of hands to reach this side of the world, Colonel."

"Well, it's useless! The fighting starts in a half hour and it's over seventy-five miles away. We won't get there in time!"

Krasilov picked up his chair and sat back down. His face showed obvious frustration.

"You're overlooking one important fact, Colonel."

Krasilov briefly studied Jack. The ends of the Russian's thick eyebrows dropped a bit. "I am?"

Jack reached for the bottle of vodka, which also had Krasilov's oily imprints, took a sip, and set it down in front of him. "Even if your fighters don't get there in time to help the ground troops, you can still get there after their German planes have exhausted their fuel and ammunition . . . and simply shoot them down."

Krasilov remained silent. Everyone else in the room quieted. For a few seconds, the only sound inside the bunker was the crack and fizzle of the stove and the constant wail of the wind outside. Then Krasilov got up slowly, glanced down at Jack once more, and then scanned the room.

"To your planes! Now!"

Men rushed outside the bunker nearly running over each other.

The room fell quiet. Jack remained seated, feeling Krasilov's eyes on him.

"Are you coming, Captain?"

"Colonel, you know I'm not allowed to engage in battle, sir. My orders are strictly to—"

"You mean to tell me you get information like this and then even come up with this clever idea, and then you, a pilot with a plane ready to fly outside, are just going to sit and listen to the radio?"

"Colonel, I've been ordered not to—"

Krasilov exhaled. "You are a virgin after all."

Jack clenched his teeth as Krasilov headed for the exit.

The Russian stopped by the doorway and turned around. "You wouldn't mind if I take your *Impatient Virgin,* yes, Captain? A plane without a pilot is like a woman without a husband. Perhaps after a few sessions with a real pilot she will grow to like me better than she likes you."

Jack tried to control his anger but failed. It was bad enough he had been sent to this desolate land to freeze to death, but he was not going to put up with the colonel's harassment any longer.

"The fuck I do mind, you hardheaded, egotistical bastard! You keep your damn hands off my plane! I'll fly it myself!" Jack stormed past Krasilov and headed for his plane.

Krasilov went after him. Jack picked up his pace and got to his Aircobra before Krasilov got a chance to catch up. As Jack stepped up to his plane, Krasilov extended his arms in the air.

"Listen, everyone! Listen!"

All the other pilots, including Natalya and three other women working on the engine of the La-3 Krasilov had flown earlier that morning, turned their heads.

"Today," Krasilov said in a sarcastic, half-humorous tone, "we'll be honored by having Captain Jack Towers from the United States Air Force come along with us!"

"Who's gonna be his wingman, Colonel?" screamed Andrei from the cockpit of his Aircobra. "We're already teamed up in pairs."

Krasilov's smile grew wide. "In that case we're going to let one of our own virgins fly with the American virgin. Natalya! You will be Captain Towers' wingman today!"

The pilots burst into laughter.

Jack glanced at Natalya. Their gazes met and Jack winked. Natalya threw down the rag in her hands and headed over to an La-3 parked next to the one she was working on.

Jack shrugged, donned a parachute, and crawled inside his Aircobra's cockpit. He was airborne five minutes later with Natalya to his right.

"Stay on my tail no matter what, Natalya," he said over the radio.

"You worry about the Germans in front of you, Jack. I'll handle the rear."

43

Stukas

Fifty Miles North of the Aksai River
December 15, 1942

At twelve thousand feet Werner Haufman held the lead of his Stukagruppen, which totaled sixteen dive-bombers flying in four-finger formations. He flew the lead formation. The other three groups of four Stukas were positioned four hundred feet to his right, left, and above him respectively.

Werner looked up and behind him and eyed the lead

Stuka of the formation above him. The undersurface of the wingtips and fuselage bands were yellow, marking the craft's theater of operation as the eastern front. All planes in his gruppe sported similar markings.

It felt good to be flying, Haufman thought, particularly in a sky cloudy enough to hide from enemy planes should the Russians send some to intercept his planned strafing run over enemy positions.

"Any sign of enemy fighters?" he asked through the intercom to the gunner in the rear cockpit.

"No, sir. Skies are clear."

Haufman glanced at the group of Gustavs escorting him back to the battlefield for a second sortie that day to delay the Soviet tank advance against the left flank of General von Hoth's panzer army.

44

Teamwork

Fifty Miles North of the Aksai River
December 15, 1942

Jack Towers watched Krasilov take the lead with his wingman, Andrei. He cut back throttle and let Krasilov get a thousand feet in front of him. Airspeed dropped to three hundred knots and the plane felt just right. The trimming on both throttle and elevators was as it should be, reducing to a minimum the effort Jack had to exert on the stick to maintain a level flight. He glanced backward and saw Natalya glued to his left.

"Germans, Jack!" her voice crackled through his headset.

"Where?"

"Nine o'clock. About three thousand feet up."

Jack squinted. Even though he wore sunglasses, the glare

from the early morning sun filtering through the curved canopy stung his eyes. A few more seconds, and he spotted them.

"Damn!" he said. In Africa he never saw more than a handful of Messerschmitts at a time. "Look at them! It must be at least . . ."

"I'm counting over thirty planes!" Krasilov shouted. *"Scramble! Work in pairs! Dive-bombers are the highest priority!"*

Jack slammed full throttle, jammed the stick back, and lifted the trigger guard case. The Gs piled up on him as his craft roared upward at great speed. The altimeter dashed above nine thousand feet.

Ninety-five hundred feet.

Ten thousand feet.

Rapidly bleeding airspeed, Jack lowered the nose by a few degrees and pointed it toward the right-most Stuka formation, but he didn't get much farther in his pursuit. The escorting Gustavs broke flight in all directions.

One of them made an inverted dive right turn and threatened to come around on Jack's tail. Jack broke left, rolled the plane on its side, and faced the incoming German head on while quickly checking that Natalya remained with him.

The clear disk of her propeller glittered in the corner of his eye.

The Gustav less than a thousand feet away and closing at great speed, Jack squeezed the trigger as he coordinated the rudder, ailerons, and elevators to keep the German aligned in his sights.

The 37mm blasts started, two per second. The mighty recoil pounded against the entire fuselage, giving Jack the impression of having a second heartbeat in his chest.

He noticed the airspeed indicator needle quivering with every burst. For a second he wasn't sure if it was just the vibrations from the recoil, or if the powerful guns actually had enough power to slow down the plane momentarily. It didn't matter. His airspeed had already gone through the roof at 410 knots, way beyond the safe envelope.

The Gustav grew larger. Jack could now see the muzzle flashes from the German's nose-mounted cannon, but registered no hits on his Aircobra.

Jack waited until the last minute before pulling up . . . and the German also pulled up!

"Jack!" he heard Natalya scream.

Instinctively, Jack swung the stick right and forward. For a second the large cross painted on the underside of the Messerschmitt's left wing filled his field of view.

As he cringed for what seemed like an imminent collision, the Gustav's gray underside grazed his canopy as he heard the loud thump from the tail wheel striking his rudder. It was over before his mind got a chance to register it all. He had come within inches of death.

Jack snapped his head back as he applied both left and right rudder. The tail was not damaged, and the Messerschmitt had gone into a steep dive.

"Stay with me, Natalya!" he said, not believing he had survived that.

Shoving aside the near-miss, Jack slammed full power and hauled the stick back, the Gs tearing at him. His vision became a narrow tunnel, but it didn't last long. The moment he reached the top of the loop, blood rushed back to his head. He continued the rear pressure until he got the nose pointing straight down, and centered the stick.

Airspeed scurried above 420 knots again. The craft trembled. The vibrations on the stick were getting out of control.

"Jack! We're going too fast!"

"Slow down now, Natalya, and he'll get away," he replied in the most confident voice he could muster.

The Gustav continued its dive, and Jack, topping nearly 450 knots, caught up fast, but at the same time, he was dropping at a staggering rate.

Sweat rolling into the corners of his eyes, Jack saw the altimeter dip below five thousand feet. The Aircobra plunged into a cloud. Jack lost the German for a second, acquiring him again as he left the cloud behind.

Five hundred feet. The gap between the planes was closing too fast.

Three hundred feet.

Two hundred.

The Gustav remained on his dive. Jack cut back power and squeezed the trigger.

The Gustav pulled up while breaking hard left. The sun flashed off the German's wings as Jack tried to follow it, but out-speeding the German by a hundred knots, Jack found his craft making a wider turn than he had liked.

Rather that cutting back power to get some relief from the titanic centrifugal force that made his limbs feel five times as heavy, Jack added throttle and instantly saw his vision reduced to a small dot—his body's warning that he was pushing maximum G-force. Anything more and he would either pass out or the wings of the Aircobra would fold.

Neither happened. Jack's gamble worked. He kept on pursuing, and as he completed the turn and leveled off, he found himself only three hundred feet from the German at roughly the same airspeed.

The Gustav pulled up in full throttle, condensation pouring off its wingtips as the Gs blasted over the Messerschmitt struggling for altitude. He stayed with it.

Another two turns, a throttle adjustment, a final dive, and Jack opened fire. This time it was easier. A few short bursts and the Gustav arched down toward the ground leaving a trail of smoke on its path. Jack saw no parachute, and glanced back and noticed that Natalya was still with him.

"Good flying, Natalya!" he said in a more naturally confident voice.

"Good shooting, Jack."

Jack pointed his Aircobra back toward the Stukas, which continued to fly in formation toward the Soviet tanks north of the Aksai River.

Werner Haufman watched in anger as two Gustavs got shot down in the first minute of the air battle. He had given strict instructions to his dive-bombers not to break formation under any circumstance. Their slow Stukas would be no match to the Soviet fighters in a one-on-one encounter. They were safer together.

Jack approached the Stukas from their most vulnerable spot: the rear underside. He focused on the right-most plane of the right-most formation.

As two small clouds of black smoke bellowed from the exhausts and wafted away in the slipstream, Jack let go several rounds. A river of holes exploded across the Stuka's right wing before it broke apart from the fuselage. Jack cut left, dove to three thousand feet, made a three-sixty, and as the Stuka spun down to earth, he advanced the throttle, tugged back the control stick, and aligned the next dive-bomber.

"Left, Jack. Break left!" Natalya screamed as she broke right.

Jack automatically responded to Natalya's shouts while moving his head in all directions to find . . .

There! Another Gustav diving toward him.

The craft caught him broadside. Natalya struggled to pull a quick three-sixty to get the German fighter before it got Jack.

The muzzle flashes started. Jack had to figure a way to get out of the German's line of fire before he got closer. He glanced at Natalya coming to his rescue at full speed, but she would be several seconds too late.

Instincts overcame surprise. As the rapidly approaching dark-green Messerschmitt became hazy behind the bright flashes of its cannon's guns, Jack idled the throttle, added flaps, and dropped the gear.

Jack jerked forward into his restraining harness as his airspeed plummeted to two hundred knots. Two seconds later the Gustav zoomed past Jack's field of view at great speed, too fast for Jack to fire but close enough for him to go in pursuit. The German went into a steep climb.

Gear and flaps up, full throttle, stick back, and the sun bathed his canopy as he pointed his nose at the heavens.

The Gustav was pushing for altitude five hundred feet above him. Jack squinted at the glare, but it was not the sun. There was something else reflecting the bright light.

Something flying very high and very fast.

45

Vantage Point

Thirty Thousand Feet, Twenty Miles North of the Aksai River
December 15, 1942

Erich Steinhoff smiled broadly under his oxygen mask as he cruised at a comfortable five hundred knots. He was untouchable at this altitude and speed, yet he could easily drop on anyone like a hawk in a matter of seconds, blast them with the powerful cannons, and cruise back up in under a minute. He now understood the reason for his superiors wanting to get the plane to the field as soon as possible to recover some of the Luftwaffe's lost prestige.

He looked directly above and to his right. The second Me 262 flew just as steady at the controls of Barkhorn. The Aryan major would fly his jet to Gruppe 3, now located a short twenty miles from Erich's Gruppe 1. Between them, they would try to maximize the number of missions in which the new jet fighters participated to achieve maximum visibility with the enemy forces—as well as with the German troops. The word would soon get out about the propellerless craft of the Luftwaffe and their devastating effects.

As the whirling twin Jumo engines shunted down to a quiet hum by the well-insulated canopy, Erich's thoughts briefly drifted to Sonja and the single hour they had spent together. The smell of her was still with him, and Erich only wished it would remain like that always, for he did not feel lonely at that moment. All he had to do was close his eyes and breathe deeply, and he felt her body next to his—

"Major Steinhoff! Major Steinhoff!" Barkhorn's voice crackled through his headset.

"Yes, what is it?"

"Tip your left wing! Look at the skies over the Aksai River!"

Erich eased the stick to the left and looked ahead and below, spotting what could have been at least fifty planes in the air. He checked his fuel gauge. Their last refueling spot had been in the port of Odessa on the Black Sea. Even with his eighty-gallon drop-tank, his Me 262 had less than thirty minutes of flying time left—much less if he engaged in a dogfight.

"Major Barkhorn," Erich began, "we don't have fuel for—"

"Follow my lead, Major!" Barkhorn shouted.

"But, Major. Our fuel situation is—"

Barkhorn inverted his plane and went into a steep dive.

Cursing the obstinate major for putting both prototypes in danger by risking running out of fuel, Erich swung the control stick to the left and back.

The earth swapped places with the overcast skies as he followed Barkhorn's tail, his airspeed rocketing past 520 knots.

46

Break Left!

Fifty Miles North of the Aksai River
December 15, 1942

Jack applied full power and slammed the stick to the right to close the gap on the departing Messerschmitt. The Gustav went into another vertical climb while executing a left corkscrew.

The palms of his hands moist inside his gloves, Jack pulled the stick back and felt his eyeballs about to burst from the Gs. His vision temporarily reddened and got cloudier while rivulets of sweat tricked down his forehead, but he did not ease on the rear pressure or throttle setting. He followed the Me 109G all the way up to eleven thousand feet before the Gustav tried to shake off Jack by executing an inverted dive to the left.

Jack momentarily eased back power, pushed the control stick hard to the left, and then rammed full power.

In the corner of his eye he spotted Natalya in the La-3 getting so close to him that for a second he thought she was going to slam into him, but she didn't. She executed the maneuver beautifully and stayed slightly behind and to his right.

The Gustav in his sights, Jack let go a short burst of the powerful 37mm nose-mounted cannon. The Aircobra shuddered with every blow as the all-aluminum structure absorbed the M4 cannon's powerful recoil once every two seconds. It took six bursts before the Gustav fell apart. Several rounds pierced through the rear fuselage, tearing off the tail and the left wing with a bright flash. The sky in front of him suddenly filled with fire. Jack pulled left and noticed Natalya breaking right. The wreckage was still too thick to fly through.

Jack scanned the skies for Natalya but couldn't find her. He half-rolled the Aircobra to the left and back in the direction of the fallen Gustav. She had gone the other way and the sky was filled with . . . there she was . . . with a Gustav diving down on her!

"Natalya! Break left! Left!"

The Soviet woman complied, barely missing the cannons of the Gustav as it leveled off behind her. The Messerschmitt closed for the kill. Jack saw Natalya desperately going for a steep climb and turn, but the Gustav easily imitated the maneuver and opened fire again.

"Invert and dive right, Natalya! Now!"

Once again she did just as Jack suggested, but the Gustav followed, and Jack followed the Gustav.

Natalya completed the dive and pulled up at less than three hundred feet aboveground with the Gustav on her tail. Jack closed the gap so narrowly that he could almost touch the Gustav's vertical fin. The dangerously low altitude at which the trio had pulled out of the dive didn't sink in until a few seconds later. Jack's concentration was so intense that he had nearly blocked everything else from his mind. Natalya's change of direction had gone from a shallow to a very intense and abrupt tight left turn. Her wingtip nearly grazed the leafless treetops.

The Gustav struggled to keep up with her, and so did Jack.

He glanced at the altimeter.

One hundred feet.

Natalya leveled off, and so did the Gustav, but Jack already had an angle on the Messerschmitt even before the Gustav's wings became flush with the horizon.

Another five bursts from the cannon at such close distance and the Gustav stabbed the forest, igniting it in a cloud of smoke and orange flames.

"Good flying, Natalya!"

"Thanks, Jack."

"No problem."

She reduced airspeed enough to let him get by and take the lead once more. Jack pulled up and began—

What in the hell is that? he thought when spotting something zooming across the sky at great speed. Whatever it was had come and gone in a couple of seconds.

"What was that?"

"I saw it too, Jack. Can't tell, but there were two of them."

Jack scanned the skies and saw Krasilov and Andrei closing in on another Gustav. There were three other Soviet pairs in the air, each with their hands full, but they were all normal—

"There they went again!" Jack shouted, this time getting a good look at them. "They're jet aircraft!"

"What?"

"Jets, Natalya. Airplanes without propellers using jet propulsion technology! Sweet Jesus!" said Jack, remembering the USAF research with the de Havilland H-1B turbojet. Word among American pilots was that Lockheed had installed the engine on some secret prototype development.

The pair of fighters dashed past a group of scattered clouds and closed in on Krasilov and Andrei.

"Watch out, Colonel! You've got two on your tail!"

Jack noticed Krasilov breaking hard left as the two jets made a quick pass from behind.

47

New Maneuvers

Fifty Miles North of the Aksai River
December 15, 1942

Major Erich Steinhoff saw the two Soviet fighters in pursuit of a Gustav break left and right respectively. He hardly had any time to fire. What had been a small dot on the horizon quickly became the tail of the fighter. He stopped firing after one second, pulling up to avoid ramming the Soviet, and started to execute a loop the loop.

The Gs crushed him. His vision narrowed. The craft appeared to take the stress well, but Erich had almost passed out. He eased back on the stick when he came back around. There were still a lot of maneuvers that he had to test carefully before executing them at full speed.

Erich bent forward to look through the sight and noticed that he had gained too much speed again. The trees and fields below flashed underneath as the tail of the Soviet plane loomed alarmingly in the sight. As his finger reached the trigger, Erich realized that the fighter was already smoking. He had somehow managed to hit him on the first pass.

Surprised at the power of his own guns, Erich pulled up, glanced at his fuel gauge, and quickly reduced throttles. He was flying on vapor.

48

Trouble

Fifty Miles North of the Aksai River
December 15, 1942

"I'm hit! I'm hit!" Jack heard Andrei scream over the radio.

"Andrei, this is Jack. Can you make it to the base?"

"I'm not sure, Jackovich. I've still got some power."

"I'll tell you what. Don't ease the throttle. We're only thirty minutes away from our base. I'll come up on your right side and guide you all the way home. Once over the field you can cut back power and glide your way in. The Aircobras float beautifully."

"Thanks, Jackovich."

At four thousand feet, Jack saw Andrei's plane ahead of him followed by a river of smoke a mile long. He was about to add power when something zoomed past him.

It was another jet, and it was headed directly for Andrei.

49

Coup de Grâce

Fifty Miles North of the Aksai River
December 15, 1942

"Time to head home, Major Barkhorn," Erich said over the radio, but got no response.

He scanned the skies and noticed Barkhorn coming around behind the wounded Soviet fighter.

"Wait, Major! That's my kill, and I say it's already going down!"

No response.

Enraged, Erich watched Barkhorn's Me 262 approaching the smoking craft from the rear and letting go a three-second burst—an overkill in Erich's opinion. In a flash, what had been a thick trail of smoke turned into a ball of fire.

"Now he's going down for sure, Major Steinhoff!"

"It wasn't necessary, Major!"

"I'm low on fuel. I'm headed back to my base. I suggest you do the same, Major Steinhoff. Over and out!"

Erich clutched the stick as he watched Barkhorn turn toward his base. Before he too made his turn, Erich glanced back at the falling Soviet craft.

50

I'm Burning!

Fifty Miles North of the Aksai River
December 15, 1942

"Turn the plane over and drop, Andrei!" Jack heard
Krasilov scream over the radio as he watched Andrei's
P-39D in a steep dive. The fighter inverted and the nose
dropped a few degrees. Jack held his breath waiting for Andrei to drop from the burning craft, but he never did.

"Get out of there, dammit!" screamed Jack.

*"I can't . . . the canopy! The bullets bent it! It's
jammed . . . it won't give . . . the flames! My back is on fire!
My legs!"*

Jack watched as Andrei's cockpit filled with smoke first
and then with fire. The Aircobra went into a deeper dive,
but to Jack's utter surprise, it was not an uncontrollable
dive.

*"I'm burning! I'm burning! Stick left! Rudder left . . .
stick forward!"*

Jack was speechless. He could see clearly the inside
of the cockpit filled with flames and Andrei's ablaze figure talking himself into the last few maneuvers. In his
agony, the young Russian had kept his hand pressed on
the radio transmit button.

Jack saw the target, a slower Stuka. Andrei's plane, now
totally ablaze, dashed across the sky like a comet and approached the Stuka at great speed. The German pilot tried
to break left, but not soon enough. Jack heard Andrei curse
the Germans with a final cry of despair as both planes went
up in a spectacular ball of flames, smoke, and scorching
debris.

51

Will to Fight

In utter shock, Erich watched the courageous Soviet pilot take out one last German airplane with his wounded fighter, and his old concerns about the enemy filled him once more. Did his pilots have that kind of will to fight and die for Germany? Did he? And if Germany lost the war, how would the Soviets retaliate to the kind of needless abuse as Barkhorn had displayed here today?

Dread overcoming him, Erich turned and headed north.

52

Hard Right

Jack saw the two jets depart the area leaving behind long and thin white contrails. He didn't attempt to pursue. Not only didn't he think his Aircobra could reach the speeds of those jets, but Colonel Krasilov was in trouble. With all the commotion with the jets, a Gustav had managed to sneak behind the Soviet colonel.

"Hang in there, sir. I'm on my way!" screamed Jack as he set the Aircobra in a steep dive and closed in on the Messerschmitt.

Negative Gs pushing him up against the restraining

harness, Jack lined up the Gustav and fired a short burst from the wings' 50-caliber guns.

The rounds missed the tail by a couple of feet.

Jacked inched the throttle a dash, closing the gap a bit more. Krasilov pulled up and rose to the sky like an elevator. The German did likewise, and Jack and Natalya followed along.

"Take the shot, Captain Towers! Get this Hitlerite bastard off my tail!"

"On my mark break hard right, Colonel. Hard right. Got that?"

"Got it."

"Three . . . two . . ."

Jack broke hard right and cut back throttle.

"One . . . now!"

Jack was now flying parallel to them. Krasilov broke right. Jack swung the stick left and caught the German broadside. The pilot realized he'd been tricked just as Jack opened fire with the 50-calibers at less than fifty feet. The Gustav came apart, breaking up in four pieces, as if it were made of paper, its sections trembling in the slipstream before the gas tank detonated with metal-ripping force.

Jack and Natalya flew through the flames and emerged on the other side.

The trio climbed to five thousand feet, where three more pairs of Aircobras soon joined them. Behind, they left the still ablaze wreckage of the Stuka and Andrei's Aircobra, along with five destroyed Gustavs and three more Stukas. The remaining Stukas were already out of sight and out of reach. Everyone had barely enough fuel to make it back to base. Not only had they lost Andrei, but they had not been able to stop the bulk of the Stuka force from reaching the Soviet front lines.

53

Sacrifice

Lazur Factory, Stalingrad Pocket
December 15, 1942

"It is an honor to share our modest supplies with you and your team, Comrade Major. Your triumphs against the Hitlerites bring hope to our people. You are an inspiration to us all!"

Zoya Krasilov regarded the massive Sergeant Melkinov with the rotten teeth sitting across from her sipping hot tea while singing praises about her and her team. They sat in a secluded warehouse within the vast complex of buildings making up what used to be one of the largest tractor factories in Russia. The right half of his face, severely scarred from a mortar attack six months ago, twitched every time he spoke, probably from damaged nerves. Facial hair only grew on his undamaged side, almost splitting his face between his prewar years and the present. Like most Russians in recent weeks—at least since trapping the German Sixth Army—the sergeant seemed in good spirits.

"The honor is mine, Kostya," replied Zoya. "And thanks again for accommodating us and also for sharing your supplies. We must conserve ours for our long mission."

Sergeant Konstantin Melkinov, about two full meters in height and weighing as much as two men, went simply by the nickname of Kostya. He was on his way back across the Volga with his platoon after three days and two nights of spreading havoc south of Mamayev Hill, mostly by taking potshots at passing German columns from the safety of the many structures in the area.

"The Germans are cowards," said Kostya, turning the scarred side away, presenting Zoya with a bearded side that was almost handsome in a rugged sense.

He produced a piece of moldy bread from a pocket and brought it up to his mouth. Blood trickled from his darkened gums as he sank his front teeth into it, taking a bite, which he then chewed slowly. Medical services were limited to those in critical condition and whom the doctors felt would heal to fight again. All others were either left to die or forced to continue fighting regardless of the pain and inconvenience that their wounds or medical situation created. And that included dental work.

The sergeant, who had to be in pain but did not display it, swallowed the bloody mass and added, "Instead of coming in the buildings and engaging us like soldiers, the Germans run away like frightened children and retaliate by calling out our position to their artillery."

"Yes," added a young soldier sitting next to Kostya, his teeth just as dark. "And they only come back after they have pounded the buildings for hours. And *always* while hiding behind a column of panzers."

"Indeed, my young comrade," said Kostya, patting the private's right shoulder. "Take away their planes, tanks, and heavy artillery, and what you are left with are men without the will to fight."

Zoya nodded while letting the tea warm her core. Tasha sat next to her also clutching a hot tin can filled halfway with something that tasted more like dirty underwear than tea, but at least it was hot.

"Where was the location of your last enemy sighting, Sergeant?" Zoya asked.

Using the rough piece of bread to scratch the jagged line on his chin where scar tissue met his beard, he replied, "Just north of here, atop one of the buildings of the Red October plant overlooking Mamayev Hill. We killed eight of the bastards before their artillery started working on our position. I lost one man in the shelling before we could reach safety. The round ripped off both his legs and he bled to death before we could get him out."

Zoya pulled a creased map of downtown Stalingrad and unfolded it in front of the sergeant, who looked with interest.

"Where exactly on the Red October plant?" she asked.

Kostya ran a long and black fingernail down the stained paper, circling the area just east of Mamayev Hill. "Right here. My men had taken up sniper positions here, here, and here," he added, pointing to what was shown on the map as factory buildings that were still standing. "There was also a lot of activity along the east edge of the hill, almost as if they were getting ready to defend against a major Russian attack. Problem is the nearest Red Army division is over ten miles away."

Zoya exchanged a glance with Tasha, who was also studying the map in between sips of tea. They were planning to take up their positions along the buildings east of the hill, which Kostya was describing as surrounded with German troops. Russian intelligence had reported German defense lines north and south of the hill, but not to the east. Perhaps the Germans suspected or knew about Chuikov's attack and had chosen to reinforce that flank, or maybe the enemy was just being cautious given the strategic importance of the hill as it overlooked most of north and central Stalingrad. It was also the place where General Paulus planned to use to coordinate a breakthrough to meet up with von Hoth's panzers.

Either way it didn't matter. Zoya had been ordered there and that was exactly where she would lead her team and wait for Chuikov's tanks to start driving south before commencing her attack.

"What else can you tell us about your experience around Mamayev Hill, Comrade Sergeant?"

Kostya nibbled at the bread, chewing and bleeding before swallowing and leaning closer to her while pointing at the map. "Best locations for sniper activity are along this wall on the third floor, though the roof is also very good, but vulnerable to mortars and artillery shells. One of the corners of this building has a protruding ledge that will give you shelter against the wind and snow, plus there is a second access to the roof here."

A rancid smell oozed from Kostya's rotting gums and

teeth, but Zoya felt nothing but admiration for this giant Slav, accepting his wounds with patriotic resignation while carrying out his orders.

"There are also stories of Russian women falling in their hands," added Kostya cautiously, almost whispering. "I must beg you and your beautiful and brave warriors to be very careful. I cannot bear the thought of those animals . . ."

Zoya smiled thinly and put a hand to his scarred cheek, which actually felt quite smooth despite its lumpy appearance. "You are a good and brave man, Comrade Sergeant. But you need not worry about me or my team. All of us have experienced firsthand German brutality and managed to survive. That is why we do not care what happens to us as long as the Rodina survives this onslaught."

Embarrassed by either her touch or her words, the corpulent sergeant dropped his gaze for just an instant, the moment broken by hastening footsteps from the south end of the warehouse.

Everyone stood in unison and reached for their weapons.

"Kostya . . . Kostya!" hissed a young recruit, probably still in his teens, his cheeks flushed red from running and also from the cold. He was clutching his stomach.

"Yes? What is it?"

"Germans, sir. An entire platoon . . . took us by surprise . . . killed my . . ." the kid collapsed.

Only then did Zoya notice the dark circle staining his jacket. He had been shot.

Kostya knelt by his side, shifting his gaze between the wounded soldier and the hallway from where he had emerged, before motioning four of his men to go and cover it. "Where, son? Where did they come from?"

Four men took off in single file as ordered, disappearing beyond the darkness in the rear of the warehouse. The rest of Kostya's twenty-some men remained put, alongside Zoya's dozen warriors.

The young soldier started to tremble uncontrollably.

"Please," Kostya said. "Where did they come from?"

"Everywhere, sir," he replied, shivering. "They just . . . appeared in the . . . room next door . . . Started shooting . . . killed my friends. I have never seen them act this way."

"But we didn't hear any shots," said Kostya.

"Silent . . . silent rifles."

"How many did you see?" asked Zoya, kneeling next to Kostya, feeling her stomach knotting.

"A dozen, at least. Maybe . . . more. They wore uniforms that blended them with the building . . . like us. Their rifles were also camouflaged . . . like ours, and silent."

Zoya and Kostya started at one another for a moment before the veteran sergeant asked, "Silent? What do you mean?"

The soldier began to cough blood as his eyes rolled to the back of his head.

"He meant the Germans have adapted some sort of sound suppressor to their rifles," offered Zoya as the boy died.

"Which means," added Tasha, standing in front of them. "That they have an edge over us."

"Not anymore," she said. "We now *know* they have silenced weapons. They should have never allowed this kid to warn us."

"Bastards," mumbled Kostya, peering toward the hallway leading to the section of the building where this soldier had been.

An ear-piercing shriek echoed inside the room.

"That's one of the men I just sent over there," hissed Kostya, his face tight with concern.

He only had to glance at his seasoned troops before the men scrambled around the large equipment warehouse, blending themselves with their surroundings. Zoya was about to order her soldiers to do likewise when Kostya stopped her.

"You must leave at once, Comrade Major. We will hold them back to give you time to escape. Then we will make our own escape."

Zoya hesitated, but then remembered Chuikov's orders.

She had to reach her vantage point east of Mamayev Hill to support the attack. Her superior had stressed that she was to avoid enemy contact at all cost and just hide until the right moment.

Slowly, she nodded while backing away, then turned to her team. "Move out."

Her troops took off in the opposite direction from the threat.

Before following them, she gave this courageous man one last look. He smiled, exposing his rotten teeth, before joining his men.

54

Shadow Game

Lazur Factory, Stalingrad Pocket
December 15, 1942

Major Christoff Halden swept his silent weapon across the narrow field of view between a towering tractor and an odd-looking machine, like the hundreds that dominated this industrial section of the city.

The bleeding Russian fifteen feet ahead of him finally stopped moving, and Christoff chastised himself for having missed the first shot, wounding him in the chest instead of in the head, which would had prevented the scream that no doubt alerted others. But at least he had killed the Russian, instead of just wounding him and watching him run away to alert this second wave of soldiers.

The third-floor machine room where he stood, on a sea of metal shavings beneath a corrugated metal roof supported by colossal rafters, connected the stairs behind him with a second workshop through a hallway lined with abandoned desks, their drawers scattered along the concrete floor. Crumpled papers littered the floor, mixed with empty boxes and more rusted shavings, fittings, and hundreds of screws, nuts, and washers.

Christoff moved out first, rushing across the thirty feet separating him from the long hallway, which ran another fifty feet before connecting to the next cavernous room of this largely intact section of the complex. Even the windows had managed to survive the onslaught that destroyed nearby buildings, providing shelter from the powerful blizzards ravaging the city.

Controlling his breathing, he approached the right side of the hallway, pressing his back against the wall, rifle held firmly in front of him as he checked his flanks before nodding once.

His well-camouflaged team materialized from behind an array of grayish equipment and dark nooks, like shadows detaching themselves from their hideouts, racing toward their leader, who constantly swept his rifle in every direction, always assuming the enemy lurked around the next corner.

Johan reached him first, followed by the rest of his hand-picked warriors, their eyes gazing about on faces darkened by engine grease, blending them with their surroundings.

Christoff pointed at himself and then at Johan, before extending a thumb toward the opposite end of the hallway. He then paired the rest of his men and extended the fingers of his right hand three times, signaling to keep fifteen feet in between them to minimize casualties should the enemy spot them as they carried out a search-and-destroy sweep through this floor.

Once more becoming the lead man for his platoon, Christoff Halden followed instincts he had acquired years ago while hunting with his father in Texas. That was well before he decided to pursue the foolish dream of becoming a part of the greatest nation on Earth—only to be propelled into a nightmare from which he so desperately fought to escape.

55

Overpowered

Lazur Factory, Stalingrad Pocket
December 15, 1942

Sergeant Kostya Melkinov searched for a target, swinging his rifle back and forth, peering into the darkness projecting toward the hallway.

A bright flash followed by a loud report coming from his left told him one of his men had opened fired at something.

Narrowing his gaze, he realized an instant later that it had been the shadow of a man rushing across their field of view.

More gunfire followed as his men tried to hit the Nazi, their multiple muzzle flashes inducing a stroboscopic effect in the room. The missing rounds ripped chunks of concrete from the wall as the dark silhouette vanished behind a large machine.

One of his men suddenly fell back, his throat ripped open by a silent round. Then another Russian soldier snapped back, crashing on the stained floor in spasms before going limp.

"What in the devil is happening?" Kostya hissed through his clenched jaw as he continued to search his surroundings, seeing nothing. "Who is firing?"

Another shadow; this one dashing in the opposite direction, triggered more gunfire from his men. Rounds screeched with clouds of sparks as they struck the metal of nearby tractors, in the same instant as two of the Russians who had opened fire dropped dead, their faces bloody masses of cartilage and shattered bones.

"Hold your fire! Hold your fire!" Kostya screamed, understanding the enemy's tactics to draw them out using the Russians' own muzzle flashes as targets.

Two of his men failed to obey, opening fire on a third

shadow, giving out their positions to other Germans assigned to shoot at the Russians firing on the ingenious lure.

It took the sergeant another moment to realize that seven of his men had been killed in less than twenty seconds, and that did not include the four he had lost minutes before and the others he had posted as lookouts before that.

"Pull back!" he finally shouted, trying to cut his losses and escape, but the moment his men began to move out, the well-deployed—and well-hidden—German snipers picked them out one at a time in wickedly silent fashion. Skulls burst, faces disappeared in clouds of blood, bodies fell to the floor like sacks of coal, and there was nothing Kostya could do to fight back. Firing at an enemy he could not see only resulted in more Russian deaths.

Cursing the lack of enemy muzzle flashes as much as their silent shots, the Russian sergeant rolled away from his hideout, keeping his head low as the cry from one of his men mixed with the doleful howl of another, both shot in the chest a few feet from each other.

The smell of gunpowder assaulting his nostrils, the sergeant dove in between two stacks of scrap metal, his left shoulder burning as he rammed it against a pipe while trying to get to his wounded soldiers.

Crawling back toward them, Kostya reached the back of the rusting heap of discarded spare parts, his rifle clutched in his hands, his wild-eyed stare struggling to discern the enemy from the surrounding clutter.

The first shot struck his upper right thigh, reminiscent of the bullet wound he had endured on the same attack that had disfigured him.

He fell, losing his grip on the rifle, watching in horror as it skittered away.

Mustering strength, he made one attempt to reach for his weapon, but a pair of gray boots stepped in between, blocking his way.

Lifting his gaze, he stared at his enemy, at a darkened face and a pair of cold blue eyes that blinked once before the German leveled the bulky muzzle at him.

"I hope you burn in hell, Hitlerite!" Kostya screamed, before gathering his phlegm and spitting at the German's boots.

The German paused, resting his index finger on the trigger but not pressing it. "That's the thing, my friend," he said in heavily accented Russian right before he fired. "We are already in hell."

56

Orders Are Orders

Lazur Factory, Stalingrad Pocket
December 15, 1942

Zoya Krasilov fought back her tears as she stared in disbelief at the slaughter taking place at the other end of the cavernous warehouse. She had chosen to remain behind with Tasha Burojev while the rest of the team regrouped in an adjacent building.

"They killed them all," whispered Tasha, kneeling next to her atop a large machine. "Let's attack, Zoya. Let's do it now, when they least expect it."

Their current position provided them with a perfect vantage point to launch a surprise counterattack, but Zoya's orders had been very specific. She had to reach her assigned post and avoid engaging German troops unless strictly in self-defense.

"We can't," she replied, hating herself. Zoya had vowed to kill any German that ever crossed her path, and here she was, not only with a clear line of sight on a group of around a dozen Germans, but those Germans had just slain a brave Russian platoon.

"But—" Tasha started to protest.

Zoya held up an open palm. "Enough, Tasha. Our orders do not allow it."

"Then the hell with the orders," hissed the young woman, tears also welling in her eyes. "They killed our comrades. We can't let them get away with that."

"My dear, Tasha," Zoya said. "If we fail to reach our assigned post because we chose to engage these Germans, and somehow were also killed like Kostya's platoon, then *thousands* of Russians could be at risk. We have to be in position to silence the machine-gun emplacements when Chuikov's tanks and infantry start their attack on the hill."

Tasha lowered her gaze.

"Now come, my brave Tasha. The best way to avenge their deaths is to reach our posts at the Red October Factory."

57

Code of Honor

Fifty Miles North of Rostov
December 15, 1942

Erich pushed open the canopy and climbed out of his jet as Mathias and several pilots of his gruppe ran up to meet him.

"The plane without propellers!" screamed Mathias, jumping by the side of the Messerschmitt like a child on Christmas morning. "Look! It's the plane without propellers! The war is about to turn in our favor!"

Erich slowly shook his head as he stepped down and helped the other men push the Me 262 under the trees to the side of the runway before heading for the communications tent. He had two messages he needed to send, the first to General von Hoth, and the second to Göring in Augsburg.

He reached the tent and saw two young corporals reading the encoding manual. They looked in their midteens, probably straight out of Hitler Youth's ranks.

"Where are my encoder and my telegraph operators?" Erich said as both men snapped to attention.

"They were requested by the Sixth Army, sir. General Paulus needed them in the pocket. Reports are flowing back and forth between General Paulus and General von Hoth at such a rate that the general requested additional experienced personnel."

Erich stared at the two soldiers in disbelief. The Wermacht was now taking resources from the Luftwaffe without asking. The German war machine was rapidly breaking down.

"How much training have you two got with Enigma?"

"About a week, sir," responded the one sitting behind the coding machine.

"Well, get going. You have those messages next to the machine, but first I need you to transfer two messages right away." Erich sat down and wrote the two one-paragraph notes and handed them to one of the Enigma operators, who began typing one letter at a time.

"You are absolutely certain that you have the wheels and plugs set correctly for today?"

"Yes, Herr Major," responded the same kid behind Enigma. "I checked them three times."

"Good. Call me when it's done."

Erich turned and left the tent. He was still upset about the incident with Barkhorn. The Aryan major had shown Erich the type of behavior Erich had fought so hard to eliminate within his flight group. Over and over he had preached to his men that there is a code of honor in the skies. He made sure they understood that they must fight with courage, but in the best knightly tradition. Shoot until the enemy shows signs that it's going down. Never shoot at a parachuting flyer, and never attack an enemy who is forced to land.

But Barkhorn, along with thousands of other Aryan fanatics in the Luftwaffe and the Wermacht alike, did not believe in such rules. They did, however, feel it necessary to murder mercilessly an enemy they considered belonging to an inferior race. Those Aryans were not German soldiers, Erich decided; they were nothing better than common criminals who had been given a rank in the armed forces.

Erich was certain that if Germany lost the war, the Russians would not stop their drive at the border. The Russians would pay back in kind, and when they did, the German nation, if it survived, would never be the same again.

58

Vodka

Kalach Airfield, Twenty Miles West of Stalingrad Pocket
December 15, 1942

Jack taxied his airplane into a three-sided shelter, turned it around, idled the engine, and cut back the air-fuel mixture. The propeller stopped. He powered down the magnetos and the master switch, released his upper and lower safety harness, removed his parachute, pulled the canopy open, and climbed outside.

He walked over to Natalya's La-3. She was climbing down with her parachute still on her back.

"Your parachute," he said pointing to her back.

She nodded, released it, and threw it inside the cockpit. "What a terrible thing, Jack," she said, jumping on the frozen ground. He noticed the lines down her cheeks. She had been crying. "Andrei's brother and I were very close."

"The one missing in action?"

"Yes. Now Andrei . . ." Natalya lowered her gaze and slowly walked away.

That afternoon, Jack walked inside the briefing bunker and saw a lonely Krasilov behind a half-drunk bottle of vodka. Jack noticed the pad and pencil next to two crumpled sheets on the side of the table.

"Mind if I join you, Colonel?"

Krasilov pointed at a chair across the table. Jack sat in it while Krasilov slid the bottle over to his side.

Taking a sip, Jack let the liquor warm his mouth and throat before swallowing it. He took a second sip and eased back into the chair.

"I'm very sorry about Andrei, sir. I understand he was a friend."

Krasilov's bloodshot eyes stared directly at him. "He was a *good* friend, Captain. He also has a mother and three young sisters. They live in Moscow. Now I'm left with the burden of writing to them, but as you can see, the words will not come."

Jack lowered his gaze and took another sip. His chest felt warm. He slid the bottle back to Krasilov, who drank some more before setting it down.

"Andrei was a fine warrior, Captain Towers."

"Call me Jack, Colonel."

Krasilov grinned slightly. "I go by Aleksandr. Now, listen, Jackovich . . . about today. What you did . . ."

"You would have done the same for me."

"Probably not before today."

Jack shrugged.

"You fly well, Jackovich. The American Air Force has good pilots and good machines."

"Thanks."

"The . . . *Impatient Virgin* . . . Why?"

Jack smiled. "Named it after a local girl I met while going to flying school. She was pretty wild."

"Hmm," Krasilov retorted as he drank more vodka. "You remind me of Andrei. Might as well enjoy it while you're young. Before life hardens your heart or the Germans kill you."

Jack narrowed his eyes as Krasilov fixated his gaze on the inch of vodka left at the bottom of the bottle.

"The war will be over soon, Aleksandr. After that we shall all be able to get on with our lives."

Krasilov leveled his stare with Jack and breathed deeply.

"Maybe that's something you can do, Jackovich, since there is no war in your homeland, but here there won't be much left for us after the war."

"But surely you must have a family, Aleksandr. A wife maybe, kids?"

Jack saw a pained expression flashing across Krasilov's face. The Russian drank the last of the Vodka, set the bottle down, and began to speak slowly and moderately. Although the context of his words was appalling, his tone never changed. When he finished, he got up, reached inside a counter, and produced another bottle of vodka.

"I'm deeply sorry about your wife and daughters, Aleksandr. I had no idea that—"

"Zoya was a brave woman, you know," he said, sitting back down, his wrinkled eyes glaring at the bottle. "Warm, beautiful, and smart too. She was a doctor as well as an officer of the Red Army."

"Why are you saying *was,* Aleksandr? I thought you said she was taken prisoner. Perhaps one day—"

"It's been over a year, Jackovich. No human can survive the brutality of the Germans in those prison camps. Besides, that's assuming they took her there. The Germans captured me too, you know."

Jack slowly shook his head. "No, Colonel. I didn't know that."

Krasilov shrugged, opened the bottle, and drank more vodka. "Not everyone knows about what happened to me at the beginning of the war. Andrei knew. Now he is dead. I think he may have told Natalya and some of the other pilots," he said, before telling Jack how he had survived the mass murder at the Babi Yar forest north of Kiev.

"Jesus, Colonel. I had no idea."

"Do you have a cigarette, Jackovich?"

Still a bit stunned from the back-to-back revelations, Jack reached for his pack of American cigarettes and handed them to Krasilov along with a lighter. The Russian briefly inspected the colorful design of the package before pulling out a cigarette.

"Marlboro?" What does that mean?"

"I have no idea."

Krasilov lighted up and took a draw. He dropped his eyebrows, exhaled, and took another draw.

"Something wrong?" Jack asked.

Krasilov stared at the cigarette, took another long draw, and closed his eyes in satisfaction. "Now, *this* is a cigarette."

Jack contemplated the burly Russian. "By the way, Aleksandr, you've got yourself one hell of a pilot in Natalya. She is very good behind the stick."

Krasilov waved a hand in the air. "But she's a woman, yes? I need someone I can depend on as my partner up there, not some shrinking violet that might come apart during a critical situation."

"Well, I'll have to say that she is *exactly* the type of wingman I would like to have. Someone who would stick with me in all kind of weather. Today she did just that, Aleksandr. You should give her a chance." Jack got up. "I'll leave you to your privacy, my friend. Again, I'm truly sorry about Andrei and about your family."

Krasilov nodded.

Jack walked outside. The morning clouds had broken and the sun now warmed the airstrip. He filled his lungs. The air was cold, but he could breathe it without much trouble. The thermometer outside the bunker marked five below zero.

Pulling up the lapels of his jacket, Jack glanced at the fighters parked along the side of the runway behind the three-sided shelters. He stopped and smiled when spotting Natalya standing with a bucket under the engine of the La-3 she flew that morning. Jack walked in her direction. Her back was to him.

"You're going to be an ace one of these days, Natalya Makarova."

Startled, Natalya spun around, spilling the contents of the bucket by her feet.

"Jack! Look what you made me do! You scared me!"

Jack smiled. Natalya was indeed naturally pretty. Her dazzling hazel eyes inspected him. Jack thought he could look into her soul through them. His attraction for her went beyond anything he'd felt before. Jack wasn't sure if it was because she was so pretty, or if it was because she was so different from any other woman he'd ever known. Natalya was a woman of substance, and she also seemed to love flying as much as Jack did—a hard combination to find.

She lowered her gaze and picked up the bucket. "Here, now you'll have to help me."

"Help you do what?"

"Just hold the bucket right under . . . here."

Jack picked up the heavy cast-iron bucket and placed it exactly where Natalya told him, beneath the La-3's radiator drainage plug.

Natalya pulled the plug and let the steamy-hot water pour into the bucket.

"What are you doing?" he asked as the bucket filled up and she reinserted the plug.

"Have you ever helped a lady wash her hair, Jack?"

"Can't say that I have, but I'd love to learn."

Smiling, she tousled her hair and leaned forward. "See that other bucket next to the landing gear?"

"Yeah, what about it?"

"It's filled with snow. Bring it over and pour some hot water into it until it gets warm."

Smiling at her ingenuity, Jack complied. Inside the large bucket was a small pint-size pot. Jack used it to pour water on Natalya's head as she leaned over.

She pulled out a bar of soap and worked up a lather as Jack poured a little more water over her head. After a few moments, he poured some more to rinse it off.

Natalya stood up, pulled her hair back, and wrapped it with a towel. "Thanks, Jack."

He smiled. "Thank *you,* Natalya."

59

New Cribs

Bletchley Park, Buckinghamshire, England
December 15, 1942

Captain Peter Myers and his apprentice, Charles Rosset, examined the latest messages intercepted from what Myers had guessed was JG52 Gruppe 1, based on the Direction-Finder point of origin. Working under that assumption, the known cribs were the location, the unit's name, and the originator. The problem was finding the right order in which each of the three cribs was located in the ciphered message.

Myers took one of the messages and Rosset the other. Myers put the first crib against the message and made a second assumption: Major Erich Steinhoff would sign his name at the end just as General von Hoth did on his messages. He tried that and found matching letters—an impossibility using Enigma. The coding machine could never turn a letter into itself.

He moved the crib one space to the left. Same thing. Four letters matched. He moved it five more times without luck; the crib and the coded message still had letters in common.

"What did you do, you bloody Steinhoff, use a nickname?"

"We don't have to use his name, sir. There's something better."

Myers dropped his eyelids at his apprentice, who showed the excitement of having figured out another way of generating cribs.

"Yeah? What's that?"

"The telegraph operator made a grave error when sending these messages, sir."

Puzzled, Myers read it again. This time he saw it, smiled, and shook his head, not believing that he had missed something so obvious. "Splendid, Charlie! Bloody good eye! I guess I'm in need of a holiday."

Two-thirds of the way down the ciphered paragraph was a part of the message that normally should have gone near the beginning or the end, but the operator had thought to put it in an inconspicuous place, and that was clever of him. However, the operator—because he was tired, had gotten lazy, was new, or perhaps had a pile of messages to transmit—had failed to spell out the numeral fifty-two. Enigma was not capable of translating numbers, only letters of the alphabet. A fifty-two in the original message was a fifty-two in the ciphered version.

"But Enigma doesn't have any numerals, sir," said Rosset.

Myers shook his head. "That's right. I find it so hard to believe someone made a mistake like that, Charlie. The Enigma operator would have had to stop encoding, after the word *JG* or *Jadgeschawader,* have the telegrapher insert a 52, and then continue with his encoding. It would definitely make his encoding faster, but at what risk!"

Myers placed the Jagdgeschwader crib against the letters preceding the 52 in one of the messages and got no matches. He did it again on the second message and obtained the same results. They now had a solid crib to feed to the bombe.

As Rosset grabbed the phone, Myers got up and poured himself another cup of tea.

60

Losing Confidence

JG52 Gruppe 1, Fifty Miles North of Rostov
December 15, 1942

Pushing away the small metallic food tray in front of him, Erich sat back on his chair, grabbed the bottle of vodka, and swallowed a mouthful. Closing his eyes, he relaxed as warmth spread down his chest.

"Easy, Erich," Haufman said across the table inside Erich's tent, where the two officers had just consumed their single daily warm meal—a half pound of boiled horse meat, bones included.

Erich eyed his friend and frowned. Their equipment situation stunk as much as their food. Of the original sixteen Stukas that left the field, only ten made it back from their attacks. The rest fell victim to a squadron of Soviet fighters that had come out of nowhere and blasted Haufman's pilots as they pulled up from their dives.

"This is not looking good, Erich," continued Haufman, ignoring Erich's silence. "We lost six Stukas and . . . how many Gustavs?"

Erich exhaled. "Five." He drank more vodka.

"Damn! Eleven planes, and all we got to show for are nine lousy burning tanks."

"And the bad news is that it is not going to get any better . . . at least not in my opinion."

"Is that why they gave you the jet? To instill confidence?"

Erich nodded. "Isn't that ridiculous? Two planes are not going to make any difference in the final equation, Werner. We are losing this war, yet Göring wants us flying the jets around the clock to maximize exposure and give the troops a morale boost. I say stop feeding us this crap, give us more winter uniforms so that our men won't have to stuff newspaper in their summer uniforms to stay warm, and more fighting gear, and Berlin would get its morale booster."

Haufman finished chewing the stringy meat off a flat bone, and reached for the vodka.

"There are those like Barkhorn and Mathi," Erich continued, "who believe these new weapons are going to make a difference, but only proper planning and hard fighting wins a war."

"What about the rockets in Peenemünde that we all hear about?"

"I don't know, Werner. My guess is that if they really come up with a new type of bomb to put on those rockets, then they might make a difference, but just random V-1 attacks on London with a few hundred pounds of explosives has proven strategically useless so far."

Haufman nodded.

Erich ran a finger along the edges of the clear glass bottle. There was only one swallow left in it. He took it, and rolled the liquid inside his mouth before swallowing it.

61

Toy Plane

Kalach Airfield, Twenty Miles West of Stalingrad Pocket
December 15, 1942

Jack Towers' first reaction when Natalya Makarova showed him one of three PO-2 single-engine bombers ingeniously hidden behind the fighters' shelters was that of skepticism. For a moment he thought that the blond Soviet pilot was playing a trick on him, but the look on Natalya's face told him otherwise. The fragile-looking biplane was her "other" craft, the type she and the other women in the airfield flew after the sun went down.

Jack watched the ground crew push all three craft to the side of the runway as the wind whipped across the open field, blowing snow flurries against the wire and canvas fuselage of the two-seater bombers.

Natalya climbed on the side of her airplane and removed the protective covers that had been snapped tight across the open cockpits.

"You know you'll be dead the moment a Messerschmitt spots you, don't you?" There was a caring tone in his voice, a bit more than what Jack wanted to show.

Natalya didn't respond, but her eyes studied him. She smiled, donned her leather helmet on top of her white silk helmet, and slid the goggles down to her neck. Another woman joined her. Jack didn't know her name, but had seen her around the base. She nodded at him, looked at Natalya, and then giggled as she crawled into the navigator's seat.

"Good-bye, Jack. I'll see you in an hour?"

"I'll be right here," he responded and winked. "Be careful."

She smiled and got in her seat. A large man dressed in overalls approached the two-seater trainer and stepped up to the propeller.

"Contact!" he screamed.

"Contact!" Natalya responded.

The heavy Russian raised his hands, grabbed the propeller, and swung it down hard. In spite of the hard freezing temperatures, the engine started immediately after coughing some smoke. Natalya put on her goggles. Jack saw the ailerons, elevators, and rudder moving in all directions as she went through the preflight check.

She waved at Jack, who stepped aside and watched the bomber pop-popping down the concrete runway and into the night.

"They'll allow fifteen minutes between each takeoff," said Krasilov from behind, startling Jack.

"Damn, Aleksandr. You scared me."

Krasilov smiled. The colonel wore a heavy long coat and a furry hat. He kept his hands inside the coat's pockets.

"Why the time difference?" Jack asked.

"To avoid midair collisions."

"Huh?"

"See, Jackovich, to ensure stealthiness, the PO-2s maintain strict radio silence and have no navigation lights. They operate alone and at low altitude. One bomber per bombing site. The only time when there's risk of collision is around our base, so we time the missions such that they are close in length. They go by the clock and know exactly the time when they should land. That way their only problem upon returning is finding the runway. They don't have to worry about another returning bomber crossing their path."

Jack shook his head in disbelief. "And I thought *we* took a chance, Aleksandr. At least we can defend ourselves if spotted. They're sitting ducks."

"Wrong, Jackovich, they're Soviet women."

Jack stared at the vanishing plane. Those were indeed the most courageous group of women he had ever seen.

62

Night Witches

Sixty Miles North of Rostov
December 15, 1942

Natalya Makarova cut back the throttle and watched her airspeed decrease to eighty knots while maintaining a steady three hundred feet aboveground. She glanced over her shoulder and watched her navigator looking down into the cockpit using maps, charts, and a stopwatch to navigate.

"Heading three three zero," the young navigator, a nineteen-year-old by the name of Ina, said over the intercom.

Natalya turned the stick to the right until the compass read the precise heading.

The night was partly cloudy. Natalya gazed at the stars surrounding a bashful moon hidden behind a small cloud. She smiled and filled her lungs with the cold air, which was somewhat mixed with the engine's exhaust, but Natalya didn't mind. This was her craft, the one that had taken her through nearly one hundred sorties in the past eight months. Most of the original canvas had already been replaced at some point or another. There was always a rip here, a scratch there, and Natalya would repair it by cutting out the damaged section and stitching a new piece in place. After a while, the craft had begun to look like a jigsaw puzzle from the different shades of canvas she had employed over time. But it was all hers, and she trusted it more than any other plane. She was the only mechanic of the twelve-cylinder radial engine. Her logic was simple: her survival depended on striking quickly and silently, and leaving before the enemy got a chance to figure out what had happened. Engine trouble at any point of the mission meant disaster.

"Five minutes to target, Natalya."

Natalya cut back power even more. The light airplane decelerated to sixty knots, just a shred above stall speed. This part of the mission required her full concentration. Flying at three hundred feet at such slow speed didn't leave much room for error if the bomber stalled. By the time she'd recover they would have crashed against the pine trees below. For that reason, Natalya kept her right hand glued to the throttle control valve and her left on the stick. She decided to give herself a little more room and climbed to 350 feet. It wasn't much, but perhaps enough to make the difference between a crash and a close call.

Natalya saw the airfield ahead.

Their targets, all within the two-hundred-mile range of the PO-2s, were selected by the Red Air Force's high command, which in turn passed the orders to the 46th Guard's Regiment—Natalya's regiment of women pilots scattered

over ten different airfields across the southern section of
the Russo-German front.

There were a few lights on the airfield, but Natalya could
spot no planes on the ground.

"Are you certain of the location?" she asked Ina.

"This is the one," came the reply from the rear. "Get
ready for—"

"Wait, Ina. Don't drop them yet." Natalya decided to
make a low—a very low—pass over the center of the
airstrip to get a better view of their target. The Messerschmitts had to be down there somewhere. There was no
sense in dropping bombs over frozen ground.

"What are you . . . you're crazy, Natalya Makarova!"

Ignoring Ina's cries, Natalya lowered the nose to gain
some airspeed while cutting back power to idle to minimize engine noise. The biplane darted across the dark sky
and glided toward the airfield.

63

Light Noise

JG52 Gruppe 1, Fifty Miles North of Rostov
December 15, 1942

Erich thought he'd heard something but wasn't sure if it
was just the gasoline engine they used to generate electric-
ity for the communications gear.

He sat up in his cot, swallowing before trying to listen
again. After a moment he decided that the light engine
noise was not stationary. That could only mean one thing:
an airplane was flying near his field, and from the sound of
its engine, he guessed it was not German.

Jumping out of bed, he grabbed his sidearm and heavy
coat, taking the precaution of buttoning it all the way up
before venturing in thirty-below. Two of his men had

caught pneumonia from failing to do just that and had to be flown out. He put on a furry hat to protect his ears and threw a scarf around his neck.

Outside, clutching his pistol, he fast-walked to the middle of the runway, his eyes peering into the dark sky trying to find the plane generating the noise.

Erich stopped breathing when he spotted something black moving across the sky at a relatively slow speed. It blended so well with the surroundings that the only way for Erich to really follow it in the night was by listening to its engine and then guessing its general location.

"Alarm!" he screamed, lifting his gun at the passing bomber and firing several times. "Sound the alarm! Turn on the spotlights!"

"What in the hell is going on?" screamed Haufman as he joined Erich by the side of the runway clutching a machine gun.

"We're under attack by those damned night witches again!"

"Where . . . wait! I see it. There!"

As Haufman raised the gun toward the passing bomber, a single thought filled Erich's mind.

The Me 262!

64

Second Pass

Fifty Miles North of Rostov
December 15, 1942

Natalya saw the fighters' propellers protruding from under the heavy foliage at the edge of the long and narrow clearing. The airplanes were hidden under the trees to both sides of the runway. She hauled enough explosives for just one side, and chose the left.

As she reached the end of the runway, the entire compound came alive with lights . . . and spotlights! One of which instantly blinded her. Machine-gun fire soon followed.

Natalya made a tight right turn and because of her low altitude, she managed to get out of the range of the lights and disappeared behind the trees.

"Let's go home, Natalya," said Ina in a frightened voice.

Natalya frowned. Stealthiness was the PO-2's only edge over the fast and powerful enemy fighters and the lethal flak of antiaircraft guns. Without the ability to hit and run before anyone spotted them, the PO-2 was indeed a sitting duck. She was about to turn back to a southerly heading when images of Andrei's burning craft filled her mind.

What if there was one of those jets in this airfield? How many more lives would it claim before someone destroyed it? And what about the Gustavs she'd just spotted hidden by the tree line? How many Soviet planes would they claim? Besides, if she didn't drop her bombs today, she would have to come back tomorrow night.

Natalya turned but didn't stop when her compass read one eight zero—the heading that would had taken her away from the compound and back home. She continued the turn until her nose was aligned with the compound.

"You're crazy Natal—"

"Target in sight, bombardier!" Natalya screamed.

"Ye-yes! Target in sight confirmed."

"Arm bombs and wait for my command."

"Bombs armed."

Not suicidal by nature, Natalya decided to reduce her exposure to enemy fire by making a short and fast pass across the field at an angle instead of her standard bomb run down the field. That was a reasonable compromise, she decided, confident that they would get at least a few fighters on each side of the runway.

She turned toward a spot almost halfway down the field and climbed to five hundred feet. As the airfield approached, Natalya lowered her nose and pushed full power.

With the sound of creaking wood and flapping canvas mixing with the purring of the engine as it puffed two clouds of smoke, Natalya accelerated the biplane to 140 knots, twenty knots above its maximum specification.

The control stick trembled. Natalya could see the wings dangerously flapping as struts and wires snapped them back in place.

"Ready to release on my mark!" she screamed over the intercom as they approached the airfield's edge.

"Ready, Natalya!"

"Now, now, now!"

"Bombs off!"

The nose cleared the trees and Natalya was engulfed by lights again. Firing began roughly a second later, but quickly subsided the moment the PO-2's fragmentation bombs struck something, which went up in a cloud of smoke and fire that temporarily cut through the night.

Natalya assumed it had been an enemy fighter, since the secondary explosion was by the edge of the forest. The two bombs that landed on the frozen runway created no secondary explosions. A final bomb landed on the opposite side of the clearing. Another hit. A cloud of fire told Natalya she had gotten at least another German plane, perhaps two.

65

Light Noise

JG52 Gruppe 1, Fifty Miles North of Rostov
December 15, 1942

Lowering his pistol, Erich cursed the bomber as it vanished over the trees flanking the left edge of the runway, but he did not order any fighters after it. Past experience had taught him that the light Soviet biplanes, flown by women,

were very difficult to find at night. He'd rather take on the
fighting in daylight. Besides, his Me 262 had not been
damaged.

While Erich and a dozen of his pilots remained in the
middle of the runway in case another bomber decided to
make a pass over his field, several men ran toward the burning Gustavs and began to shovel snow onto them to quench
the flames.

"Night witches again, sir?" asked Mathias as he walked
behind him.

Erich removed the ammunition clip from his pistol and
inserted another one, his eyes shifting from the men putting out the fires to the dark sky. He doubted another
bomber would come tonight. The Russian witches attacked
alone.

"Yes, Mathi. It was them again."

"Are they after the plane without propellers?"

"Doubt it," Erich said. "They're just doing the same thing
they've been doing for months: terrorizing us at night."

Although Erich was angry at the Soviets using such tactics, he couldn't help but feel a certain degree of respect for
those female pilots. Using World War I biplanes in the
middle of the night at treetop level? It was just another sign
that the Soviet fighting spirit was far from dead. If anything, it appeared to be on the rise every day while slowly
eroding Germany's ability to wage war.

66

Whistling Wind

Sixty Miles North of Rostov
December 15, 1942

Natalya left the smoking airfield behind and turned toward their base. "Heading one eight zero, Ina?" she asked.

There was no response from the backseat.

"Ina? Can you hear me?"

No response.

"Are you all right back there?"

The only sounds were those of the engine and the whistling wind.

Natalya climbed to five hundred feet and trimmed the plane such that she could let go of the control stick. The PO-2 remained on the same heading and speed while Natalya released her safety belt and turned around. She took one look at Ina, whose body leaned forward, supported only by the restraining harness.

With her back to the control stick and her knees on her seat, Natalya reached for her. The slipstream battered her back. Natalya's right hand moved toward Ina's head. She saw the large hole in Ina's helmet. Natalya removed her glove and poked a finger through the torn leather. She felt sick the moment her finger came in contact with a warm soggy mass that slithered away at her touch. Ina's brains were exposed and sliding out of her skull.

Natalya jerked back in terror, lost her balance, and fell on the control stick.

The nose dropped. Natalya quickly turned around and pulled up the nose as the treetops swatted the landing gear. She applied full power and climbed back up to five hundred feet.

She strapped herself and did not look back again.

67

Shadow vs. Shadow

Red October Factory, Stalingrad Pocket
December 15, 1942

Major Christoff Halden knew the humid and frigid night air would chill him in spite of his thick coat when he reached the roof of the building, but he felt it paramount to check the surrounding streets for any signs of Russian patrols before allowing his team to spend the night here.

The building was colossal, extending roughly four city blocks. Its steel and brick structure, a classic art deco architecture, had remained pretty much intact—aside from having most of its windows broken. He guessed that it would likely take the concentrated effort of an entire wing of the Luftwaffe to bring down its sheer mass.

He stepped away from the roof-access stairs and onto the vast flat surface littered with dozens of equipment sheds, ventilation fans, abandoned antiaircraft batteries, hundreds of feet of pipes, several smokestacks, and mounds of debris from the collapsed building next door, which amazingly enough had not brought down this section of the structure.

The muffled thump of Russian and German artillery echoed in the distance a few seconds after the muzzle flashes splashed the snow-covered steppe beyond the city limits with stroboscopic light. From this fourth-story vantage point, Christoff could not only survey most of the buildings in this former tractor factory complex, but could see the glowing lights of the Russians' 62nd Army across the frozen Volga, strategically out of the range of German artillery units.

Small fires burned all around the factory complex from recent strafing runs, illuminating the rubble-littered streets.

Large arrays of pipes and ducts, some at ground level and others elevated, snaked their way in between buildings. Heaps of bricks and steel beams nearly buried the remnants of three panzers and two Russian tanks, ironically still facing each other muzzle to muzzle. Smoke coiled skyward from the open hatch on one of the panzers, amid the charred figure of a crew member with half his body out of the hatch, arms stretched forward in a silent plea for help.

Shivering from the extreme cold, Christoff considered abandoning the rooftop search and just heading back down where it was relatively warmer. He wondered if the tank crews had been able to fire any rounds before a section of the building behind them collapsed, probably as a result of a misplaced artillery shell. The glowing flames below, however, provided another explanation for the partially destroyed structure: the unmistakable landing gear of a Stuka projected from beneath the smoldering debris, along with a section of the tail.

It must have crashed while trying to provide air support to the panzers, he decided shifting his weight from one leg to the other to keep warm while staring at the bodies strewn around the tanks. There were dozens of them, plus the typical assortment of loose limbs, heads, and torsos— Germans and Russian alike.

According to his intelligence sources, a fierce battle had been fought below four days ago, resulting in German control of this section of the factory, only to lose it a day later to a Russian counteroffensive. Then a German attack drove the Russians back to the other end of the factory yesterday, leaving this section once more in German hands.

For now.

Staring at the madness below, Christoff questioned the tactical value of this nightmarish back-and-forth, of this circle of death, of the nonstop fighting for the same ravaged piece of land, advancing today and retreating tomorrow, only to repeat the cycle again and again while consuming entire divisions of men, while eroding the Sixth Army's ability to defend itself against the increasing Russian threat.

Stalingrad must hold at all cost.

The führer's words came to him as he inspected the vacated buildings illuminated by pulsating flames, their walls peppered with machine-gun fire, stained with powder burns.

Christoff frowned, recalling the speeches, the promises, the assurances that Russia would fall, that the Bolsheviks would become servants of the Aryan race, that the German empire would stretch into the far reaches of Asia, into the oil-rich regions of the Caucasus, meeting up with their Japanese allies.

The Slavs lack the will to fight! Their weapons are obsolete! We shall be in Moscow by the fall of 1941!

Christoff frowned.

Chest-thumping monkey.

He wasn't sure what he detested most, Adolf Hitler or this forsaken city—if it could still be called a city. The jagged outline of the buildings still standing—many mere facades lined with rubble—was a burning testament of the unbending will of the Russian people to defy the Nazi invasion. The Soviets resisted at all cost, even if it meant destroying every city that the Germans occupied. Even if it meant sending hordes of young soldiers to their deaths as long as they took some Germans along with them. Even if it meant enduring a kind of human suffering that even the most veteran and rugged German soldier found intolerable.

Christoff had seen the Russian will to fight on the first day of the invasion, and that will had only grown stronger with time, with every square inch of soil that they lost to the Wermacht, to the Luftwaffe.

The distant artillery continued to pound unseen enemy lines, their reports reverberating across the complex like a band of drum players in slow motion, beating their stretched skins methodically, round after round, lighting the night before the noise bounced off the unstable buildings.

Satisfied that the street below was clear on this side of the building—and also that he had better start moving or risk freezing to death—Christoff headed for the east side.

He walked near the waist-high wall bordering the edge, slowly, carefully, close enough to survey the scenery below, yet far away enough to avoid becoming the target of a Russian sniper on this clear night.

Christoff saw a shadow shifting in the corner of his right eye.

Instincts overcame surprise, forcing him to drop behind a meter-wide ventilation duct connected to a huge fan, shiny icicles hanging from its dark blades.

He glanced up at the glowing moon, looking for a passing cloud that may have cast the shadow, but night over Stalingrad lacked clouds.

Gripping his rifle, the adrenaline searing his veins momentarily making him forget the appalling cold, he rolled away from the fan but remained behind the duct, which ran for another three meters before curving up ninety degrees. The shadow had been roughly twenty meters away, near a cluster of sheds surrounded by a maze of pipes and ventilation ducts.

But if the Russian bastard saw me, why didn't he fire? Why am I still alive?

Perhaps he didn't see Christoff. Or maybe he did and was trying to position himself for a better shot. Or it could be that the Russian didn't want to give out his position for just one German and was waiting for Christoff to rejoin his group and then take them all out at once. Or maybe he was facing one of those demented Russians he had read about who wandered the city alone at night looking for isolated opportunities to hunt down Germans, frequently killing them silently with bayonet strikes or knife blows. More often than not, a German patrol would find these poor bastards missing their eyes, or their ears, or even their genitals, which the Russians apparently enjoyed stuffing into their victims' mouths following the field emasculation.

Or, he thought, *it could have been just my imagination, or the moonlight playing tricks on my mind.*

Silently cursing the growing number of possibilities, each calling for a separate course of action, Christoff assumed for now that the Russian had seen him and was waiting for Christoff to make his move first, which, of course, Christoff could alter by *not* making a move until the Russian did, turning this into a fatal waiting game.

Until one of us dies of exposure, he thought, his face becoming numb, as well as his feet and hands.

Time.

Christoff waited, listening while the bone-chilling temperature began to take its toll, inducing a slight tremble in his hands. Soon hypothermia would set in, making it difficult to move, until he was totally paralyzed, incapable of defending himself.

Perhaps the Russian has better clothing, though he could not imagine that. Christoff and the rest of his team wore the finest that Germany had to offer in winter gear, yet nothing seemed to help for a prolonged period of time when the air temperature dropped below forty degrees Celsius.

Making his decision, opting to risk a bullet in the head by the well-hidden Russian rather than slowly succumbing to the winter, he rolled away from his hideout, his nearly frozen limbs protesting the effort. But he had to move them in spite of the pain, had to get the blood flowing again. His body had the energy to keep warm as long as he remained in constant motion.

Rising to a deep crouch, he peeked toward the spot where he had seen the shadow, realizing once more that the enemy had very likely already moved to a new position, just as Christoff had.

Based on the direction that he had seen the shadow moving, Christoff guessed that the Russian was headed for the same access staircase that he had taken to reach the roof— the only one for the entire structure, at least that he knew of based on an earlier search of the area.

Surveying his surroundings, he made his move by rushing in the opposite direction from the roof access staircase, keeping a steady speed down the narrow space between the waist-high wall bordering the edge of the building and another ventilation duct. His goal lay just ahead: an equipment shed surrounded by two rusting antiaircraft artillery units draped in bright icicles, marking the position on the rooftop directly on the other side of the access staircase.

The back of his neck tensing as he ran partially exposed, Christoff cut right at the shed, ducking under a thick steel pipe and pausing a moment, looking now in the direction of the access staircase in the hope of spotting the back of the Russian as he headed for the only way to reach the warmer floors below.

But he saw nothing except several piles of spent casings from the antiaircraft emplacements, more pipes, a collapsed shed, and a Russian boot, from which a femur stuck out along with frozen chunks of flesh and scraps of white cloth. The leg had been severed cleanly just below the waist. A second leg projected beyond the first, also wearing a boot plus a portion of the hip and groin, surrounded by frozen viscera.

Christoff stared at macabre sight and then tensed when spotting a figure hidden in between two heaps of casings just past the legs.

His instincts made him roll across from it while leveling his silent weapon at the frozen remains of a Russian soldier who had been cut in half most probably by the cannons of a German Stuka, the winter capturing his contorted face as he had screamed in agony.

He exhaled while shaking his head, before getting back to his feet and continuing his sweep toward the access staircase, finding nothing but more abandoned hardware, most of it layered with ice.

Wondering if the moonlight had played a trick on him, Christoff doubled back and resumed his search of the rooftop, his limbs slowly warming up as he rushed past the dead Russian, as he once more glanced at those terrified eyes, like a wax statue, the pale skin glistening from the ice filming it.

Reaching the edge of the roof, he inspected the street below, just as he had done on the other side, slowly, with caution, looking for signs of the enemy, convincing himself of their absence before checking the third side.

Rumbling artillery units continued to hammer each other's front lines, the intermittent flashes providing him with opportunities to peek into trenches and crevices amid the rubble covering the wide street.

Nothing.

He could see absolutely nothing in this—

He sensed something behind him and dropped to a deep crouch while pivoting on his left leg and bringing his rifle around, aiming it at another ventilation shaft.

Damn. You need to relax, he told himself.

Perhaps the abysmal cold and the distant grumble of artillery shells, plus the incessant flashes, were making him too paranoid on this frosty night.

Inhaling the bitter air, which burned his lungs, Christoff turned around and resumed his search.

68

Smooth Operator

Red October Factory, Stalingrad Pocket
December 15, 1942

Her body protesting the cold seeping through the insulating layers of her thick coat, Major Zoya Irina Krasilov remained motionless behind an exposed steel beam, merging her slim figure with the shadow cast by the wide rafter, waiting until the German had turned around and continued searching the street below from the edge of the roof.

Silently, her gloved hands clutching her rifle, she tiptoed away from her hideout and followed him once more, moving only when he did, pausing when he slowed down to check his surroundings, mimicking his movements—all the while always keeping an immediate place to hide within reach should he turn around. Zoya focused on the soldier's torso, the first place that would shift if he were to check his rear, giving her a second or two before the eyes would follow.

The German was good, Zoya thought, nearly spotting her twice; once soon after he had reached the roof, and again just now.

But Aris Broz had honed Zoya's skills to near perfection after her rescue in Poland. The Yugoslav-born partisan had turned the Russian officer into a guerrilla. He had shown her how to stalk her enemy stealthily, without him realizing he was being hunted. Aris Broz had taught her the destabilizing power of hit-and-run missions against a stronger enemy. He had taken Zoya under his wing during countless sabotage missions against the Germans. And he had made Zoya realize that the most powerful of enemies could be brought down to its knees by striking at its weaknesses, by constantly nibbling at its Achilles' tendon.

Zoya had spotted the German soldier and his group of silent assassins two hours ago, when they had arrived at the factory and settled down near the center of the first floor, one below her well-deployed—and well-hidden—forces. Zoya had ordered them to maintain total silence until she gave them the signal to open fire on the machine-gun emplacements spread along the east end of Mamayev Hill. Under different circumstances, the Germans getting ready to sleep downstairs would have been already dead, but killing them carried the risk of someone firing a shot, telegraphing her position to other German patrols in the area, compromising her mission.

Zoya regretted having to hold back, to keep from doing what had become so natural for so long, especially since this group was the one that had slaughtered Sergeant Kostya Melkinov and his team back at the Lazur Factory. But after she had counted thirty-two German machine-gun emplacements and half as many mortar teams lining this side of Mamayev Hill, she could not justify taking such risk. In addition, her sharpshooters were already positioned such that they had a clean line of sight on the flanks and rear of those German forces. She had to keep her team in place so they had the best chance of preventing heavy losses to the Russian infantry.

Besides, the Germans on the first floor were apparently just staying the night before resuming their patrol.

On the other hand, stealing the enemy's silenced rifles presented her with a great advantage when firing on those machine-gun emplacements. The spotters on Mamayev Hill would not be able to see the muzzle flashes from Zoya's team if she had access to those German rifles. She remembered vividly how the Germans had overran Kostya's positions the day before. Their lack of sound or muzzle flashes made it impossible for the Russians to launch an effective counterattack.

Perhaps when they are sleeping, she thought, wondering if she was just looking for an excuse to attack them. Would the silent rifles really make such a difference in her attack when there would be far louder racket coming from Chuikov's tanks and the Germans' own machine-gun emplacements?

Stick to your mission, she told herself while watching her quarry complete his round and head back downstairs via the main access staircase. According to her orders, the initial attack from Chuikov would start in the morning by way of air strikes, followed either later tomorrow or the day after by some elements of the armored divisions and infantry of the 62nd Army. She had to stick to her plan and wait for the right moment to attack. Anything else was in direct violation of her orders.

Zoya waited until he vanished from sight, pausing for a moment to make sure he would not be coming back, before returning to her observation post on the south end of the roof—the side where German patrols coming from the downtown area were likely to appear.

Settling into a recess in the wall overlooking the rubble below, Zoya grinned. The late Kostya had been right. The thick concrete flanking her plus the overhead ledge cloaked her presence and also provided her with shelter from the wind and the harsh cold. However, the primary reason she could withstand the extreme temperature without moving for extended periods of time was the thick coat, hood, gloves, and boots she wore—plus the dark-wool sniper cape she threw over her to further conceal her presence and trap her body heat.

Inspecting the scenery below through the narrow slit on her cape, Zoya resumed her watchful post, her eyes inspecting both the street below and the starry skies.

Chuikov's bombers will start pounding this area in the morning to clear the way for the ground troops. Although she had deployed her team exactly as described in her orders, there was still the chance that one or more of the bombers could drift off course by a kilometer—or even less, since the foot of Mamayev Hill was less than five hundred meters away—and inadvertently drop bombs on this building. It had happened many times before, resulting in the death of Russians as well as Germans.

Zoya tightened the cape around her while silently praying that the Germans would move on by first light. Their presence here further complicated her team's already delicate situation.

69

Casualties

Kalach Airfield, Twenty Miles West of Stalingrad Pocket
December 15, 1942

Jack anxiously waited for Natalya's return. It was past midnight and the other two bombers had already landed and taxied away. Natalya's was supposed to have been the first to arrive.

Apprehension drying his throat, he continued to scan the skies expectantly, hoping, praying.

Then he heard it, faintly at first, like a whisper beyond

the horizon, growing in intensity until he spotted the PO-5 making a final turn to get its nose lined up with the end of the runway.

Jack immediately noticed something wrong. The other bombers had made flawless approaches and short landings. Natalya's craft started to drift left as she neared the runway. She overadjusted and glided above to the opposite side of the clearing, perilously close to the trees.

He let go of the breath he had been holding the moment she finally got the biplane over the wide runway after gobbling up five hundred yards.

The plane floated five feet over the concrete surface and abruptly plummeted, bouncing twice before finally landing. She taxied behind the shelters.

Jack ran to its side and saw Natalya pounding the instrument panel. Puzzled, he climbed up the lower wing and approached her cockpit.

She was in tears and murmuring incoherently.

"Calm down. What's wrong? Are you all right?"

She pointed behind her. Jack saw the bullet hole on the navigator's helmet and, understanding, released Natalya from her seat and helped her down.

Colonel Krasilov came running from the briefing bunker.

"What happened? Where were you?"

Jack could smell the vodka on his breath.

"The navigator's dead, Aleksandr," responded Jack before Natalya had a chance to say anything. Krasilov paced around the plane, checking for damage, while Jack took Natalya to the briefing bunker, where he removed her leather and silk helmets, and sat her down next to the burning stove.

"It was my fault . . . we should have turned around and . . ."

"Shhh . . . be quiet, Natalya. Control your emotions before the others get here," Jack said as he poured her a glass of vodka and handed it to her. To his surprise, Natalya downed it in one gulp.

The alcohol had the desired effect. Natalya breathed in

and out deeply and was much more calmed by the time Krasilov stormed inside.

"What happened out there? And why were you in shock when you arrived?"

"Cut her some slack, Aleksandr," Jack said. "She was half frozen by the time she landed. Look at her. She's still thawing. I'd like to see how you would weather out there in one of those planes without a cockpit in forty below. You'll probably be stiffer than her."

"The Germans spotted us, Comrade Colonel," said Natalya in the cold and controlled voice that she used to relate the rest of the incident. She spoke for only a few minutes. When she'd finished, Krasilov nodded and got up.

"You have done well, Natalya. You achieved your objective and brought your plane back in one piece. Remember that this is war. Casualties are always expected."

"Yes, sir."

"Now get some sleep. We start early tomorrow. Jack, until you leave, you will fly with her. I need all the pilots I can get."

Krasilov turned and left the bunker.

Jack leaned back and studied her pale face in the flickering light from the stove. Her eyes were once more on him.

"Thank you, Jack. I wasn't myself when I landed. I promise you Ina's death won't affect my flying."

Jack smiled. "It will, Natalya, but hopefully in the right way. What are we anyway, if not the product of our experiences? I think you'll do just fine."

She stared at him. "Is every man in America like you?"

Jack looked away. "You mean compassionate to the woman I care for?"

She dropped her gaze. "Please don't do this, Jack. I don't know if I could handle another . . ." She got up and walked outside.

"Natalya, wait . . . I . . ."

She ran away, hugging herself while leaving fine footprints in the snow.

Jack watched her in silence.

70

Back-Breaking Defeat

Bletchley Park, Buckinghamshire, England
December 16, 1942

Captain Peter Myers was confused. He rubbed his eyes and drank from a cup of tea. The message from Major Steinhoff acknowledged a recent request from General von Hoth to provide air support to a new panzer advance thirty kilometers south of the Mishova River in exactly five hours, but for some reason the message from Hoth to Steinhoff was never intercepted. Myers had read reports of bad weather in the Aegean Sea. Perhaps it was that, or perhaps the Germans had switched frequencies on him again. It was hard to tell.

He glanced at Rosset, who was peacefully snoring away on the small cot on the side of the room. Myers could use some sleep himself, but before he could do that, he had to pass this information to the USAF adviser in Hut Three.

Time was running out for the Germans captured in the pocket. The only way to defeat them was to keep the lifeline severed. General von Hoth's panzers had to be stopped at all cost. Doing so would cause Stalingrad to fall, breaking the Germans' back on the eastern front.

71

Partisans

Firmly clutching a weathered machine gun he had taken from a dead German soldier weeks ago, Aris Broz moved swiftly and quietly in a dry ravine that bordered the road where he was certain German panzers would soon be traveling.

His sheepskin-covered boots sank deep in the snowbank as he struggled to keep his balance and move forward for another three meters before stopping to listen. His trained ears searched for noises other than the howl of the wind sweeping through the trees, yet they detected nothing.

He continued.

Trained in the classic hit-and-run partisan tactics by his father, who was posthumously named a hero of the Soviet Union for taking out an entire squadron of Germans before turning the gun on himself to avoid being captured alive, and by his uncle, the famous Yugoslav Josip Broz, known by his comrades in arms as Tito, the thirty-year-old Aris considered himself a true partisan.

He was not Russian by birth. He was Yugoslav, although no one could tell by his accent—a useful asset during recruiting trips. And of course, he was a Broz. Tito himself had sent Aris to Poland, Ukraine, and Russia with orders to recruit fresh troops among the surviving population and train them in the art of guerrilla warfare to fight the Germans in the region.

Most of the recruits were peasants, people who had lost everything to the Germans, including loved ones. They had nothing to lose and an uncompromising will to fight to the death. Aris had seen fifteen- and sixteen-year-old girls turned into women overnight after Germans had raped them. They had subsequently joined Aris' partisan force with a desire to learn to fight back that even Aris himself found extreme. Those were his soldiers, his guerrillas, his partisans. Missions ranged from minor ambushes of German motorcyclists carrying messages to and from the front, to the destruction of bridges, roads, railroads, and anything else that disrupted the flow of supplies to the German forces.

To accomplish these tasks Aris would spread his warriors in small groups of six or seven, following a simple logic: if the mission backfired, the loss of volunteers and equipment could be easily replaced in a week's time. It also allowed him to strike multiple targets in synchronized fashion to give the enemy the impression of being attacked by a much larger force.

Sometimes a mission called for a large number of partisans, as in the case of breaking into a concentration camp to rescue prisoners and perhaps find a few recruits. In such large-scale attacks, Aris would be careful enough to divide the large group into small subgroups, or packs, each with its own independent escape route.

For Aris and his guerrillas stealth and surprise meant survival. Capture meant torture, mutilation, and hanging. That was the grim fate of detained partisans. In addition to the risk of his soldiers being arrested, the Germans had recently added another dimension to the partisan war. They had set a strict set of guidelines that defined how many innocent peasants—women and children included—were to be executed on the spot for a particular type of partisan crime. The loss of one German soldier usually meant the hanging of a dozen civilians picked at random off the streets of cities or villages. The directive, created to force the partisans to slow down or even stop their attacks, had had the opposite effect in the months since its implementation. More and more peasants had approached Aris with the desire to become partisans.

Yes, the Germans would butcher captured guerrillas, but they also feared the partisans. Aris had seen many

German soldiers putting pistols to their heads when surrounded by his fighters.

His partisans were many in number, but none of them accompanied Aris on this chilly and humid morning as he continued uphill for another hundred meters before checking for enemy tanks once more. This time he heard them coming.

A grin on his bearded face, the Yugoslav guerrilla leader rested his machine gun by a tree and removed a sack hanging from his back. He carried a handful of explosives; not enough to destroy a tank, but that wasn't his mission today.

Aris had chosen a task far more dangerous than that and had opted to do it alone. The risk was too high, and besides, he moved better alone. He knew the forest—every square inch of it. He knew where to find the hideouts, sources of food, shelter, and weapons caches.

Aris always kept weapons hidden everywhere, and all his soldiers knew of their exact locations—a contingency that had saved many lives in the past.

Cautiously walking up the side of the ravine, he reached the edge of the frozen road, his heavy gloves making his work cumbersome, but he had no choice. At forty below, his fingers would have crystallized and fallen off after a few minutes of exposure.

First, he strapped a grenade to the trunk of a large tree that leaned toward the road. He attached a thin wire to the safety pin and ran it across the narrow road to the other side, where he secured it around another tree. He walked back across the road and slid an explosive pack between the grenade and the tree. He lifted his head and looked down the road. The tanks were getting closer. Any moment now the lead panzer would clear the turn in the road.

Quickly, Aris removed two bottles filled with gasoline. He poured half of the contents of the first on the booby-trapped tree, then ran a river of gas toward the middle of the road, where he emptied the second bottle.

Aris quickly stepped around the large puddle of gas and ran to the side. He slid down to the ravine and sprinted away from the trap until he estimated he'd put a few hundred yards in between them. Then he stopped, climbed up to the side of the road, and waited.

He didn't have to wait long.

Bellowing clouds of blue smoke from its engine exhausts, the first panzer swept down the road closely followed by several soldiers on foot while others clung to the sides of the armored turret. The inky haze swirled over the soldiers' heads and soon joined the smoke from two other panzers along with several open trucks carrying loads of soldiers. Aris could see the rows of steel-helmeted heads behind the truck.

He held his breath the moment the tank got near the wire.

The bright explosion flashed in the morning air, igniting the surrounding woods. The tree plummeted over the lead tank, rolled in front of it, and caught on fire. The river of gas turned into a river of fire that ended under the tank. In seconds, the entire underside was in flames, along with the burning tree blocking the road and the flanking forest.

The driver and the gunner pushed open the hatch and quickly crawled outside. Two of the soldiers hanging onto the sides caught fire. Aris could hear their guttural screams drifting across the frozen woodland while other soldiers threw snow over them.

Aris smiled broadly and slid back down to the bottom of the ravine. His father and his uncle would have been proud of him.

As he left the screaming Germans behind, Aris heard something overhead, like a whir, but the thick forest prevented him from getting a visual. The sound definitely didn't belong to any plane he had ever seen.

72

Air Support

Fifty Miles South of Stalingrad Pocket
December 16, 1942

At five thousand feet, Erich zoomed over the snow-covered countryside and noticed the explosion below. He inverted the Me 262 and dove toward the source of the flash, frowning when realizing what was taking place. Someone had blocked the road with a burning log. A panzer burned next to it. It would take some time before the caravan could move it out of the way. He spoke into the microphone attached to his headset.

"This is Major Steinhoff, JG52, Gruppe 1. Stand back from the burning tank! Repeat, stand back!"

He made a low pass over the road while the caravan began to pull back. Most soldiers pointed in his direction, waving their arms in the air and shouting.

Erich smiled.

He reached the end of the panzer line, made a tight one-eighty turn, and came back around. This time he pulled back throttles and lowered ten degrees of flaps. Airspeed decreased to 250 knots. Erich lined up the wrecked tank in his sights and fired. The four cowl-mounted 30mm machine guns began vomiting rounds at the rate of two per second each. The massive projectiles carried enough energy to puree the side of the tank, which went up in a bright ball of flames, splitting the log in half and shoving it to the side of the road.

Erich inspected his work, raised flaps, and pushed full throttle. Airspeed quickly increased above five hundred knots as he made a propaganda victory pass over the area, rocking his wings.

Satisfied, Erich pulled up and headed back toward the

advancing Soviet lines. He reached twenty thousand feet and scanned the skies for his flight of Gustavs and Haufman's Stukas, spotting them in the distance, roughly three miles north of his position. He also noticed other planes a thousand feet above the German formations. Erich inverted and dove. This time he had a full load of fuel.

73

Sighting

Fifty Miles South of Stalingrad Pocket
December 16, 1942

Aris' smiled washed away the moment the strange German plane cleared the way for the panzer column. He was furious and surprised. He had never seen a plane like that. Not only did it lack propellers, but it had the fire power to slice a panzer in half.

It didn't matter. For Aris, a plane was a plane, and it was coming back down again. Aris pulled up his machine gun and aimed it at the incoming plane.

It rushed past his field of view at such speed that Aris didn't have time to let go a single shot.

What kind of fighter was that? Did the Germans finally come up with some of the wonder weapons that their propaganda officials kept advertising? Aris was not a pilot, but he could guess the type of damage a craft like that could have on the Red Air Force.

He slid back down the ravine and raced toward his camp. The word would be sent out. If the German propellerless craft were hidden somewhere in the region, Aris had no doubt his partisans would find them.

And destroy them.

74

Dogfights

"Stay with me, Natalya!" screamed Captain Jack Towers as he set his Aircobra in a vertical dive. The Me 109G Gustavs flew in formation several hundred feet below, creating a shield around the Stukas.

Information on the German attack had come sooner this time around, giving Krasilov's free hunters plenty of time to prepare. There were a total of five pairs in the air from Krasilov's fighter wing alone, including Jack and Natalya.

The Gustavs scrambled while the Stukas remained in formation. Jack picked a Gustav and closed in. The Aircobra trembled as he pushed it beyond four hundred knots. The wail of the engine ran in his ears and the soul-numbing vibrations made it harder for him to get the right angle.

The German went into a vertical climb. Jack swung the stick back, pointing the nose toward the tail of the vertical Messerschmitt.

The Gs blasted on his shoulders. His vision reddened and his palms moistened, but he remained on the Gustav's tail.

At five thousand feet the Messerschmitt went for a dive. Jack almost pulled back throttle to avoid ramming it, but decided against it.

Reduce throttle now and you'll never catch him, Jack, he told himself as he floated his plane right up to the Gustav's tail and opened fire with the 50-caliber guns and the 37mm cannon.

The tail blew up in pieces and went into a flat spin.

Jack broke right, Natalya still glued to his side.

He spotted another Me 109G to his left and swung the control stick in that direction. The wickedly tight turn pressed him against the seat with such might that Jack could barely keep his hand on the throttle control valve.

The Gustav's tail was a few hundred feet straight ahead.

"All yours, Natalya!"

"Wh-what?"

"Go, go! It's your kill!" Jack pulled back the throttle just a dash to let her take the lead.

The Gustav went for a dive. Natalya waved as she sprung past him, inverted her plane, and dove straight down on the German. Jack had a hard time following the maneuver, but he remained on her tail.

The Gustav went for a turn and climb. Natalya remained locked on its tail but was not firing yet. She got closer, apparently wishing to take the Messerschmitt in one burst.

She did, and smoke and fire abruptly engulfed the Gustav's nose.

Natalya broke left and so did Jack as she searched for another target and found it: a Gustav on Krasilov's tail.

"Break left, Colonel! Left!" Jack heard Natalya scream.

Krasilov and his wingman turned in opposite directions but the Gustav stayed with the Russian colonel, who turned, dove, and executed a perfect loop-the-loop.

Natalya inched her way toward the Gustav until she was less than fifty feet away. As she opened fire, Jack spotted something in the corner of his right eye. It came and went in a flash and for a instant Jack also heard a thundering machine gun.

When he looked down at Natalya's Aircobra, he noticed that smoke was coming out of the rear of her craft. He shifted his gaze to the sky and saw the German jet again.

Bastard!

"Get out of there, Natalya!" he screamed as the fire spread down the Aircobra's fuselage. "Jesus! Get out of there! Jump, dammit. Jump!"

"Damn!" screamed Krasilov. "It's that black-clove Hitlerite jet again!"

They were flying at three thousand feet. Natalya inverted her plane and lowered the nose. Jack held his breath and saw her drop as the jet came back around, this time in Jack's direction.

As her bright-red parachute opened, Jack went for a vertical climb to seven thousand feet. The German zoomed past him. Sensing that he might also be forced to jump out of his plane, Jack released his restraining harness and turned his plane in its direction, but by the time he had done that, the jet had already completed a two-seventy turn and was approaching from his right. Jack veered the Aircobra to the right until he saw the jet head-on.

Erich couldn't believe the audacity of the Soviet pilot. In spite of the massive show of power that he had just displayed, the Soviet plane still had the boldness to face him and his four 30mm cannons head-on. Erich opened fire, and so did the Soviet.

Jack's craft shook violently. He ducked under the windshield and continued to press the trigger of the cannon and machine guns. The glass windshield shattered, showering him. The firing lasted but a handful of seconds before Jack saw the grayish underside of the German jet dart over him. He sat up and put on his goggles. The windblast from the propeller nearly jerked his head back, and the frigid air numbed his face.

Jack looked for the German jet. He tilted his wings both ways but the jet was out of sight. He looked down and saw Natalya reaching the woods.

The sky was still filled with planes. "Aleksandr! Aleksandr!"

"Jackovich, I saw what happened."

"She's fine. She made it down."

"Jackovich! Behind you! Break right! Break—"

Krasilov's words were cut short by roaring cannons. Jack ducked again. The rear windshield, rated to sustain a direct hit from a 20mm round, was successful in deflecting the first few rounds before it collapsed, taking the overhead glass along.

Once more crushed glass bathed Jack Towers. The German scurried past him on his right side.

"Son of a bitch!" Jack cursed over the radio. The German had left him with a convertible Aircobra.

Erich couldn't believe just how easy it was. He was merely picking and shooting targets at will. He noticed the Soviet plane was not going down yet. He made a long sweeping turn and came back around on its tail.

Jack saw the jet returning for another pass. This time he had a plan. He put his craft in a shallow dive while pushing full throttle. Airspeed rocketed past four hundred knots. He let the German get on his tail.

Erich smiled at the Soviet plane trying to gain speed by going for a dive. He pushed full throttle as his finger caressed the trigger lever.

Jack peeked behind him and saw the German approach at great speed. He waited.

"Break left, Jackovich! Break left!" Krasilov's voice crackled through his headset. Jack ignored his Russian friend and remained in a leveled flight. He waited just a little longer . . . *now!*

In the same swift move, Jack pulled back throttle and lowered flaps and landing gear. His airspeed plummeted by almost two hundred knots in under ten seconds. Because he had already released his restraining harness so he could easily bail in an emergency, he crashed against the control panel, bounced, and slammed his back against his flight seat.

The tail of the Soviet craft abruptly filling his front window panel, Erich pulled back hard to avoid ramming it. He felt the bottom of the fuselage scraping the Soviet craft's rudder.

Partially disoriented from the blow, Jack tried to turn the nose in the direction of the departing jet, but the rudder wouldn't respond. He threw the stick to the left and tried to force the nose in its direction with ailerons, but instead, he wound up inverting the plane. For a second, the nose temporarily turned in the German's direction just as Jack's plane turned upside down.

Jack pressed the trigger and managed to fire a few rounds before the stick slipped away from his hand. He was not wearing his restraining harness and the canopy had been blown off. With the Aircobra inverted, Jack dropped out of the plane.

Shit!

In a flash, the powerful windblast crushed his chest as he glanced up at his plane, which continued upside down above him.

The earth and sky switched positions as Jack, disoriented, fell toward the forest at great speed. Struggling to find his ripcord, he slapped his right hand against his back but could not find it.

It has to be back there somewhere, Jack. Reach, reach, dammit!

The peaceful sound of the wind ringing in his ears, he plummeted toward earth at a speed of 150 knots. His right · hand was so far behind his back that he thought it was going to snap.

There!

Jack found the cord and pulled hard.

The canopy opened a few seconds later with a hard tug. He was roughly a thousand feet up and saw his Aircobra slowly arching down toward the ground. It disappeared behind the trees and the orange ball that followed foretold the end of his *Impatient Virgin*.

He tried to search for Natalya's canopy and spotted it about a mile to the north. He steered his parachute in that direction.

For Erich that had been the closest call of his life. His hands still shook from the short but intense battle with the stubborn Soviet pilot, whom he now watched reaching the forest. However, Erich's jet had not escaped the dogfight undamaged. White smoke spewed out of his left turbine, a result of the few rounds that the Soviet was able to fire before dropping from his airplane.

The white smoke, however, didn't seem to interfere with the turbine's performance. Erich decided to remain in the air battle for just a little longer while Haufman's flight team made their dives.

One by one, the Stukas inverted and dove over the column of Russian tanks, amid a shower of antiaircraft fire that would take the commitment out of everyone but the most courageous pilots.

75

Antiaircraft Fire

Forty-Five Miles South of Stalingrad Pocket
December 15, 1942

Werner Haufman and his four-finger formation reached the Soviet frontal attack on the German panzer's left flank. Haufman flew solo today. His gunner had developed pneumonia.

He inched back the throttle with his left hand and spoke in his radio. "Formation attack. Repeat formation attack. Stay with your leader."

"Yes, Gruppenkommandeur!"

At five thousand feet, the indicated airspeed marking 150 knots, Haufman rolled the Stuka on its back and dove, and so did the other three craft of his schwarm. He glanced both ways and noticed with satisfaction his team remaining with him as they dropped toward the column of Soviet tanks directly below them.

As speed increased to 190 knots, Haufman checked his distance from his right wingman, and also checked his angle of dive. He knew the other pilots would not be doing that. They would be following him blindly to the point that if he made a mistake and ran aground, the other three Stukas would most likely follow him down.

He achieved an eighty-five-degree dive at full throttle, without air brakes.

The flak started. Airspeed dashed above two hundred knots, and the Jericho trumpets started their loud whine, but in the midst of the massive ground fire, the sirens lacked the impact they had during the earlier stages of the war.

Two hundred twenty feet and the vertical speed indicator showed they were dropping at the rate of five thousand feet per minute! Way too fast, but the ground fire . . . he had to go even faster to minimize the risk of a hit.

Dark clouds of flak peppered the sky. Haufman flew through several of them as the earth came up to meet him. Two hundred seventy knots. The vibrations started. The fuselage began to tremble under the excessive windblast crashing against air surfaces designed for lower speeds, but the robust Stukas remained in one piece and accelerated closer to three hundred knots.

One thousand feet. Flak clouds were everywhere, some appearing right in front of him. A second later he flew through the harmless smoke. A second earlier and his canopy would have been vaporized, but he didn't have time to think about that now. The tanks were below—the infamous tanks that were threatening to cut General von Hoth's flanks to pieces, jeopardizing his drive north to liberate Stalingrad.

A squeeze of the trigger and the cannon thundered across the sky while Haufman used both hands to ease the control stick back and pull out of the dive.

The deafening reports blasting in his ears, Haufman felt the Gs piling up on him as he leveled off three hundred feet above the column and began to wrestle for altitude.

A loud explosion on his underside, accompanied by a powerful but brief vibration that rocked the craft, almost made him lose his grip on the stick.

Puzzled, he scanned the gauges and saw nothing abnormal. Oil pressure, engine temperature, fuel levels—all read normal.

His Stukas pulled up alongside of him.

"I need one of you to check my underside for damage."

"Right away, sir!" Haufman heard his right wingman say as the Stuka dropped several feet.

"Your underside looks darkened, sir, like it was hit by flak, but I can't see any physical damage. It appears intact."

"Any damage to the landing gear?" Haufman asked. If there was, he would try to parachute down over their base. The Stuka was a very volatile craft when it came to crash landings.

"Ah, no sir. It looks intact."

Haufman raised his eyebrows and frowned. "Very well, come back up. Thanks."

"You're welcome, sir."

The formation headed back to base.

76

Russian Winter

Near the Mishova River,
Forty Miles South of Stalingrad Pocket
December 16, 1942

Captain Jack Towers untangled himself from the silk parachute and pulled off the sections caught in overhead branches. He gathered it onto one large bulk and buried it in the snow.

As he looked about him, he quickly began to feel the effect of the thirty-below weather. To both Krasilov's and Natalya's disapproval, he had not worn the heavier, and therefore bulkier, coat that was standard for all Soviet aviators. Instead, Jack had chosen his standard-issued USAF leather jacket, which was good for keeping him warm in freezing temperatures, but not in the extreme cold of the Russian winter.

Snow clinging to the sides of his face, Jack began to move quickly to stay warm, heading in the direction where he had seen Natalya go down.

After a couple of minutes he spotted three figures roughly fifty feet ahead. Instinctively, Jack dropped to the snow and reached for his handgun, a Colt .45, flipped the safety, and cocked it.

The steel helmets protruding over the line of bushes told Jack the enemy was looking for him.

He remained still as their guttural sounds filled the air. Jack didn't speak a word of German, so he had no idea what they said, and besides, the German language was so rough that he couldn't tell if the soldiers were shouting or simply talking to one another.

The soldiers got closer. His initial assessment had been accurate. He saw three Germans and, to his relief, no dogs. The trio walked fifteen feet to his right. Jack had to move quickly or risk losing his limberness to the cold, which stung him hard. His arms and legs were shockingly cold. His hands were stiffening and his fingers losing sensation. A few more minutes and he probably would not be able to move them.

He took a chance. The Germans were thirty or so feet behind him now and their backs were to him. He got to his feet and took a few steps forward.

Snap!

A weathered branch under a thin layer of snow had given under his weight. The guttural voices intensified.

The Colt firmly gripped in his right hand, Jack took off in the opposite direction, aiming for the darkness behind a thicker section of forest.

One, two, three bullets cracked the silence, their reports echoing in the frozen woods. Near-misses buzzed past him like hornets from hell, exploding in clouds of bark as they struck a pine tree to his right.

Jack cut left and kept on running for another hundred feet as the noise behind him intensified. The trees to both sides of him turned into solid walls as his boots kicked the snow . . . *The snow*!

Only then he realized that no matter how fast he tried to get away, the Germans would merely follow his tracks. Sooner or later they would catch up with him.

Jack continued to run, but this time he searched for a break in the snow-covered woods, something clear of snow.

He found it moments later: a frozen ravine.

As two more shots whipped the frigid air, Jack raced past the frozen underbrush that led to a ten-foot-wide ravine. He could see water flowing under the ice, and he could not tell how thick the layer was, but he had to take a chance.

He jumped over the ice and tried to run over it but instead slipped and fell face-first.

The blow stung him, disoriented him. He felt a warm trickle of blood running down his forehead.

The world around him blurred, Jack blinked to clear his sight, the cold air burning his throat as he breathed through his mouth.

Regaining focus, his limbs trembling, Jack grabbed onto an exposed root on one side of the ravine and used it to propel himself down the narrow and winding channel, sliding on his belly, slowing down, and grabbing onto another object to lurch forward again, repeating the process several times until he had put about a hundred feet from the last place that he had left snow tracks.

He stumped his feet against the ice to push himself to the opposite side of the ravine and managed to reach a branch, which he used to pull himself up.

Next came the tricky part. Jack grabbed a higher branch with both hands and used it to swing himself over the edge of the ravine, landing on his back several feet away, behind knee-high bushes, out of sight from the Germans, whom he heard reaching the opposite end of the rift.

Jack slapped his waist holster, his gloved fingers reaching for his Colt . . . *my pistol*! The last time he had it was when he'd fallen.

"Amerikaine? Amerikaine! Hello, Amerikaine!"

Jack saw the German raise his Colt .45 in the air. Jack had his name, air force rank, and serial number engraved on the handle.

"Captain . . . Jack Towers of the United States Air Force?" said one of the Germans in heavily accented English. "If you are indeed Captain Towers, come out with your hands above your head and no harm will come to you! The Third Reich respects Americans! But if you resist, you will be shot like a Russian dog!"

In spite of the appalling cold, Jack wiggled his body into the snow, taking time to cover his legs and back. Numbness spread down his arms and legs. His fingers swelling inside his gloves, Jack cursed the cold wresting control of his body, quickly stripping him of life-supporting heat. If his temperature dropped any lower, Jack feared he would lose consciousness.

"Very well, then. Have it your way, Captain Towers!"

The Germans split three ways. Two went back to the opposite side of the ravine while the third entered the forest twenty feet from where Jack hid.

Slowly, Jack reached down to his boot and gripped his numbed fingers around the black handle of a ten-inch steel blade. The pain from his fingers as he forced them to clutch the handle hurt more than the wound on his forehead from falling on the ice.

He narrowed his eyes as the German, wearing a bulky white coat that dropped to his knees, turned in his direction. The muzzle of the machine gun held by the tall and slim soldier pointed in his direction.

Half buried in snow, Jack remained still as the German scanned the forest around him with the weapon before taking two more steps in Jack's direction.

The cold began to cloud his judgment. For a second he forgot the German's threat and simply stared in envy at the soldier's thick coat.

Jack forced his mind back to his situation, praying that the snow over his legs and back was thick enough to disguise his presence.

It appeared that way, because the soldier, after taking two more steps, turned his back to Jack.

The German now less that six feet away from him, Jack hesitated about attacking. Would his achingly cold body move swiftly enough to reach the soldier before he turned around?

Jack wasn't sure, but he was certain of one thing: if he didn't move quickly he would freeze to death. He had to make his muscles work to get his circulation flowing.

The German remained still. The weapon pointed away from Jack.

He breathed the cold air once, exhaled, and breathed it again as he inched his legs forward to see how they would respond. They moved.

He recoiled and lunged.

The German must have heard him, because halfway through his attack, the soldier began to turn around, but too late.

Jack kept the knife aimed for the chest and drove it in hard. Both men landed by the edge of the rift. The blade had only gone halfway inside the soldier's chest.

Their eyes locked.

Staring into the terrified light blue eyes of the soldier— a kid in his late teens—Jack jammed his numb right hand against the soldier's mouth as he fiercely palm-struck the knife's handle.

The blade cut deeper into the German's body until the handle met the soldier's uniform. He knew that his palm should be hurting from the blow against the handle, but it didn't. Although he could still move his hands, he had lost sensation below the wrist.

The German went limp. Jack stood up and dragged him away from the ravine, realizing as he did so that this was the first time he had killed someone outside of aerial combat. He had just killed a kid.

Guilt should have overwhelmed him, but the bitter cold took its place, shoving away anything but the most primal survival instincts.

His lips trembled and his cheeks twitched. Realizing that hypothermia was slowly setting in, Jack shifted his priorities from evading the Germans to finding shelter—protection from the harsh elements before he froze, before the cold seeped deeper into his core.

He leaned the dead kid against a tree and pulled the knife of the German's chest. The jagged edge cut a wider track on its way out, jetting blood over Jack's legs. He ignored it, dropped the bloody weapon by his feet, and released the straps of the soldier's heavy jacket. He removed it and quickly put it on. Next he slung the machine gun and—

"Hans? Hans?"

Jack snapped left. The other two Germans were back in the ravine, catching him in plain view kneeling in the snow.

One of the Germans looked straight at Jack and waved for a moment before realizing that he had stolen the German's coat.

He leveled the machine gun at Jack.

Clutching the dead German's machine gun, Jack jumped away as the slow rattle of the German's weapon cracked in the woods, followed by multiple explosions of snow.

He got to his feet and reached a thick cluster of trees. The firing subsided as his back crashed hard against the trunk of a tree. Breathing heavily, he clutched the machine gun and glanced over his left shoulder.

Gunfire erupted once more, shaving off bark, stinging him.

His face bleeding from the flying bark, trying to control his quivering hands, he dropped to the ground, rolled away, and blindly opened fire in the Germans' general direction.

It had the desired effect. Both Germans ran for cover, giving Jack enough time to reach a fallen log.

On his belly, Jack spread both legs, set the muzzle over the log, and waited. And waited.

Time.

Minutes went by. Jack kept the gun trained on the trees protecting the soldiers, his face growing numb.

The jacket didn't seem to help. Enough heat had escaped his body before he put it on to keep him from getting warm again.

Jack understood what that meant: he had lost the ability to warm himself back up. He had to get to a source of heat fast, before his body fell deeper into hypothermia.

One of the Germans ran to an adjacent tree. Jack tried to fire but his index finger didn't respond fast enough. He missed the soldier by a few feet.

The second soldier now ran. Jack fired and missed again. He tried to shift the gun toward the new German hideout, but now his arms wouldn't respond; his body wouldn't respond. He was convulsing.

One of the Germans came into plain view. Jack tried to fire but couldn't. He pressed his lips together and forced his index finger against the trigger, but it wouldn't move. It was frozen stiff!

Jack found it harder and harder to breathe now. Every gulp of air that entered his lungs felt like a hard cold hammer squashing his chest and forcing the last remnants of heat out of his exhausted body. His vision became foggy, cloudy. The shadowy figures loomed in front of him.

Jack heard laughter mixed with the dreaded guttural words he couldn't understand, but this time he decided they were screaming, and in the middle of all the shouting he picked up the only word that his ears recognized: *Hans. Hans.*

Jack had killed their comrade in arms. He knew the Germans would not be merciful.

His thoughts became fuzzy, irrational. His ears picked up several shots, and he tried to brace himself, but his arms only moved part of the way. His rigid body didn't feel any impact. He could be bleeding to death at that moment and wouldn't know it. He searched in vain for the silhouettes of his executioner. They had shot him and left him to bleed to death.

A shadow then loomed over him and began to lift him to his feet.

Why are the Germans dragging me away?

Why not just let me die in the woods?

Jack tried to open his mouth to say that he didn't care anymore, but he had pushed his body past the brink of exhaustion and it would not respond to his commands. A sense of desolation overwhelmed him as he sensed life slowly escaping.

Slowly, very slowly, Jack surrendered himself to the Russian winter.

77

Nerves of Steel

Red October Plant, Stalingrad Pocket
December 16, 1942

The distant humming grew into the unmistakable rumble of Russian twin-engine bombers—dozens of them, sent by General Chuikov ahead of the main echelon of tanks and infantry.

Zoya saw them materialize on the northern horizon, first as mere dots, which slowly flattened as they approached the German defenses dotting Mamayev Hill.

Petlyakov Pe-2 twin-engine bombers.

Here we go, she thought when the first wave raced across the sky over the hill, their engines growling as pilots revved them up to minimize their exposure to the expected antiaircraft fire. It ignited a moment later in an ear-piercing crescendo that reverberated across the entire factory complex.

The acoustic energy of the detonating shells rumbled the building. Zoya remained at her observation post, which in addition to providing her with a clear view of the streets also gave her a great vantage point on the German defenses.

To Zoya's disappointment, the German patrol had not yet left the building, meaning her team would not be able to seek better cover in the center of the structure. They would have to weather the developing battle from their window posts along the building's third floor or risk being discovered.

Those pilots had better remember their orders, she thought as clouds of flak peppered the blue skies from the German antiaircraft fire, whose thundering drowned the engine noise of the Petlyakovs.

Four bombers maneuvered through a steep dive in tight formation, amazing Zoya that they could remain so close despite their size. Flak exploded all around them as their revving engines suddenly roared above the German guns when dropping below five hundred feet a few blocks from where she sat frozen in amazement at the surreal sight.

For an instant, Zoya saw the face of one of the Russian pilots as he frantically checked his flanks before focusing his attention on the approaching targets beyond the nose of his plane while his bomb-bay doors opened.

As if connected to an invisible rubber band, the bomber shot skyward the moment a dark cluster of bombs dropped from its belly.

The bombs arced toward the side of the hill, detonating in flashes of yellow and crimson flames amid towers of black debris and billowing smoke.

One of the four planes released its cargo just as an antiaircraft shell tore off its left wing. The giant engine attached to the severed wing continue to turn the propeller, shooting off in the opposite direction of the maimed craft, which went into a spiral, crashing beyond its exploding bombs, erupting in a sheet of flames that dwarfed its detonating cargo.

The wing momentarily hovered over the stretch of land between the factory and the hill, almost defying gravity, before plummeting to the ground near two German pillboxes. The fire from the exploding fuel in the wing's tank swallowed the machine-gun emplacements. Ablaze figures rushed out of their positions, collapsing moments later as the flames consumed them. The three surviving planes gained altitude and turned back north as the next wave made its dive amid considerable ground resistance.

Spellbound by this display of raw power, Zoya remained at her post, cringing as numerous explosions rumbled across the factory complex, making concrete and steel structures tremble.

A small three-story building a block away collapsed when a Russian bomber, its cockpit in flames from a direct hit, crashed into its first floor, bringing the whole structure down in a boiling cloud of dust and debris that momentarily blocked the madness surrounding Mamayev Hill, where Russian bombers continued to make their runs.

Zoya cringed. This close to the ground, there was no time for bomber crews to bail out. Once entering the dive, the pilot and crew were committed.

A northern breeze swept away the haze, revealing the crash sites of several bombers, flames and columns of inky smoke rising up to skies still dotted with flak clouds.

And so it went, bomber after bomber, some making it through the wall of antiaircraft fire unscathed, most perishing even before they were able to unload their cargo, often spiraling out of control, like the one that had taken out the building a block away. Their impact spread acoustic energy across the ground, shaking all of the structures in the area.

A second building collapsed two blocks away, this one four stories high, rumbling the very foundation of her building, which trembled under the extreme stress. She felt a secondary vibration a few seconds later coming from within the building, and for a moment wondered if it would collapse.

It didn't, holding together—though it did sound as if something had collapsed internally.

In spite of the heavy pounding by the bombs dropped over the hill, the Germans continued their powerful show of force, firing a wall of explosive rounds in front of the incoming Russian planes.

The air raid is not being too effective, she thought while watching the destruction with apprehension, praying that her building remained untouched, and also hoping that her team maintained the nerve required to sit tight even though at any moment one of those bombers could stray their way, vaporizing them with violent intensity. The German patrol was still in the building. Remaining hidden was paramount to the success of her mission, particularly in light of the Red Air Force's apparent failure to dislodge the Germans.

The last of the bombers made their run, only to end up in flames and crash well off their intended target. Zoya realized that taking the hill—thus preventing the German Sixth Army from breaking out of the pocket from this section of the city—would be up to Chuikov's tanks and infantry. It also relied on her timely sniper support, a mission that she was determined to carry out just as she had been ordered.

Or die trying.

78

Decisions

Red October Plant, Stalingrad Pocket
December 16, 1942

"It has stopped, Johan," said Major Christoff Halden while remaining in a crouch behind an array of steel machinery in the middle of the building's first floor.

"Is it safe to move out, sir?" his subordinate asked, his light blue eyes flashing genuine concern on a face darkened by camouflage cream.

Christoff slowly nodded, trying to convince Johan, and himself, that it was prudent to head out into the open now. The nearby battle had been fierce, at times shaking the very structure of this factory. On one occasion it had triggered the collapse of a section of the roof, which had come crashing down roughly thirty feet away, leaving a gaping hole between the first and second floors.

His well-honed guerrilla tactics were useless when caught in such savage display of destruction. But it did appear that the battle was over—at least for the moment—providing him and his team with the opportunity to resume their hunt.

"Tell the men to get ready to move out."

"Yes, sir," said Johan, relief relaxing his tight features as he stood and began to pass the orders.

Within a few minutes the group was already gathering by a hole on the wall facing the west side of the building, lined by fallen brick and chunks of mortar mixed with tangled rebar. Huge flames flickered on Mamayev Hill. Columns of smoke marked the attempt by the Russian bombers to dislodge well dug-in elements from the General Paulus' Sixth Army.

"It's going to take more that an air raid for the Russians

to retake that hill," Christoff said reassuringly to his team, his eyes already focusing on a two-story building to the far right, adjacent to one that had apparently collapsed during the raid. He pointed at the German soldiers already out of their foxholes and bunkers swarming the strategic hill, almost like ants crawling out of their hideouts after an attack on their mound, quickly repairing the damage.

"Those soldiers on that hill are doing their job, gentlemen," Christoff added. "They are protecting the interests of the Sixth Army by holding onto the hill that will enable us to coordinate our planned breakthrough to meet up with General Hoth's panzers. Now let's go and do *our* job and find this elusive group of Russian fighting women and make them pay the ultimate price for daring to kill German soldiers."

Setting the example, Christoff ventured through the hole first, inspecting his surroundings. Debris and dust swirled in the air from the fallen structure as well as from the smoke blowing in their direction by the prevailing winds. Soon they would all be caked in dust, which would actually work to their advantage because the brownish powder and falling ashes would cover everything else as well, further concealing his team.

You must become a chameleon, he thought, stepping away from the building and onto the rubble littering the wide avenue. Turning around, he motioned his team to remain put until he reached the middle of the avenue. No sense in giving a potential Russian sniper more than one kill.

He watched in satisfaction as Johan and the others remained huddled by the jagged opening, watching with a mix of admiration and anxiety as Christoff continued to live up to his reputation of placing himself in the line of fire ahead of his men, taking the largest risk by venturing out alone.

Debris partially covered many frozen corpses of unrecognizable origin, some scattered around wrecked panzers as well as Russian tanks from a battle that was already ancient history in this city, just like the air strike that had nearly wiped out his hideout would be forgotten by tomorrow.

Insanity, Christoff thought as he pressed on, ignoring the death surrounding him, his mind focused on the job, on making it alive to the next building, on hoping that the light haze and his camouflage would protect him from the bullets of a Russian sniper.

He looked over his right shoulder as he reached the remnants of a fountain near the halfway point. The statue in the middle was missing most of its torso. Christoff looked toward the building where his troops hid and raised his left arm.

A moment later Johan came out into the open while the rest of the men remained, as ordered.

Christoff surveyed the terrain behind him, mostly bricks, wood, and metal debris amid old tanks and bodies—though he recognized the landing gear of a Stuka just off to the right, probably shot down while attacking the tanks with its nose-mounted cannons.

The statue once adorning the fountain must have been of some general, at least based on its military boots and the sidearm hanging from its waist. The rest had been long lost to the same war that had turned this city into a—

Christoff froze the moment he spotted the glint of glass reflecting from a shadowy corner of the roof of the building he had just left.

Binoculars?

His stomach knotted as a worse possibility flashed in his mind: a sniper's scope.

But if it was a sniper, why was Christoff still alive? Was the Russian waiting for more Germans before opening fire? Was the hidden Russian the shadow Christoff had seen the previous night? But again, if that was the case, why was he still alive? Maybe the Russian was alone, posted there to observe and report rather than to kill.

Options rushed to him. His trained mind struggled to assess the situation without reflecting it on his physical appearance. He had to pretend he had not seen it or risk

tipping the sniper that he had been spotted, in which case
Christoff was certain that a bullet would follow.

Slowly, realizing that both Johan and he were exposed
and out of choices, the German major turned around and
continued his advance toward the building as if he had seen
nothing abnormal, the back of his neck itching in anticipation of a bullet that could come at any moment.

79

Facial Expressions

Red October Plant, Stalingrad Pocket
December 16, 1942

Zoya Krasilov lowered her weapon the moment the German
soldier stared in her direction. The eye contact had not lasted
but a second or two, but his facial expression, as seen clearly
through her sniper scope, told her he had seen something
strange on the roof near her position when inspecting the
building from that fountain near the middle of the avenue.

But an instant later the German had turned around and
continued his march toward the building across the square
as if nothing had happened. He had not signaled the second
German in the street to rush back or seek cover. He had
simply turned around.

Zoya frowned.

Weird.

Either the German truly hadn't seen anything alarming
enough to react, or he had chosen to *pretend* he had not
seen it to avoid telegraphing this new knowledge.

*You should have killed them last night when you had the
chance.*

She grimaced again, watching the German reach the
next building as a second man approached the fountain,
when a third soldier ventured into the open.

Zoya watched as the cautious German patrol crossed the clearing with no more than two men exposed at any one time, minimizing the damage a sniper could do.

When the last German disappeared inside the distant building, Zoya leaned back and forced her mind to relax— at least momentarily.

Her instincts, however, told her that this would not be the last time she would come across this bizarre German patrol that waged war in a style that rivaled her partisan tactics.

80

Vital Signs

Near the Mishova River,
Forty Miles South of Stalingrad Pocket
December 16, 1942

"Is he alive?" asked Natalya Makarova while she helped Aris Broz hoist Jack over the back of a horse next to the ravine.

"Barely," he responded, securing thick blankets over him. "I don't think he is going to make it."

Natalya looked at the craggy partisan who had rescued her from a German patrol less than thirty minutes ago, before going after Jack Towers. Together they had killed the Germans before they shot him. "How far do we have to go?"

"It all depends," replied Aris while leading the horse away from the ravine. "The nearest place where he could get any type of medical attention is over two hours away. I can tell you for certain he's not going to last *that* long."

"Dammit, Jack," Natalya cursed as she put a hand over the blankets. "I told you to wear warmer clothing!"

She exhaled and looked back at Aris. "Where is the closest place that's protected from the elements?"

"The caves, but again. There is no medical—"

"How far away is that?"

"Just minutes away."

"Please take us there. We have to get him out of this weather."

81

Hard Choices

*JG52 Gruppe 1, Fifty Miles North of Rostov
December 16, 1942*

Major Erich Steinhoff walked outside his tent the moment he heard the Stukas in the distance. Right away a cold breeze made him shiver even though for the past thirty minutes he had warmed up by the fire sipping vodka.

"They're coming back, sir!" he heard Mathias shout.

Erich nodded, his eyes trying to get a count. Twelve Stukas had left that morning. Erich could only see ten circling overhead.

He walked toward a barrel filled with burning logs. Several of his pilots gathered around it as they tried to thaw between sorties. It was barely past breakfast and most men on the base had completed at least one sortie, some two.

The first Stuka landed and taxied to the clearing adjacent to the runway as another craft made its final approach.

For the next five minutes, one after the next, Erich and the other Gustav pilots watched the dive-bombers land, until only one plane remained airborne, Haufman's. Just as it was customary among Luftwaffe fighter wings, the flight leader always took off first and landed last.

Erich followed the dark Stuka all the way down, as it gracefully cleared the pines by the edge of the runway, floated over the clearing, and gently descended over the runway. The approach was one of the smoothest that morning in spite of the heavy crosswind.

The landing gear grazed the runway for a second before touching down. Then it gave.

Erich stared in total awe as the Stuka's belly crashed over the runway in a cloud of sparks. The gigantic propeller stabbed the ground before breaking apart. The Stuka skidded sideways along the runway, dangerously close to the trees, while trailing bright yellow flames from its underside.

"It's gonna blow! You and you!" he screamed at the top of his lungs. "Get the shovels and follow me!"

The pilots ran to the side of the runway and grabbed the large shovels lying by the edge of the mess tent. Erich clutched one and raced after the decelerating plane, whose nose was already on fire.

"Hurry, hurry!" he shouted as he sprinted after his friend's plane.

The flames intensified when the Stuka's right wing crashed against a tree and broke off in a ball of flames that swallowed the cockpit right before the plane came to a complete stop.

Erich and the pilots got there seconds later and began to shovel snow over the burning canopy.

"Quicker, dammit. Quicker!"

Tears filled his eyes as Erich breathed heavier, throwing shovelfuls of snow along with a dozen other men.

Then something emerged through the flames.

Werner!

No!

He had pulled the canopy back instead of waiting for Erich and his men to put out the fire out.

"Bury him! Hurry!" Erich shouted.

The pilots tried to throw the snow in his direction, but Haufman was moving too fast. Erich dropped the shovel, ran toward him, and tackled him from behind, forcing the Stuka pilot face-first into the snow.

The flames rapidly went out. The smell of burning flesh filled his nostrils, nauseating him. Haufman was convulsing. It took four men—one per limb—to hold him down.

Erich padded his friend's body with more snow to cool

the blistering skin while leaving his face buried in the snow. He was afraid to turn him over for fear of what he would see, but he couldn't show any weaknesses in front of the men. He tried to remove the charred helmet but it was stuck to Werner's head.

He turned to Mathias. "Get the medic! Quick!"

Mathias ran off. Erich breathed deeply before saying, "All right. Let's roll him over."

They did.

Some closed their eyes. Others took a few steps back. Erich remained with the men holding Haufman down.

His eyes filling with rage, Erich started at his friend's horribly disfigured face. The flames had consumed the hair, and his eyes . . . they were twice the size and no longer blue, but dark and glassy . . . the eyelids were gone. The rest of the face resembled fried bacon.

Erich fought a stomach spasm.

"Erich . . . Erich . . ."

"I'm here, my friend. I'm here. You're all right. You've made it."

"The . . . pain . . . pain . . . Erich.   I   can't   see . . . Erich . . . the pain . . ."

Erich turned to the medic, who had just arrived alongside Mathias. "Morphine! Where is the damned morphine?"

"But, sir," replied the young soldier. "He is not going to make it. I have other men who—"

Eric grabbed him by the lapels. "Now! Dammit! Give it to him!"

The medic complied, shooting him up.

"Erich . . . the pain . . ."

Erich breathed heavily, feeling a lump in his throat. He wanted to save his friend, but Haufman couldn't possibly survive those wounds. All he could do was make his final moments as painless as possible.

"Shoot him up again!" Erich barked.

"But, sir. The overdose will kill him."

Erich leaned closer, hissing, "He's *already* dead! Do it now, soldier!"

The medic complied, injecting Werner in the leg a second time.

"Erich . . ." came the whisper again in between raspy sobs.

Erich held him, tried to console him, to tell him that it would be all right, that the right medical attention was on the way, that he would now get to go home to a hero's welcome.

Then his breathing ceased.

Erich embraced his childhood friend for a long time, eyes closed, ignoring everyone around him, before setting him down on the snow.

He finally stood. "Get his body bagged and ready for the next cargo plane that stops here on the way to Germany. Oberstleutnant Haufman *will not* be buried in Russian soil."

As his men carried out the order, Erich gave his childhood friend one final glance.

You're going home, old buddy. You're going back to Augsburg.

82

Body Heat

Near the Mishova River,
Forty Miles South of Stalingrad Pocket
December 16, 1942

Assisted by three partisans, Natalya Makarova dragged Jack's freezing body inside one of several huts built against the side of a rocky hill overlooking the Mishova River.

"Get me some vodka!" she screamed as she set Jack down over some blankets next to a gas lantern.

Aris ran outside, leaving the door open. A gush of cold air rushed inside the hut. Natalya cursed and closed it.

Jack was still unconscious and extremely cold. She

removed both his jackets, his boots and pants, and began massaging his stiff legs and arms, trying to get some blood to his purplish feet and hands to prevent frostbite

Aris came in, closed the door behind him, and handed Natalya a small dark bottle. She removed the cork, took a sniff, and brought it to Jack's lips.

"Drink it, Jack."

She got no response. She put a few drops on his lips and saw his tongue move.

"He needs immediate medical attention," offered Aris. "A fire would probably help him, but I'm afraid it's out of the question. There's too many German patrols in the area. There is, however, another option to get heat into his body fast, but that's really up to you, Natalya." Aris then left them alone in the room.

Natalya knew what she needed to do if she was to save his life. Jack's body was so cold that his core could not produce enough heat on its own to bring his body temperature back up. Jack needed another heat source to radiate warmth back into his system.

Natalya quickly removed the rest of his clothes. Jack braced himself and shivered. She covered his body with blankets before removing her own clothes. First the wet boots, thick aviator pants, and jacket, followed by her undergarments. Her nipples stiffened the moment she snapped off her brassiere.

Natalya maneuvered her pale body beneath the blankets and pressed Jack against her. Her body tensed the moment his cold chest came in contact with her breasts but she forced herself to remain. The skin of her stomach was against his; his face buried in her neck as she breathed heavily over his face to smother him with warmth.

She parted his cold thighs and wedged her right leg in between his while rubbing her arms up and down his back. Heat radiated from her onto him.

Minutes went by. Natalya didn't stop. She continued to rub her entire body against him, until slowly, very slowly, Jack began to respond. His body became soft, still cold, but soft, relaxed. His breathing steadied. She could now feel his heartbeat pounding steadily against her chest. She felt his arms pulling her tighter against him. She was his heat source. His body needed more of her to survive.

Time.

Natalya saw Jack open his eyes, inhale deeply, and close them again, obviously drifting in and out of consciousness.

83

Dreaming

Near the Mishova River,
Forty Miles South of Stalingrad Pocket
December 16, 1942

Jack Towers felt as if he were dreaming. The harsh cold wind had been replaced by a rhythmic warm breeze that caressed his neck. There was heat around him, and it felt good, cozy, intimate. He opened his eyes and was instantly comforted by Natalya's hazel stare inches away.

He tried to speak, but she put a finger to his mouth.

"Shh . . . Rest, my dear Jack. Rest."

Jack stared at Natalya's eyes as they reflected the flickering light of the gas lantern, which cast a yellow glow on her white Slavic face. The high cheekbones, full lips, and small chin looked majestic in the twilight of the room. Her powerful embrace was the most intimate Jack had ever felt. He never thought he could feel such complete union with a woman, and yet there was no sex involved, just the thrust of her lifesaving heat into him.

Slowly, all faded away. The face, the yellowish light, the eyes. Jack quietly surrendered himself to the warm and soothing comfort of Natalya's nearness.

84

Guilt

Kalach Airfield, Twenty Miles West of Stalingrad Pocket
December 16, 1942

Krasilov jumped out of his plane and raced for the communications bunker. Their Aircobras or La-3s were no match for the German jet. The Soviets had not been able to stop the advancing Hitlerites. The jet had taken four of his planes, injecting confidence in the Gustav pilots, who shot down six more Russian fighters. A third of his pilots didn't come back. The Germans effectively had prevented Krasilov's squadron from reaching the front lines.

Lacking air support, the 62nd Army of General Vasili Chuikov had no choice but to retreat. General von Hoth's panzers were now only forty miles from Stalingrad. If a corridor got established, he knew Paulus' 250,000 soldiers would get enough supplies to keep the city through the rest of the winter.

Krasilov inhaled the relatively warm air inside the communications bunker. They needed additional planes if they were to provide any type of air support. More planes and also a way to get rid of the annoying jets.

Krasilov frowned. He also needed to make two more calls. One to the U.S. Air Force adviser in the Kremlin, and a second to Colonel Chapman, who was currently training another air regiment one hundred miles north of Stalingrad.

85

Letters

The day had been a marginal victory for the Luftwaffe. A total of ten Soviet fighters and a dozen tanks had been destroyed in the Mishova River region. The drive to the Stalingrad pocket continued. Erich wrote it all in a message that would be encoded and sent to Berlin. The Me 262 was a superb fighter, although it was temporarily grounded until the left turbine could be repaired.

Erich passed the message to the Enigma operator and walked back to his tent. He was depressed, exhausted, and terribly hungry. He had not only lost his best friend today but the single hour he had spent with Sonja had changed him more than he'd originally thought. She was on his mind constantly now—not that she wasn't before, but it was different. They had shared the deepest kind of intimacy a man and a woman could have. He wondered if he would see her again, or if fate had something else in store for him.

He reached his tent, pulled out her picture, and began to write her a letter. He told her about the pain, the solitude, the anger, the frustration. He told her about Haufman's death, leaving out the details of exactly how he'd died. He described to her the feeling of emptiness after arriving from a mission to nothing but a frozen airfield in the middle of nowhere with thirty other exhausted and lonely pilots, all wishing to be someplace else. *Why does it have to be this way, my dear Sonja? Why? Is all of this necessary?*

Erich wrote for nearly half an hour. Writing to Sonja always took a long time. Those yellowish pieces of paper represented his opportunity to vent, to let go of it all and go back to the days when nothing mattered but flying his mother's gliders and spending time with Sonja. Back to the days when his family would get lost in their Alps winter chalet and ski for days without end. Ski, fly, Sonja. That had been Erich's life. Yet, all of that seemed a lifetime away as a tear smeared the ink at the end of a sentence. War had brought it all to an end. War had killed Haufman— a war created to satisfy the obsessive desires of a single man.

Erich put down the pen, folded the sheets of paper, and stuffed them in an envelope. After sealing it, he stared at it and wished he could go along. He wished there was a way that he and Sonja could just disappear from all this madness. For a moment he even wondered if he could use his jet to escape, to fly to Germany, pick up Sonja, and truly disappear until after the war. Thoughts of defection crossed his mind.

But then the soldier in him emerged. Yes, he loved her, but he also loved his Germany, and his country needed him now more than ever. It didn't take a fool to realize that this was not the victorious Germany of 1939 and '40. Erich could see through all the Nazi propaganda so carefully fed to the soldiers in the field. He knew what was going on, and the fact that he had an Me 262 prototype jet parked right outside his tent was living testimony of his superiors' level of desperation.

Erich reached for the bottle of vodka. This time around he wasn't physically cold. His body was warm, but his heart ached.

"Are you all right, Erich?"

As he swallowed a sip of vodka, Erich looked up and saw Mathias' thin figure in the doorway. The African carried a food tray. Erich motioned him to come in and close the tent's flap. Mathias did so and set the tray on the table. Erich eyed the boiled horse meat and looked away. No wonder his flight suit felt looser.

"I'm sorry about Werner, Erich. He was a good pilot."

"He was a friend, Mathi. I'll miss him." He took another sip. Mathias lowered his gaze. "What is it?"

"The jet . . . I saw the damage in—"

Erich exhaled. "Yes, Mathi. Some crazy Russian got me. He set the trap beautifully and I fell for it. He did go down, though, but not before one of my turbines." Erich saw fear in the African's face.

"We need the jet, Erich. We must have it to win the war."

"Relax, Mathi. One plane is not going to make a difference." Erich noticed that his words had no effect on Mathias. In the African's mind the jet played an instrumental role. Erich would have agreed to that opinion if the Luftwaffe had entire squadrons of them, but not just two.

"We'll get it fixed, Mathi. The spares arrived this morning and Augsburg is sending a mechanic over in a couple of days."

"But—but . . . we must have the jet operational right away."

"Get some sleep, my friend. We'll talk in the morning. And here, give this letter to the dispatcher. He'll know what to do with it."

The African took the letter, mumbled a few incoherent words, and slowly left the room.

Erich stared at the bottle of vodka, but in his mind he saw the woods south of Augsburg. He saw the sun shining on Sonja's hair, the smile on her face, the promise in her eyes. Then his mind shifted to the day when he'd met Haufman, the bullish kid from Augsburg.

Werner. Erich exhaled. *Dear God.*

They had gone through school together. They had flown gliders together. They had joined the Hitler Youth's ranks and then the Luftwaffe together. They had fought together first in Poland and now in Russia.

And now you are gone.

His body had been loaded into the same transport plane due to leave in a couple of hours that would carry the letter he had just written.

Erich glanced at the horse meat again and felt nauseated. He opted for the vodka and took another sip, set the bottle on the table, and lay down on his bed to get some rest before his next sortie.

86

Instincts

Red October Plant, Stalingrad Pocket
December 16, 1942

"Are you sure you saw someone?"

On the second story of their new hideout, Major Christoff Halden regarded his bearded friend, whose narrow face arranged into a mask of curiosity and concern.

Without an explanation for his actions, Christoff had ordered the rest of his men along the windows facing the suspicious building as well as this side of Mamayev Hill, which continued to swarm with activity as the Germans used old Russian tractors to clear the damage done by the bombers. Men refilled sandbags and stacked them around their machine-gun emplacements and antiaircraft batteries, getting ready to fend off anything else the Russians decided to throw at them.

Shrugging, Christoff, who had only shared his suspicions with his trusted subordinate, said, "Had I not seen— or *think* I'd seen—that shadow last night on the roof, I would have dismissed what I think I saw an hour ago. But that's two unusual observations, Johan. When you put them together, you get a pattern, and I simply can't bring myself to ignore that. My instincts are screaming at me that something is seriously wrong."

"But no one attacked us last night. And they could have while we were sleeping in shifts. And they also didn't try when we were crossing."

"Perhaps the enemy only has one sniper who doesn't want to give out his or her position yet. Maybe the sniper was posted there for a reason *other* than to attack a single German patrol."

"If that is the case, then shouldn't we be returning to the building and searching it, especially the place where you saw these shadows?"

Johan was right, of course—at least according to the German infantry manual, which also required the German patrol to call in an air strike on the building. But if the hidden Russian was indeed waiting for something bigger to develop, then Christoff stood the chance to gain much more by turning the situation around and taking up an observation post himself on the possible Russian hideout—at least for a day or so to see what developed.

He told this to Johan, who sighed while looking away and replying, "But doing so will only delay us from accomplishing our true objective. We need to find and terminate this group of rogue female warriors. That's our ticket out of this hellhole."

Christoff nodded slightly before saying, "I can't argue with your logic. But I can say that my instincts are telling me to remain here for the time being and see what transpires. I know it goes against our training and our orders, but sometimes a soldier has to follow his instincts. Judiciously doing so—and prudently, to avoid getting court-martialed—could mean the difference between a live soldier and a dead one."

Johan gave him the same intrigued look he had shot him at the Pitomnik Airfield when Christoff had refused to execute those who had inflicted wounds on themselves. A German soldier didn't last very long in the Wermacht by defying orders and acting on one's initiative. Yet, Christoff seemed to have figured a way to accomplish that while not only avoiding prosecution, but also getting promoted. His instincts had prevented him from becoming a murderer in Poland by making him sign up for the most dangerous missions, thus fighting soldiers instead of slaughtering civilians.

His instincts had then kept him from killing Germans, but rather giving them an opportunity to rejoin the fight if they survived their self-inflicted wounds. And his instincts now told him to set up an observation post when he should be on the move looking for his target.

Christoff stared at his friend, placed a hand on his shoulder, and said, "Never ignore your instincts, Johan. No one has more knowledge of your current situation in the field than yourself. Those who sent you here probably have never seen battle like you and I have and therefore can't possibly tell you what is right and wrong at this moment. We are in the best position to do so."

Johan nodded while staring at the building where they had spent the night. "Have you seen anything abnormal yet?"

Christoff surveyed the side of the building using his sniper's scope.

"No. Not even by the roofline, where I saw the reflection a moment ago."

"None of the men have also seen anything unusual."

"So we wait," Christoff said, standing up. "We wait and see what transpires. In the meantime, I'll make a round and make sure this building is clean."

87

Unexpected Visitor

Kalach Airfield, Twenty Miles West of Stalingrad Pocket
December 16, 1942

That late afternoon, Krasilov stood by the side of the airfield as the visiting Aircobra landed and taxied toward the bomb shelters. He walked up to the plane as the propeller stopped turning and the pilot slid the cockpit open.

The visiting officer, a tall heavy man with broad shoulders and a square face, climbed down the side of the plane.

He removed his helmet and scanned the base. Krasilov approached him.

"Colonel Chapman?"

"That's right, I'm Colonel Kenneth Chapman. You must be Colonel Krasilov."

"Yes, sir."

"Well, Colonel, I gotta tell you. I wasn't pleased to hear that you've used one of my bilingual trainers to fly in your sorties."

Krasilov did what he could to contain his temper. He simply stared back at Chapman for a few seconds. "We all make our mistakes, Colonel. And we all learn to live with them."

"What in the hell happened? You are running short on pilots?"

"Among other things."

"What do you mean? The Kremlin's not sending you enough men to fly the machines we're giving you?"

"I must make do with what I have at my disposal, Colonel. Unlike your country, we don't have unlimited resources available to us at a moment's notice. We have to fight back for the survival of our country and use whatever is available at the time. Captain Towers was available, and I used him. You may include that statement in your report of the incident."

The two pilots stared at one another for a few seconds.

Chapman exhaled and looked away. "Do you have a place where I can get a drink, Colonel? I nearly froze my ass off tonight trying to get here."

Krasilov nodded. "This way, Colonel."

88

Small World

Near the Mishova River,
Forty Miles South of Stalingrad Pocket
December 16, 1942

That evening Captain Jack Towers sat by the fire outside
the hut where he had slept most of the day. As Natalya had
explained to him, at night they ran little chance of someone
spotting the smoke.

Jack felt rested, and to Natalya's amazement, he had survived without the need for an amputation. His fingers and
toes had regained their natural color and elasticity. He had
indeed been lucky. His mother had warned him about the
Russian winter. He now understood her fears.

Jack took another drag from the strongest cigarette he
had ever smoked in his life. At first, Aris and Natalya had
smiled when he nearly turned green while smoking one
earlier that afternoon, but as the day went on, he'd grown
accustomed to the locally made unfiltered cigarettes.

"You're going to be all right, Jack," said Natalya, sitting
next to him and smiling.

"Thanks to you."

She looked away and frowned.

"Hey, hey. What's the matter?"

Natalya didn't respond. She simply gazed down at her
boots. Jack gently pulled up her chin. She was in tears.

"Look, Natalya. I'm really sorry you had to do that. I
just want you to know that—"

"You were wonderful, Jack. You didn't take advantage.
That's what makes it so hard . . ."

Now Jack was really confused. "Makes what so hard?"

"I promised myself I wouldn't fall for another pilot,

Jack. Don't you see the kind of life we live? I lost a loved one once. I'm afraid to get close again!"

Jack put an arm around her and pulled her close.

"Look, Natalya. The way I see it is that you must live life today, now, because there might not be a tomorrow. You're absolutely right. What we do up there is dangerous. Don't kid yourself about it. It's *damned* dangerous, and for some reason the powers that be decided that you and I are among the lucky ones who get to do it. That's our fate. Our destiny. And it will happen regardless of what you do today. So live for the day, Natalya. Worry about the future after the war is over."

Natalya lifted her head and kissed him on the cheek. "Thanks, Jack. You're all right."

She got up.

"Where are you going?"

"To get some coffee. Want some?"

He slowly shook his head. "But thanks for offering."

Jack watched her walk away before turning his face toward the fire. Natalya was a fine woman. A fine woman . . . and a hell of a pilot.

He pulled on the cigarette and exhaled through his nostrils.

Pilots.

It had taken him only a couple of days to form a different opinion about Russian pilots. Unlike American and British pilots, who got to go home after a certain number of missions, the Soviets—and also the Germans for that matter—continued to fly until they got killed. There were no minimum number of missions or a fixed-length tour of duty. Here you fought until it was over or you died, whichever came first.

"How are you feeling, Jackovich?"

Jack stared up at the nearly emaciated Aris Broz. The Yugoslav held a bottle in his hands, offering Jack a sip, but Jack kindly declined. Aris sat next to him.

"It's going to be another cold night, Comrade Jackovich."

"That seems to be the norm around here."

"That was a good job you did with the knife on the Nazi pig."

Jack frowned as he remembered the young German soldier he had killed in the forest. "Can't say that I'm very proud of it. He was just a kid, you know. A teenager. But I had no choice."

Aris smiled and patted Jack on the shoulder. "You have a lot to learn about the Hitlerites. They are not humans, you know? They are . . . the devil incarnate. The things they do to people, to civilians. They are demons, Jackovich, and must be exterminated at all cost."

"I think I'll just keep calling them the enemy."

Aris took a swig from his bottle, rolled it inside his mouth for a few seconds, and swallowed it. "Whatever you say, Comrade Jackovich. Oh, by the way, Natalya told us how you two got shot down. I saw the jet too."

Jack narrowed his eyes. "Oh, really?"

"Yes. It has no propellers and it's very fast."

"Please tell me what you know, Aris."

The Yugoslav described his encounter with the panzers in a tone that lacked emotion. He explained how he saw two German soldiers burn to death, and how upset he had been when the jet blew away the roadblock.

"That's a very special plane, Aris."

"Yes, and my people are trying to find it."

"I've seen two so far. I wonder how many more are there."

"One of our contacts near Rostov thinks he saw one."

Jack's eyes narrowed. "Hmm . . . how far away is that from here?"

"About a day's walk. Less if we drive, but that could be dangerous. This is no-man's-land. There is no telling what we'd find on the roads."

"Could you take me there?"

"Take you where, Jack?" said Natalya from behind. She sat next to Jack with a cup of coffee in her hands. She pressed her shoulder against his. He liked that.

"Aris here tells me he thinks where there might be one of those German jets." Jack stared into her eyes.

Her eyes blinked understanding before she said, "You are crazy, Jack Towers. Absolutely insane."

He shrugged.

"Okay, okay . . ." she added, dropping her stare while showing Jack her open palms. "Assume we *do* find it and manage to steal it from the Germans. Have you ever flown one like it?"

He slowly shook his head.

"All right," she continued. "*Assume* you can fly it. What then? Where are you going to take it?"

He shrugged again and said, "To our base. Where else?"

Her eyes widened as she said, "You are going to fly a German jet into Colonel Krasilov's base? Are you insane? You will be shot down before—"

Aris interrupted. "Did you say Colonel *Krasilov's* base?"

Jack and Natalya turned toward him.

"Yes," she said.

"Why do you ask?" said Jack.

Aris dropped his eyebrows at the pair. "Colonel *Aleksandrovich Nikolai* Krasilov?"

Jack nodded. "Yes, yes. The Red Air Force colonel. He's the one responsible for the shit that I'm in by talking me into fighting the Germans instead of sticking to my instructor role."

As Natalya slapped his shoulder in jest, Aris Broz looked away while mumbling, "I'll be damned. Small world."

"What do you mean?" asked Natalya.

"I know his wife . . . Zoya."

"You do?" asked Jack. "But . . . I thought that she was imprisoned by the Germans, perhaps even dead."

"She *was* in a German concentration camp in Poland. But we rescued her and dozens of other women prisoners back in the fall of 1941."

Jack and Natalya both said in unison, "Are you sure?"

"Of course," the partisan replied. "Very brave woman. Pretty too."

"What . . . what happened to her?" Natalya asked.

Aris took a few minutes to explain how Zoya Krasilov had talked him into heading toward Russia to sabotage the German supply lines. She had fought alongside them for a few months, until parting company near Vyazma, during the first winter Russian counteroffensive to prevent the Germans from taking Moscow. "I last saw her at a Red Army base near Moscow on Christmas of 1941. About a year ago."

Jack and Natalya exchanged another glance before he said, "Colonel Krasilov . . . he thinks she is still in that concentration camp."

"Or worse," she added.

"She *could* be dead for all I know," warned Aris. "Remember that over a million Russian soldiers have perished in the last year across the entire eastern front."

"Good point," Natalya said. "But at the very least the news that she was freed, plus that she made it back to Russia, would surely give the colonel some hope."

"But then again," said Jack, frowning. "Wouldn't she have made some attempt to write by now? Why hasn't she tried to make contact for this past year?"

Natalya smiled. "You're thinking like an American, Jack. I'm sure that in your country the government makes it a high priority to keep soldiers in touch with their loved ones to maintain high morale, to make them fight harder. But that is not the case here."

Aris nodded. "The Russian high command believes that a soldier is better off not getting distracted with letters from home. The quicker a soldier breaks away from family and friends, the sooner that individual becomes the killer machine that Moscow expects all Russians to be, especially when fighting against such a terrible enemy."

"The only motivator that our government uses," added Natalya, "is fear."

"Fear?"

She nodded. "You either fight the Germans or get executed. It's their bullets or ours that will kill you, Jack. What is important is the survival of the Soviet Union, even at the cost of millions of lives. That is why the colonel's wife may have not been able to contact him."

"And even if she tried to send out queries, it's very likely that those requests for information never made it past Moscow."

"Well," Jack said, standing, still amazed at the vast differences in their cultures. "The colonel still has the right to know that his wife survived the concentration camp and made it back to Moscow in one piece, and I will personally deliver the good news the moment I land that German jet on his runway."

89

Sins of War

Ten Miles South of Rostov
December 17, 1942

Jack Towers and Natalya Makarova followed Aris and a dozen other partisans as they made their way north. The sun had already broken above the horizon, casting enough light inside the murky woods for Jack to get a better feel for where he was.

Following Aris' advice on proper breathing in forty-below weather to avoid excessive heat loss, Jack kept a scarf around his mouth and nose, forcing himself to breathe slowly. Under no condition was he to open his mouth unless he had to talk to someone, and even that was kept to a minimum to maintain their stealthiness.

The group walked single-file with ten feet in between,

preventing an enemy mine from hurting more than one or two of them. It would also allow them to have ample warning to seek cover if someone in the group spotted a German patrol.

The road narrowed as it began to veer its way up the side of a hill. Jack struggled to keep his balance. His aviator boots lacked the necessary traction for a smooth ascent. He slipped on an icy slab, landed on his back, and began to slide down the hill.

Flapping his limbs to find anything to hold onto, he crashed against a tree, stopping. He looked up and noticed the partisans' grim faces.

Jack slowly nodded at their silent reprimand. With likely German patrols in the region, the noise could have easily given away their position. Embarrassed, he struggled to stand and continued moving uphill under the watchful eye of the guerrillas.

Only after reaching the edge of the bluff did Jack realize how high up they were. From where he stood he could see several miles of white, desolate countryside extending beyond the jagged edge of the frozen rimrock.

As they neared the summit, Aris, who was the lead, abruptly raised his hand.

The caravan stopped, and the Yugoslav dropped to the ground and crawled forward to take a glimpse at the other side of the hill.

The group remained still. Jack heard shouting or screaming.

Slowly, the team crawled up and took a spot at the edge of the hill. Jack lay down next to Natalya and shoved aside enough snow to get a clear view of a small village below. It didn't take him but a few seconds to realize what was happening.

Like most villages in the region, the people sympathized with the partisans. One truck and a dozen German soldiers gathered at the center of the village, where around thirty villagers gathered off to one side.

A German officer, probably their leader, grabbed an old

woman from the group and forced her to her knees. He then screamed in Russian for the partisan collaborators to step forward.

None did, but most pleaded with the Germans. That had no effect. The German officer grabbed his pistol, pressed it against the old woman's head, and fired.

"Jesus! What in the hell—"

Natalya squeezed his hand, hissing, "Keep it down, Jack."

"But that son of a bitch just—"

"This goes on every day, Jackovich," said Aris as he knelt next to Jack and put a hand over his shoulder. "Demons. They're nothing but demons."

"Are you going to let them get away with that?"

Aris grinned, his eyes burning. "Justice will prevail, my American friend. *Partisan* justice."

Aris then signaled his men to follow him. Jack and Natalya were about to get up but Aris motioned them to remain put.

"We can't afford for either one of you to get hurt," said the partisan leader. "You are air warriors. We belong to the land battle."

Jack wanted to go along anyway, but Natalya pulled him down. "We might be more of a burden than help, Jack. They have trained together. Let them do what they do—"

Jack heard something, like the muffled cry of a woman, but it did not originate from the village. His head turned toward a road just below them, snaking its way down to the village in the valley. Jack crawled back until he was out of sight from someone in the small town, raised to a crouch, and, weapon in hand, began to move down the side of the hill.

"Jack? What are you doing?"

"Shh . . ." Jack motioned Natalya to follow him.

She looked down at the village, back to Jack, and then reluctantly crawled toward him.

"What is going on?"

"Trust me. Come."

"First tell me where we're going."

Jack ignored her and continued to head down.

"Damn you, Jack," she whispered as she began to follow.

This time Jack was careful when making his way toward the road below. He had seen Aris and the other partisans using the land to their advantage by selecting their foot- or handhold before moving, and avoiding hesitation midstride. The terrain was slippery, but as Jack quickly realized, as long as he remained in slow but constant motion, he could make reasonable and controlled progress. After the first hundred yards his confidence grew to the point that he started coaching Natalya. His breathing also slowly became one with his moves. He inhaled before moving, held his breath during transition, and slowly exhaled as he reached his next rest point.

The sound of a woman struggling got louder as Jack approached the unpaved road, but with trees in the way, he still couldn't get a clear view.

The slope changed to almost forty-five degrees, forcing Jack to change his strategy. He opted to slide on his back, using his arms and legs to hold onto roots and branches to control his descent, until he reached the edge of the trees, where a thick underbrush prevented him from seeing what he feared he would see. He looked up hill and watched Natalya catching up with him, kneeling by his side.

Jack parted the foliage enough to see two German soldiers on the bed of a truck parked around the corner from the village. One soldier had a girl, who appeared to be around fifteen, pinned against the flatbed while the second, the trousers of his uniform down to his knees, forced himself into her from the top. The first soldier held her arms and kept a piece of cloth over her mouth as the girl's head snapped back with every thrust.

"Bastards," Jack hissed, glancing over to Natalya. There were tears in her eyes.

He holstered the pistol and grabbed a double-edge knife. "Cover me, Natalya, but don't fire."

"But, Jack, Aris said not to—"

"It's gonna be all right. Trust me. Now cover me," he whispered.

Natalya pulled out her pistol as Jack moved down the hill until he reached a spot directly above the kneeling German holding the girl down. The fingers of his right hand curled around the handle, Jack jumped over the side and landed on the German.

His blade entered the base of the German's neck at an angle. Bones and cartilage snapped as he crashed against the soldier and pushed him to the side.

The corpse rolled away.

The second German jerked in surprise, still inside the girl.

He jumped off and reached for his pants, but his fumbling hands never made it past his knees. Jack lunged, slitting his throat. The soldier whipped both hands up as blood jetted from a wide gash. He tried to scream but couldn't, finally dropping to his knees while staring at Jack, then at the bloody knife in his hand, before collapsing.

The girl, obvious in shock, had not moved during the entire incident. Misted by the blood of his victims, Jack pulled up her heavy pants and waved Natalya over. She climbed up the rear of the truck and reached the girl's side while Jack walked up the road to see if someone had heard him.

A hair-raising scream made Jack rush toward the village, hiding around the corner, his eyes narrowing in anger at the sight.

The German officer dragged a young woman away from the group, ripped off her dress, and tore down her undergarments. Holding her from behind, he stabbed her temple with the muzzle of his pistol as she braced herself, shivering. If he didn't kill her, the Russian winter would.

Protests erupted from the villagers, whom the soldiers held back with the butts of their rifles.

"Partisans! Enemies of the Reich! Come forward and spare the life of this woman!" the officer screamed to the mob of crazed villagers.

"Butchers! Butchers!" came the unanimous response.

A gunshot splattered across the frozen tundra.

The girl now stood screaming while hugging herself. The German officer lay on the ground, his face smeared with blood. The soldiers appeared momentarily confused.

Jack grabbed his Colt, flipped the safety, and lurched around the corner while the Germans raced for cover behind their truck. Half of them never made it. They fell victims to Aris' sharpshooters. The rest began to exchange fire with the partisans.

Jack approached the Germans from behind. He knelt down, cocked his weapon, and fired. The first German jumped up in shock as his hands tried to reach behind his back, where Jack's bullet had struck. Before he fell, Jack already had a second German lined up in his sights, firing twice. The German crashed against the side of the truck. The other three Germans swung their machine guns in his direction. Jack dove behind a tree as bark and snow exploded all around him, but it didn't last long. As he placed both hands over his face to protect himself from wood chips stinging him, fire ceased.

Slowly, warily, Jack got up and looked around the tree trunk. Aris stood over the bodies of the Germans. Jack picked up his gun and walked in his direction. Two of the Germans—their chests covered with blood—were moving their heads from side to side. Aris shoved the muzzle of his weapon inside the mouth of one of the Germans and fired once. The German jerked for a second, then remained still. The Yugoslav did the same to the second fallen German. Jack felt no compassion for the soldiers, whom on closer inspection appeared to be not older than twenty.

An hour later, with all the corpses buried under the snow behind the village and the trucks driven into the woods and covered with branches, the villagers brought out loaves of bread and bottles of vodka for Aris and his rescuing band.

The men ate outside in front of the fire while the women, Natalya included, tended the assaulted girls.

"Demons, Jackovich," said Aris while sitting next to him by the fire, a bottle of vodka in his right hand. "I told you they are nothing but demons."

Jack stared back at his bearded friend. The Yugoslav stuffed a large chunk of bread in his mouth and washed it down with a gulp of vodka. Jack's view of the Germans had definitely taken a turn for the worse during today's events. He no longer saw them as the enemy but as the most depraved of criminals.

"Jesus. What kind of war is this anyway?" he muttered, extending his hands toward the fire.

Aris took another swig of vodka and passed the bottle to Jack, who took a sip.

"Their plans have been clear from the start, Comrade Jackovich. The Hitlerites seek the total destruction of this country. They have no regard for Slavic lives and take them without a second thought. See that young boy over there?"

Jack spotted a kid biting into a large piece of bread he held with both hands.

"What about him?"

"He saw his entire family get executed while he returned from the forest with a pile of firewood. The Germans raped his mother and two older sisters before hanging them. And the worst part of it was that they weren't partisan collaborators. They were simply picked at random and executed."

Jack narrowed his eyes. "Why?"

"To create terror. For every German killed by partisans, ten innocent peasants will hang. The rule, of course, is aimed at trying to force the people to do what the Germans themselves have not been able to do: stop us."

Jack couldn't think of anything to say to that. Aris continued after he grabbed the bottle from Jack and took the last swallow.

"We see that as an act of desperation. The Germans are resorting to forlorn measures to try to bring the situation under control, and it's not working. That frustration, of course, drives them into committing more and more atrocious acts of violence, but it will all soon end."

Jack stared at the fire. "How can you tell for sure? I mean, there are still, what? More than two million Germans in Russia. I call that far from being over."

Aris smiled. "You are correct, my friend. It is not over yet, but when it is, there will be two million dead Germans. Justice will prevail. The German high command will regret the day they decided to attack the Soviet Union. Soon, the thought of Soviet reprisal will haunt every living German. It will be their nightmare."

Jack didn't know how to respond.

"Justice will prevail, Jackovich," Aris added. Justice will—"

A boy came running to their side, leaned down, and murmured something into the Yugoslav's ear. Aris lowered his gaze.

"What was that all about?" Jack asked as the kid ran away.

Aris looked at Jack. "Come. I want you to see for yourself the agony that this people must endure."

Jack followed Aris to one of the shacks at the edge of the village, his skin shivering at the thought of anything worse than the horror that he had already seen today.

He walked a few steps behind Aris. The leader of the partisan band reached the shack—a round structure made of stone, clay, and straw. It had an opening at the top, where he could see a trail of smoke from the burning stove, probably also used as a heater.

Aris pulled the canvas flap hanging at the entrance and held it open to let Jack in. Through the yellowish light, Jack saw a man in his early twenties lying in bed. Two old women sat by his bedside as a child held his hand.

Aris turned to Jack and whispered, "We were about to engage a German detachment of soldiers two weeks ago. As we planned our attack in this village, he and three others were in an adjacent shack readying the weapons. It appears that a grenade slipped from one of the commandos' hands and went off by his feet, lightly injuring the others, but mangling his right leg.

"Because we knew the Hitlerites were coming, we all fled and left him in the care of the villagers. We hoped that maybe the Germans would leave him alone since he was wounded. Instead, they tortured him for information, and when he refused, instead of just killing him, the bastards rubbed horse manure on the open wound and left. The villagers tried to clean the leg as best they could. I got a report on his condition every few days, and from what I heard it seemed that his leg had stopped bleeding and was healing fine. I saw him an hour ago, and he claimed to be feeling better, but that boy just whispered in my ear that he saw his leg without the bandage, and it looked blue and smelled like rotten cheese."

Jack looked away.

Aris approached the young commando.

"Hello, Sasha."

The women and the child moved to the side of the room.

"Hello, Aris."

"You don't mind if I take a look at that leg, do you?"

A half-smile appeared on Sasha's face. "Wh-why? It's all right. I already told you it has healed. I might even walk back with you tomorrow."

Aris' expression became harsh. "The leg, Sasha. Let me see it."

The young man turned his head to the side as Aris lifted the cover. Aris removed the cloth wrapped around it. The leg was blue with gangrene from the ankle all the way up past the knee.

"Call the others," Aris said to the child, who promptly ran outside. "That leg has to go, Sasha."

If Jack could ever describe what fear looked like, it would be what he saw in that young man's eyes at that instant.

Sasha's lips quivered and his face contorted with anguish. "No, Aris, please. No. Look, I can move the foot and the toes. Look—"

"I'm sorry, son. It's either that or you'll be dead in a week. That gangrene is going to eat you alive and you know it. It has to be done."

Three other partisans arrived. One carried a black case. Aris opened it and removed a green bottle, two small rags, a thick piece of leather, and a hand saw.

Jack stopped breathing, nausea worming in his stomach. Aris made Sasha drink a quarter of a bottle of vodka.

Then it was time to start. Aris' men took their positions around the stunned and half-drunk fighter. Jack turned around, not relishing the thought of seeing this. The women and child ran outside in tears. Jack started after them.

"Comrade Jackovich?"

Jack stopped in midstride, inhaled deeply, exhaled, and faced Aris Broz.

"Please hold his leg while I amputate it."

Jack froze. *For the love of*—

"Now, Jackovich. I need your help." Aris' face matched the seriousness of the life-and-death decision he had made for the young commando.

Jack gripped the decomposed foot and wedged it in his armpit to hold it tight. Then he used both hands to force the knee against the bed while fighting the nausea induced by the rotten smell that assaulted his nostrils.

Jack's gaze met with the young warrior's for a moment. His pleading eyes touched Jack's soul, but what could he do? The damage had already been done by the Germans. The manure had created an infection that could have been stopped had Sasha been administered an antibiotic, but the rudimentary cleaning of the leg after the Germans had smeared it with excrement had not been enough to prevent it.

Jack's legs quivered when Sasha lifted his head and stared at his leg one last time before one of the partisans forced the young man's face down against the bed while jamming the piece of leather in between his teeth.

Aris soaked the serrated blade with vodka and brought it to the fire. Jack watched the blade burn for several seconds before looking down at Sasha's chest rapidly swelling and deflating as the young man mentally prepared himself for the amputation.

Aris brought the saw down next to the leg and used his

other hand to feel the skin on Ivanovich's thigh, apparently looking for the safest place to make the cut without robbing the young man of a healthy section of his leg. His finger stopped feeling on a spot roughly three inches above the knee, about an inch from the decayed skin.

Aris lifted his head and scanned the room. "Keep him steady! He must not move no matter what happens or he might bleed to death!"

"I'd rather die, Comrade Broz!" Sasha screamed after managing to free one hand and remove the piece of leather from his mouth. "Please, just shoot me. Please!"

"Quiet!" Aris shouted. "Everyone quiet!"

"What is the use of living if I can't—"

"Keep that leather in his mouth! What's the matter with you, men? Can't you hold one man down?"

The partisans brought him under control once more as Jack saw Aris pressing the disinfected blade over the selected section of flesh.

And began to cut.

90

Sacrifice

JG52 Gruppe 1, Fifty Miles North of Rostov.
December 17, 1942

Erich Steinhoff flew so fast that he felt out of reach of any other aircraft in the sky. White plains blended with the brownish woods to create a solid floor as he dashed across the sky faster and faster. A large bomber approached, its many gun turrets swinging in his direction. Erich decided to engage, lining up the huge flying fortress in his sights. He fired for what seemed like an eternity, but nothing would happen. The aircraft simply continued in its path. Erich scanned the ground below and saw Sonja waving at

him. Then he saw the bomber's payload bay doors opening. He continued to press the trigger, but it had no effect.
The bomber maintained its run dropping dozens of bombs,
their high-pitch sound mixing with Sonja's shrieks as she
ran for cover. The bombs went off and Sonja disappeared
behind a sheet of fire that reached up to the sky and engulfed him as well. The fire . . . the burning fire. The heat
was intolerable. It burned the flesh off his face . . .

Erich kicked the sheets and bolted out of his cot, soaked
with perspiration. He gazed around the inside of his tent
before exhaling heavily and rubbing his eyes with the
palms of his hands.

The nightmares worsened as the war progressed.

"Major? Major Steinhoff?"

Erich heard one of his pilots calling from outside the
tent.

"Yes! What is it?"

"Please come outside, sir. We have a problem."

What now?

"What are you talking about?" he asked as he put on his
boots and heavy jacket.

"It's about your mechanic, sir."

Erich hurriedly buttoned up his coat and stepped outside.

"What is going on? And where is . . ." Erich saw the pilot pointing at a few men gathered around Erich's jet.

The cold stinging his cheeks, Erich ran to the side of
his Me 262 and shoved the pilots aside. Mathias lay dead
on the frozen snow. His hands still clutched a wrench and
a wire from the recently arrived box of turbojet spare
parts.

"He must have been here all night, sir," said a pilot, but
Erich was hardly listening anymore. His eyes were fixed on
the stiff, frozen body of his black friend.

"The engine is fixed, sir," reported another mechanic.
"Mathias fixed the engine! Your plane is ready to fly!"

Erich just gazed at Mathias' dead stare, his heart aching
for the African.

"You and you," he finally ordered to a pair of pilots. "I want you to dig a grave this minute."

"But, sir," one of the pilots replied. "The ground is frozen. You really don't expect us to—"

"*Now.*"

The pilots lowered their gaze. "Yes, sir."

91

Bloody Airfield

Bletchley Park, Buckinghamshire, England
December 17, 1942

REF: CX/MSS/T262/67   HP4646

ZZZZZ

(HP 4646 & 4646 CR ONA GT QX YKE GU 7 & 7)

Results at two two zero zero hours sixteenth. Prototype 1 engaged in two air battles with positive results. Minor engine damage. Received spares. Awaiting arrival of mechanic. Jagdgeschwadern 52 Gruppe 1 prototype one max. vel. 534 knots. Second prototype undamaged with Gruppe 3 xxxxx. Maj. E. Steinhoffzzzzzzzz

PM
CR   17/12/42

Peter Myers read the note as Charles Rosset looked on.

"Is this for real? Five hundred and thirty-four bloody knots? The bastards must have perfected jet propulsion."

"It appears so, sir."

"Send a message to the eastern front. Give them the coordinates of the bloody airfield with instructions to blast it to hell while the bastard is grounded!"

"Yes, sir!"

"Now we need to figure out where in the hell is the second bloody jet!"

Myers sat down with a map of the Stalingrad area. "Where are you hiding little friend? Where?"

92

Bomb Run

Fifty Miles North of Rostov
December 17, 1942

A thick layer of gray clouds extended as far as the eye could see, turning the midafternoon sky gloomy and depressing.

Red Air Force Lieutenant Mikhail Petrov lowered the nose of his Petlyakov Pe-2 twin-engine bomber until his altimeter read two hundred feet. He shifted his eyes from his controls to the southern Russia countryside, hating the fact that he and his crew of three flew alone this chilly afternoon. No escorts accompanied him to provide a shield against enemy fighters, and no backup bombers followed him to complete the mission if something went wrong with his machine.

But there was a good reason for the added mission risk, Petrov reflected as he trimmed the wheel to keep the nose level with the horizon. Additional planes would only increase the risk of the Germans detecting what Petrov considered so far to be a stealth approach. Stealth, however, was not the only reason Petrov kept his heavy bomber flying at such dangerous altitude. His Pe-2 was a well-designed bomber with one exception: the engineers at Petlyakov had failed to include an underside gun turret. His plane was defenseless if approached directly from underneath.

Such oversight puzzled him as much as the very unusual last-minute change of orders that pulled him away from his squadron approaching the Stalingrad pocket and diverted him to attack a lone airstrip.

Someone must have one hell of a bug up his ass to pull a stunt like this, Petrov thought while scanning the terrain ahead. In all his years with the air force, he had always been able to plan missions properly at least a few hours in advance. A mission should never be modified after it had started, unless, of course, bad weather developed over the target, in which case Petrov always had a secondary target for his squadron. But pulling the lead bomber at such short notice to do a search-and-destroy run based on some British intelligence report about a German plane without propellers qualified as insane.

In Petrov's opinion, his new mission had all the makings of a disaster.

Erich silently stood by Mathias' grave not knowing what to say. Even though his mother had been a devoted Catholic, Erich never really had gotten into religion. At first the Fascists convinced him to do otherwise, and after he had realized the farce of the Nazi system, he had been too busy flying to worry about praying.

Now Erich wanted to pray for his friend, but he didn't know any prayers. He did remember his mother telling him once that he didn't actually have to know a specific prayer to reach God.

Closing his eyes, Erich began to pray for his friend.

"Major Steinhoff!"

Erich stared at the intrusion.

"Major Stein—"

"Damn it, man! Can't you see I'm—" Erich jumped to his feet and raced for his Me 262 the moment he heard the engines in the distance.

Petrov scanned the ground, but at that altitude it was difficult for him to see beyond a few hundred feet. He was about to climb to get a quick glance of the area, but decided against it. *Do that Mikhail, and you'll have every available German fighter on your tail in minutes.*

On the other hand, if he remained over enemy territory for too long, he was bound to run into some fighters anyhow.

He silently cursed his superiors for placing him and his crew in such a predicament.

Erich was confused. The engines got progressively louder, and then faded away.

He reached his jet, climbed in, and in a few minutes he taxied to the end of the runway.

Petrov checked his watch and fuel gauges. Time was running out and he still had not found the German airfield. One of the problems with bombing targets identified by Direction-Finder during message intercepts was that the error of the target coordinates could vary as much as few kilometers.

Certain that he had swept the area several times and had not seen anything that resembled an airfield—much less a plane without propellers—he decided to risk a quick higher altitude scan of the area.

Petrov didn't have to climb for long. The moment he reached seven hundred feet, he saw the field at ten o'clock, and immediately dropped the nose and pushed full throttles to start his run.

"Bombardier, target in sight!"

"Bomb bay doors opening, comrade!"

"Thirty seconds to target!"

"Bombs are active. Ready to drop on your command, sir!"

Erich pulled back on the throttle handles and the Me 262 sprang forward as three Gustavs lined up behind him. Airspeed scurried above 150 knots. He kept the craft on the ground for another ten knots before slowly easing the stick back. Mathias had done a superb job with the turbine, which delivered thrust smoothly.

The fighter left the ground. Erich slapped the gear handle and pulled up the nose by a few degrees to clear the forest.

Petrov knew the clearing would appear at any moment. He checked his airspeed. Two hundred twenty knots!

The large bomber shook under the strain as sweat trickled down the sides of Petrov's forehead. The airfield loomed beyond the trees. His lips curved upward when he noticed the long line of fighters on both sides of the—

Petrov instinctively broke left when a plane filled his windscreen.

Erich cut hard right, pushing the Me 262 to the design envelope. The G-forces hammered him. He screamed in pain as the extreme pressure reddened and tunneled his vision. Both hands clutching the control stick, he focused on the artificial horizon. He could not let the nose drop a single degree during the tight turn while flying at just one hundred feet doing three hundred knots—an impossibility in a Gustav.

The palms of his hands sweaty, Erich kept the rear pressure and slowly leveled off. He turned his head to see what he had just missed.

Petrov knew he was in trouble when the nose of his bomber dropped below the horizon. He had turned too fast while pushing maximum airspeed. The left wing grazed the treetops while his hands clutched the wheel and pulled hard. The muscles in his arms ached from the effort, but the nose would not come up. The wingtip dipped further into the trees until it struck something solid and detached itself from the fuselage.

The forest crashing against his windshield, Petrov let go a shriek of anger. In ordering him on such mission, his superiors had put the gun to his head. The Hitlerites had merely pulled the trigger.

Erich saw the forest igniting a few hundred feet from the airfield and realized how close they had come to total destruction. He climbed to three thousand feet and scanned the skies for more enemy bombers but saw none.

Puzzled, he headed back to the airfield.

93

Jet Propulsion

Twenty Miles Southwest of Rostov
December 17, 1942

Captain Jack Towers lifted his gaze and saw the crystalline, southern Siberian sky. The majestic view contrasted sharply with the desolation and suffering below it. This was Jack's first war, and the romance had long been lost. The glorified posters of fighter squadrons flying into the sunset was just the mask of a voracious beast with an insatiable appetite for young men. There was nothing to be gained by war—Jack was now certain of that. Not for the soldiers that fought it, anyway.

He reached the top of the hill and crawled next to Aris. The Yugoslav scanned the airfield with the set of binoculars he'd stolen from the German truck earlier that morning. He passed them to Jack, who slowly searched the edge of the forest outlining the German airstrip, carefully inspecting every plane and then continuing to the next one when he spotted its propeller. The unpaved airstrip measured roughly two thousand feet long by seventy feet wide. The Germans had done a fairly good job of keeping it clear of snow, and the surface appeared reasonably flat. Tents lined both sides of the airfield.

"You're sure about this place, Aris?" Jack asked as he finished searching one side and saw nothing but Gustavs and a few larger planes.

"Our contacts tell us this is where they saw one landing yesterday afternoon. Maybe they moved it to another airfield."

"Maybe, maybe not," Jack said, smiling. He handed the binoculars to Aris and pointed to a spot directly behind a tent halfway down the airfield.

Aris pressed the binoculars against his eyes. "Is that it? The one without the propeller in the nose?"

"That's the one," Jack responded taking the binoculars back from the partisan and studying the plane once more. It was dark, but there were enough lights by the edge of the clearing for Jack to see the streamlined outline of the German jet clearly. It looked like something out of a science fiction magazine, but it wasn't. The plane was for real, and Jack had already witnessed what it was capable of doing.

"Are you sure you want to do this, Jack?" Natalya asked as she leaned down next to him. He returned the binoculars to Aris, who used them to scan the rest of the field.

"There is no other way." He stared into her pleading hazel eyes and put a hand over her cheek. "I know what I'm doing. Trust me."

Without waiting for a response, Jack got the binoculars back from Aris and stared at the German jet once again. An officer emerged from the tent right next to it. Jack put down the binoculars and looked at Aris. "Let's do it."

A cold wind sweeping across the clearing, Major Hans Barkhorn quietly strolled by the edge of the runway while proudly admiring the sleek nose of his Me 262 barely sticking out from the forest. In spite of the harsh cold, he managed a smile. After two days and fifteen victories, Barkhorn had long decided the jet aircraft was everything his superiors claimed it would be, and more. The jet was untouchable in the skies.

News of Steinhoff's engine trouble had reached Barkhorn

early that morning. Barkhorn had not been surprised. The young major took too many chances by getting close to the enemy before shooting it down, especially with the jet. Barkhorn could only hope his former subordinate learned from his mistake and developed a different hunting tactic before he destroyed the valuable prototype.

He turned around and headed back for his tent. The air was too cold tonight. Barkhorn could usually take it, but not tonight. It hurt too much to breathe.

Firmly gripping his double-edge hunting knife, Aris Broz approached the base from the east—the side where they had spotted the jet. Jack, also clutching a knife, remaining a few feet behind him. Their weapons were slung across their backs.

Natalya was not with them. She had reluctantly agreed to head back to the nearest Soviet air base the moment she got the signal that Jack's plan had worked. Aris had placed two partisans on either side of the runway. The rest were with Natalya at the top of the small hill.

Hit and run, Jackovich. Stealth and surprise are our main weapons, he recalled Aris telling him ten minutes before.

Jack felt much more comfortable in the woods now. He felt he blended well within its protective cover. He moved only when Aris moved, and stopped when he stopped. He used the same foot- and handholds as the Yugoslav guerrilla, and managed consistently to pace himself such that he could sustain his body's oxygen needs by slowly breathing through his nostrils.

He was about to take another step when Aris abruptly stopped. The bearded Yugoslav didn't have to say or point to anything. Jack nodded the moment he spotted the German sentries some fifty feet ahead. The soldiers were smoking.

Jack tilted his head. Given the forty-below temperatures, he couldn't blame them for doing that, although if it had been him, he would had chosen hot coffee—or anything else that wouldn't give away his position.

Aris pointed at Jack with his index finger and made a circle in the air with his hand.

Jack nodded. The two men split. Aris's tactic was both simple and clever: surprise the enemy from the place it would least expect an assault to come.

Jack made a wide semicircle to the right of the guards while Aris made one to the left. Now Jack had to be extra careful. He didn't have Aris to guide him through the forest. He was on his own, and well aware that one false move could blow everything. The Germans were too close.

Jack developed a new rhythm, moving only when the gusts of wind swept through the trees, stopping the moment the breeze died down, and moving forward once more with the next gust. After a few minutes he could almost anticipate when the breeze would come again, and how long it would last.

The rustling of branches and leaves mixing with his own movement, Jack kept the pace for another five minutes, reaching his objective on the other side of the guards—so close to the edge of the clearing that Jack could see the tail of the jet about forty feet away. Aris already waited for him.

The partisan leader pointed at the guards. Jack nodded and followed him, slowly closing the gap to twenty feet. The guards continued to smoke while their weapons hung loosely from their shoulders.

The constant whirl of the wind through the trees masking their sounds, Jack and Aris dropped to a crouch and quietly—

The guards turned in their direction and began to walk.

Jack froze. Aris had to drag him down behind a thick pine.

The Germans stopped. Jack gazed at Aris, who brought a finger to his lips. Jack complied, remaining totally still. He didn't even breathe.

The guards, clutching their weapons in front of them, inched closer until they were directly on the other side of the tree. Aris motioned Jack to go around at the count of three.

Aris extended his index finger.

Jack recoiled.

The Yugoslav extended his middle finger.

Jack leaned his body forward.

Now.

Jack shot around the tree and caught the German broadside, stabbing him on the side of the neck at an angle. Jack pushed into the knife, driving it in while nearly lifting the soldier off his feet. By the time the German dropped, Aris was already wiping the blood off his own blade.

He smiled at Jack, who felt sick. It was one thing to pull the trigger and watch the enemy go down in a smoking plane. It was a different story to watch them roll on the ground gasping for air with a severed windpipe.

Jack shifted his gaze toward the clearing and saw the long cylindrical turbines hanging beneath the wings of the German jet.

"It's all yours, Comrade Jackovich."

Jack carefully walked by the tail while Aris, left hand clutching his knife and right hand on the handle of his machine gun, warily surveyed the deserted airfield. Most pilots were inside their tents.

Major Barkhorn heard a strange noise and went back outside. He scanned the airfield but all seemed quiet. He was about to return to his tent when he noticed two sentries roaming around his plane. He frowned. Barkhorn had given them strict instructions not to touch the jet and to guard it from a distance. Yet, he saw them inspecting the wings and looking into the jet exhausts.

He threw his cigar on the ground and marched toward them. They were going to get the reprimand of their lives.

As the German approached, Aris stopped Jack from squeezing the trigger of his machine gun. Instead the partisan grabbed his knife by the blade and waited until the officer was almost out of sight of the clearing.

The German stopped next to the wing and froze. He had

recognized them, but before he had a chance to turn around and yell for help, Jack watched the glistening shape of Aris' knife streak across the chilly air and imbed itself in the German's chest. The German dropped to his knees, but not before he let go a loud shriek, which Aris quickly stopped by jamming a hand over the German's mouth while he finished him off.

"Go, Jackovich! Do what you must! Hurry!"

Jack climbed onto the wing and walked up to the cockpit. He opened the canopy, crawled inside, and closed it, locking it from the inside.

He spotted three Germans racing across the field. Jack pulled off his heavy gloves and scanned the cockpit. The basic instrumentation was as it should be. The artificial horizon to the left, next to the airspeed indicator and above the slip-turn indicator. On the right side were the directional gyro, clock, and dual engine gauges. The jet's controls were standard stick and rudder with a built-in trigger and radio buttons on the upper section of the control stick. The landing gear lever was to his right above the small elevator trim wheel.

His head snapped up the moment he heard gunfire, quickly followed by a loud scream. Jack glanced to his right and watched Aris' body tossed by enemy gunfire.

Jack turned around and watched Aris dragging himself into the forest, but the Yugoslav guerrilla didn't get far. Another burst across his back killed him.

Gunfire erupted from both sides of the hill as the partisans began their coordinated attack to draw fire away from Jack.

Natalya knew something had gone wrong the moment she'd heard a scream and gunfire, but no sign of jet engines.

"Stay down!" one of the partisans shouted moments before a loud explosion caused three of Aris' men ten feet behind her to arch back and fall face up. The remaining two opened fire on the squad of Germans coming from their rear.

Natalya reached the fallen warriors, but in a moment she realized there was nothing she could do for them. Their chests had been ripped open with shrapnel.

She pulled out her pistol and was about to get to her feet when the remaining two partisans flew over her head riddled with bullets. She was trapped between the airfield and the advancing squad of Germans.

The steel helmets looming behind a line of bushes twenty feet away, Natalya rushed downhill toward the clearing. She was well aware of the fate fighting Soviet women faced in the hands of the Germans.

Jack saw five soldiers less than fifty feet in front of the plane, but for some reason no one would open fire. Three were busy returning fire from the hills. The others simply stared at the jet.

Jack threw what he guessed were the electronic switches to power the avionics. The cockpit came alive, giving him readings on fuel, oil, and turbine temperatures.

He pressed the dual set of buttons above the engines' gauges, and the turbines began to make a high-pitched whirl. Jack let go and the turbines died down.

He pressed them again until the turbines engaged. The jet briefly jerked forward. Jack pushed the dual throttle controls forward, but they didn't move. Puzzled, he pulled them back and the craft lurched forward.

"Shit! This thing works backward!"

The Germans took a few steps back as Jack left the clearing behind. One of them leveled his machine gun at him, but before he could let go a single shot, Jack lifted the trigger guard casing and fired for three seconds. Actually he had wanted only to fire for one second, but the powerful recoil nearly stopped the craft's momentum. Jack crashed against the control panel, bounced, and slammed his back against the seat while his finger remained on the trigger.

"Jesus!"

Half startled, Jack leaned forward and all he could see was a pile of body parts where the five Germans had been.

In disbelief at the kind of power packed in the nose cannons, he pulled back the throttle handles and the Messerschmitt lurched out of its hideout and onto the frozen runway. He quickly reduced throttle, deciding that it would take some time to get used to the volatile engine response.

The airstrip blared with sirens. Pilots ran for their craft as Jack slowly added more throttle. Two of them tried to climb onto the wings of the jet, but with additional power he left them behind and quickly taxied to the end of the strip and turned the jet around.

Now this is when the real test begins, Jack.

He had no idea of the takeoff or stall speeds for this jet. Furthermore, Jack had no idea what was the takeoff run. He had already estimated the runway was two thousand feet long. Did such a short runway require him to perform a special takeoff technique? Jack decided he would try a modified version of his Aircobra's short takeoff maneuver, and searched for the flaps' handle.

He spotted a vertical lever with three different settings. He lowered it to the first, and watched in satisfaction as the hydraulically driven flaps lowered. Suddenly, a spotlight blinded him. It came from his left.

Jack pressed left rudder and let go another burst the moment the nose lined up with the source of light. The light blew up in a bright flash. He realigned the nose and began to pull—

He glanced at the Me 262's built-in rearview mirror and saw Natalya running in his direction.

Natalya?

She reached the tail of the plane. Jack turned his head toward the runway and saw a truck loaded with soldiers racing toward him. He lined it up using rudder and throttle while stepping on the brakes, and let go another burst.

The guns were impressive. The truck stopped dead in its tracks, flipped, and went up in a ball of flames. Once more, Jack lined up the craft with the runway.

Natalya made it up the wing and began to bang on the canopy.

Jack unlocked it and she pulled it up.

"Are you crazy? You want to get us both killed?" he screamed. "You were supposed to have gone with—"

"They're coming, Jack! The Germans!"

"Wh-what are you—"

"They got the partisans! It was a massacre! They're right behind—"

He pulled her by the collar and sat her between him and the stick over his left leg. He closed and locked the canopy as more machine-gun fire erupted from the front. Several rounds ricocheted off the bulletproof glass.

Jack pressed the brake pedals, pushed full right rudder, and added throttle. As the Me 262 pivoted clockwise at great speed, Jack pressed the trigger.

The whole world seemed to catch fire around him as the Messerschmitt showered everything in sight with 30mm rounds.

Jack lifted his finger off the trigger. Gunfire ceased. He lined up the nose with the runway once more, and while pressing on the brakes, he pulled back the dual throttle handles.

"Hold on," Jack said, placing his face over her shoulder to get a better view of the runway. The jet trembled as Jack gave the throttle handles a final pull. Full throttle. The engine whirl became deafening.

The craft plunged forward the moment he released the brakes.

Natalya's body crushing him against the seat from the powerful acceleration, Jack tried to get a glimpse of the airspeed indicator, but her head was in the way.

"Read out the airspeed!"

"Seventy knots . . . eighty . . . Jack! There's a tank blocking the runway. Slow down!"

Jack shifted his gaze directly ahead and saw a panzer rolling onto the center of the runway.

"Just read the airspeed!"

The tank and a number of Germans were roughly one

thousand feet ahead. The massive turret turned in his direction. Jack lined up the tank and squeezed the trigger. The thundering cannons shook the entire craft.

"Airspeed!"

"Ninety knots . . . one hundred . . ."

The soldiers were cut to pieces by the guns and the tank caught fire but it remained there blocking the way. He estimated it was no more than seven hundred feet away.

"One hundred ten knots!"

Jack pulled back on the stick but the craft didn't climb. He decided they were too heavy and were not accelerating fast enough. He needed a way to reduce drag . . . the landing gear!

"One hundred twenty knots . . . Jack, the tank!"

Jack let go another burst. The tank exploded, but he could not see if it was out of the way or not. "Speed's down to one hundred ten knots . . . fifteen . . ."

The tank's turret was gone while the bottom half burned, but Jack decided that enough of it was still there to spoil his takeoff run. Using guns, however, was out of the question. The brutal recoil would only slow him down even further.

"One hundred twenty knots."

The scorching wreckage rapidly grew in size. In the corner of his eye, Jack noticed the muzzle flashes of Germans on the side of the runway emptying their machine guns on them.

Bullets bouncing off the glass, he reached for the landing gear lever and pulled it up as he eased back the stick. The jet trembled but left the ground. The landing lifted and locked in place.

"One hundred thirty knots!"

Flames filled his windshield. Jack pulled on the stick hard, and the Messerschmitt rose by a few feet. The bottom of the fuselage scraped the wreckage, but he had cleared it.

"Ninety knots, Jack! We're gonna stall!"

The stall buzzer went off. Jack lowered the nose and gained back some airspeed, but the jet dropped a few feet.

A cloud of sparks engulfed them the moment the jet's belly bounced off the runway before coming back up. Jack lowered the nose even more, keeping the plane just a couple of feet over the runway.

"One hundred forty . . . fifty . . . sixty."

Jack waited. He couldn't afford another stall. A wall of trees rapidly approached.

"One hundred seventy . . . eighty! The trees, Jack!"

A dark green wall nearly engulfed him. Jack pulled back on the stick and the jet sprang skyward at a steep angle. He waited for the impact of branches against the underside, but it never came. He had somehow cleared the forest. The stars were the only thing visible through the armored glass—the stars and the tiny cracks left by the rounds that had struck the sides of the bubble-shaped canopy. Jack quietly thanked the engineers at Messerschmitt for making the canopy bullet resistant. There were over a dozen cracks in all.

As he watched the altimeter reach five hundred feet, Jack eased the stick forward and reduced throttle, but the plane continued to climb. He reduced throttle once more, and the plane leveled off at a thousand feet. He trimmed the elevators and relaxed the pressure on the stick.

The craft now felt very smooth. Only the quiet hum of the turbines told him they were airborne. There was no trembling, no piston-induced vibrations, no turning propeller or black smoke coming out of the exhausts. The jet was indeed a work of art. The elevator trim worked perfectly. He let go of the stick and the artificial horizon confirmed his suspicion—the plane remained perfectly leveled.

Natalya rested her head against his shoulder as Jack briefly closed his eyes.

"You're crazy, Jack Towers. Absolutely crazy."

"We're not out of the woods yet, Natalya. We still got to land this thing."

She turned her head and smiled. "The Germans don't call us night witches for nothing, Jack."

94

After-Hours Visit

Krasilov and Chapman sat inside the briefing bunker and read the official report of the attempted surprise bombing of the German airfield.

The Red Air Force colonel pounded his fists on the table and stared into Chapman's bloodshot eyes. Neither of them had slept much in the past twenty-four hours.

"Damn! The bastards have probably moved it to another field by now. We lost our chance to blow it to hell!"

Chapman sat back on the wooden chair and quietly studied Krasilov through the smoke of the cigarette hanging off the side of his mouth. "We'll find the jets again, Colonel."

"Yes, but every extra day that those infernal planes remain in action costs the lives of my people, not yours."

Chapman stared into Krasilov's weathered eyes.

Krasilov frowned. "Sorry. For a moment I forgot about—"

"Don't worry about it," said Chapman. "Look, you've been under a lot of stress. Why don't you take a break for a few hours and get some sleep."

"I can't. I need to prepare the reports of today's sorties for Moscow, and plan tomorrow's sorties."

"You're burning out, Colonel. You should take it easy."

Krasilov leaned forward and put both elbows on the table. "*I'm* burning out? My *country* is burning, Colonel." He stabbed his chest with the thumb of his right hand. "*My country.* Do you understand that? Those Hitlerite bastards have taken everything from me. My wife and daughters; my home; *everything,* except my will to fight. If Russia loses, you'll go back home and perhaps prepare for an invasion of the mainland, but we lose what little we have left, our dignity, our lives, our traditions. The Nazis have sworn to tear this nation into small pieces and use the people as slaves. So if I'm burning out, then I'll just burn out." Krasilov reached for the bottle of vodka next to him, took a swig, and handed it to Chapman, who turned it down.

Krasilov abruptly stood. "Do you hear that?"

Chapman shook his head. "Hear what?"

Krasilov headed for the exit while shouting, "Alarm! Sound the alarm!"

Chapman went after him, finding him by the side of the runway staring at the sky.

"Hear it now, Colonel?"

"That's a jet engine," said Chapman a moment later. "Looks like the bastards have decided to pay us a visit after hours!"

95

Challenging Approach

Kalach Airfield, Twenty Miles West of Stalingrad Pocket
December 17, 1942

"Why can't we just contact them and tell them it's us?"

"Because, Jack, all radios are off. Radio silence is essential to the night bombers."

Jack frowned and reduced throttle even further. He couldn't see much. Below, the ground was pitch black. There was not a single ground reference he could use to guide his jet. On top of that, without a moon, there was no horizon to tell Jack if his wings were leveled. He had to depend fully on the artificial horizon—something he didn't do often. The Aircobra was a day fighter. Jack had flown at night before, but only when he had no other choice.

"Where is the damned runway?"

"You'll have to drop below one hundred feet to see the approach lights. We set them very low so the enemy can't see the airfield at night unless they know to fly this low. Something very unlikely."

"Below a hundred? At night? I'll say that's *very* unlikely, Natalya. If the altimeter isn't properly calibrated we're gonna run right into the trees!"

"Do it, Jack!"

Jack cursed but dropped the nose by a few degrees while shifting his gaze between the darkness below him and the altimeter's needle. One hundred feet.

"There," he said. "Now all I got to do is sneeze and we're dead. What's next?"

"We look for the lights. They should be around here. Blue over green, Jack. Look for them."

Jack felt the wings tilting to the right. Instinctively, he inched the stick a bit to the left to compensate.

"Jack! What are you doing?"

Jack shifted his gaze to the artificial horizon and noticed he was flying at a twenty-degree angle of bank. He had allowed spatial disorientation to take over his judgment. Spatial disorientation came in when the brain, confused from lack of visual inputs, decided on its own which way was up, and forced that false reference on the pilot. The only way to fight it was by forcing his brain to accept the artificial horizon as the real reference.

Feeling the nausea induced by spatial disorientation, Jack clenched his teeth and eased the stick back until the artificial horizon told him his wings were leveled again. It felt awkward, but he did it anyway. His instincts were lying to him.

"Sorry, I had vertigo."

"There, Jack. See them? See the lights?"

Jack squinted and spotted the bluish glint in the distance, but because it was dark he couldn't judge distance very well.

"How far away is that?"

"About three thousand feet away. I know where I am now. Turn left for thirty seconds, and then right to one seven zero. The nose should be lined up with the runway."

"How do you—"

"We do this every night, Jack."

Jack eased back the throttle controls and inched the stick to the left.

Krasilov was about to order the searchlights on, but decided against it. It had been over two minutes since he first heard the jet engines, and he could still hear them, but faintly.

"Alarms off! Turn off all the lights, including the approach lights!" he shouted. The siren died down, and the only sounds left were those of the jet in the distance and the wind swirling across the concrete runway.

"What are you doing?" asked Chapman.

"Trust me, Colonel. The bastards won't be able to find us. Besides, I don't feel like losing more fighters to those damn German jets."

"There, Jack! See them?"

Jack completed the right turn, narrowed his eyes, and saw the dim bluish glow a few thousand feet ahead. The lights suddenly went off.

"What happened to them? Damn!"

"They turned them off, Jack. Krasilov thinks we're the enemy."

"Lower flaps, Natalya!"

She reached for the lever on her side and pulled it down to the second setting.

"I did this once without lights, Jack. At least we got to see the general location."

"Great," he said while squinting to see something. "Airspeed?"

"One hundred fifty knots."

Jack Towers decided that if the jet took off at around 140 and stalled close to ninety, an acceptable approach speed should be somewhere in the middle. He cut back power and lowered the landing gear.

"One hundred forty . . . thirty-five . . ."

Krasilov was puzzled. The jet engines became louder, but still did not appear to sound as high-pitched as they did during his two encounters with the German fighter.

"Look, Colonel! There it is!" shouted Chapman.

Krasilov pulled out his gun and so did most of the pilots on the field, Chapman included. Krasilov leveled it at the incoming craft, but stopped the moment the landing lights flooded the concrete runway.

"Hold your fire! Hold your fire!" Krasilov shouted.

"What are you doing? The bastard—"

"Is trying to land, Colonel! The German is trying to land!"

The runway rushed up to meet him as Jack fought the controls. For every adjustment in power and stick, he found himself readjusting in the opposite direction, failing to obtain the proper response from the German fighter.

"One hundred twenty knots, Jack . . . fifteen . . . ten . . ."

Jack added just a dash of power to maintain 110 knots.

"One hundred twenty knots, Jack."

"Dammit! This plane!" Frustrated, Jack reduced power again and eased the stick back trying to descend and slow down at the same time.

"One hundred ten knots. Holding at one ten."

Jack exhaled, but the brief surge of confidence was washed away by a gust of crosswind that brushed the craft to the side of the runway. Jack swung the stick in the opposite direction.

Krasilov sensed something wrong with either the jet or the pilot. The plane drifted over the side, back over the runway, over to the other side, and finally back on the wide runway.

Someone panicked and opened fire.

Jack momentarily lost control when three rounds bounced off the armored canopy.

"Damn. Someone's firing at us!"

His left wing got dangerously close to the trees by the side of the runway.

"Right rudder, Jack! Quick!"

Jack pressed the right pedal and eased the stick to the right, bringing the craft back over the concrete.

"Hold your fire!" Krasilov shouted as he ran toward the young pilot who had his pistol leveled at the German fighter, and pushed his hand up in the air. "You idiot! All of you hold your fire! Now!"

Krasilov grabbed the weapon from the pilot and shoved him aside. He shifted his gaze back to the jet.

Jack had consumed half the runway's length and still had not landed. He tried to cut back power, but instead of pushing the throttle controls, he automatically pulled them back. He realized his mistake the second after the jets kicked in full power and pushed the craft back up.

"The other way, Jack. It's the other way! Airspeed one hundred sixty . . . seventy . . . eighty . . ."

Jack was about to reduce throttles but it was to no avail. The end of the runway was too close.

"Imbeciles!" shouted Krasilov. "You have scared him off! The next man that opens fire will have to deal with me!"

He shifted his gaze back toward the plane slowly floating seemingly out of control over the runway.

Jack pulled up, climbed to one hundred feet, made a one-eighty turn, and came back around for another pass.

He kept the stick dead centered while decreasing power

steadily. Once again, the runway came up to meet him. Jack felt the light crosswind blowing across the runway. This time around he had a better feel for the finesse required to control the jet during the last phase of the landing approach. He decided to change tactics, and eased the stick to the right to fly into the wind while applying left rudder. The conflicting commands tilted the jet's wings a mild fifteen degrees, but with the payoff of keeping the nose aligned with the runway.

This time instead of overcorrecting, Jack barely moved his hand on the stick, making minimal adjustments.

The right gear touched down first. Jack centered the stick, and the left wheel bounced against the concrete once before settling down. The tail dropped as Natalya read seventy knots indicated airspeed.

Krasilov, Chapman, and the other pilots ran behind the German jet, which managed to stop at the end of the runway, turned around, and came to a full stop next to the fighter shelters.

Krasilov was the first to reach it. He jumped on the wing, pistol in hand, and was about to bang on the canopy for the pilot to push it open when he froze.

Jack and Natalya waved at him from inside the cockpit.

Krasilov remained silent for a few seconds before bursting into laughter.

96

Fronts and Flanks

Sixth Panzer Mechanized Division, Thirty Miles
South of Stalingrad
December 17, 1942

The cold night air clashed against General von Hoth's position with an intensity that matched the fierceness of the Soviet tanks that had pounded his flanks hours ago. The fifty-two-year-old general glanced at three soldiers huddling between two stationary panzers to get away from the cutting gusts.

He had prohibited the lighting of any fires to prevent giving out his position to the dreaded night witches that General Paulus had mentioned to him so many times. At first, von Hoth had been skeptical about the reports, but after ten destroyed panzers, he too had chosen to protect his advancing army with total darkness.

He brought both gloved hands to his face and rubbed off the ice crusting his beard. Temperatures rapidly approached fifty-below. Von Hoth cursed those Soviet women pilots that were not strategically significant to destroy his army, yet posed enough of a nuisance for all fires to be put out on what he considered to be the coldest night of his life.

He shook his head and walked toward the communications truck parked near the middle of the three-mile-long line of tanks.

Along the way the general strolled by a pair of medics standing by a soldier who had made the mistake of removing a glove and then touching one of the metal levers of a field gun being towed by a truck. His hand had stuck to the cold metal.

Von Hoth walked on, not wishing to witness another field amputation, especially one caused by not following orders.

Every soldier had been instructed to keep all body parts covered when the weather became extreme. He reached the communications truck, and he noticed that the engine was on.

"Why is the engine on?" von Hoth asked as he opened the rear door and climbed in. Due to shortage of fuel from constant partisan attacks of supply lines, he had given strict orders that no engine was to be turned on for the sole purpose of heating. The fuel was needed to reach Stalingrad.

"Heil Hitler, General!" replied one of the operators. "It's thirty degrees below zero outside, sir. The telegraph and the Enigma machine. We're not sure how cold they can get before malfunctioning."

Von Hoth relaxed. The operator was right. He couldn't afford malfunctioning equipment at that moment. Besides, the operators had to remove their gloves to type—something they could not do in this weather lest they risk frostbite plus their fingers sticking to the metal keys.

"Well done, Corporal," he replied. "Now get ready to transmit a message to all Luftwaffe gruppes in the southern eastern front."

As the operator rushed through the coding manual to set the wheels and plugs according to that day's instructions, von Hoth stared out the side window. Somewhere out there were General Chuikov's hordes of seasoned Soviet soldiers ready to cut his army to pieces with an attack on the flanks of the German panzer column. Von Hoth couldn't afford such attacks, for they could break his rescuing army into isolated pockets. If that happened, all hope would be lost not only for Paulus' army but for his own. Once encircled, the Soviets would wait a few weeks until the German troops were frozen and starved into a nonfighting mode, and then close in for the kill.

Von Hoth closed his eyes at the thought of the massacre that would result from such an attack. He knew Hitler would not allow capitulation, which explained why Paulus had secretly agreed to attempt to break out of the pocket and try to meet von Hoth halfway.

"Ready, sir?"

The general shifted his gaze to the Enigma operator holding a pencil and paper in his hands. The operator was so young. All his soldiers were so young, and all were dying in such a harsh place.

Slowly, he began to dictate his message.

97

Gibberish

HMS Liverpool, *Aegean Sea*
December 17, 1942

"Got that, mate?" asked the intercept operator as he fiddled with the knobs on his radio while jotting down the last few letters of the Morse-code message. He did it with such speed that his brain worked nearly in automatic, not even paying attention to the meaning of the words he wrote down. That would come later. First it was important to get every single letter down in the precise order as it was received.

"Think so. Looks like another German gibberish message," responded the second operator as he used the Direction Finder to point toward the source.

The intercept operator glanced at what was supposed to be a German message before Enigma coded it. "Well, I've known bloody German for ten years, and that is definitely *not* it."

"In that case it looks like we got us another intercept for the chaps at BP."

"Got a bearing on the bastards?"

"Well . . . it looks like . . . well, what do you know? It's coming from a region roughly thirty miles south of Stalingrad. I believe our old friend, General von Hoth, is broadcasting again."

The intercept operator began to smile when another message came through. He automatically began to scribble each word on a piece of paper while his colleague telegraphed the first message to the BP relay station in Athens.

98

Terrific News

Kalach Airfield, Twenty Miles West of Stalingrad Pocket
December 17, 1942

Colonel Krasilov sat back, stunned, the drink in his right hand falling to the ground, splattering vodka over his boots. A few pilots sitting by the makeshift bar on the other side of the room glanced in his direction before returning to their drinking.

"Jackovich . . . what are you saying? That Zoya . . . *my* Zoya is . . . *alive*?"

Sitting next to Natalya, Jack locked eyes with the colonel across the weathered surface of their table before glancing at the pilots in the room celebrating the capture of the German jet. None of them noticed the shocked expression flashing across the colonel's scarred face while regarding Natalya and him with utter disbelief in the corner of the loud room. Chapman and the Russian pilots were toasting and laughing by the bar, cracking joke after joke about Hitler, Himmler, von Hoth, Paulus, and other top German officials. Jack even heard an old one about Churchill.

"She was rescued, Colonel," said Natalya.

"By partisans," added Jack. "Over a year ago."

Krasilov remained in shock, his lips barely moving as he mumbled, "A year . . ."

Jack proceeded to explain everything that the late Aris Broz had conveyed to him, including Zoya reaching the outskirts of Moscow in December 1942 and rejoining the Red Army.

"Then why," Krasilov started. "Why hasn't she made any attempt to . . ." his voice trailed off as his face became blood red.

Jack and Natalya exchanged an alarming look. The colonel looked like he was going to explode. After the explanation that Aris and she had given Jack the day before, he knew what was going through the colonel's mind. The reason he had not heard from his wife—assuming she was still alive—was probably because her multiple requests to get in touch with him were cluttering the desk of an overworked clerk in some forgotten war office in Moscow.

Like an angered bear, the massive Russian jumped to his feet, lifting the table, which he flung to the side, sending it crashing near the crowd by the bar.

The room quieted an instant later as all eyes gravitated toward the veteran colonel, who stomped away in the direction of the communications bunker.

Jack and Natalya stood up as Chapman joined them. "What was that all about?"

Jack tilted his head in the direction of the exit. "I think all hell is about to break loose in Moscow."

99

Spread Too Thin

JG52 Gruppe 1, Fifty Miles North of Rostov
December 17, 1942

A very irritable Erich Steinhoff grabbed two messages from one of the rookie radio operators who had just entered his tent.

Rubbing his eyes, he sat on the side of the bed and read the first one. It was from General von Hoth.

The commander of the Sixth Panzer Division had requested an unprecedented amount of air support from all Luftwaffe gruppes in the southern eastern front. Von Hoth was less than thirty miles from Stalingrad. If he could drive his army north for another twelve or fifteen miles, perhaps General Paulus could have a chance to meet him halfway.

The stakes were high. Von Hoth's failure to reach Stalingrad would mean the certain capture of Paulus' Sixth Army. Air support was required to hold back Russia's divisions attacking the flanks of von Hoth's column, while von Hoth concentrated on the drive north. Additional air support was needed in Stalingrad to support General Paulus' attempt to defend a strategic location called Mamayev Hill from an approaching Russian division of tanks and infantry. Paulus' control of the hill had been weakened the day before by a massive Red Air Force strike. Now the ground troops were getting ready to move in and take the hill away from the Germans.

Erich frowned. He barely had enough aircraft to handle one location, much less two.

That was the first message. The second message was from High Command in Berlin. It expressed the great disappointment at the loss of one of the prototypes, and a warning that loss of the second would not be acceptable.

Erich just rolled his eyes.

What are they going to do? Fire me?

Berlin's warning, read here in the middle of this frozen hell, carried very little impact.

The Luftwaffe had spread too thin. The army in general had spread too thin. The Soviets were overwhelming in numbers and lately also in weaponry. And now Berlin, the culprit of this mess, was wiring over these borderline-amusing threats.

Erich put both messages on the table, stepped outside, and gathered his pilots.

100

Revelations

Kalach Airfield, Twenty Miles West of Stalingrad Pocket
December 18, 1942

Jack was exhausted. The debriefing with Krasilov and Chapman—after the colonel had gotten a chance to vent and ream certain people in Moscow—had gone well, but had lasted an hour longer than Jack would have liked. He went over everything from the time he got shot down to the moment they landed.

Both Krasilov and Chapman had taken extensive notes, particularly about Jack's description of the strengths and weaknesses of the German jet. Even before he had completed giving them his impressions of the exotic fighter, Chapman had already made the decision to get the plane flown to England immediately, where it would be thoroughly inspected by a joint USAF and RAF team. Jack had been assigned as the pilot, and he was to leave in another twelve hours. Refueling stops were already being set up along a route worked out by both Krasilov and Chapman.

"Well, so much for my little tour of the eastern front," he murmured as he reached his tent behind the fighter shelters by the edge of the trees. Things were moving too fast for Jack. Much had happened in the four short days since his arrival here, and now he was being requested to leave for England.

He opened the canvas flap and quickly closed it to keep some of the heat still trapped inside the tent from last night's fire. Each tent had a small wood-burning stove and ventilation pipe.

He walked up to the stove, reached for a few logs, piled them up, soaked them with kerosene, and threw in a match. He knelt in front of the fire while his face thawed.

Jack removed his gloves and cap, and began to unbutton his coat when a gust of wind nearly put the fire out. Convinced that he had closed the canvas flap, Jack turned around.

"Hello, Jack."

"Natalya. What are you—"

"I heard you were leaving tomorrow to fly the German plane to England. I came by to wish you luck, and also to say thanks. What are your plans after England?"

"Sit down, please. And close that flap."

The Soviet pilot snapped the canvas shut and removed her furry hat. Her hair hung loose over her ears, framing her beautiful face.

"I'm not sure what's going happen to me after I deliver the plane. Chapman mentioned something about training another group of pilots. There are three shipments of Aircobras on the way."

She lowered her gaze. Jack knelt down next to her and lifted her chin. "I'm going to miss you too, Natalya Makarova."

She tried to move his hand away, but he softly cupped her face. "Look at me, Natalya. Please."

Slowly, she raised her gaze until it melted with his. Jack smiled. "I knew it."

"Please, Jack, stop. You know there can never be anything between—"

"Says who? Our governments? The hell with them. Something has happened to me in the past few days, Natalya. I've never felt this way about anyone. I—"

"Don't say it, Jack . . . please." She got up to leave.

"Natalya. I might not see you for some time."

She stopped. "That's probably for the best."

"Why do you say that? I know that you care for me."

"Jack, please. You won't understand."

"Try me, Natalya. Is it differences in cultures? Religion maybe? What? Tell me, please."

She slowly turned around. Tears rolled down her cheeks. "His name is Boris Nikolajev. He was a pilot with another

air wing and was reported shot down during the battle of
Moscow a year ago. We were married the same day that he
was sent to defend Moscow, Jack. We never even had a
honeymoon. After several months, I figured he was dead
and decided to get on with my life, and then you came
along and . . ."

Jack didn't like the way this was headed and steeled
himself for the worst as he asked, "And?"

"A message arrived from Moscow an hour ago. I guess
Colonel Krasilov screamed at the right people. Messages
from most of our loved ones began arriving on the telegraph an hour ago."

Jack closed his eyes.

"It was a miracle, Jack. Boris and a handful of others
were the only survivors out of hundreds of prisoners taken
by the Germans during the battle last December. After being in prison for months, he was liberated and taken to a
hospital outside Moscow, where he is right now struggling
to recover from the subhuman conditions in which the
Nazis kept him for all those months."

Jack was confused. "Boris *Nikolajev*? Is he—"

"Yes, Jack. Boris is *Andrei's* brother. My husband needs
me. Please understand."

Jack fought the pressure forming behind his eyes as he
searched for the right words, but there weren't any. He
lifted his gaze and stared into the hazel eyes that had somehow taken possession of his feelings—of his very soul.
Now those same eyes told him that it could never be. They
had been promised to someone else long before he'd gotten
here.

Natalya leaned down and kissed him on the cheek.

"Good-bye, Jack Towers. You'll always have a special
place in my heart. Thank you for giving me my life."

Jack softly pulled her face close to his and inhaled
deeply. "Thank you for giving me mine," he responded as
he tried to bring her lips next to his. Natalya gently pulled
away.

"Please, Jack. Please understand. I can't . . ."

Jack lowered his gaze. She turned around and reached the entrance flap.

"Natalya . . . that day in the hut after we got shot down, when you . . . did you feel what I . . ."

"I will treasure that day for as long as I live, Jack. Goodbye."

A gust of cold wind blew inside the tent as she left. Jack felt the bitter air cut through his soul.

101

Door Slam

Bletchley Park, Buckinghamshire, England
December 18, 1942

Peter Myers read the deciphered messages. The one about the stolen jet was old news, although he had to admit that it felt good knowing how upset the German High Command was about the loss of one of two prototypes. It wasn't the most elegant way for the Allies to move ahead technologically, but heck, all is fair in war, Myers reflected. There was no prescribed set of rules . . . at least not when it came to fighting the Germans anyway.

The second message, however, required their immediate attention, for it was to be what Myers considered von Hoth's final drive to rescue Paulus. Soviet units were already in place to stop the drive. Myers' intelligence report indicated that the 62nd, the 63rd, and the 64th Army Divisions were already deployed to flank the Germans as well as clash against the column head-on. The numbers were appalling. Von Hoth had less than seventy thousand men and five hundred tanks. He faced a formidable force of 150,000 Soviet troops, along with tanks and artillery. The Soviets, however, did not know exactly when the attack was to take place.

The message was a desperate call from von Hoth for air support. Myers understood the need for the Luftwaffe. If there was a way for the German air force to hold off or perhaps even delay the flanking attack of the Soviet army, von Hoth might have a chance of establishing a corridor for long enough to get supplies to Paulus' army. Once fully armed, the Sixth Army might be able to fight its way out.

Myers frowned. If the trapped army escaped, it would be just a matter of time before the soldiers launched another offensive in the spring. He knew that Hitler's lust for control of Caucasus as a way to reach Persia and India would not stop unless the Soviets slammed the door on him.

The message had to reach the eastern front immediately.

102

Bear Hug

Kalach Airfield, Twenty Miles West of Stalingrad Pocket
December 18, 1942

The flap of his tent flew open just as Jack Towers had fallen asleep. A rush of cold wind stung him.

He sat up, rubbing his eyes, before staring at the bulky figure of Colonel Krasilov.

"Jackovich!" he screamed, leaning down over him.

"Colonel!" Jack said as Krasilov wrapped his large arms around him and nearly lifted him off the cot. "What is the meaning of—"

"She is alive!" Krasilov said, stepping away, smiling. "My Zoya is alive!"

Terrific, Jack thought, leaning back down while exhaling heavily, his mind still in havoc from his last conversation with Natalya.

The Russian colonel, too happy to realize that Jack wanted to be left alone, explained how Zoya had been trying to make contact for the past year but Moscow never relayed the messages due to *other* priorities. But thanks to Jack, Krasilov had used his rank and influence to cash in many favors and find the right people, who in turn found not just the stalled queries from Zoya but those from every member of his flight squadron.

"I'm very happy for you, Colonel," he said, wishing he had already left this godforsaken place. "I'm *really* happy for you."

103

Final Letter

JG52 Gruppe 1, Fifty Miles North of Rostov
December 18, 1942

An hour before dawn, Erich finished writing Sonja what he thought would be his last letter for some time. The battle for control of Stalingrad would be a fierce one. More than three hundred fighters, Stuka dive-bombers, and conventional bombers had been called to provide air support for General von Hoth's advancing panzer army as well as for the Germans defending the pocket from a confirmed column of Russian tanks and infantry from the 62nd Army.

Erich sealed the letter and put it in his coat pocket along with the letter he had written the day before. He made a mental note to stop at the communications tent before he left. A supply plane headed for East Prussia was due to arrive at the airfield for refueling in a few hours.

104

Beauty Sleep

Kalach Airfield, Twenty Miles West of Stalingrad Pocket
December 18, 1942

Jack Towers felt someone pulling on his shoulder.

"Get up, Jack. Rise and shine!"

Jack opened his eyes and stared into the gold-capped teeth of Colonel Kenneth Chapman. The sun had already come up.

"Sorry I had to interrupt your beauty sleep," added the colonel, grinning. "But there's a war out there, son."

"Damn. I must have passed out." He checked his watch.

"Go grab some breakfast if you can find anyone, Jack. You're leaving in thirty minutes."

Jack narrowed his eyes. "What do you mean if I can find anybody, sir?"

"All of your Russky friends left a half hour ago."

"Left? Where?"

"Son, you must have been half dead or something. Didn't you hear the planes taking off?"

"Ah, no, sir. What's going on?"

"Big-time offensive, Jack. The Soviets are gonna try to castrate the German advance at the Mishova River and also sting them hard in Stalingrad to keep them from trying to break out of the pocket. We got the word a couple of hours ago from our British friends. Heck, from what we were told, half the Luftwaffe is gonna be up there."

"Sir, the jet, we gotta use it to help them—"

Colonel Chapman raised his right hand. "Don't even think about it. The Russians got their orders and you've got yours. You must get that plane to England in one piece."

Jack exhaled. "Got a light, sir?"

Chapman handed him a cigarette and pulled out a lighter. Jack tore off the filter, lighted up, and took a long draw.

Chapman dropped his brows at him before shaking his head and getting up. "Thirty minutes, Jack. Our people are already waiting in England to dissect that baby sitting outside."

Jack nodded and rubbed a hand through his hair.

105

Sniper

Red October Factory Complex, Stalingrad Pocket
December 18, 1942

From her rooftop vantage point, Zoya Krasilov watched the planes arrive over the pocket. But to her dismay they were German, flying very low, their engines screaming as they shot across the sky separating them from the advancing elements of General Chuikov's army.

Where is our air support? she thought, watching fighters and Stukas drop over the 62nd Army's main echelon like hawks, peppering tanks and troops with a mix of machine-gun fire and bombs.

From her vantage point, she could see the infantry units swinging their rifles at the incoming planes. Several armored vehicles, topped with higher-caliber machine guns, also followed suit, blasting a wave of antiaircraft fire at the threat in the skies.

A few planes burst in midair, but the rest continued their dive, pounding the ground troops, many of which perished in gruesome displays of exploding body parts. Tanks burst in flames as the Stukas' cannons pierced their armor, igniting fuel and ammunition, incinerating their crews as well as any infantry running by their side.

But the Russian forces continued their drive despite heavy losses. Several divisions remained behind fending off the wave of Luftwaffe fighters to allow the rest of the

62nd Army to continue its planned attack on Mamayev Hill. But another wave of German planes appeared on the horizon, swarming toward the front of the Russian lines like a cloud of angered bees, further decimating the ground troops.

Anger swelling in her gut, Zoya forced her attention to the ground, to the enemy pillboxes, which abruptly came alive as the surviving front end of the Russian advance got within their range. In an instant, the entire hill burst into a fury of machine guns and artillery, turning the field in front of the Russians into a hell of uncountable explosions.

Taking careful aim, she opened fire on the closest machine-gun emplacements, a move that would signal her team to commence the attack. She watched through her scope as her rounds struck the backs of the soldiers manning the pillbox.

Fire broke out all at once from the floor below.

106

Sniper vs. Sniper

Red October Factory Complex, Stalingrad Pocket
December 18, 1942

Major Christoff Halden had been momentarily distracted by the massive display of firepower erupting from Mamayev Hill as General Paulus made an attempt to fend off the initial enemy wave.

He had ordered most of his soldiers to the rear of the building, which faced the fields where Russian troops were getting slaughtered by the Luftwaffe's impressive display of power. Christoff was concerned about protecting his rear should Russian troops shift their attack on the hill and try to take refuge in this building, which was the nearest one to the rapidly developing battle.

He had remained behind with only Johan, who was also looking toward Mamayev Hill from a broken window ten feet away from him.

That's when Christoff first noticed something wrong. One of the German machine-gun emplacements—the one closest to him—had just gone silent. Then a second followed suit, and a third. The fact that Germans on the hill were taking casualties didn't surprise him. After all, the 62nd Army continued its attack on the hill despite the Germans' best attempts to stop them. What concerned Christoff was his observation that the Germans in the third pillbox to go silent didn't fall back, as they should have if shot by the nearing Russians. The Germans had fallen forward, as if shot from behind.

His stomach suddenly tightening, Christoff shifted his attention to the building he had been supposed to be guarding, and that's when he saw them.

Muzzle flashes!

"Johan!" he hissed, gaining his subordinate's attention before pointing at the building. "Over there!"

The two Germans swung their weapons in the direction of the flashes originating out of multiple locations across the entire third floor of the building.

107

Lucky Break

Red October Factory Complex, Stalingrad Pocket
December 18, 1942

Zoya Krasilov had stopped firing the moment she spotted the first group of Russian fighter planes in the distance. There were more than two dozen of them, flying high before inverting and diving over the unsuspecting Germans, who continued their attack on the Russian lines.

It's about time, she thought before getting ready to resume her attack on the machine-gun emplacements, but something stopped her.

She noticed that her team was no longer attacking the German pillboxes even though there were still more than a dozen of them fully operational firing on their comrades.

What is wrong?

As she was about to stand up and head downstairs, she noticed two German soldiers—wearing the same camouflage uniforms and large sniper rifles as the team from last night—stepping away from the building.

Confused, Zoya wondered why her team was allowing this to happen.

Why aren't they firing on those two Germans? And why have they stopped attacking the machine-gun nests?

The standing order was to fire on any German target after Zoya had given her signal. Yet, the two Germans were standing there pointing at her building.

Her heart sank as the realization of what could have happened ripped through her like the silent bullets those Germans had certainly fired against her team. There could be no other explanation for their sudden silence when the battle roared at Mamayev Hill.

As Russian planes dove into the mass of enemy fighters, Zoya took careful aim at one of the two Germans and fired a round into his chest.

108

Encounters

Two Thousand Feet over Stalingrad Pocket
December 18, 1942

Colonel Krasilov didn't know where to start. The overcast sky seemed peppered with enemy aircraft attacking General Chuikov's tanks and infantry as they drove south toward the pocket.

He set his sights on an Me 109G Gustav, inverted, and dove.

"Stay with me, Natalya!"

"I'm right behind you, Colonel!"

The Gustav went for a left turn and climbed as Krasilov engaged the Aircobra's 37mm cannon, but couldn't get the angle. The Gustav came out of the roll and started a vertical dive. Krasilov came up so close to its tail that he could have touched it with the propeller hub.

He opened fire again. This time the Messerschmitt's fuselage separated from the wings and plummeted toward earth, but a section of the burning wreckage broke off in a cloud of sparks before crashing right over another Aircobra.

Tears of rage filled Krasilov's eyes as he felt the shockwave from the fierce midair collision roughly one thousand feet below.

"Who was that?"

"I don't know, Colonel. He wasn't from our unit, sir."

"Dammit!"

"Colonel! Behind us!"

Krasilov turned and saw two Gustavs leveling out of a dive. Instinctively he broke left and Natalya to the right.

"Let's see how good you are, Hitlerite," Krasilov said, swinging the stick toward him while pushing full power. The Aircobra spewed smoke before pulling up to six thousand feet while Krasilov executed a corkscrew. The Gustav remained on his tail.

At the top, Krasilov cut power, bled airspeed until the plane stalled, and as it went into a right spin, he added right rudder and full power. Now he was falling at a staggering rate. The airspeed blasted past four hundred knots.

The Gustav remained with him.

The altimeter read four thousand . . . three thousand . . . two . . . fifteen hundred.

The Gustav closed in.

Krasilov decided that the German was either crazier than him, or simply wasn't paying attention to anything but Krasilov's tail. He banked on the latter, and as the plane rushed below five hundred feet, Krasilov simultaneously cut power, lowered flaps and landing gear, and pulled back on the stick.

The extreme G-forces hammered him. The wings trembled. Krasilov hoped that the American design was strong enough to sustain the abuse.

The Gustav failed to slow down in time and darted past him. Krasilov watched the altimeter scurry below three hundred feet . . . two hundred.

The pressure became unbearable. He felt light-headed.

One hundred feet.

An orange ball of flame roared under him when the Gustav crashed into the frozen steppe.

Krasilov watched his nose hoist over the horizon at . . . fifty feet! He breathed deeply and pulled up the gear, flaps, and added full power.

Two down and plenty more to go. He had survived the dogfight, but he had lost sight of Natalya.

He scanned the skies for her La-3 and spotted a squadron of Stukas.

"Natalya? Where are you?"

"Right above you, Colonel. I'm coming down."

"Don't. Head for the Stukas. I'll catch up with you."

Krasilov jammed full power and the Aircobra belched black smoke before responding. Airspeed darted past three hundred knots. Krasilov pointed the nose at the sky and started a vertical corkscrew. One thousand feet . . . two thousand . . . three . . .

He lowered the nose by a dash and took the lead slightly ahead of Natalya. The Stukas were less than a thousand feet above.

Krasilov counted sixteen in groups of four. He picked the right-most group, set his craft in a shallow climb, and approached the Germans from the rear.

"Keep an eye for fighters, Natalya!" he ordered as he brought the first dive-bomber into his sights and pressed the trigger. Three seconds of fire, and the Stuka, now less than four hundred feet away, burst into flames, rolled on its side, and arched down to earth leaving a trail of smoke.

With two hundred feet left, Krasilov aligned the next Stuka and was about to fire when the entire squadron of dive-bombers inverted and started their dive. Krasilov rolled the plane upside down, pulled the stick, and dove after them.

Airspeed shot above three hundred knots. Too fast. The tail of the Stuka filled his front pane. Krasilov pressed the trigger and the 37mm cannon blew the tail section before Krasilov had to pull up, which he did and followed with a loop-the-loop.

Heading straight back down toward the falling dive-bombers, Krasilov opened fire on the next Stuka for a few seconds before he saw something zooming past him at great speed.

"It's that damned jet!" Krasilov fumed at the sight of the German jet.

The revolutionary jet always caused a greater loss of Soviet lives and planes. Also, the German pilots seemed to fight harder when the dreaded plane appeared.

Krasilov decided to continue firing until smoke came out of the Stuka before breaking left to go after the jet. Sooner or later, the German pilot would get careless, and when he did, Krasilov would be right there waiting for him.

109

Side Trip

Ten Miles West of Stalingrad Pocket
December 18, 1942

Jack Towers reached sixteen thousand feet and put on his oxygen mask. He had maintained radio silence as Colonel Chapman had instructed, but as he flew close to Stalingrad, he couldn't help but wonder how his friends were doing. He knew the frequency, but hesitated. He knew he couldn't trust himself, but he had to find out.

Jack dialed the frequency.

"Break left . . . break . . . I'm hit. I'm hit." The voices caused the impact Jack knew they would cause. He saw them as his family now. A deep sense of remorse overwhelmed him. He had abandoned—

"It's that jet . . . dammit! He's just too fast! I can't get to him! Out of the way! Everyone get out of its way! Use the clouds for cover!"

Jack recognized the voice. It was Krasilov's. Jack held his breath for a moment. He had to do it. There was no other way now. The Germans would have the advantage as long as that jet was present.

"This is Jack, Aleksandr. I'm on my way!"

"Jackovich? Are you insane! You have your orders. Get that jet out of here!"

"And do what? Let the other prototype take out more of your men? I've made my decision. I'll be there in thirty seconds." Jack pushed full throttles and set the jet in a shallow dive. Airspeed climbed to 535 knots.

"Natalya, Aleksandr, where is the jet? I'm scanning the skies, but there are too many planes!"

"He's executing a vertical climb, Jackovich. Bastard just shot down another one of my men."

Jack saw him at three o'clock about a thousand feet below him. "Got him. You guys stick to the Gustavs. It's about time that German plays with someone his own size!"

110

Prototypes

Skies over Stalingrad Pocket
December 18, 1942

Erich Steinhoff leveled off at ten thousand feet and looked around for his next target. He selected a—

What in the world?

He blinked in surprise, and blinked again when realizing he wasn't imagining things. He saw the second Me 262 prototype zooming overhead. It had American flags painted on the wings and on the fuselage.

Bastards!

111

Negative Pressure

Skies over Stalingrad Pocket
December 18, 1942

Jack Towers noticed the German snapping his head as he dashed in front of him. Jack went into a tight turn to come back around, but by that time the German had also turned. They were headed nose to nose. Jack pushed full power and began firing.

Only now did he realize the meaning of a combined

closing speed of a thousand miles per hour. One second the German was a speck in the skies. The next, the entire craft filled his windshield. He didn't even get more than few rounds out before he had to break left. The German also broke left and pulled up. Jack lost him in the clouds.

Jack shot up and as the altimeter scurried past twenty thousand feet, he also entered the thick cloud coverage. It lasted only a minute. At twenty-four thousand, he squinted when the bright morning sun shone in his eyes as he left the cloud bank below.

The Messerschmitt was out of sight. Jack did a three-sixty but could not see it. Did it go back down and engage with a few more propeller planes? Jack didn't think it likely. That move would leave him open if Jack wanted to surprise him.

The sound of machine guns told him the German had managed to sneak up behind him.

Instinctively, Jack inverted and dove.

Bad move, Jack chided himself an instant later. The German was far away enough to slow down and follow him down with the gun.

As the first rounds ricocheted off the armored glass, Jack pushed the stick back and the negative Gs filled his head with blood as his body was thrown against the unyielding restraining harness. His vision got so red he thought his head would explode. He pulled out of the dive inverted, quickly leveled off, and added full throttle.

The German closed in at great speed as Jack grazed the cloud cover, turbines whining. He decided it was time to reverse the trap and let the German get even closer. The pilot had not opened fire, yet. Jack felt certain that he wouldn't until he had gotten close enough.

He was right. The German jet closed in for the kill. Jack waited until the last minute, before inverting and diving. This time he disappeared behind the clouds and maintained the dive until he broke through, then pulled the stick back.

The negative Gs crushed him once more. The wings trembled and the fuselage struggled to remain in one piece.

Jack leveled off less than five hundred feet from underneath the clouds, pulled up until he could almost touch the base of the clouds, and waited.

The German broke through a moment later, but to Jack's surprise, he was not diving, but simply descending. The tactic didn't work. In fact, it backfired due to sheer luck. The German just happened to descend directly behind Jack while in total control of his plane.

"Shit!"

Jack pushed full power, but not before the German's guns opened fire.

White smoke began to trail out of his right turbine. Jack decided not to shut it off yet. He kept the pressure on the throttles until he reached five hundred knots and climbed back into the clouds, but not by much though, just enough to hide in them as he swung the stick to the left and right.

Gunfire ceased. The German pilot would not fire unless he had the perfect shot.

Jack cut power and dropped flaps for ten seconds, before raising flaps and diving while reapplying full throttle. This time it worked. When the haze cleared, Jack stared directly into the German's tail.

He opened fire. Several rounds went through the rear fuselage.

112

Final Dogfight

Skies over Stalingrad Pocket
December 18, 1942

Erich felt his jet tremble and went for a dive as several rounds ripped through the metal skin of his right wing.

The American was good. Real good.

Erich dashed past five hundred knots and glanced back.

His craft still puffing white smoke from its left turbine, the American kept the pressure, blasting away with the cannons.

Erich swung the stick to the left while applying full right rudder, throwing the jet into a steep corkscrew dive.

The American did not let up.

Three thousand feet.

Erich waited just a little more.

Two thousand feet.

Fifteen hundred feet.

Erich pulled back on the control stick, but the nose wouldn't come up as fast as he'd expected it to.

Five hundred feet. The hollowed buildings of downtown Stalingrad filled his windscreen.

The American still locked on his tail, Erich applied rear pressure hard. The nose began to level off and he braced himself for the Gs.

They came with appalling force, squashing him down against his flight seat as his vision went blood-red and his arms tingled from lack of circulation.

Two hundred feet.

Firing stopped. The American either realized that he needed to get closer, or . . .

Erich did a mental calculation. Twenty seconds at three rounds per second per gun. The American probably had depleted over half . . . wait a second. The report he'd read said that the Me 262 had literally blasted away trucks and a tank before leaving Barkhorn's airfield.

Is he out of ammunition?

Erich decided to take a chance. Instead of adding full power and climbing, he leveled off and accelerated to five hundred knots.

Jack let go of the trigger when no more rounds came out. He couldn't believe he had depleted his load so soon, and the German probably knew it, for he was simply flying a straight line without regard to what Jack did.

Suddenly, the German went vertical. Jack followed . . .

the smoke from the damaged turbine intensified, but it still provided him with enough thrust to stay in the—

Fire!

As the tail of the German disappeared in the clouds, Jack saw his right turbine catch on fire. He turned it off, but in doing so his plane stalled a few seconds later. One turbine was not powerful enough to maintain a vertical ascent. He pressed right full rudder to avoid a spin while letting the nose drop to get back some airspeed.

He broke through the clouds and decided it was time to leave. The German had won. At least he had the—

"Break left, Jack! Left!" Natalya's voice crackled through his headset as the German jet came back around with its cannons blasting.

Jack broke to the left, but not before a shower of 30mm bullets impacted the armored canopy. The first few rounds were deflected, but that didn't last long. The canopy collapsed under the powerful stress. Jack released his safety harness and ducked just in time. Glass showered him.

"Dammit, not again!" he cursed into the radio as the Me 262 blasted past him and made a left three-sixty to come back around.

Jack rode in an open cockpit once more. He strapped only the bottom harness so that he could duck if he needed to, but he wouldn't fall off if he inverted.

The German approached at great speed. Jack inverted the craft and set it in a shallow dive to gain airspeed.

Had that been another type of plane, Erich would have stopped firing long ago. In his mind the rules of engagement called for gunfire until the enemy was disabled. The jet was disabled. Not only couldn't it fire back, but it was flying on one engine. But the plane was a prototype, and short of getting it back, Erich would much rather destroy it than see it in the hands of the enemy.

Erich decided to give the American one final chance. His objective was simply to destroy the plane, not kill the pilot, especially one as brave as the one piloting the jet.

He followed the wounded jet's dive, and floated his craft wingtip-to-wingtip next to it.

Jack continued to glance back but the Messerschmitt was out of sight. He was puzzled. Did the pilot decide Jack was no longer a threat and had decided to engage the rest of the planes fighting the Germans over Stalingrad?

He spotted something from the corner of his eye, and looked to his left. The sight chilled him. The German was right next to him. In his current wounded situation, Jack knew he was no match for the undamaged jet, but for some reason the pilot was not shooting him down but . . . signaling him to bail out! It was obvious that the German was offering him the chance to save himself

Jack shook his head emphatically.

The German saluted him and pulled right behind Jack.

Erich was moved by the bravery displayed by the American, refusing to bail out for the chance of saving the plane. He adjusted throttle and waited until he had the perfect shot to conserve ammu—

Muzzle flashes!

Erich spotted muzzle flashes to his right. He broke left and pulled up.

Krasilov cursed out loud the moment the German jet rapidly left his field of fire. The infernal plane was just too fast.

Erich executed a loop-the-loop, and briefly considered going after the Soviet plane but decided against it. He still had unfinished business with the prototype.

"Break right, Jackovich. Quick! Quick!"

Jack ignored Krasilov's shouts as airspeed reached 450 knots. The windblast was strong. He glanced behind him and spotted the German jet closing at great speed.

Jack waited, realizing he would only get one chance at this.

Five hundred knots at four thousand feet.

The German was almost on top of him.

It had to be now.

As the enemy cannons came alive, ripping holes across his wings, Jack inverted the plane, pulled back throttle, lowered flaps and landing gear, and unbuckled his restraining harness.

Erich reacted too late. Not in his wildest dreams did he imagine someone pulling a stunt like this on him.

He swung the jet left, but could not avoid striking the inverted tail with his right wing, which was torn away as it severed the tail section from the fuselage of the inverted jet. Both craft caught on fire.

In a flash the world and the skies disappeared and became a blur. He slid the canopy back and released his harness.

Smoke filled his eyes, but didn't last long.

Erich fell.

He waited a few seconds before pulling on the ripcord. The white canopy extended with a hard tug. Erich looked down and noticed the burning remnants spinning down toward the forest below. The American pilot was still inside his cockpit.

113

Rage

Stalingrad Pocket
December 18, 1942

Holding back tears of rage, Major Christoff Halden held Johan in his arms as he began to tremble uncontrollably.

"Cold . . ." Johan mumbled, blood spurting from his chest, where a bullet had punched a fist-size hole.

Christoff forced savage control, fighting the urge to roll away from his temporary shelter—a large tractor wheel where he had dragged Johan after the shooting—and open fire on the bastard who had shot his friend.

Johan coughed blood as his eyes rolled to the back of his head, expiring a moment later.

Christoff remained there for what seemed like an eternity, his mind in chaos while the battle for Mamayev Hill raged on.

Deciding to test his situation, he silently apologized to Johan as he lifted his friend's face over the edge of the wheel.

The bearded face disappeared in a cloud of blood as the Russian sniper scored a perfect hit.

Dropping Johan, Christoff decided that one Russian sniper had indeed survived the one-minute silent attack that Johan and he had carried out, firing into every window that showed a muzzle flash, just as they had been trained to do.

Pondering his next move, Christoff looked behind him at the nearby German troops battling the incoming Russians, and he doubted they would be able to help him, at least not while the 62nd Army continued to drive south.

Then he heard noises coming from the building.

Shouts in both Russian and German, along with gunfire.

Christoff frowned. He had been right in sending his team to cover their rear. Russians were running for cover into the building, but based on their sheer numbers, he didn't think his troops would last long before running out of ammunition and getting run over.

And he couldn't move, at least not while the sniper had him pinned down. But Christoff then heard a noise above him, and what he saw quickly made up his mind for him. Raising to a deep crouch, he rushed away from the tractor wheel and toward a second hideout behind a panzer still smoking from a recent battle. To his surprise, no one fired on him.

114

Ripcord

Skies over Stalingrad Pocket
December 18, 1942

His craft still inverted, Jack Towers pounded on the safety belt, but the buckle was jammed. The heat intensified. There was fire behind him and to his right. Through the smoke, he glanced at the altimeter. Two thousand feet and dropping fast. Jack reached in his right boot and pulled out his hunting knife. He pressed it against the belt and began to cut.

One thousand feet.

He wasn't cutting fast enough. Fire erupted from the floor of the cockpit. His feet burned. Images of Andrei's final moments flashing in his mind, Jack kept hacking at the belt but didn't have the right angle. The belt was pressed hard against his legs. Jack jammed the blade flat in between, cutting into his leg.

Seven hundred feet.

He turned the double-edge blade vertically and pulled hard. The belt gave and he fell, but the burning jet was falling right over him. Jack extended his arms and legs and slowed down enough to let the plummeting craft catch up with him. He kicked his legs against the fuselage and pulled the ripcord.

The ball of fire zoomed down past him as the main canopy fully extended for several seconds before the trees engulfed him.

Jack saw the German's stark-white parachute above him and the jet exploding a few hundred feet in front of him.

Then he felt crushed. Branches and leaves smothered him as he continued to fall. A stinging pain from his leg followed by a heavy blow to his head. Jack's vision clouded. He felt disoriented and had finally stopped falling, yet his feet were not on the ground.

The heat . . . Jack felt heat, and he saw a translucent image of flames nearby. Artillery rounds were going off all around him, and he realized that he had fallen in the middle of the battle.

He looked beneath him and saw white. He was hanging from his parachute harness and adjacent trees were on fire.

115

Missed Opportunity

Stalingrad Pocket
December 18, 1942

Zoya Krasilov had the German in her sights as he sprung away from his hideout.

Just as she was about to press the trigger, the tractor wheel and all surrounding debris disappeared in a cloud of fire.

For a moment she thought the position had been hit by a bomb or artillery round, but through the billowing smoke and pulsating flames she could see the tail section of a plane.

Frowning at the luck of the German soldier, Zoya tried to reacquire, but before she could do so the German dove behind a wrecked panzer twenty meters away.

Bastard!

Options rushed to her. She could remain put and wait for the German to show himself again, or she could go after him in the streets—and along the way check on the condition of her team, though something told her they had been terminated.

She also had a third option.

Lifting her rifle, she centered the crosshairs of her scope

on the next German pillbox on her list and opened fire, scoring a direct hit before shifting her aim to the second German behind the machine gun and shooting him as well.

She was about to switch to the next emplacement when she spotted a parachute slowly descending toward the city. It belonged to a German pilot.

As she thought about shooting him in the air, she watched in horror as the muzzle of the machine gun in the German pillbox swung in her direction. She had been spotted.

Instincts overcame surprise.

Clutching her rifle, Zoya jumped to the side, away from the recess in the wall at the edge of the building an instant before dozens of rounds tore chunks of concrete where she had been. She fell on her side on a rusted corrugated metal plank that had fallen loose from a nearby equipment shed.

The machine gun continued pounding the side of the building as she crawled away from the edge, her right shoulder and torso burning from the fall.

She rose to a deep crouch once she had reached a spot several meters away from the edge. Sighing with relief, she took off in the direction of the emergency stairs, the ones that the Germans had not found the night before.

116

Who Are You?

Stalingrad Pocket
December 18, 1942

Jack Towers slapped his hands over the release strap. It gave and Jack fell once more. He crashed on his side over the snow . . .

"Aghh!"

It was a rock . . . many rocks covered with snow. The blow made him tremble in pain. He couldn't move his right arm and leg. Just the smallest motion shot agonizing streaks of pain through his body. Something had broken, but his vision was too foggy to see what it was.

Then a figure loomed over him. The figure spoke in German.

German!

Jack inhaled the cold air through his mouth. He knew he shouldn't, but he did it anyway. It didn't matter. He felt certain that the warm liquid that dripped on his forehead and flowed over his right arm and leg was his own blood.

Although his mind grew cloudy, Jack realized that he would most likely bleed to death in a matter of minutes. The fall had been too extreme. The parachute had not opened in time.

The figure kneeled down next to him, took his arm, and began to bandage it.

Jack was confused.

Who are you? I can't see your face.

He tried to speak, but couldn't even grunt in pain when the German twisted his arm to reset the bone. His mind had drifted back to Natalya. The sweet Natalya. Her hazel eyes crinkled as she stared back at him in the yellowish light of the cave. Her body pressed next to his. So close, so warm, but a body that had never belonged to him. But Jack could still feel her now. Her warmth slowly revolving around his body.

Another tug. This time from his upper leg. The German must have reset a broken femur.

Why are you doing this? Can't you see I'm dying?

Other voices joined in with the German, but they were not guttural. They were . . . Russians. The German quickly opened Jack's coat, stuffed something into it, closed it, and ran away.

The Soviet voices got closer.

Jack slowly faded away.

117

Warrior and Doctor

Stalingrad Pocket
December 18, 1942

Zoya's boots thudded hollowly on the metal steps as she raced down to the third floor, anxiety filling her when violating one of her cardinal rules and simply charging into the cavernous machine room where her team hid without checking for the presence of enemy soldiers.

The fact that she reached the first sniper post alive told her there were no Germans on this floor, but she did find one of her snipers.

Dead.

She was one of Zoya's youngest recruits, a girl from Kiev, her dead eyes staring at the ceiling. A round had struck her in the neck, nearly severing the head, now twisted at a grotesque angle.

Mustering strength, Zoya moved on to the next post, finding another dead Russian soldier, a seasoned recruit from the Urals. The round had shaved the top of her skull, exposing her brain, which was steaming in the extreme cold.

Realizing the futility of her situation, and also aware of the fact that the longer she took checking for survivors the greater the chances that the Germans responsible for this would escape, Zoya went straight for Tasha's post, finding her sitting back, away from the window, hands on her stomach.

"Tasha?"

The young soldier slowly raised her eyes toward her commanding officer as she tried to reply but vomited blood instead.

"Oh, dear God," Zoya said, the doctor replacing the warrior as she dropped her rifle and rushed to Tasha's side, moving her hands away from her abdomen, staring at the crimson circle surrounding a bullet hole.

Slowly, Zoya laid Tasha on the floor before unbuttoning her heavy coat enough to get a better look at the damage. An instant later she buttoned her back up. There was nothing she could do even if they were at a field hospital across the river.

"Cold . . ." Tasha managed to mumble while spitting blood on her legs.

Zoya cradled her just as she had done long ago in that concentration camp. "It's all right, my dear Tasha. It's going to be all right. Just rest, my dear. Close your eyes and rest."

And her subordinate did, resting her head on Zoya's shoulder, closing her eyes as the Russian major rocked her back and forth, back and forth while fighting the tears, struggling to control the anger boiling up inside of her, while the battle beyond the window intensified.

Tasha died in less than a minute amid a convulsion. Zoya gently set her on the ground before crawling to the window, inspecting the scene below, observing the machine-gun crew still keeping their weapons pointed in the direction of the building, but higher than her position, apparently expecting Zoya to show herself on the rooftop again. She also noticed a pair of parachutes in the sparse forest between the clearing and the foot of Mamayev Hill but could not spot the pilots.

Wedging her weapon on a crack along the bottom of the window, Zoya centered the German to the right of the machine gun in her sights. Without hesitation, she fired once, turning his face into a mass of blood. Before his colleague could react, Zoya had already shifted her aim in his direction and fired again.

As she rolled away from the window, she heard the unmistakable sound of a near-miss buzzing past her right ear, like an angered hornet.

The German sniper!

She stood, keeping her back against the wall, narrowed

eyes staring at the window just half a meter to her right. The bastard had been waiting for her to make a move on the hill so he could kill her just as he had killed her team.

Weighing her options, Zoya ran toward the interior of the building, cut left when reaching the halfway point, and continued all the way to the end of the warehouse before turning left again and settling herself behind the closest window. But by the time she got the chance to inspect the clearing below, Russian troops were emerging from the building where the German snipers had been hiding.

In the minutes that followed, the forward elements of the 62nd Army reached the foot of Mamayev Hill, driving the Germans deeper into the pocket, until all she could see were Russian soldiers in the streets and Russian aircraft in the sky.

Standing, Zoya Krasilov said a short prayer for her fallen comrades before heading down to join her people.

118

Departures

Moscow
February 6, 1943

Although the cast on his right leg and arm made every move awkward, Captain Jack Towers sat up in bed for the first time in weeks. The casts were something that should come off soon, according to the Soviet doctor in charge of that wing of the hospital. His recovery had taken a turn for the better since Jack regained consciousness two days before.

He put down the copy of *Pravda* a nurse had given him earlier that day. General von Hoth's Sixth Panzer division had been unable to break through to the pocket and had been forced to turn back. Paulus' Sixth Army, unable to break out of the pocket, capitulated a few days later, bringing to an end Germany's last offensive. Stalingrad had broken the German spirit in the eastern front.

"Feeling better, Jack?"

Jack lifted his gaze and saw Colonel Kenneth Chapman peeking through a crack in the door. Jack inhaled and got ready to get the reprimand of his life for disobeying a direct order.

"Ah, yes, sir. The doctor seems to think so anyway," he responded in a weary tone. Chapman walked into the room, pulled up a chair, and sat next to Jack's bed.

"Looks like you're doing pretty darn good. Food here any good?"

"No, sir. It stinks."

"Better than the rats the Germans were eating in Stalingrad."

"I've just read about it, sir. I guess it's all relative."

Chapman stared at Jack for a few seconds before saying, "Well, I gotta tell you, Jack, a lot of people in London were quite pissed at you for getting shot down, but this kind of shit happens. Colonel Krasilov gave us a full report of the incident. He stated that you tried to avoid a dogfight but the Germans went after you and you had to defend yourself."

Jack smiled inwardly. "Although I'm sure Colonel Krasilov was accurate in his report, I still feel pretty bad about losing the jet, sir. I wish things had turned out differently."

"Don't worry about it. You tried to avoid it as much as you could. It ain't your fault the bastard came after you with the second prototype. At least you also got him before you went down. In a way, that probably helped the Soviets regain air superiority over the pocket."

Krasilov had definitely saved his skin.

I owe you one, Jack thought as he asked, "How's Krasilov, sir?"

Chapman smiled. "Last I heard he was flying his ass off somewhere near Rostov. The Germans are in retreat, Jack. Those Russkies are not taking any more shit. Their morale is sky-high."

Jack ran a hand through his hair. "What about his wife, sir? Any news on that front?"

Chapman shrugged. "Word I got was that she was in the same battle that you were in, only on the ground."

Jack made a face. "Are you shitting me?"

"Nope."

"So, are she and the colonel back together?"

"Not sure, Jack. I think they are corresponding, or so I heard from one of the Russian pilots from your old airfield."

Jack grimly nodded, not certain why he cared so much that those two were reunited. Perhaps because a part of him wanted the brave colonel to have what Jack could not.

"So," said Chapman. "The word out there is that you're very lucky to be alive."

"So I've been told, sir," Jack responded, turning his head and glancing at the translated version of the two German letters the Soviets had found inside his jacket after rescuing him near the foot of Mamayev Hill. They were from a Major Erich Steinhoff to a woman named Sonja living in Augsburg. The German had most likely been the figure that Jack vaguely remembered resetting and bandaging his wounds and stopping the bleeding.

Chapman looked at the pieces of paper on the nightstand. "Our sources tell us that this Steinhoff was the pilot of the other prototype. Looks like he was one of Hitler's special boys with a special mission. Too bad you blasted him right out of the sky."

"He probably saved my life, sir."

"Yeah, right. The bastard goes after you, shoots you down, and then out of the goodness of his heart he stops by to cure your wounds? I'd say the Nazi saw the Soviets coming and did what he could to make himself look good in their eyes."

"But the letters—"

"He's still the enemy, Jack."

"What's gonna happen to him?"

"The Russkies ain't being kind to German POWs, and

frankly, can't say I blame them. The pilot is probably on his way to Siberia by now along with the survivors of General Paulus' Sixth Army. Can't help but feel sorry for them bastards. Word from my contacts here is that they're headed into hell itself. Siberia is the place Stalin reserves for his worst enemies."

Jack looked away. Even before Steinhoff had shot him down, the German pilot had offered Jack the opportunity to bail out. That was the signature of a professional soldier, not of a criminal. Somehow it didn't seem fair for Steinhoff to be treated the same as Nazi garbage, but as Natalya had told him earlier, this was war, and war was hardly fair.

Jack closed his eyes as her face loomed in his mind. Her hazel eyes crinkled as she laughed. Her body snuggled next to his. Just as it had happened dozens of times during the past forty-eight hours, a deep sense of desolation briefly engulfed him. His feelings for the Russian woman were deeper than he had imagined, but Jack knew she belonged to another man.

"Ah . . . sir?"

"Yeah?"

"There was a woman pilot with Krasilov . . . Natalya Makarova?"

"Yes?"

"Do you know what happened to her, sir?"

Chapman shrugged again. "No, but I think I can find out. Why is that important to you?"

Jack didn't respond. Chapman grinned. "No problem, Jack. I'll see what I can find out of her whereabouts and have the info passed on to you before you leave."

"Thanks, sir, but the status of her well-being is not for me."

Chapman narrowed his eyes.

"His name is Boris Nikolajev. He is supposed to be here in Moscow recovering from wounds received while in a German POW camp. See what you can do to keep those two in touch. It's very important to me."

Chapman gave Jack a puzzled look. "You want to tell me what it's all about?"

"Long story, sir."

"All right, Jack. But I can't make any promises. Personal requests are way low on the priority list."

"I understand."

"Wanna smoke, Jack?"

"Please. There are no cigarettes in this place. I'm going nuts."

Chapman pulled out a pack and a lighter, and handed them to Jack, who hid them under the blankets. "Consider it a going-away present."

"Excuse me, sir?"

"You'll be here for another two weeks before going back to the States."

"The States?"

"You're going home, Jack."

He nearly bolted out of bed. "But . . . but the training, sir. The Soviets—"

"The Russkies are kicking German ass. We're not needed here any longer. You're off to the States for good . . . unless you want to keep on fighting that is." Chapman winked. "We can always use someone like you in the Pacific."

Before Jack could say a word, Chapman got up.

"These are your papers," he said, holding a folder in his hands. He placed it on the nightstand. "I'm leaving in less than an hour. Gotta report to duty in Britain in a week. Got me a job escorting B-17 bombers over France and Germany. Believe that shit? Well . . . so long, Jack."

Jack shook his hand. "Take care, sir."

Chapman left the room.

Jack stared out the second-story window and saw the somber streets of Moscow while he heard Chapman's footsteps disappearing down the hall.

Snow flurries lazily floated past the glass panes and onto the sidewalk below, where a virginal blanket of white attempted to cover the brutal results of a war that should have never been.

119

Cattle

Three Hundred Miles Northwest of Moscow
February 7, 1943

The cattle train chugging its way northeast seemed like the same train Erich Steinhoff had seen long ago, when Germany had the glorious army and the Soviets were in desperate retreat.

He felt someone bumping into him. Erich turned and stared into the dead eyes of a German boy not older than eighteen. The kid was being cradled by a bearded soldier in his forties, his blue eyes filled with tears.

"Here's another one," the bearded stranger said, loud enough to get the attention of the two Russians guarding the chained German prisoners, who were packed like rats with barely enough room to breathe much less sit down.

One of the massive Russians plowed his way through pale and emaciated Germans in ragged uniforms, reached down for the boy, unchained him, and threw him over his shoulder. He walked to the side door, opened it, and kicked him out. Erich watched the boy disappear in the deep snowbanks of the southern Siberian plains, through which the train snaked on its way to its final destination: a group of islands in a place called Gulag.

Erich stared into the eyes of the bearded man, whose uniform displayed the rank of a major in the Wermacht. He slowly nodded at the fellow officer, and he nodded in return before extending an open palm.

Realizing that where they were headed he would need all of the friends he could find, Erich pumped the stranger's hand.

"I'm Christoff Halden," the stranger said.

"Erich Steinhoff," Erich replied while inhaling the frigid air.

The stranger returned his attention to the scenery outside, and so did Erich as he tried to pull himself away from the futility of his situation, but the repulsive smell of urine, vomit, and feces kept jerking him back.

He looked toward the west; toward his home, somewhere beyond the thousands of miles of cold desolation, where he knew his Germany would be; his Augsburg . . . his Sonja.

Erich stared at the thin trail of black smoke left behind by the coal-burning steam engine. The smoke slowly surrendered to the hazy and overcast skies of the Russian winter, until there was nothing left but white; pure white and crystalline snow that seemed to reach up to heaven . . . and down to hell.

He cried in silence.

120

Light at the End of the Tunnel

West of Rostov
March 22, 1943

The spring sun had begun to melt the snow, exposing more and more of his beloved countryside. A partly cloudy sky reigned over a land recently liberated by the immense sacrifice of the men, women, and children of the Soviet Union. In many sections of the country people were already busy rebuilding a new nation out of the ashes of destruction, and Stalin himself had started a national campaign to create a new Soviet Union.

But there was still much more territory to free, more Russians to rescue from the atrocities committed by the Germans in the occupied territories. So Colonel Aleksandrovich Nikolai Krasilov flew. He flew mission after mission to assist the Red Army in its drive west, pushing back the invading force, recovering inch after precious inch of soil, and holding it back with brutal determination.

Krasilov flew his machines with the same intensity as the first day of the invasion, never holding back, never hesitating to push the limits—even after receiving the first letter from Zoya. And the second. And the third. Even after realizing that there was a chance for a new start after the war.

Flying a brand-new Aircobra, Krasilov circled his field one more time before starting his descent. He was tired. The Germans still held a few isolated pockets of resistance in regions west of Rostov, and he had been supporting the latest attempt by his country to dislodge them.

He set her down gently, just as his old friend Jack Towers had taught him back in December.

Krasilov smiled with affection as he taxied the plane to the shelter beneath the trees flanking the muddy runway, shut off the engine, slid the canopy back, and released his harness just as a ground crew member approached the plane.

"Colonel, you have a visitor this afternoon."

Krasilov frowned. Visitors usually meant new orders, and at the moment he had enough to keep him busy for weeks.

"Who is it?"

"I don't know, sir," replied the young mechanic. "Someone from Moscow arrived an hour ago and is waiting in your tent."

Krasilov marched past the mechanic and headed straight for his quarters, pushing the green canvas flap aside.

Right there, standing in the middle of the tent, was Zoya Krasilov.

Epilogue

Checkpoint Charlie,
West Berlin, Federal Republic of Germany

Under an overcast and chilly midafternoon sky in January of 1961, East German and Soviet workers busily labored around the clock erecting and connecting concrete plank after concrete plank of what was being labeled as the new symbol of the Cold War. The snow blizzard that crashed against a recently finished section of the wall seemed to exhibit the same defiant boldness of countless border crossers who'd lost their lives trying to breach the unfinished sections, and into the freedom of the West.

The Wall of Shame.

Colonel Jack Towers, still limping from the one-year-old leg wound he'd sustained while ejecting from his F-86 jet over South Korea, quietly glanced at the East German soldiers goose-stepping beyond the slalom barriers.

He took a deep draw from his cigarette. A hundred yards beyond the Wall was another concrete barrier just as oppressive. Someone had thought to call the space between the concrete walls no-man's-land, where free-fire machine guns, land mines, and armed patrol guards gave potential defectors second thoughts about trying to reach the West.

Jack briefly closed his eyes as he used a walking cane to approach the bridge. The multiple fractures of his upper leg—the same leg he'd broken in Russia a lifetime ago—had long healed thanks to a ten-inch-long stainless-steel rod and four screws that held his femur together, but drastic changes in temperature caused the rod to expand and contract, reminding Jack that perhaps some wounds were never meant to heal completely.

Jack was not alone on that frosty day. He could hear the footsteps of a woman he'd known through the mail for some time, but whom he had only met hours previously. The attractive middle-age German woman walked quietly to his right, although Jack could hear her breathing rate increasing as they got closer to the middle of the bridge.

To his left was a man Jack had never seen before—the son of a Soviet party leader who had gotten shot down while violating Alaska's airspace.

Jack slowed down when he spotted four figures at the other end of the bridge, several feet from a parked sedan. He motioned the woman to slow down. She did. He narrowed his eyes to get a clearer picture of their faces. Two wore Soviet uniforms, the other two were in civilian clothes. One of the officers only walked a fourth of the way before stopping. The second one escorted the civilians all the way to the middle of the bridge.

Suddenly, the civilians began to walk faster. The Soviet officer tried to stop them, but the men pulled free and ran toward Jack. The young Soviet to Jack's left, who Jack didn't think was older than thirty, broke into a run toward the Soviet side, and quickly disappeared inside the dark sedan.

Erich Steinhoff kicked his legs so hard, he thought his feet would go through the wooden floor of the bridge. He had spotted her . . . his Sonja. She ran to him. The two embraced.

Erich tried to say something, but couldn't. Instead, he simply held her tight. In a moment it all returned to him. The smell of her brought him back to the last time they'd been together in Augsburg, so many years ago. But he had survived. The Siberian cold had not broken him. He had endured the long prison term imposed on him by a Soviet postwar committee.

Erich gazed into her eyes, convincing himself that this

was not one of those dreams he'd woken up from just to face another grim day working behind a sewing machine stitching leather gloves along with a thousand other prisoners. He had actually made it, and so had his dear friend Christoff Halden, whom he now introduced to Sonja as his blood brother.

She hugged Christoff and kissed him on the cheek.

The trio walked back in the direction of the American wearing a blue uniform and holding a walking cane in his right hand.

Jack saw the Germans approach him, saw tears in their eyes.

Steinhoff stopped as they walked by Jack, who stared into the weathered blue eyes of someone who had helped him long ago. The former Luftwaffe major briefly nodded, brought his right hand up, and touched the middle finger against his temple. Jack took a deep breath and returned the salute.

The trio walked past him and toward a waiting black limousine. Jack shifted his gaze to the uniformed officer twenty feet away. They stared at one another in silence for several seconds.

"I never got the chance to say thank you for the story you fed Chapman, Aleksandr. It probably saved me from getting court-martialed," Jack said as he took a few steps forward.

"You didn't have to, Jackovich. You saved many Soviet pilots' lives—and you helped me find my Zoya. It was the least I could do."

Jack grinned at the sight of an old familiar face. The Soviet colonel, a general now, looked nearly the same as he'd looked a dozen years previously save for the white streaks along his full head of hair. Even the scars on his forehead remained the same, lending credibility to the many decorations on his uniform.

"The years have treated you well, my friend," said Jack in a more relaxed tone. "I could only wish our governments would allow us the opportunity to meet under more friendly circumstances."

Krasilov slowly nodded. "As you can see, Jackovich, tensions are only going to get worse. I can only hope that one day I do not find myself chasing you across the skies."

"Hopefully it won't get to that."

"Hopefully, yes. Jackovich?"

"Yes?"

"Someone else came along to say thanks."

Jack dropped his eyelids halfway as Krasilov tilted his head in the direction of the second uniformed officer twenty feet behind the Soviet general. His back was to Jack.

"Who is he? I can't . . ."

"It's a *she,* my friend."

Jack felt his pulse rocketing as he walked past Krasilov and approached the Soviet officer, who suddenly turned around and stared into his eyes. Jack froze.

"Hello, Jack."

He was at a loss for words. The hazel eyes gazed at him. The beautiful eyes, the glistening-white skin and red lips . . .

"Natalya . . . you . . . how did you . . ."

"Krasilov told me what you were trying to do, and I begged him to let me come."

Jack smiled as he got close to her. He couldn't help himself and brought a hand to her face.

"It's good to see you, again, Natalya."

She smiled. "I'm glad you are well, Jack."

Jack exhaled as his hands cupped her face. "Right now it feels as if we were all back in that airfield in the middle of nowhere."

Natalya lowered her gaze and pushed his hands away. "I wish we were, but we're not, Jack."

Jack nodded. "Is he a good husband?"

"And a good father."

"You have a child?"

"Two," she responded while brushing away a tear. "Jackovich Aleksandrovich is three and Boris Andrei will be five in March."

His throat constricted.

"I came to say thank you for helping Boris and me stay in touch during the remainder of the war."

Jack swallowed hard and said, "You know I would have done *anything* for you."

"You were a good man back then, and you still are." She pointed at the departing limousine.

He shrugged. "He saved my life."

"Good-bye, Jack Towers," she said, hugging him, before whispering in his ear. "I hope you find happiness in your life. You deserve nothing less."

Before waiting for a response, Natalya let him go, turned around, and headed for the sedan. Jack briefly closed his eyes to hold back the tears, and he felt a hand on his shoulder. He turned around. It was Krasilov, who walked past him and smiled without saying a word. Jack understood. There wasn't much left to be said. He was their enemy now. The world had taken a different turn.

Jack saw his old friends disappear inside the sedan, which promptly drove away the moment the doors were slammed closed.

The sounds of bulldozers and trucks rang in the distance while snow flurries turned into a light rain that chilled his face. Jack felt the cold rain drown his soul as it mixed with his tears.